LOST INDIGNATION
a novel
by Becky McAuley

Cover illustration by Chris Wilson
Book & Cover design by Shining Life

Second printing, 2022
ISBN 978-1-7364991-1-5
Shining Life Press
Washington, DC

This is Shining Life number 37

To Mike, Ellie and Goose

"We're gonna be forgotten, and that's OK,
'cause we don't live for anyone but ourselves anyway."
-Eaten Alive

"If there were a race among all artists to the human heart,
my money would be on music to win. It knows a shortcut."
-Marie-Helene Bertino

Prologue
2006

Ryan Marnell stood on the railroad bridge, waiting for his oldest friend. It was a humid August night, just after 11 p.m. on a Monday. Over the usual evening noises, he could hear the sounds of the Hudson River hitting the shores of Bare Ass Beach on the other side of the bridge. Waiting out here, Ryan was simultaneously excited and apprehensive, like walking into a hardcore show with the idea that anything could happen.

A few minutes later, he saw headlights sweeping down the hill, first on the long driveway down from Palisade Street, then around the side of the building, and finally stopping in the small parking lot below where he stood. The bridge was situated between two old industrial buildings, part of a complex that spanned the Metro North tracks and connected the main structure to assorted outbuildings and garages on the narrow strip of land between the tracks and the Hudson River. Sometimes, artists with studios here worked late, but Ryan didn't see any lights tonight. There was no one around.

The complex was more populated these days than when they'd hung out down here in the '80s. Ryan had vivid memories of this place, including the day he had first met Christine. Skateboarding on the loading docks, hanging out at BA Beach: it was the Rivertown equivalent of spending time at The Abyss. When Ryan had returned last year, he was half surprised that everything was nearly the same as he'd remembered. Still stubbornly dilapidated, the narrow bridge was now closed to vehicular traffic but nominally safe for pedestrians.

Ryan heard an engine shut off and the headlights died. He couldn't see the car, but he knew it would be a MTA police vehicle. His best friend— who still loved to see how much he could get away with by almost breaking the rules while somehow staying within them, who had once enjoyed writing graffiti here—was now a transit cop, charged with monitoring the exact type of miscreant he had been a generation earlier. After 9/11, some people had the tendency to reinvent themselves.

A moment later, Ryan heard a car door slam in the parking lot, and then saw a shadow on the entrance to the bridge.

Chapter 1
2017

Looking back, you could say it all started with the message board. This was frequently the case with hardcore lore, beefs, legend, and intrigue—at least in the early 2000s. In 2017, message boards had nearly faded from popular consciousness, or at least relevance, even in the corner of the internet inhabited by Mo McGraw and her musically congruous peers. But a message board was the catalyst for the unlikely events that unfolded over the course of that fall. Technically, it all stemmed from Mo's compulsion to check the board just one more time when she was supposed to be finishing her homework. Or more accurately, a compulsion to always be doing something she wasn't supposed to be doing.

It was Thursday, September 21: Rosh Hashanah. Mo McGraw curled over her desk in a Skarhead shirt and basketball shorts. Sun streamed in through the window of their third-floor apartment on Overlook Street in Mount Vernon. Out on Gramatan Avenue, the 52 bus sang its half-tone departure melody that sounded like the end of Operation Ivy's "Knowledge."

At her desk, Mo was flanked by a mug of black coffee, a liter of seltzer, and a teetering stack of unopened mail. CC prowled at her feet, while Brett was no doubt off causing destruction elsewhere in the apartment. It was oddly exhilarating to be home writing while Pat was at work. But this was one part of the new arrangement. Work in the morning, school in the afternoon, while Pat worked full time at a residential school in his first real job obtained via his psych degree. He was pretty distracting in general, and they had way too much fun when they were both home, even with Pat's desk in the living room and Mo's in the bedroom. Mo had observed the holiday by staying home from her office in Chelsea, yet she was still now just frantically finishing a story for her 3:30 class. Somehow, she had convinced herself to go back to school for an MFA in fiction writing from Sarah Lawrence, as impractical as that might be. New year and fresh starts aside, her second stint as a student was beginning remarkably like the last, featuring bursts of inspiration, procrastination, and the inevitable sprint to arrive at class with an assignment in hand.

Before she could make any more headway on the story, her cell phone buzzed. Now that Mo worked part-time, there was an amorphous agreement regarding when the office could or couldn't call her: she would pretty much always pick up if she wasn't in class or underground on the train. A 212 number flashed across the screen, presumably one of the various lines associated with her employer.

Colette Foulard had gotten a lot more than she bargained for when she tossed the life preserver of a job offer to Mo in 2011. With Pat out of work and credit card debt mounting, Mo hurled herself from her humble if interesting admin role at a book wholesaler in the suburbs into the rarified landscape of Manhattan public relations. She had no idea what she was getting into, and her employer probably didn't either. Over the past six years, she had tamed her boss's unwieldy database of contacts, hired some great people that Colette would have overlooked, started an intern program, sort of turned into the HR person, and was occasionally pressed into guest list management for high-profile events.

Alongside the neverending variety of tasks, when not consumed by heart-pounding anxiety generated by various short-lived catastrophes, Mo had managed to thoroughly enjoy herself. She snuck Kool Keith into the database after looking up his contact info for her own wedding's guest list before realizing that it wasn't worth it to pay for the calligraphy of an extra invite that would merely languish in the office of Keith's agent. (Though it was an *Our Man in Havana* moment when he started spontaneously appearing on guest lists shortly after, even attending the Futura exhibition Colette had staged during Fashion Week 2012.)

There was a surprising amount of crossover between her preferred subcultures and work world, and she reveled in the intersections. Only Pat, vicariously steeped in the drama and minutiae of her office, and Tony Gerson, their former office manager that Mo had recruited from her previous job in Dobbs Ferry, understood the humor in any of these references. Not only did former hardcore kids occasionally appear as artists, journalists, gallery owners, or art handlers, but they also popped up on guest lists for events.

Somewhere around 2014, Mo had realized that far from something to be avoided when describing one's extracurriculars, hardcore punk had become hip and brought her a certain accidental cachet and currency at work. Over the years, while she had attempted to present as blandly normie as possible, her rivals were maximizing or fabricating their alty roots. In this new world, "punk rock" was an aspirational adjective. Mo still wasn't sure how she felt about all of this, as it was at times both amusing and uncomfortable, though she was alright with being able to wear a Supertouch shirt to work.

And most importantly, the job was alright too, especially since Colette had been nicer since Mo went part-time. There was a fair amount of chaos, and cigarette smoke, and long hours, but she did in fact get to look at *names* all day (both in the database and on resumes), names that she could then twist and transmogrify for fictional purposes. While most days she barely had time to refill her water bottle, use the bathroom, or eat lunch, at least every day had been interesting. And when Colette was yelling, for the first few years at least, Mo herself had rarely been the target of her ire.

There wasn't anything else in particular that Mo yearned to be doing professionally (besides writing all the time, which was out of the question financially). Her only regret was that she had always been too busy to be "paid to post," in message board parlance. She had never had a job where she'd had the luxury to be bored! It was a blessing and the curse of finding everything interesting.

Mo was correct in her assumption that the 212 number was indeed one of the Colette Foulard Associates office lines, though her boss did not identify herself by name.

"Hello, Maureen?" she opened in her precise yet accented English. "Are you enjoying your holiday?"

"Yes, thank you! It's been nice so far," Mo replied, upbeat, not letting on that she might be enjoying her holiday more if she were a) not taking work calls on a holiday and b) not trying to clandestinely finish homework that she shouldn't have been doing on a holiday either.

"Listen," Colette continued, a trademark opener, usually indicative of some missive or musings about the state of their personnel. Mo braced herself and hit "Save" on her Word document. Colette's customary "listen ..." always reminded her of the beginning of the Jawbox song "Reel."

"Listen, Elvis is busy with 93 Morton and the Sheikh. And he does not do events. So I was thinking of putting Aaron on Vedomedy."

"Wonderful," Mo affirmed, her voice revealing both enthusiasm and trepidation. Aaron Overton was her third-favorite person at CFA, as he was orderly, adept and kind. She always enjoyed working with him, as this series of seated dinners would necessitate, but she was unsure how Aaron would feel about joining the Vedomedy project. While technically a real estate endeavor—the type of client ordinarily wrangled by the very adept yet very commercial Elvis Fregosi, CFA's only current VP and true adult besides Colette and their bookkeeper—there would also be a heavy events component due to the dinners. Mo could already visualize the profusion of misspelled names, hard to find addresses, and assorted other tedium unfurling over her and Aaron's other fall commitments like a gym class parachute.

Starting in 2014, Colette had become acquainted with Ludo Vedomedy, minor aristocracy from a miniscule European nation state no one had ever heard of, who was building a collection of residences on West 20th Street. After myriad delays, with the building still unfinished, CFA was hosting a trio of dinners in its honor, along with a slate of press appointments, a panel discussion, and a closing party (scheduled for November 4, a date on which Mo was already fortuitously booked elsewhere, not that she worked events.) It was, on top of Mo's own personal commitments, shaping up to be an interesting fall. Mo had a strong premonition that the Vedomedy project would overshadow every other extant retainer client and office occurrence, in the way such extended fiascos often did.

"So I finally have a moment to dive into the list and wanted to confirm everything we have received has been entered so I can start coding my names."

"Of course," Mo replied, though Monica Marquez would have also been able to field this inquiry with aplomb. Monica, a water polo aficionado/theater nerd from Texas with cropped pink hair and boundless enthusiasm, had been Mo's right hand woman since 2015 (despite sitting on different floors, due to the quirks of the limited seating in Colette's townhouse office). Monica had swum quite nicely into the database portion of Mo's role at CFA, first when Mo had taken on other tasks, and then later when she reduced her hours for school.

"So you got the first list from Ludo, and we entered that last week."

"Correct," Colette affirmed.

"And we actually have seven different groups from the gallery, plus the one from Bottega Veneta ..." Mo endured ten additional minutes of instructions and interrogation from Colette before managing to extract herself from the call. At least she wasn't at the office today! While some of her tasks were legit important and time-sensitive, Mo often theorized that at least half the crap that people summoned her for in a frenzy could be resolved without her expertise. Of course, that was job security: people thinking they needed you for shit for which you were absolutely not required.

Already distracted from the call, Mo now checked her phone for dispatches from the outside world or urgent missives from non-Colette members of the office. "Happy New Year!" her mom had texted, along with a blue heart and a squirrel emoji, which Mo supposed was intended to convey greetings from central New Jersey's finest fauna. Mo wasn't going home for Rosh Hashanah this year due to its occurrence in the middle of the week. Yom Kippur fell on a Saturday, as it often seemed to in the last few years, and she and Pat would be scooping up her brother Max in Washington Heights on their way to the McGraw family home in Lawrence, NJ. Thankfully, the Raybeez memorial show in Tompkins Square Park had been scheduled for the day after.

"How are you feeling?" Mo then texted Kenza Dixon, her best friend from home, who was in the midst of her first pregnancy. Sometimes Mo couldn't believe that Kenza was going to have a kid. It felt like she and her husband were adults in ways that Mo and Pat were not.

"Vomitrocious," came back the near-instantaneous response, with a corresponding emoji to match. The term was a throwback to their

Lost Indignation

track team days, during which they had sometimes hid at the bagel shop on Route 206 and then attempted to trot surreptitiously back to school as if they had indeed completed a full training run. Now Kenza was the development director for the National Institute of Radio, and—in addition to working full time and being pregnant—was teaching a college class on Saturday mornings about the psychology of mass communication. Mo, who was having enough trouble writing this damn story for someone *else's* college class, wasn't sure how she was doing all of it and still looking like her fab Kenza self, if Instagram could be trusted.

Speaking of Instagram, Mo now opted for a quick circuit of the other distractions on her phone and computer. Instagram, Twitter, Facebook, and of course the Controlled board. She still had ... aah crap, only three hours left before she had to be done with this story and leave for class, which was a 30 minute walk from Overlook Street. Usually she came straight from the train after work in the city.

Sometimes Mo could hardly believe her good fortune that she was going back to school to study something so frivolous as creative writing at the age of 31. It was the kind of thing that happened to other people, not someone who had just finished paying off a mountain of credit card debt. People from richer families, or with superior skills for thrift, or who hadn't been the primary breadwinner since the recession had wiped out Pat's job in 2009 (hence the debt). And yet the tables had turned, and Pat—with his entry level but very real salary—was contributing enough to keep Mo in peanut butter sandwiches and frozen vegetables for the foreseeable future. But at other times, it was like what the fuck was she doing, trying to cram two entirely different full-time brain roles into her already overtaxed brain.

And yet, as overjoyed as she had been when accepted to the program and as hard as she was trying to take it seriously, she was still falling into the same historical traps of procrastination and avoidance. Maybe if you were a "real" writer you had more time to think about your projects; Mo's writing was shoehorned into whatever moments she was not at her day job, or at least thinking about her day job. Or maybe she liked the idea of sitting at her desk and writing way more than the actual practice of sitting at her desk and writing. Or maybe it was easier to make yourself do work in an office where you sat by the front door and any moment an interloper could pop up over your shoulder? Here, in the comfort of home, Mo restarted the End It demo, reflexively opened a new Chrome tab, and entered the address for the Controlled board.

The Controlled message board was one of various independent offshoots of the Bridge 9 board for those who were fed up with the topical sprawl and lack of focused music discussion. Bridge 9, a record label from Boston which had been around for like 20 years now, had become intrinsically linked with its eponymous message board, the notoriety of which had eclipsed the popularity of the label, at least during the board's heyday in the mid-aughts.

Message boards had been on their way out for a while, replaced by Instagram, Tumblr, Facebook groups, Google groups, group texts, and who knows what else. Mo—and Pat to some extent, who had reigned over (but not reined in) great mischief as a moderator on various hardcore and rap message boards—were patiently awaiting their return as a retro phenomenon. If kids were DJing parties with CDs, and JNCOs and assorted '90s accoutrements had made their less-than-welcome return, could the humble message board not be reanimated?

The board was a mix of enigmatic old heads, people around Mo's age, people in their 20s with active bands and zines, and the odd teen with discerning taste. It was invite-only, but not so cliquey that there weren't a variety of groups represented. Here and elsewhere, Mo had a decent chance of persuading people about what was the superior WNYU set or the relative quality of the Warzone s/t LP. People actually seemed interested in what she had to say and were willing to buy her zine to read it. Mo's username was SomethingMaur, a combination of her name and the Bad Trip track on the *New Breed* comp. Her avatar was a picture of Raybeez in his Wise Potato Chips hat.

Due to the constraints of life, money, and scheduling, Mo and Pat had been attending fewer shows, but she still *thought* about hardcore all the time and was just as susceptible to the charms of a message board in 2017. Well 2014 really, which was when she had first spotted a post by AJ McGuire seeking contributions for the second issue of his zine, *Gratitude Fanzine*.

GRATITUDE FANZINE *ISSUE #2 IS IN DEVELOPMENT*

Tentatively scheduled for release Fall of 2014.

Do you want to contribute? If you want to write essays on any of the following topics please get in touch. Generous compensation is available (although unlikely).

1. Contrary to popular opinion, the best songs on the New Breed comp are the live Beyond songs.

2. Warzone & Insted are the most popular bands to become straight edge after already being a band for a while. Here are others you might have overlooked.

Lost Indignation

3. Top 10 recorded covers of HC songs that are better than the original.

4. The Abused "Loud and Clear" 7" cover is the best use of bricks in the history of HC artwork. Here are numbers 2 through 10.

5. The Warzone self-titled LP has been overlooked for 24 years. It deserves a second look.

5. [sic, this was also numbered 5] All three mixes of "Break Down the Walls" are equally worthwhile. Here is what is best about each of them.

Intrigued by the idea of defending the Warzone s/t, Mo promptly forgot all about the post until AJ ordered a copy of her newer zine, *How About Some Hardcore #2*, in March 2015. Was perhaps the Warzone topic still available, she inquired? Sure enough, it was, and 2,700 words later, her contribution was complete.

Mo was no stranger to advocating for things with minimal perceptible support, from spare parts baseball players such as Chris Dickerson and Greg Golson to the Henry Wiggen books, but hardcore was different. The unturned stones were increasingly scarce and fewer truly obscure topics remained each year. And when the previously unheralded bands became popular, it wasn't the lack of rarity that bothered her, but more the homogeneity that resulted from everyone aping these previously unique specimens. People online actually *liked* the Warzone s/t now, as opposed to the general sentiment when she had bought her LP copy in 2004. And not just the prior demo versions, which she, too, would admit were a lot better.

AJ being a fellow adult with responsibilities, who—just like Mo—took a few years to put out an issue of a zine, *Gratitude #2* had just recently been completed. The reaction to the Warzone article had been positive overall, with a handful of orders arriving for *How About Some Hardcore #3*, and had inspired a lighthearted debate on the Controlled board regarding the record's merits. As Mo scrolled through topics such as "Does anyone have recordings of THE MOB first demo, 1980?" and one descriptively named "zines," she saw there was a new post in the "*Gratitude #2* out now" thread. Originally intended to announce the release of the issue, the thread had devolved into a discussion of riff-stealing in general, which, with only so many different chord configurations available, was an art within hardcore. Warzone had repurposed assorted Altercation riffs throughout the record, which technically wasn't stealing, as Paul Canade had authored both iterations.

At the bottom of the thread was a new post under the moniker "ShadowOOT." Mo didn't recognize the username or avatar, but it had five total posts since joining in 2016, so their output had been sporadic at best. Mo was used to these obscure handles, as hardly anyone—from graffiti writers on Instagram to even the insular group who frequented this invite-only message board—commented under their actual name in her circles. Then again, everyone generally knew who everyone else was, if not their real names. She recognized the user as a nod to either the Icemen song, the Lovecraft story, or both, with "OOT" as a twist on "OOP," or "out of print." The contribution was as follows:

"Of course Warzone were known borrowers—from Altercation, Waylon Jennings, and probably others. But that's nothing compared to how much Ministry of Fear sounds like the Indignation demo from the '80s. Though it's up for debate who wrote those Indignation songs—and who really copied who?"

Before she had a chance to reconsider, or go back to her paper, Mo quickly hit reply. "Word, have never heard Indignation but would love to hear the demo and compare—am intrigued!" Mo was always telling someone she was "intrigued" and had resolved to dial that back a bit as her default response to new bands or releases. She had never listened to Ministry of Fear either, but knew they were one of those '90s Boston bands that were slightly too metal to be on her radar. Metallic '90s hardcore wasn't her area of expertise, beyond like, later Zero Tolerance and Merauder. And not only was she intrigued by accusations of plagiarism, but also by late '80s bands of a certain style—a category which Indignation likely fell into. There were lots of bands who had started off as regular hardcore bands and then veered in varied directions in the advent of the new decade.

Mo had never thought about Ministry of Fear very often, but when she had come across their name in the past, she wondered if the Graham Greene reference was intentional. Plus, she was a sucker for mysterious demos that may or may not exist—like how the first Merauder demo with Minus was merely a rumor for most hardcore kids who had only heard those songs during the Live at CBGB's set. Mo had finally tracked down Bob Riley when Stigmata played with Billy Club Sandwich in Long Island last summer, and he had admitted to owning a copy, but Mo was no closer to hearing it. With any luck Indignation might be easier to find, if only half as interesting.

Refreshing the board one last time, she clicked back to the Word doc and her faltering story. But five minutes later, a private message popped up from ShadowOOT:

If you want to hear Indignation, the demo is hard to find. I have a videotape with one of their live sets, which I'd sell if you're interested.

Lost Indignation

Also has a bunch of other sets including Raw Deal.

Mo hit reply. What did she have to lose? "Nice, would love to hear them. How much for the tape?" At least if this Indignation band was less than inspiring, there might be other interesting shows on the tape.

OK, back to her story, which was called *The Oldest Baseball Player on Twitter*, and likely to be dissed and dismissed, Breakdown style, by most of the class. They weren't much of a baseball-loving group over at Sarah Lawrence, but baseball had been on her mind, along with hardcore, which she wasn't touching yet. Maybe later in the semester. All she could do was write as much as she could while waiting for the next reply to arrive. It was the usual paradox: when Mo had limited time, like with a meeting or interview looming at the top of the hour, she was able to buckle down and get as much work done in that short window as time allowed, without the ability to drift towards more enticing distractions. When she didn't receive an immediate reply from ShadowOOT, Mo kept at the story, marginally more confident she might be able to finish before class, until she saw another new message from ShadowOOT:

I'm in NY for a conference but I'm staying with my family in Yonkers. I've been on the road a lot and bringing the tape with me just in case someone is interested. Are you available later today?

Damn, this was escalating quickly. Dude must have seen her message board location listed as Mount Vernon. Ironically, this was the first time that info had been relevant to another poster. And based on his initial contribution to the thread, Mo had just assumed that Indignation might be from the Boston area too, like Ministry of Fear. It added another level of intrigue that this Indignation band might have some Westchester connection, if ShadowOOT's family lived in Yonkers. Though it was disconcerting, imagining messaging with this person and assuming they were hundreds of miles away, when they'd been nearby all along.

"I have class until 5:30," Mo typed. "Maybe tonight? I live in Mount Vernon," she added, superfluously, as why would he have even mentioned Yonkers if he hadn't seen her nearby location? She almost included another sentence about being glad that the board was entertaining him while he was at the conference, which must be boring. This dude was living the dream and being paid to post, even if he wasn't at his usual work site.

Mo jammed her chin-length reddish hair behind her ears and petted Brett (Gardner) as he stalked by her desk. Her hair was fucking atrocious, but she was getting it cut on Saturday. The days of having a long ponytail to whip around while moshing to Biohazard were a thing of the past.

Mo was slim but solid, the perfect size for someone to run around the pit with her on their back or shoulders, but was surprisingly heavy when picked up, kind of like their other cat, CC (Sabathia). These days, now that she was married to Pat, no one was scooping her up to use as a battering ram, nor was she leaping onto any random dudes' backs. She still jumped on Pat from time to time when she needed to see better (Mo was 5'2") or for a quick ride to the front of the room. It was the fastest way to cut through the crowd: Pat wasn't a huge dude, but people definitely got out of his way much more quickly than hers. At almost 35, he was a robustly-built bald guy (maybe more of an actual fat guy these days) with a medium amount of tattoos. And while he had mostly retired his aggressive '90s mosh style, he still looked like the type of person that you wouldn't want to get in the way of.

With 15 minutes to go, Mo inhaled a protein bar and an applesauce packet while executing final revisions and coaxed the full assignment from their balky printer, which was the single most nerve-wracking aspect of coming straight from home rather than printing her homework at work. She jettisoned the Skarhead tee—taking care to store it out of the reach of Brett, as he was known to masticate unsecured garments—wrestled into a floral dress and Adidas Gazelles, grabbed her purse and cardigan, locked the door, and galloped down the stairs as quietly as possible, trying not to wake their downstairs neighbor, Mr. Boxhill, who worked nights.

There was still no reply from ShadowOOT about tonight; perhaps the conference was less boring than he had previously indicated, or the boring bit had ended. Mo would keep an eye on her phone over the next few hours, but until there was anything definite in the calendar, she would not warn Pat about upending their night to meet up with some strange dude to execute a videotape transaction.

And, after all, it was 2017: Mo was no longer tethered to a computer for message board access, like when riveting stuff was going down on the Bridge 9 board in college and she was either in class or busy at her retail job. As she was crossing Bronx River Road, Mo checked again and saw one new message.

8 p.m. work? $25?

$25 for some old videotape she had never heard of earlier today? No way dude. Mo resolved not to reply right away, though now she did want this tape.

But as she passed under the Cross County Parkway to continue towards campus, Mo felt compelled to respond. "How about $15?" She dropped her phone back into the detritus of her purse and resolved not to check the board again before class, though of course she would do one last

Lost Indignation

round of Twitter and Instagram perusal before heading in.

The nondescript houses on Kimball Ave. quickly gave way to the grander buildings of the Sarah Lawrence campus, and soon Mo was striding into her Thursday night workshop. In general, these MFA classes were more engaging than her undergraduate courses, and the two hours went by rapidly. But tonight, she struggled to keep her mind on her classmates' stories as she wondered if the Shadow was going to reply to her most recent DM. At least they were communicating via the archaic form of message board DM, rather than something like email or Instagram that would generate a notification, so it would be a surprise whenever she opened the board to check for an update.

Finally, around 4:30, she slipped out to use the bathroom and check her phone. Her work email revealed various updates, none of them positive. A candidate who had been offered a job at CFA had impolitely declined—Mo would have to assuage Colette's frustration and incomprehension tomorrow. She was cc'd on a couple confusing emails from Aaron Overton about a mailing for their Americans for the Arts event, though Monica seemed to have a handle on that one. There was something wrong with their Masterplanner subscription—why was this even being directed to her and not new office manager Drew Flowers? Fed up with her work email, Mo switched to her personal. Inexplicably Verizon had raised their bill another $10. This month's ConEd bill had been high, too. Library books were coming due. (And she would have to give up and return a few of them—after reading a passage from *A Naked Singularity* for craft class, she was now attempting to read the remaining 600+ pages, which might take anywhere between six weeks to six years.) There was a reminder to pay her car insurance. Fuck! Why was everything so annoying?

Everything besides hardcore, that is: always the best escape from your society and/or your reality. The Controlled board revealed one new DM. Of course she had been waiting to check this last, like waiting to open a Myspace message from one's crush in the pre-Pat section of her life.

> *How about $20?*

OK, $20 sounded fair. After all the back and forth, she did want to hear this tape. Mo checked her wallet. She had $47, Shane Spencer style, and wouldn't even need to hit the bank on Gramatan Ave. to make this transaction a reality.

"$20 is good," Mo typed back. "8 p.m. still work for you?"

She checked her watch: she had now missed five minutes of class. Before she headed back in, Mo opened Gchat and messaged Pat. "You down for a mysterious adventure later?"

His bifurcated reply arrived moments later. "Hi lady, how is class?

What kind of adventure?"

"Buying some videotape from a dude on the internet? Will fill you in when out of class. Love you!" Mo stowed the phone in her purse and snuck back into class, somehow managing to focus through the rest of it, including while facing some harsh commentary about her story. After dismissal, she pulled up the Controlled board and opened the latest message.

8 is good. Where should we meet?

"There's a park on the corner of Primrose and Summit in Mount Vernon. Let me know if you need more info." Mo typed back. Just then, there was a new Gchat from Pat. "Haha ok lady, whatever you want to do."

Pat was the fucking best. He may have been rolling his eyes at the change of plans for their evening, yet he unquestionably accepted his role in the adventure. He didn't say "I'm so fucking tired" or "But we don't even own a VCR!" He just agreed to meet the video purveyor at the park at 8 p.m.

On the north side of Mount Vernon, at the intersection of Primrose and Summit Avenues, there is a small park that does not appear on any maps. It has no name and appears to be an afterthought from the time when the neighborhood was designed. Maple Place, a one-block street, runs southwest to intersect with Primrose, the southern border, while Summit Ave. makes the third side of the triangle. Elvis Fregosi had once pitched a whole article about one-block streets in NYC to get one of CFA's clients into *The New York Times*, but couldn't have used this one, as Mount Vernon is just across the border from the Bronx and not part of NYC, though spiritually and spatially it has much in common with the outer boroughs.

When Mo had set the location with ShadowOOT, she hadn't realized it wouldn't show up on Google Maps as a park. She'd never set up any meetings there or hung out there with anyone from outside the neighborhood. It was only after she had described its whereabouts that started to realize this might have been a poor choice. Why couldn't she have named a more conventional meeting place, such as Slave to the Grind or the Bayou?

"So this guy just PM's you out of nowhere and says he has this tape?" Pat inquired as they strode down Primrose to the park. While they walked, Mo had filled him in on the developments of the last few hours and why his presence was required. As usual, she had the feeling of being a leashed dog itching to bound ahead in comparison to his more measured temperament and gait. Plus, by walking ahead of him, he got to look at her ass.

"Yeah, I said something about wanting to hear Indignation and he messaged me that he's willing to sell me this video," Mo confirmed. She had changed out of the floral dress and was back in the Skarhead shirt and basketball shorts.

They crossed Summit Ave., with the park ahead and to their left. It was already dark, but a couple of insufficient streetlights surrounded the triangular green space. Mo and Pat walked in alongside the line of bushes that led to the slate circle in the center, Pat fiddling with his phone as usual. There was a person waiting in the slate area, but it was too dark and too far away to see if this was the guy with the tape. As they got closer, Mo decided this was likely him, as he looked like he was waiting for someone, rather than someone from the neighborhood just hanging out. Also, he was watching them.

The Shadow looked slightly put off for a second as they approached. Did he not know that she was going to be female, or that there were two people coming? Mo tried to think back to their interactions. She'd said something about "getting out of class"—had he thought she was going to be closer to the age of the average college student? Not that Mo looked much older than the average college student. Whatever the reason for this guy's surprise, she was glad she had brought Pat.

The seller looked to be in his 40s, and seemed somehow diminished and unassuming. He was wearing small, fussy glasses, and the hair escaping from under his baseball cap could use a trim. Mo peered at the hat: Pat had a prodigious collection of arcane and outrageous minor league flat brims, but this was some ancient curved brim thing with a cryptic "B" logo. He wore a windbreaker zipped up to his neck (despite the warm night), jeans, and running shoes. Mo clocked him as an aging '90s type.

"Hey! Are you the Indignation guy?"

The park dude suddenly looked happier. "I am indeed the Indignation guy."

"Cool, I'm glad I didn't just ask some random guy in a park if they were here to sell me a videotape. I'm Mo, and this is Pat." Mo gestured to her right.

"Nice to meet you. I'm Max Malkin."

"Oh, my brother's name is Max." Mo smiled, despite the disconcerting vibe emanating from the video salesman.

"An auspicious sign," Max Malkin solemnly agreed.

"So ... is your Controlled board username an Icemen reference?" Mo wasn't going to miss an opportunity to talk about the Icemen.

"Or Lovecraft?" Pat countered.

"A little bit of both," Malkin replied.

"Did you ever see the Icemen?" Mo continued eagerly.

"Yes, but only one time." He didn't elaborate. What was this guy's deal? Most other people that Mo had met while buying or selling hardcore items were more willing to bullshit about their shared interests during the handoff. And if *she* had seen the Icemen, she would sure as shit be describing the show to a member of the younger generation.

"Anyway, there are a bunch of sets on this tape," Max explained as he handed Mo the item that had brought them to the park. "I think Indignation is the third band."

"Good to know. I'm excited to see what other stuff is on there too."

"Raw Deal? Or some shows at Streets? I haven't watched it in years." OK, so that narrowed down the general era that Indignation was from: the late '80s, by the sound of their contemporaries and the venues at the time.

"Were you the one who shot the video?"

There was a beat of silence before he answered this simple question. He almost seemed offended she had asked. "Yup, that was me. Put a bunch of different sets together on this one tape."

"Can you tell me a little about Indignation? Who was in the band, and how long were they around?"

"Dion, the singer, lives in Florida," Max started to recite in a curiously dispassionate tone. "Ryan, the guitarist, he died a few years back. Eric, the bassist, I think he moved out west. And Matt Zimmer was the drummer. Kid was really into wrestling and kind of a pain in the ass. But I bet now he's all grown up and working in an office somewhere.

"He didn't play on the demo, Zimmer," Max continued. "But he was the original drummer. They weren't around long enough to have a bunch of different dudes in the band."

"Why did they break up?"

"The usual shit." He shrugged. "Anyway, the demo is hard to find now. Who knows what happened to those tapes, since it's not like they played many shows after they recorded." Mo could only imagine how much shit had disappeared over the years, cassettes unwittingly trashed that would have been sought by future generations of hardcore coveteurs.

"So it's a good thing you got this video," he continued. "You might be one of the only people in the world with Indignation material now."

"Do you think the band themselves would still have any copies?" It wasn't a terrible guess, as the internet would sometimes explode when some former band member, presuming his output to be long forgotten, discovered a cache of remaining records or shirts.

"It's possible," Max responded. "There weren't that many made. There might be some sitting in someone's attic, but I haven't seen a copy in years."

Lost Indignation

"And how about Ministry of Fear?" Mo continued. "If I don't have any of their releases? I'm just intrigued by the idea of one band borrowing from the other. Do you know if it's been re-released, or if there is stuff floating around on Discogs or Ebay?"

"I'm sure there is. Though I hear they're trying to get it reissued."

"How did you know the Indignation guys?" Mo blurted. What she meant to ask was, how had this strange guy ended up with this tape? And why did she not necessarily believe he had shot the video?

"I used to be friends with one of them back in the day." Malkin didn't elaborate further.

"Well thanks so much for bringing the video and introducing me to Indignation. I owe you twenty dollars?" Mo pulled a pre-separated bill from the outside pocket of her purse.

"Yeah. I'm glad you want to hear these guys. You know kids these days are pulling every random band out of obscurity. I have a feeling that Ministry of Fear is next. So someone would have been after this tape sooner or later, if they knew the connection."

"I know all about that," Mo grinned. She was caught between generations on these issues: too young to have seen the original Dynamo, she had been one of approximately three people going off at the reunion in 2006, compared to the hundreds of Dynamo fans that had proliferated worldwide in the decade since.

"Like Alone in a Crowd only played a couple shows, but people have always hyped them? And then the 7" got re-pressed again a few years ago?" Max continued. "I guess you just need the right combination of time, distance, and circumstances."

"Time, distance, and friends!" Mo said automatically. Max looked nonplussed.

"It's a Strength691 song," Mo explained. "Did you ever see them?" Another band she had only caught during a reunion, though unlike Dynamo, they seemed to not have attained worldwide popularity since.

"Oh yeah, I think my old band played with them."

"What band were you in?" Pat interjected, lurking on the periphery of the conversation.

"Disregard." They waited, until he clarified, "That was the name of the band."

"Noted." Mo laughed. "Or, uh, regarded. Guess I'll have to look into them, too."

"Good luck. That stuff is even harder to find than Indignation, and for good reason."

There was a pause. The only sounds were the usual insect and night noises emanating from the park and the faint rush of traffic from the Cross County Parkway a few blocks north. It was totally dark, besides the feeble gleam emanating from the small streetlights that surrounded the perimeter.

Pat gave her a look. "Alright Mrs. Strength691, let's get you home to watch this video." He turned towards Max. "It was nice to meet you, man." He extended his hand and after a moment of hesitation, Max shook, probably surmising, accurately, the intensity of the handshake to which Pat would subject him.

"I feel like I'm entering into some sort of contract," Mo joked as she extended her own diminutive digits. "Thanks again for coming out here and parting with this thing. I'm so excited to watch it."

Malkin smiled. "Don't forget to look out for those Ministry of Fear riffs."

"Don't worry, I will!" Mo turned away. Malkin crossed to the southern edge of the park, presumably towards one of the cars parked along that stretch of Primrose, and Mo and Pat headed across Summit Ave. toward home.

Or to Mo's car, more precisely, because there was no fucking way she was buying this video and not locating the appropriate implements to watch it immediately. Before arriving at the park, Pat had confirmed with his grandmother in Eastchester that they could temporarily borrow one of her VCRs. Thursday was a dicey night to request a loan, packed with prime viewing, but she had assured Pat she was covered: she had the living room DVR recording one show, bedroom DVR assigned to another, and the living room VCR was likewise employed; she could, however, part with the bedroom VCR for a few days.

"Lucky indeed," Mo grinned, when Pat had recounted this arrangement. "I wouldn't want her to miss any of her shows."

"Trust me, she wouldn't have. She would have told us to come watch the tape this weekend or something." They both grinned, imagining his grandmother's reaction to the mysterious Indignation.

Lynn Sullivan was a night owl anyway, but it was only 8:23 as they walked from the park towards the car. Mo felt as if they had been in that park much longer, that it was much later at night. Back when she was working full time, she'd probably be on the 8:20 train home, which would have just left the platform at Grand Central Station—or worse yet, preparing to spring from her desk and up the steps from Colette's townhouse and bolt to the subway to hopefully catch the 9:00.

"I hope I can remember all those names of the dudes in the band! I should write down some notes now." Mo fumbled in her purse for a pen and a scrap of paper as they walked.

"Hey, idiot." Pat shot her a sideways glance. "You honestly think that I wasn't recording that whole thing on my phone?"

Mo stopped, agape, in front of a pair of stone lions standing

Lost Indignation

sentinel in someone's yard. "Damn, you're good."

Pat jostled her shoulder. "You'll be saying that later. I just hope the audio quality is decent."

"Can we put it on in the car to check it out?"

"Nah, but I'll send you the whole recording. Where are you parked anyway?"

"On Primrose. Just on the other side of Westchester Ave." Last night she had indeed secured a prime spot in the block between Westchester and Gramatan Avenues, a Wednesday street cleaning spot in front of that house that looked haunted by night but mundane by day, a description that in fact could be applied to a lot of the big old multifamily houses in this part of Mount Vernon.

"Guess who I saw today?" Pat asked once they were heading north on the Bronx River Parkway. "Shane Perry!"

"No way!" Mo replied, though Shane was often encountered in all manner of places one would not expect him. Plus, he drove a cab in between acting jobs, so he was likely to be found at a train station.

"At the White Plains train station. When I missed my connection from Hawthorne, I went downstairs and was considering taking the 40 bus." Mo knew, from her few years in Westchester, that one should never rely on the 40 bus. "Someone yells my full name from the parking lot, and it was Shane."

"How's he doing?"

"Same as usual. He was rambling about the shell corporation that bought Skinwalker Ranch and who he thinks is involved."

"I'm glad he was able to entertain you while you were waiting!" They passed the Garth Road little league field, which was quiet and dark. Pat's grandmother's apartment building was halfway up the block. Mo executed a U-turn at the next break in the diagonal parking spaces and pulled up by the curb with her flashers on.

"I'll just run up. You can stay down here. Maybe we can come back to visit this weekend?" Pat was already halfway out of the car.

"Sounds good. I'll be here!" Mo hit the button to turn on the car radio: if there were no Yankees tonight, she could at least listen to the Mets. Baseball that was not your team was still better than no baseball, especially when the regular season was nearing its end.

A few minutes later Pat was back, VCR in hand and cables trailing over his shoulder.

"Thank you, my love. How's your grandmother? Does she think I am totally insane? And did you thank her for me?" Mo started the car.

"She has known you long enough to know you are more than a little bit insane and was happy to help." Mo swung the car out onto Garth Road.

Becky McAuley

"I just realized we forgot about dinner." It was now after 9 p.m., and only truly exciting circumstances could make either of them forget about dinner. "What do you think, BBQ Rib House?"

Pat was always down for BBQ Rib House, as there were a lot more options for him than for Mo, a vegetarian who got almost the same thing every time: a veggie burger with either zucchini sticks or curly fries. "Sounds good to me. I'll order now."

After dropping off Pat with the VCR, tape, and dinner, Mo finagled her beloved 2002 Toyota Camry into a spot a few blocks away, then scurried back up the hill on Overlook Street to eat and watch. Pat unpacked his Cajun chicken sandwich, Mo's veggie burger, and the curly fries to be split indeterminately. "OK, just let me eat my sandwich and then I'll set everything up." There was no question that they were going to watch the tape immediately.

The kitchen table was in the corner of the living room, next to the TV, but it was barely big enough for two people, so Pat often ate at his desk in the opposite corner of the room. Mo granted her veggie burger a quick death, then moved over to the couch and coffee table with her remaining fries for a better line of sight once Pat set up the VCR.

The label on the tape said "Summer 1988." OK, so that answered what exact era Indignation was around, along with the clues that Max had mentioned in the park.

Pat popped it into the VCR and rewound. Whoever had last played it had gotten about a third of the way through.

The first band was indeed Raw Deal, at what Mo thought was the Anthrax in Connecticut, but she couldn't be sure since the feature that stood out the most about this tape so far was that the audio and video were absolutely fucking terrible. She might now own a Raw Deal set not otherwise available on the internet, but what was the point if you could barely see or hear it? Mo hoped the Indignation footage would be a little better.

"Do you think this is the tape itself, or that particular set?"

"I have no idea." Pat did not look psyched.

After Raw Deal, the setting was an outdoor show, where some sort of surf rock sounding band was playing in their bathing suits. The singer was wearing a snorkel and wielding an inflatable flamingo.

"I think that's the Scarsdale Pool!" Pat exclaimed. "I saw Stressboy there when I was eleven!"

"Whoa! I wonder if the Indignation set is from the same show?" This band was evidently not Indignation based on their style, though Mo's anticipation was heightened knowing they were up next. The audio was so poor that they couldn't hear any of the lyrics, nor the name of the band, though they didn't seem eminently memorable. Pat fast-forwarded through the rest of their set.

But the third band wasn't good either. The scene shifted to a rental hall with a decent stage, and about 10-15 kids crowded near it at the start of the set. Mo couldn't hear the band's name when the singer introduced them, though she swore it was a two word name. The longer their set progressed, the more she hoped that this wasn't Indignation. It was the opposite of when she had heard the Show of Force 1990 demo for the first time, after years of hunting, and its quality had equaled if not exceeded that of their track on the *New Breed* comp.

In contrast, this band was absolutely nothing she was hoping for. They were boring. They were sloppy. Their song structures (from what she could hear) were uninspired. There were no instant earworm riffs, no side-to-side mosh parts (or, alternately, Side BY Side mosh parts), and none of the sinuous bass lines often present in songs from this era. The audience at the hall show seemed equally unenthused. Kids had moshed for the intro, but otherwise no one was interested after the second or third song.

"Is this really them?" Mo asked. "Ugh, you can skip the rest of their set." Pat picked up the remote to fast-forward.

"He did say it was the third band." Pat was wearing an odd expression, like he didn't want to say "I told you so" to his impulsive wife who had just dragged him to a park to buy a videotape.

"Could he have been wrong about it being the third band? He did say he hadn't watched it in years."

"I dunno, we can keep going. Maybe he meant third from the end?"

The lackluster set finally concluded, followed by some blank tape. Pat kept fast-forwarding. But for what was probably 15 minutes of tape, there was nothing.

Then, action: a bald guy wielding a microphone stand among a sea of clambering kids, yelling what sounded like the words "my only!" Just then, a huge dude launched himself across the stage, upending the mic and a monitor, and the tape went black again. From the few seconds she heard, that band actually sounded pretty good, despite the poor quality. The venue looked like the same hall where the last band had played.

"Is that it?" Mo looked around, confused. "Do you think there's more stuff recorded here, and the tape just got messed up, or what?"

"That guy stagediving almost looked like a young Warren Yatrofsky," Pat mused. "If he was ever that young in his life." Pat and Warren, who was a Yonkers lifer, went way back; they had originally met in the '90s at the Low Down, a club right here in Mount Vernon that used to book hardcore shows when not hosting other groups of local reprobates.

"We'll have to ask him," Mo grinned. "Hey, did you happen to stagedive and flatten an entire crowd approximately thirty years ago?"

Becky McAuley

"I can assure you, he stagedove and flattened entire crowds on a regular basis and probably doesn't remember half of it."

Pat continued to fast-forward, but no other bands appeared on their screen. Finally, he gave up and rewound.

Mo sighed. "Well, I can't believe I just spent twenty bucks on this shit. At least we got BBQ Rib House." And at least it wasn't a few years ago, when every $20 had been of vital importance. And there was the rare Raw Deal set. "I'm sorry I made you go with me. And that we took your grandmother's VCR for nothing."

"Hey, you didn't know the band was going to suck. Or that the tape was going to be fucked up. And if you hadn't bought it, I know I'd have had to hear about it for days. Or weeks."

"But I don't know if I even believe that was Indignation. Why would someone appropriate riffs from a band that no one liked in the first place?"

"People reuse riffs all the time from bands that no one liked in the first place. But I see your point."

"If the quality was better and we could hear the name of the third band ... also what if the fourth band was them? That set that only played for a few seconds?"

"I could ask ZT to take a look at it," Pat offered. While one might assume "Ziti" to be a sobriquet for someone of Italian origin, it referred to Donald Ziskin-Tavarez, one of Pat's oldest friends and the drummer in his former band Blind Giants, who were reuniting for a benefit show in November. Don worked in IT for ConEd (and supported Mo's office in a freelance capacity during the occasional catastrophe), but he also recorded local bands on the side and might have the appropriate software to clean up the audio.

"That would be nice, if he has time," Mo allowed. She hated waiting for absolutely anything, and who knew when Don would have time to work his magic with the tape, or if he'd be able to improve anything at all. Either way, it sounded like they wouldn't be resolving the mystery of Indignation tonight. Halfheartedly, she claimed one final fry before putting them away for tomorrow's lunch.

Pat shook his head at his wife's stubborn determination to hear this band that before today she hadn't even known existed. Once Mo got into a mystery, it was difficult to divert her, even with more worthwhile topics or tasks competing for her attention. And technically, it was his role as spouse and fellow hardcore kid to enable this quest. Wasn't that part of what being into hardcore was all about—chasing after mysteries that you didn't know about before yesterday and following them to their logical, or illogical, conclusions?

Chapter 2
2017

It is a phenomenon oft acknowledged that if your hair is becoming increasingly out of control, it will somehow resolve itself to be the best it's looked in ages on the day of your haircut. That law was not in effect today: Mo's hair was wild as always, jammed under a Yankees cap as she headed to Elektra's on McLean Avenue in Yonkers. Not that she ever ventured down to the metered parking on McLean: she usually parked a few blocks up the hill on Woodlawn Ave. The parking was getting worse here every year! Elektra was worth it, and the only person who could make Mo's hair look half decent when it wasn't corralled by a knit cap or something. Maybe if she brushed it more than once a month it would have looked better.

As Mo walked down the hill, the reason for the hectic parking revealed itself: McLean Ave. itself was closed for some sort of street festival. The appointment was for 11:30, but Elektra's was already packed when she arrived.

"How you doing, Mo? It will just be a few minutes," Elektra greeted her, gesturing to the second chair, which was the only open spot. "You want coffee?"

"I'm good thanks, and no rush!" At Elektra's they always brought you coffee if you wanted it, and there was plenty to look at while you waited. If you were sitting in one of the spots closer to the window, not only could you watch people walking up and down McLean, you could see them approaching in the reverse via the extra mirrors at the side of each station. Today there was extra excitement afoot due to the fall festival. From Mo's spot in the chair, she was technically watching people approaching in reverse, seen through the mirror in front of her as they ambled past the plate glass window of Elektra's.

Mo made the most of her spare moments and sent Instagram messages to people who might be familiar with Indignation. First she composed a query to her German penpal, Henry, with whom she'd been trading zines and records for over a decade, and then to Edo in Italy, who was a more recent acquaintance, but was interested in a lot of the same bands as Mo. And finally, she DM'd Freddy Alva, who had released the *New Breed* comp and documentary. Mo didn't know him super well, but he was always accommodating and willing to answer questions.

"OK, Mo—we're ready for you; we'll wash you in the back." Mo stashed her phone in her purse, hopped off the chair and headed for the back of the salon, towards a new staffer she hadn't seen before. Outside, a band started up, playing something with the same chords as the beginning of a Last Resort song, but patently not a Last Resort song.

Hair washing complete, the new girl draped a fresh towel on her shoulders.

"Actually, do you mind if I use the restroom while I'm back here?" Mo headed towards the bathroom behind the chairs. She didn't know that right then, three people familiar with Indignation were steps from the door of Elektra's shop. But by the time she was back in the chair and could have seen them in the mirrors, they were gone.

After her haircut, Mo continued to the Will Library on Central Avenue to return some overdue books and prowl the New Fiction section. Westchester branch libraries varied considerably—from Mount Vernon, which had seen better days; to Bronxville, which was one of the nicest libraries on earth; to Eastchester, which was the closest thing to Mo's hometown Lawrence Library. The Will Library also had a similar vibe, though it was larger and nothing ever seemed to be shelved in the right place.

Leaving the library, you had to rejoin the local service road and turn onto Tuckahoe Road as if you were heading toward the Wretched Spaniel (where hardcore shows were very occasionally booked), before making the equivalent of a U-turn to go south. Mo had just turned onto Central when she saw them: two boys on skateboards heading north past the tattoo shop, with identical fades and camo shorts. In a prior decade they could have been on their way to Rockin' Rex, a record store that had existed just across the street in the '90s. Perhaps she had lost her grip on reality and they were indeed phantoms from another era.

There was something about their look and location that almost compelled her to pull over and shout at them to check out Warzone or Side By Side, but Mo kept driving. How do you think these kids would feel about a 31-year-old woman in a Brett Gardner t-shirt leaning out of a Toyota Camry to dispense musical knowledge? 30 years ago, Raw Deal's PO box had been just across the street at the Centuck post office. But Mo had yet to see any evidence of current local teenagers interested in that subset of hardcore.

Pat was on the phone with his mom when she got home, but hung up soon after. "My mom says hi!" Pat set the phone down on his desk as Brett sprang from his lap.

"Hi to your mom." And Mo meant it—Ellie, who lived over in Nyack, was a supremely kind woman and the easiest possible mother-in-law.

"She'll be at my grandmother's for dinner tomorrow, so we can go up there to see everyone and return the VCR."

"That works! Maybe we could walk first, on the Bronx River path or something? Though if we're doing that tomorrow, I should go grocery shopping today." Mo heaved a sigh and balanced her library books on the

Lost Indignation

coffee table, already a sea of Conde Nast publications, assorted hardcore zines of international birth, and newspaper clippings from her mom—half of which Mo had read and was saving for Pat, who claimed he would someday read them, and the other portion which she kept forgetting to bring to work to update the database. The assortment evoked the words from Jay McInerney's protagonist from *Model Behavior*, Connor McKnight: "How could any one person read, let alone own, so many newspapers and magazines?" Pat, to his credit, had been surprisingly tolerant, though Mo knew at some point she would have to clean up her act, or at least their table. Ever since Pat had finished school and started working full time, he hadn't had friends over for game night as frequently, which was the only time the magazines were culled and corralled. That or moving apartments, but Mo and Pat had moved to Overlook Street in 2013 from their tiny sublevel in the Bronx and hopefully wouldn't be relocating again for a while.

"Fuck grocery shopping, we can do that tomorrow on the way up to Garth Road. What are you thinking for dinner?"

Mo hesitated for half a second before producing her frequent answer, in which she sometimes substituted Burrito Poblano or Mont Olympus: "Thai House and Uncle Louie G's?"

Mo and Pat had gone from years of not having any money at all to being able to go out for Thai food on Saturday nights without experiencing spasms of intense economic guilt, though overall they were still trying to be frugal due to the astronomical cost of her MFA. And at this point they hardly ever got takeout during the week, or at least *she* didn't, since after class she was actually home for dinner after years of eating at her desk at work.

"I'm with it," Pat assented.

"What's Ally up to today?" Mo inquired once the Thai plan was finalized. Ally ZT, Don's twin sister, lived in northwest Yonkers, not far from the Thai House in Ardsley.

"I don't know, but I'm texting her brother right now. I can hit her up next. He's going to pick up the tape tomorrow."

"I'm glad Don's able to look at it. Even if he can't do anything, at least we tried to fix it."

"Yeah, he wants to see what he can do. He said we can meet him at Slave tomorrow. We can stop there on the way up to my grandmother's."

"Works for me." Mo would rarely have passed up a chance to hit Slave to the Grind, the best coffee shop in Bronxville and perhaps all of Westchester.

So the Indignation tape and the borrowed VCR would be departing their home on the same day. So far Mo had resisted rewatching it, due to the overwhelmingly underwhelming quality of the set. She wondered if she

Becky McAuley

should, if only to try to pick up on some last clues in case something got messed up during the restoring process. But rewatching it would probably just rankle her further.

As they were walking to the car, Mo saw a new Instagram message from Freddy Alva. He had never heard the Indignation demo, didn't know anyone who had it, and wished her luck. If someone as helpful and knowledgeable as Freddy had never heard of Indignation, who would have? Mo was aware this could be a protracted search, but she expected that in her wider circle, which encompassed people of multiple countries and generations, someone would know *something* about Indignation.

"Should we see if Tony is here?" Mo inquired as they were leaving the Thai House. Her former coworker Tony Gerson was known to take some weekend shifts at Petraske's, the bar downstairs, or else frequent it as a patron.

"Nah, let's keep moving. Though we should get dinner with him soon."

"Or we can see if he's around if we visit the goats in Dobbs," Mo added. The village of Dobbs Ferry, the town next to Ardsley, had recently imported some goats to denude a hill near the train station, and Mo and Pat had yet to see them in action.

"Don't get ahead of ourselves for tomorrow," Pat cautioned. "We'll play it by ear." He and Mo were known for making unrealistic plans and then running late or having something else come up, such as the acquisition of mysterious video tapes.

On the morning of the last Sunday in September, Mo called Kenza in one of the rare times in which they were both free to talk. While on the phone with Kenza or her mom, Mo usually tended to otherwise neglected household tasks, like dealing with the laundry that they had hauled home from the laundromat on Grand Street and never put away, but today's weather was so perfect that she was walking while talking: first in her immediate neighborhood and then through the grounds of A.B. Davis Middle School, back toward the asphalt track where people were playing soccer in the infield, and then—hey, she had never seen the gate open to those feral stairs that led down to another school on High Street. ("Feral stairs," in the McGraw-Catalano terminology, were any public stairs that led from, say, one dead-end street to another, especially if a large drop in elevation separated the two, which meant they were all over Yonkers, with a few in Mount Vernon.)

45 minutes later, Mo was off the phone and back on Overlook Street. Pat was at his computer, playing *Civilization V*, and Brett and CC eyed her from the couch.

"How's Kenza?"

Lost Indignation

"She's good. Well, frustrated about apartment stuff. Which I would be too." Kenza and her husband were trying to buy an apartment in DC before the baby was born but kept getting beat by buyers who could put down more cash. Mo glanced at the couch, weighing her chances of wedging her butt in without dislodging the cats, then instead sat down on the living room floor to stretch.

"Oh, and those feral stairs behind A.B. Davis? I have never seen the gate open before! We should go walk over there later."

"Not a long walk, since we also have to go grocery shopping, meet up with Don to give him the tape, and get up to my family's place. And I thought you wanted to see the goats too?"

"Oh yeah, the goats." Mo had totally forgotten about them. "We could just walk over to the stairs real quick on the way up to Bronxville."

Somehow, "later" always came way too quickly, especially on the weekends. Before they knew it, it was mid-afternoon, with no time for a walk and about a 50-50 chance of seeing the goats and/or grocery shopping, depending how soon Don arrived at Slave to the Grind. Mo wasn't sure how much longer the goats, borrowed from a farm upstate, were going to be at their current freelance assignment in Dobbs Ferry. Today was their best chance to see them, though she wasn't entirely sure if Pat would follow all posted rules when they arrived.

"You think they'd let me in with the goats, maybe ride one around a bit?"

"I've got my cards, we can say we're doing research if anyone complains. Well, if people complain. I'm not sure the goats can read." Due to Mo's penchant for caution and anxiety (which were technically antithetical to participating in hardcore), she had often joked that if they were caught trespassing somewhere, she would claim to be a location scout from Remove This Doubt Location Scouting. "Remove this Doubt" had always been one of Mo's favorite Supremes songs, but what really elevated it to canon was hearing it sampled on the M.O.P. song "Rude Bastard."

Just after starting his new job, Pat had ordered her a set of business cards emblazoned with "Remove This Doubt: Location Scout," adding further substance to their inside joke, along with a real email address: mo@removethisdoubt.com. While removethisdoubt.com did not exist besides a cryptic landing page, the email address forwarded to her regular personal email. Mo hoped that she'd never have any use for the cards in a real-life situation, but she did like to distribute them to generate a reaction from her recipients, almost like the "Occult Researcher" card deployed by Julie Jaffe in *Telegraph Avenue*.

"Look who's here." Pat angled his head as they walked down Pondfield Road after parking over by the library. It was J.P. Sydenstricker, hanging out outside of Slave to the Grind. You were semi-likely to find him here, as he lived nearby, and if so, you were more than likely to become ensnared in a long and interesting conversation. Sydenstricker was both a caustic grouch and voluble enthusiast, depending on the topic and setting. He had played in various bands, most notably Shock of Pain in the early '90s—who were more of a grindcore band and not Mo's style—and had inspired various rabid fans on multiple continents. On the more straight-up hardcore side of things, he had toured Europe with Rejuvenate, and now worked as a guitar tech and an electrician, occasionally filling in for classic New York bands.

Sydenstricker hung out here ostensibly by himself, though there was always someone wandering by and ending up in conversation with him, as there was now. While it was a gamble to insert themselves into his existing discussion, as they might end up stuck here for a while, Mo figured it was worth it to ask him about Indignation, especially if they were already waiting for Don.

They ducked into Slave to the Grind to buy coffee beans and two iced coffees. As Pat was paying, Mo headed outside and waited until J.P.'s present conversation partner wandered away down Pondfield Road towards the train station. "Hey J.P.! What's happening?"

"'Sup, Mo. Just enjoying the day." It was indeed a great day to be out in Bronxville.

Mo decided to dispense with formalities and just ask him. "So, I thought you might be a good person to ask ... do you remember anything about this band called Indignation? From around here, in the late eighties?"

"Wow! Indignation! Why the hell do you care about Indignation?"

"Well, I didn't, until a few days ago. I got this videotape, but we're not sure if they're even on it ... it's a long story. But I would love to know more about them or get a copy of their demo." The door opened, and Pat joined them outside, handing Mo her coffee.

"I knew the singer." J.P. shook his head. "Oh, man. Fucking Dion! I haven't thought of that dude in years. He used to drink with my dad. Even though he was, like, my age!"

"He used to hang out with your dad?"

"Yeah, at this place called Goose Bruno's. Over by the racetrack. I used to have to go there and pick up my dad sometimes." Sydenstricker reflected. "I only sort of knew the other guys in the band. The drummer was kind of annoying. And I went to school with the guitarist for a year or two. He was a year below me. Him and that kid who always looked like he wanted to be in the band but was just their friend."

"Max Malkin?" Mo ventured.

"No, his name wasn't Max ... maybe Dan? Something with a D. Anyway. I only saw Indignation once, and then almost saw them at CB's, but they dropped off the show the day of. And I never had the demo. Probably not worth chasing." He looked shrewdly at Mo. "If it was, wouldn't you have already heard it?"

Mo smiled at the backhanded compliment. Sydenstricker often teased her for being a devotee of arcane side projects and her assorted irrational enthusiasms for third-tier NYHC bands. Why would this quest seem any different?

"I used to see that other guy at Rockin' Rex sometimes, their friend who wasn't in the band. And then years later, I was on a job over by Murphy's Law, on Midland" (Mo knew he meant the bar, not the band, though she was pretty sure he had also filled in for the band), "doing some work on a house there. And I think I saw that guy in the driveway next door. But does he still live in the area now? I don't know."

Sydenstricker seemed alternately amused by and contemptuous of Mo's historical hardcore obsessions. Maybe it was just a difference in perspectives due to the generation gap: one of them having lived it and laughed at some of these supposedly vaunted acts, and the other exhibiting the archeological attitudes of the younger generations. Fuck, there were now multiple generations interested in hardcore, including people far younger than Pat and Mo. Mo herself was somewhere in the middle, and was used to seeing OGs like Sydenstricker or Rich McLoughlin just walking around Bronxville on a regular basis; they were just part of the local atmosphere.

With the Indignation portion of the conversation concluded, J.P. and Pat had moved on to other topics, with Mo as the observer and occasional interjector, a role she often occupied. There was still no sign of Don. Pat had mentioned that he was on his way up from some extended family event in Queens, but he wasn't exactly the timeliest person anyway. At this rate they definitely weren't going to make it to Dobbs Ferry for the goats.

Finally, 15 minutes later, Don appeared, double-parking and hustling toward them, his customary trenchcoat flapping and his wild black hair streaming behind him.

"Hey!" he swooped in, kissed Mo on the cheek, high-fived Pat, and nodded to Sydenstricker.

"Took you long enough," Pat remarked, but he was grinning. After knowing the dude for at least twenty years, he hadn't really expected him to be on time.

"Thank you for coming to get the tape!" Mo didn't let Don's tardiness dampen her appreciation. "Can I buy you a coffee or something? In trade for looking at it?"

"You might need to buy the man a lot more than a coffee in return for listening to some of the bands that might be on that thing," Sydenstricker remarked acidly.

"It's no problem at all. And I gotta run," Don gestured to the car.

"Same, we're trying to get groceries before we head up to my family's place."

"Though I'm always looking for an opportunity to avoid grocery shopping," Mo said quickly, lest Don feel bad for being late. "Anyway, here it is." She pulled the tape from her string backpack. "They're supposed to be the third band, but it's so hard to hear, and then there's a gap right after that. So anything you can recover from that area of the tape would be awesome. And no rush of course," which pained her to say, since Mo McGraw was always in a rush, particularly about a new hardcore mystery. But Don was doing her a favor and maintained a busy schedule between ConEd, the recording stuff, and sometimes CFA. Mo prayed Colette wouldn't engender any computer catastrophes over the next few weeks that would siphon Don's spare time from the tape.

While there were many times that Mo wished she were somewhere else instead of at work, particularly when there was somewhere else she needed to be, she didn't actually hate her job. Why else would she feel that wave of contentment every time she turned and walked down the three steps that ran parallel to the townhouse and opened the heavy oak door?

Then again, it was always a relief to sit down at a desk with your coffee after over an hour on various trains and then walking the last ten minutes to the office, down a block that somehow either seemed to be hotter or colder than anywhere else in the city in whatever iteration you least preferred. And her new hour-plus commute from the Fleetwood stop on the Harlem Line was better than the 80-90 minutes each way via the 6 train and walking across town back when she and Pat had lived in the far reaches of the Bronx. So yes, the descent down the stairs into the dark, cool townhouse was a satisfying moment, no matter how odious the rest of the day might turn out to be. Today, she almost collided with Drew Flowers, the office manager, as he was stepping out with Pierre, Colette's mastiff and the office mascot (mastiff-cot?) for their morning work. She always savored being alone for the first few minutes of the day, at least in their section of the office by the front door, before you squeezed past the bathroom and closets into the larger room where the important people sat, Colette included.

The environs of Colette Foulard Associates deviated from nearly every norm of a Manhattan workspace. This was no sleek office tower imbued with Conde Elevator intrigue. CFA worked out of the first two floors of Colette's home, which had its very own pros and cons, from killer mosquitoes in the garden to constant street noise, especially now with the construction down the block. And while it was technically an open-plan office, there was not enough room for a true open plan: the desks tended to

Lost Indignation

hug the walls and inhabit every bit of available space. There were currently eight people sitting downstairs, and twelve on the second floor, far more than one would expect from looking at the exterior. Not only were there 20 people packed into two floors of her boss's four-story townhouse, but it was also one of the only buildings in the block that looked remotely like a home. Hemmed in by Root Studios to the east and the Chelsea Modern condos to the west, the CFA office was a staunch holdover from an earlier era when the block had been full of townhouses before the rest were demolished to make way for a NYCHA parking lot, which in turn was being torn up and turned into mixed-income apartments. The existence of multiple housing projects this close to Chelsea Market and the High Line was one of the many incongruous facets of this neighborhood.

With the new building rising down the block, Root Studios was the only thing separating them from the cacophony of the construction and its associated debris. You couldn't even walk down their sidewalk on the north side of 18th Street anymore—you had to start on the south side and cross mid-block in front of the hardware store, as Mo was doing now, deftly swapping her coffee to her left hand and covering the lid from dust, as if palming a basketball. The only good thing that had come out of the construction was a robust customer base for the new bodega on the corner, which did a legit egg platter for $5.50 and the best iced coffee this side of Elio at the Fleetwood train station or Pat's coffee at home.

The closest parallel for Mo's office was the townhouse that had been affectionately memorialized in the George Gurley article "My Love Affair with the *New York Observer*." Besides the physical comparisons (townhouse, close quarters, bathroom strife), the article itself was the best analogy to how Mo felt about Colette Foulard Associates, in its justification for staying through so many protracted shitstorms and calamities of great variety.

At CFA, most people sat on the second floor, with the admin staff wedged in by the front door: Mo, their bookkeeper Anna, a nice Russian mom who was only there in the afternoons, and new office manager, Drew Flowers, who had replaced Tony Gerson and kind of looked like Alfred E. Neuman. Life was never dull by the front door, and while the office manager was technically responsible for welcoming all clients and deliveries, Mo was also right there, exposed and attempting to finish a plethora of tasks in half the time required.

A handful of others in Colette's inner circle sat in the room behind them that opened onto the small back garden. Elvis Fregosi, the head of the real estate practice, had the first big desk on the left, between the stairs and the fireplace. The French doors to the garden were nearly always open, as Colette sat adjacent and smoked constantly at her desk. Besides the cigarette smoke, Colette also hated air conditioning, and through

Becky McAuley

this open-door policy, Mo had learned all about the ferocity of Chelsea mosquitoes.

Head up the treacherous stairs to the left of Elvis's desk (which had seen a few high-heeled wipeouts over the years), and you would find more staffers packed into a narrow space. At the top of the stairs, along the front of the townhouse, was the arts & culture team, including Aaron Overton, extremely gay and potentially CFA's first Blasian, if you didn't count that temp in 2012. Then, as you head towards the back of the house: Oona Velissard, who appeared vaguely continental but was rumored to be from Illinois; Emily Chen, who handled the Museum of Sex and various cantankerous individual artists and was Oona's work wife and fellow oddball; and above them, a precarious collection of magazines.

Past Oona and Emily was Monica Marquez, Mo's right hand woman on the database who was also starting to take on account work, like helping Emily with the Museum of Sex, and Shannon Fahey, their former summer intern who had been elevated into permanent service, half to support on the database when Mo went part-time, and half to take over social media. Behind Shannon and Monica was the overflow seating: technically a desk or two, it housed the microwave and coffee maker, though if anyone sat there, there would have been barely three inches between the back of their chairs and those of the database team. Colette was currently agitating to add another media strategist before the fall season got truly wild, while Mo was either being pessimistic or realistic about the probability of finding someone in time who would fit Colette's high standards, mesh with staff, and appreciate the odder aspects of this crazy place rather than being repelled.

Then, in the back room visited the least frequently by Colette, and therefore also the messiest region of the office, was the team that handled hospitality, food & beverage, and events. Tati Allen, head of events, had been there almost as long as Mo. While her desk faced out over the garden, she always had one eye on her team of events understudies and Keith McTigue, who also supported on restaurant clients.

There was a high rate of turnover at CFA, and in PR in general. They'd lost some good people in the past year, and you couldn't expect this current crew to stay together forever. Someone would get burned out or get a better offer, move back home or go back to school. But Mo enjoyed the current tight-knit group, which had begun to solidify over the summer, and was glad to see most of these people every day, rather than hoping to escape them entirely.

There was only one problem with her office, in the times when Colette was treating her fairly. Well technically three problems:

1. It took too long to get there, which was now compounded by her new

short day;
2. it could be stressful as hell;
3. and, if left unchecked, it could take up every moment of her brainpower and waking life.

There were some Sundays when Mo's "Sunday night anxiety" was worse than others, but in general, she seemed to have a comically short memory about work and remained relatively optimistic about each coming week. Mo and Monica had in fact joked that this form of work-brain repression was kind of like that phenomenon in which your brain forgets how bad childbirth is, so you'll be more likely to go through with it next time. But she also recognized this as an essential tenet of surviving at a place like CFA. You had to assume each week, or event season, wasn't going to be so bad, or else the anticipatory anxiety would absolutely crush you. Inevitably, no matter how good each week's calendar looked going in, everything went to shit due to surprise projects, surprise departures, a surprise yelling-fest from Colette (one of the key components of the surprise departures), surprise events, indecisive clients, rush mailings, and other incidents that ranged from insidiously irksome to truly terrifying.

This year Mo was most concerned about how to balance her CFA schedule against classes and homework: about getting her work done in the allotted time, about not letting work take over her brain after hours, and about not being bothered by misdirected questions or manufactured crises in the evenings after class, when the office was often still in full swing despite technically closing at 6 p.m. Living in the Bronx, it hadn't been as much of a problem if you left work at 7:48 p.m. vs. 7:54, since the subway ran continually. But now a difference of those few minutes could mean missing the 8:20 Metro North train home, since it took 30 minutes to get to Grand Central, and the Metro North trains only ran every half hour. On the later nights, it was also stressful trying to get to anything on time after work, especially hardcore shows where you were trying to see the first few bands.

Colette's moods were another variable in Mo's office quality of life. They had fought nonstop for about six months from fall 2014 to spring 2015, before Colette mysteriously resumed being respectful in 2015. Fall 2015 and spring 2016 were two of the busiest seasons Mo had experienced at CFA; not terrible from a yelling perspective, just full of nonstop wackiness.

Periodically, Mo would see people bragging online about switching jobs to something more rewarding but less remunerative. But she'd never had the option to take a pay cut while they were barely hanging on already, and where were these mythical 40-hour-a-week jobs anyway? And how could she be sure that the grass was greener elsewhere?

Becky McAuley

The CFA experiment could have gone on indefinitely if not for the events of fall 2016. This was the first year that Colette had behaved truly egregiously to Mo and the rest of the staff, while the events in her non-work life made her less likely to tolerate the outbursts. Just after Mo had survived Fashion Week and Pat had started his senior year, Mo's paternal grandfather had died. He had been sick for a while, and Mo knew how fortunate she was to have made it to 30 with all her grandparents still around, but that didn't make it much easier. Soon after, Pat found out that his estranged father had passed away, though no one had informed his side of the family for two weeks. His dad had been a musician and an addict, mostly simultaneously, and Pat hadn't seen him since he was six. He had only learned where his dad had been living and working at the time of his death from the obituary. Mo sensed he had a lot of complicated feelings on the subject, but hesitated to dig too deeply, as they were both trying to hold on and get through the fall. Besides his senior year at Hunter, Pat had also been working four days a week at Generation Records. This was an unsustainable commitment, though Mo welcomed his financial contributions, access to hardcore discounts, and the stories he brought home at the end of each day to beat back the sadness that might otherwise engulf them.

Mo's great uncle Harry died in November, followed by Pat's mom's cousin. In mid-November, they attended Uncle Harry's funeral on a Sunday, a friend's wedding that next Saturday, and the other funeral the day after. There was no time to rest or unwind, though Mo joked that at least she was getting to see her family a lot that fall. And it wasn't like she'd been asking for special treatment at work—just the understanding that with all these things happening she wasn't going to clean up someone else's mess at 9 p.m. or be as patient with someone's bullshit.

And that fall, with its cavalcade of events, there was *so* much fucking bullshit. Even Tony Gerson, usually a rock during event season— from emergency FedExing to prepping the iPads to ordering the Ubers— had been semi-quit-semi-fired after a blowout with Colette at the end of June, though he would have left that fall anyway for his student teaching. He and Colette had weathered a George Steinbrenner-Billy Martin relationship since his initial hiring, with him leaving and being rehired at least twice over various spats, but he was still the best office manager they'd ever had. Mo hoped that he would somehow return to them, which ended up happening in January, before he left again in summer 2017—this time for real—in order to take his first teaching job.

Pat was scheduled to graduate with his bachelor's in 2017, after getting his associate's degree at Westchester Community College and transferring to Hunter. While there was no guarantee of him securing a job in his field right away, they could finally start to plan around his eventual full-time salary and benefits. Every time Mo came home in tears from a fresh berating by Colette, or something else unjust that had befallen one of her coworkers, he assured her that once he was done with school, he would do everything he could to get her out of CFA, even if it meant her taking some less stressful, low-paying job while she researched something better. (Mo was not entirely convinced that non-stressful jobs existed.)

There was one final incident at CFA that pushed Mo over the edge into knowing she would never be able to stay there full-time and subsequently applying for school. Art Basel and the weeks leading up to it were always the craziest period of the year, but in the past, it was almost an enjoyable chaos, with the whole office pulling together for one big push before half of them went off to Miami and triumphantly wrangled their events. This year, Colette had been in a bad mood for weeks, and Mo couldn't wait for her boss and the Miami crew to be 1000 miles away.

Once Colette and co. arrived in Miami, the situation did not improve. There was a mishap with the wristbands for the Aby Rosen dinner, a new safeguard for 2016, which ended up with Tati herself renting a car and driving around Miami to distribute them after two terrified temps quit on the spot. An influencer was kicked by a horse and had to pull out of hosting an event at The Setai. A last-minute party at the Teixeira Hotel inadvertently siphoned half of Aaron's guest list for his event at Locust Projects. During the best Art Basel weeks, Colette was on edge and never got a lot of sleep, but this year seemed worse than the past few combined. And that was before the thing with the Zywica Foundation people. What had seemed on the surface a reasonable request (the foundation wanted CFA to send out an eblast about some upcoming reception) somehow provoked a torrent of inquiries and then outright ire from Colette. As an intermittent client, there was no account executive assigned to the foundation at the time, so Colette inexplicably decided the admin staff could handle it rather than someone in Arts & Culture. For the entire afternoon of Friday, December 2nd, Colette was constantly calling the office to scream at either Lily, the confused new office manager (who would soon quit anyway), or Mo, who was supposed to be helping her with the script and blast list. Though there wasn't so much she could do when their boss was mostly calling her to rant about other employees without taking a breath or providing additional instructions.

Colette always had her favorites and favorite targets, but now it had seemed like no one was off limits. Today, she made an abrupt transition from mocking Tati and Aaron, two of the most essential people at CFA, to screaming that Mo herself was making her life so much harder. And if she was talking shit on Tati and Aaron, she was probably doing the same about Mo.

As the tension and frequency of calls escalated, all Mo's other tasks

Becky McAuley

were pushed by default either to Friday night or early Monday morning. At 5:45 p.m., Colette was yet again on the line, complaining about how Lily and Mo were making her life so much harder, when Mo snapped back: "We're trying to do you a favor! I didn't ask to be involved in this, and if we can't understand what you need, you should ask someone else!" There was silence. Mo had never spoken like that to her boss. Colette was sufficiently shocked: she muttered for a bit and hung up. As Mo slammed down the receiver on her end, she heard applause ringing throughout the office.

Mo was still steaming when she locked the office at 8:29 p.m. and started running towards Grand Central to catch the 9:00 train home. On the train she was so distracted that she could barely focus on reading *Back to Blood*, which was set in Miami during Art Basel. CFA had always seemed like the type of place she could stay long-term, as long as she could deal with the commute, the crazy hours, the cigarette smoke, and having to clean up other people's disasters. But today had made clear that the present situation was unsustainable and that she needed to focus on making a change rather than merely ameliorating the situation. In general, Mo was more like the Life's Blood song in that she would *never* make a change in any area of her life where she didn't need to, from replacing an ancient computer to applying for jobs. Getting a new job had always sounded difficult and time-consuming. She hadn't updated her resume in years. There was probably no similar combination of database and HR at another firm. But how else could she break away from scenes like today without securing another source of income? Pat wouldn't be out of school for another six months. And if she did manage to find something slightly less terrible, Colette would probably make her life a living hell during the final weeks of the transition, which Mo had witnessed during departures of various previously-loved employees.

But what if the answer was to escape via another route entirely?

A few weeks ago, she had found herself on the website of Sarah Lawrence College, looking longingly at the description of its MFA program. Imagine being able to go to school for fiction writing! Maybe she'd be better at grad school than she'd been at undergrad, when she couldn't wait to get out and find a real job where she didn't have to work on the weekends. Due to assorted retail jobs during college, Mo had missed a ton of weekend shows, or at least the first half of every CBGB's show on a Sunday. And yet now she was either working so late she missed evening shows or too stressed and tired to attend.

At 31, school now seemed a novelty rather than mandatory drudgery. And Mo, usually so averse to change, had an intrinsic urge to blow up her life, to alter every aspect besides Pat and cats and apartment. She was so sick of this shit. But imagine being able to walk to class! (Sarah

Lost Indignation

Lawrence was within a mile or two of their apartment.) Imagine going to school for something inspiring, rather than rationalizing that at least she didn't *really* hate her job? It seemed like the type of thing that happened to other people, she reflected. But why not me?

Back to Blood forgotten, Mo pulled up the admissions information and learned that the deadline was December 15th, just under two weeks away. Was it crazy to try to get everything together in time? By the time she had stomped home from the train to Overlook Street, she was dead set on applying to this program. She had no idea if she'd get in, or how she'd pay for it if she did, but they'd figure that out later.

Generation didn't close till 10 p.m. on weekends, so she sometimes waited for Pat on Fridays so they could catch the 10:32 train home together—or during Art Basel season, he might even be waiting for her. But today, Mo had been propelled straight from office to home. Which meant she had time to start working on her application. With Brett and CC looking on worriedly that she might forget to feed them, she sat down at the computer to get started.

When Pat got home at 11:15 to find Mo still wide awake at her desk, he supported the idea, being used to Mo setting her mind on something in a matter of hours, if not minutes. If Pat had hesitated, maybe she would have rethought this brash path. Now she just needed to get everything together for the application. She emailed two former professors to ask if they'd provide references—though if she couldn't get two, she could ask her old boss from the book company—and contemplated if she had any existing stories that would make a sufficient writing sample. The personal statement would be harder, though they only wanted 250 words about why she wanted to pursue a graduate degree at Sarah Lawrence in this field of study. She had a feeling that "I hate my job and decided to blow up my life" would not suffice.

Mo wondered if it was worth applying to other programs if she was already gathering all the required materials and polishing her writing samples. But she knew that if she was accepted to another program in the city, it would be hard to escape for class or avoid being dragged back in at the end of the work day.

When Colette returned from Miami, she operated like Mo didn't exist, which was fine with Mo. Like many PR companies, the CFA office was traditionally closed between Christmas and New Year's. In January, Colette made a show of being nice, chasing her out the door by 7 p.m.—no matter that they closed at 6:00. But soon she was being berated almost daily and receiving all caps emails after midnight. And when she wasn't being castigated or reprimanded, another staffer was on the hot seat.

Didn't Colette realize, Mo stewed, that the more cruelly she treated her staff, the more people quit, which made Mo's job harder when she had to replace them? This hadn't always been the case, Mo overseeing all things hiring, but in the last few years, it had all fallen in her lap, like an upended dinner or an exceptionally ill-tempered pet. Tony Gerson seemed to be the only one who could take everything in stride. After his student teaching ended and Lily inevitably quit with no notice, he made a much-heralded return in January to his office manager role. He was now on his third stint at CFA and had made it known that would be his last year no matter what, as he was graduating in May with his master's and hoped to secure a teaching job that fall.

Mo's one secret sustenance was her application to the MFA program, of which she would receive the results sometime that spring. Even if she didn't get in, it was proof that she wasn't willing to let things stay the same forever. And once Pat graduated, perhaps she could take even more concrete action towards finding another job, even if it paid less. But she was spared from thinking about alternative jobs when her application to Sarah Lawrence was accepted. Mo could hardly believe it, and she immediately knew she would have to find some way to make it happen. At least someone thought she was good at something else besides whatever the hell she did all day at CFA.

By April, Mo had already accepted her place in the writing program and was assuming/hoping she would be able to register for classes that met in the afternoon or evening, allowing her to potentially continue at CFA for the first half of the day. At some point she would inevitably have to tell Colette, a moment that she had been worrying about for months. It was always hard to pin down her boss into a private conversation unless you had the pretext of discussing something else. Colette always seemed to sense when someone was about to resign and needed to give notice in a timely fashion, and therefore pretended to be too busy to meet. In the meantime, Pat managed to graduate from Hunter and secure a full-time job, with benefits, at a residential school for kids with behavioral problems in Hawthorne. Mo was overjoyed for Pat that he would be using his new degree, but it also represented one more piece of her plan falling into place: she'd be on Pat's health insurance and wouldn't have to worry about losing her CFA insurance if she went part-time.

Finally, after Tony Gerson had departed and Drew Flowers had been installed as the new office manager, Mo worked up the courage to inform her boss. She managed to lure her upstairs with a stack of resumes, purportedly to discuss staffing and hiring for fall. But as soon as Mo sat down on the couch, she blurted out that she was going back to school and wondered if it would be possible to continue working at CFA on a limited basis.

Colette was surprisingly calm regarding this development and instructed Mo to work out the practical details with Anna the bookkeeper.

Lost Indignation

And after that conversation, she reverted to treating Mo the way she had from 2011-2014, and the intermittent good times after that. Was Colette so convinced that Mo was going to quit when she asked her to have a conversation upstairs, and so happy that she was staying that she had agreed to let her work hourly with shockingly minimal fuss? Or was she triumphing over the fact that if Mo was going to school, she would be unlikely to look for a new full-time job if she was accommodating Mo's schedule? Either way, Mo was enjoying the new atmosphere and surprised she'd been able to pull off the transition. It was all arranged quite quickly: Shannon was asked to stay on at the end of her internship, and it was announced to staff that Mo would be going part-time. Everyone was still a little shell-shocked after the final departure of Tony Gerson and transition to Drew Flowers, Mo reflected, so the timing had worked in her favor.

So while Mo had managed to extricate herself from full-time duties at Colette's, she had only engineered a tenuous and temporary solution. And she tried to enjoy the general air of chaos along with the stress, like Andres Serrano's memorable visit to their office to discuss his collaboration with the Vedomedy project, or Pierre eating the sticky for Table 8 on the seating chart for an upcoming dinner. ("He ate Table Eight!" Keith had squealed in horror.) But she knew she had to appreciate these moments while she could and that she might not be able to keep this up for long. Maybe she was just waiting for an event that would tip her work/school balance in one inevitable direction.

Becky McAuley

Chapter 3
1988

Saturday was Ryan Marnell's favorite day of the week. On weekends, Ryan often hung out with his best friend and neighbor David Eckley, but this Saturday, Eckley (pretty much everyone called him Eckley) was off taking the SATs. Eckley's dad was a chemist, and his family was more academically inclined than Ryan's, who hadn't thought that far ahead yet. He wasn't sure he needed to take the SATs; he probably wasn't going to college.

This was one of those early March days that held hope and promise for spring. In Westchester County, just north of New York City, they could easily get hit with more snow after the first hint of warm weather. But people were eager to enjoy the sunshine while they could. As Ryan rolled along Tuckahoe Road towards the Will Library, a favorite skate spot, he saw people washing their cars, walking their dogs, and otherwise taking advantage of the suddenly merciful temperatures. Skateboard under his feet and a tape of Token Entry's *Jaybird* in his walkman: Eckley or no Eckley, it was shaping up to be a decent day.

The library was just south of Colonial Heights, a neighborhood in Yonkers which had spawned a bunch of hardcore kids, but they were all a few years older than Ryan and David and didn't really know them, though they would sometimes see those kids at shows or Record Stop in Hartsdale. Ryan and Eckley lived in Crestwood, which was north and east of the library, closer to the Crestwood train station.

The back of the library parking lot was relatively quiet, though there was one kid in a Bad Brains shirt with floppy hair whom Ryan had never seen skating there before. He looked younger than Ryan and while his form was a little awkward, he was unselfconsciously having a great time. Ryan didn't want to interrupt him and waited till he was taking a break to walk over and say hi.

"Nice shirt!"

"Thanks, dude! I'm Matt."

"And I'm Ryan. Do you go to shows around here?"

Matt launched into a description of the last show he had seen at the Anthrax in Connecticut, which had featured Zombie Squad and Wide Awake.

"I wanted to come up for that, but my friend didn't want to go." David Eckley wasn't big on Wide Awake. "The last time I was there was for Sick of It All and Token Entry in January."

"Oh man, I was there too!"

"Token Entry is playing CBGB's tomorrow," Ryan offered. "If you want to ride down on the train with us."

"No way! I haven't been to CBGB's yet. I don't turn sixteen till next month. Next time!"

"Yeah, you're almost there!" This guy definitely didn't look 16, so Ryan doubted he would have been able to sneak in.

"Do you want to come over? I live up Central Ave.," Matt offered. "I have wrestling and skate videos."

"That sounds fun." Ryan wasn't into wrestling, but was down for the skateboarding videos and down to keep hanging out with this kid, especially while Eckley was otherwise occupied.

"Where do you go to school?" Ryan asked, as they skated to Matt's house on Eisenhower Drive. It was one of those Yonkers neighborhoods built in the 1950s, brick split-level homes where every house looked the same. In Ryan's neighborhood of Crestwood, there was more variety, from old Victorians to newer, smaller homes.

"I go to Roosevelt. I got kicked out of Solomon Schechter," Matt explained almost proudly.

"I go to Fordham Prep," Ryan offered.

Matt looked intrigued. "That must be cool, taking the train and being halfway to the city." Fordham was located in the Bronx, in between Westchester and Manhattan.

"It's a lot of work. The school part, not the city part. You're lucky you don't have to dress up."

"Do you ever get to talk to the Fordham University girls?"

"We don't really see the college kids," Ryan explained. "Though my friend David is always trying to get to know them." Somehow a few months ago, Eckley had deduced that some of the members of the bands Uppercut and Raw Deal resided in an old house near campus affectionately known as the Hotel Camberling, which had resulted in a handful of attempts to ingratiate himself with these bemused older members of the hardcore community. That was just like Eckley, trying to charm both adults and contemporaries/near-contemporaries, resulting in hardcore connections that more than once had benefited both him and Ryan.

Ryan was just happy to collect records and go to shows, not really caring who he met along the way, but appreciated the fruits of his friend's gregariousness. At most shows he was content to stand in the back and listen, besides the occasions where a band moved him so undeniably that he would burst into the pit or launch himself towards the action for a stagedive or pile-on. He would rarely remember the specifics afterwards, entering what was almost a fugue state, until reemerging flushed, sweaty, and exhilarated at the end of the set. Eckley, of course, was a more stylish stage-diver, and never got as red-faced as Marnell.

Matt's dad was in the living room reading *The Herald Statesman*

Lost Indignation

when they arrived. His twin younger sisters, whom he had mentioned on the walk over, must have been out with his mom, as there was no sign of anyone else in the house. Before heading upstairs to check out the wrestling videos, they stopped for snacks in the kitchen.

"Won't your parents wonder where you are?" Matt inquired as he scrutinized the contents of a disorderly cabinet.

"Not really. They're used to me being out on a day like this." His parents weren't the worrying type, especially now that he was 16, and were wrapped up in their own lives. Ryan's mom slept a lot these days, and when he himself had woken up this morning, his dad had already left for his shop. And if they had known where he was, they probably would have appreciated that he was hanging out with a new friend. Ryan had to give them credit: they were pretty much the best type of parents that a 16-year-old could have, in terms of what he was allowed to get up to. Though the older he got, the more he worried about their own problems. His mom had been drinking more than ever in the last few years, and his dad seemed constantly consumed with worry about the state of his business, where, since the late '60s, he had been selling pool tables and dart boards and doing custom trophy engraving from a small storefront on Saw Mill River Road. But what was hardcore for, besides a way to forget your problems or channel them into something you could use, either for yourself or to connect with other people who were feeling the same way? Ryan followed Matt up the half flight of stairs to his room, carefully toting their sodas and snacks.

The first thing he noticed was the wall of flyers above Matt's bed. Ryan had a similar display at home, but these went back years and featured a ton of cool shows at the Anthrax and even venues down in the city.

"These are awesome!" Ryan was legitimately impressed. "Did you go to all those shows?"

"Some of them. But my cousin Liz is two years older, and she made me copies of some of her favorites once I started getting interested in this stuff." Ryan spent a few minutes studying the flyers before they moved on to watching a Bones Brigade video on Matt's little TV and looking through his stack of vinyl. Matt's room was a mess of records, tapes, videos, and wrestling memorabilia, but he knew exactly where everything was located. As he showed off his records, Ryan asked questions about the bands he hadn't heard of (mostly older Connecticut bands he'd only learned about via his older cousin), and made mental notes of which bands he mentioned that Matt wasn't familiar with so that they could trade tapes. They were having such a good time that he hardly noticed that hours had passed, until Matt's mom stopped in to say hello when she and the girls returned home. Ryan realized he should probably head home himself before his own parents made any similar inquiries.

44

Becky McAuley

"Thanks for showing me the flyers and the videos. I have a bunch of flyers and records too if you ever want to come to Crestwood."

"For sure, dude, and you're welcome back here anytime. But I need to show you one more thing before you go!" They headed downstairs, passed through the kitchen, and Matt opened the door to the basement.

At the bottom of the stairs, next to the water heater, was a drum set.

"My drums!" Matt exclaimed proudly. How had it not come up earlier in their conversation that this kid was a drummer?

"Damn, next time I'll bring my guitar!"

It was late afternoon when Ryan got home. His mom was upstairs and his dad was still at work. He wondered about dinner, though if his mom wasn't cooking, his dad would probably bring home a pizza. From his bedroom window, he looked out towards the Eckleys' house, across the street and two houses down. He thought about calling or going over to say hi, but the house was dark. It was just Eckley and his dad these days. Maybe they had gone out to eat after the SATs. He would see David tomorrow anyway, as they were heading down to CBGB's together to see Token Entry, Wrecking Crew, Swiz, and Beyond.

Ever since Ryan had moved to Crestwood at age seven and met David Eckley, who had moved in a few years before, they had done pretty much everything together, from Little League to playing their guitars. They told each other everything, too. And yet something stopped him from spilling the details on his strange and wonderful day. He wasn't quite ready to elaborate on his new friendship with Matt. When Eckley met new people, he sometimes made things all about him and tried too hard to impress them. And Matt was the first friend that Ryan had met through hardcore who wasn't someone they had grown up with, like Andrew Rompanelli, who had lived nearby on Hollywood Avenue before moving to White Plains, or kids that he and David had met simultaneously at shows.

Ryan and David had gone to Annunciation School together through eighth grade, and were still together at Fordham Prep. Sometimes, Ryan felt that David was as much a part of his life and routine as his mom and dad and their house on Crestwood Ave. Maybe more so, in that both of his parents had been distant lately—his dad working long hours at his once thriving, now faltering business, and his mom drinking when she wasn't doing the books for his dad. The boys were together almost every day: skateboarding, listening to records, arguing about the Yankees vs. the Mets, sneaking into the city after school, and hanging out in the Abyss—a clearing in the woods just across the Bronx River Parkway. So there were plenty of chances to tell him. But for whatever reason, over the next few days, he kept stopping short of mentioning his new friendship, and more importantly, the fact that Matt played drums. What had been a half-joking comment about bringing his guitar the next time he came over had turned into a nonstop daydream about playing in a band, which was only fueled by attending the CBGB's matinee the next day and imagining himself onstage. Ryan had been impressed with Beyond, the opening band, and had bought their demo tape after their set.

It helped that Monday was Eckley's first practice of the baseball season. Ryan had played too, joining the freshman team at Fordham Prep, but hadn't gotten much playing time when he moved up to junior varsity last year. This year, he had decided not to try out for the team. Ryan reasoned that it didn't make sense to devote that much time if he was barely going to get into any games.

He and Matt had exchanged numbers, and, with David at practice that Monday and Ryan at loose ends, he called Matt to ask if he was interested in getting together sometime that week to jam. Matt was down, and didn't seem to have a lot going on after school either. So that Wednesday, Ryan convinced his mom to drive him to Matt Zimmer's house, so he didn't have to walk a mile and a half over steep hills with an amp and a guitar. Maybe if things went well and they started writing songs together, he could even start leaving the amp at Matt's to make it easier to get back and forth to practice.

The Wednesday meetup had been arranged casually enough, so Matt probably had no idea what he was in for. At school on Monday and Tuesday, Ryan couldn't stop thinking about the idea of playing in a band. He drew notes and lyrics and wild lettering in the pages of his notebooks, and thought about lyrics on the train home. It helped that he had already been thinking about this stuff for a while, but the catalyst of meeting a potential drummer had pushed him into overdrive. And they hadn't even talked about starting a band! But ever since their conversation, Ryan had imbued both Saturday's meeting and Wednesday's "band practice" with a new significance.

After school on Tuesday, Ryan broke out the guitar as soon as he got home. He had scraps of songs written, lyrics and guitar parts he'd thought of, and some ideas about how he would want the drums to sound. He and Matt hadn't discussed playing original music, but he wanted to be ready with practically fully-formed songs in case the opportunity came up. After dinner with his parents, he headed right back upstairs to continue writing. Hours later, homework forgotten, he forced himself to fall asleep while still thinking about tomorrow.

When Ryan arrived at the Zimmers' house on Wednesday, he had come prepared with his guitar, amp, and notebook full of lyrics. His backpack also contained two blank tapes, along with a tape he had dubbed based on records they'd discussed on Saturday that Matt didn't own or hadn't heard. He was excited to be in charge, not only in terms of sharing his favorites with Matt, but also being out from under the shadow of Eckley's judgment. He and Matt could create whatever they wanted, if Matt was indeed equally on board with writing original songs without anyone to critique them, at least at first.

After Ryan dragged his equipment into the basement, he and Matt had started out playing covers—Negative Approach, early Agnostic Front, and some of the Bad Brains songs that were easier to handle. But after a short snack break in the Zimmers' kitchen, they returned to the basement, and Ryan introduced another idea.

"I've actually written a bunch of songs," Ryan said quickly. "If you want to hear them."

"Hell yeah, of course I do!"

So Ryan started playing the riffs he had perfected last night, with Matt drumming along and Ryan shouting lyrics at appropriate moments. The rest of practice passed quickly as they started to work out the structures of songs, and Ryan couldn't believe it when Mrs. Zimmer came downstairs to announce that it was 6:00 and to ask if Ryan had a ride home. They hastily wrapped up, with Ryan dubbing the best part of their practice tape on Matt's boombox after calling his mom to come pick him up. He had a good feeling that Matt was going to be as interested in this band thing as he was.

While Ryan had always thought offhand about playing in a band, it was never the all-consuming obsession that it had suddenly become. He and Eckley had started playing the guitar around the same time, as they were both getting into metal bands like Slayer and Nuclear Assault. But once they had discovered hardcore, after Ryan ordered an Agnostic Front record on a whim from the Combat Records catalog, they had both gravitated in that direction. But neither had ever specifically talked about writing their own songs or having a band.

Ryan knew it was possible to just start a band with people you happened to know: Breakdown was from near here in Yonkers, though the singer was from New Rochelle and the drummer was from White Plains. And Ryan and Eckley had struck up a casual friendship with the guys from this band called Power Structure, who were from the Peekskill area but had opened a show at the Anthrax last year. Power Structure evidently loved Rest in Pieces, who also had members from Westchester, but weren't as good as Rest in Pieces. Ryan had a feeling that they were only tolerated because they were nice dudes and enthusiastically supported shows at the Anthrax, even if they seemed to have no musical talent whatsoever. Or maybe people kept booking them because they mixed them up with Power Surge, a more established band from Connecticut who also played the Anthrax.

Lost Indignation

In some circles, hardcore kids were supposed to renounce all traces of their metal past, whether it be selling their Metallica records or cutting their hair. But in Westchester, a certain amount of metal was permitted, even appreciated. There were still a bunch of kids with long hair at the shows at Streets in New Rochelle, though Ryan and David had already cut their hair short before their first Streets show.

While Ryan wasn't going out of his way to deny his metal roots, he also couldn't deny that he liked hardcore better. When he saw Supertouch for the first time at a show in Mahopac with Rest in Pieces and the Gorilla Biscuits, it felt like his whole life was leading up to this and all his other prior musical choices had functioned primarily to point him in the direction of this sonically perfect band. Eckley wasn't that impressed with Supertouch, but he did like Rest in Pieces, and who wouldn't have liked the Gorilla Biscuits?

Ryan and David kept going to shows through the rest of 1987, sometimes venturing into the city but mostly seeking out lineups closer to home, like when Agnostic Front played Streets the day after Christmas. Despite any divergence in their musical tastes, they pretty much always went to shows together, both for the strength in numbers and the logistics of having to convince only one of their parents to give them a ride. Sometimes they took the train to White Plains and then Andrew Rompanelli's dad drove all three of them to the Anthrax. Either way, Ryan was glad to have lenient parents who weren't grilling him about what went on at these events, even when he came home covered in bruises.

Band practice was different: unlike a show, you weren't going to come home with a black eye (or a new t-shirt), so there was no outward evidence to Eckley that Ryan had started a secret band. But did Matt even comprehend that they were starting a band? He probably had no idea what he had just gotten himself into: that Ryan had already written so many songs and was going to seize this chance to make them into a reality.

Ryan also knew that he would have to tell Eckley about the band eventually, as he would surely notice he was spending so much time with a new friend. Maybe he would think Ryan had been hanging out with a girl! At least Eckley and his dad would be travelling during spring break, Mr. Eckley to some sort of conference in Florida, and David along for the vacation. Hopefully they could write some songs and assemble the rest of the necessary members while Eckley was away, if not before.

"Are you going anywhere for spring break this year?" Matt asked after another practice.

"Nah, we never go anywhere for spring break," Ryan replied. "You?"

"Not this year," Matt shook his head. "We usually go see my grandma in Florida, but we went in February." So spring break would

Becky McAuley

indeed be an Eckley-free time for them to write, and even for Ryan to attend his first Seder. Matt had invited him, along with two school friends, Marshall and Alex. Ryan was looking forward to this glimpse into Matt's other life and quietly relished the validation it brought him as a new friend who was being welcomed into the fold along with Matt's longer-standing compatriots.

"And anyway, my grandma is moving back up here, so we won't be going to Florida anymore. She's moving in with my uncle. Liz's dad," Matt continued. Ah, the famous Liz Zimmer, the catalyst of Matt getting into hardcore! Ryan would finally get to meet her at the Seder, which was part of his anticipation. Matt had mentioned after they started jamming that once they had a demo recorded (which at this point sounded like a remote possibility) he would make sure to get a copy into her hands. Matt was excited about capitalizing on her social currency with the kind of cool older guys for whom she could play the demo. Ryan, however, was more curious about Liz's female friends, especially the possibility that some of them might like hardcore too.

Ryan had seen groups of girls hanging out at the Anthrax and knew there were girls who liked the same bands that he did, even if he didn't know any of them. His experience with girls was limited in general. He'd made out with Erica Macaluso sophomore year and had then gone on exactly one date with her afterwards. And he always had a thing for Allison Syzmanski, who lived down the street from the Crestwood Library, but she seemed to prefer David Eckley. But these were neighborhood girls, from his town and his world. Meeting a girl from Connecticut or the city or even White Plains who liked hardcore would have been something else entirely. The idea of dating someone who would listen to the same bands or hang out with him at shows seemed just as remote as recording a demo.

With fine features, light brown hair, and hazel eyes, Ryan wasn't bad looking, but nor was he the most arresting in a pack of boys the way that David Eckley was. Ryan was the kind of kid who would have done fine with girls if he had been the one asking them out, which he wasn't, and which Eckley definitely was. Eckley had both the looks and the audacity: an effective combination. Along with his dark hair and striking blue eyes, he also projected an overall glow that had been passed down more from his Portuguese mom than from his British dad. In Lower Westchester, families with one parent dark and the other fair were most likely to be Irish-Italian. Trust Eckley to represent a more unusual combination of Portuguese and British.

The two friends had been lucky to go to school together despite their different backgrounds. Mr. Eckley was a scientist and an atheist, but acquiesced to his wife's suggestion of sending David to the local Catholic school that most of the neighborhood kids attended. After all, they might

Lost Indignation

not have been able to afford a house like theirs in a neighboring town like Eastchester or Scarsdale with better schools than Yonkers. Eckley's house was awesome—this half-haunted looking three-story thing with a porch and freestanding garage in the back. Even though they were a few houses apart, Ryan could see Eckley's window from his own street-facing bedroom on the second floor of the Marnells' more pedestrian three-bedroom. The Marnells had moved to the neighborhood when Ryan was seven and his dad's business was flourishing, providing a steady supply of rec room furnishings to lower Westchester and beyond. By 1988, his pool tables and recreational decor had fallen out of fashion, with most of his remaining sales coming from bars and mail order. Ryan had the feeling his dad was hanging on to the business because he didn't know what else to do with himself. He wondered if his parents would sell the house and move to an apartment once he graduated, like where his paternal grandmother lived on Bronx River Road in Yonkers. Ryan was pretty sure that he was only still at Fordham Prep due to his grandmother chipping in for tuition.

Within a week or two, Ryan and Matt had written enough songs that Ryan started to think of them as a real band. But if they were going to be a band, they needed a name, especially if they were going to post a flyer to try and attract more members. Once Ryan suggested this, he and Matt had started coming up with names nonstop, but none stuck. They had half kicked around some wrestling related names like Chokeslam and Spinebuster, but Ryan wanted something a bit more serious and universal. Matt was just happy to be in the band at all, and as long as Ryan considered his ideas, he was willing to go along with Ryan's vision. Ryan was unused to wielding this position of influence; he was usually in the thrall of Eckley, bending to his authority and ideas.

This show of confidence from Matt was one more reason that Ryan had been taking the naming very seriously and had, in fact, started noting ideas in his history notebook. History with Mr. Galvano was one of his favorite classes, but lately he hadn't been able to concentrate anywhere, history included. He'd even fallen asleep in class twice last week, then jerked awake with a momentary sensation of not knowing how he had ended up there. After the second incident, Galvano had made a joke out of it—"Looks like Marnell was up a little too late last night." Ryan had shrugged it off, but vowed to try to break the habit before it became a regular occurrence. Though he'd been up late on St. Patrick's Day again. For weeks, Ryan had looked forward to Supertouch appearing on WNYU and rushed home from his grandmother's apartment ahead of his parents to start taping by 9 p.m. He had captured every moment of the set, then when *Crucial Chaos* ended at 10:30, rewound and listened to the entire show again. Eckley didn't like Supertouch, but Ryan had dubbed him a copy as a last ditch effort to convert him, along with making one for Matt.

Becky McAuley

And here he was, jerking awake in class yet again. Ryan looked around. There was something wrong with the classroom. He looked down at his notebook, where he'd been writing the word "Indignation" over and over again, in increasingly unintelligible form. He raised his hand to ask a question ...

Ryan was abruptly awakened—this time for real—by his alarm clock. It was 6:30 a.m. He and Eckley usually met outside around 7:10 to walk to the 7:27 train down to Fordham, and he'd have to jump in the shower shortly or risk being late. Ryan lay motionless for another moment, still in the grip of his dream, trying to recapture both the creepy atmosphere and the series of events. He had been writing something repeatedly in history class and then raised his hand to ask about it. "Indignation"—that's what he had been writing. Which was actually a pretty good band name. Ryan wondered what Matt would think of it. He wouldn't have another chance to talk to Matt all day, but he also couldn't call the Zimmers at 6:30 in the morning.

"What do you think of Indignation? As a band name?" he asked casually the next afternoon while they were playing *Skate or Die*. Eckley was at baseball practice. Ryan sent another silent thank you to whoever had convinced him to drop baseball this year.

"Indignation?" Zimmer queried. Ryan held his breath. He could feel him turning it over in his mind, trying to find an objection.

"That's pretty good. I dig it. Hang on," Zimmer instructed as he unsuccessfully attempted to sneak through a gap in a fence in the Downhill Jam. But the topic was settled, at least temporarily.

Ryan expected Matt to come up with another name 30 minutes later, but somehow, it stuck. Perhaps they were both just relieved to be a band with a name, if only an interim name, but it crept gradually into their lexicon before they made an official decision. Matt started calling him to schedule "the next Indignation practice" or going on tangents about "when Indignation starts to play shows" and which of his friends could be counted on to attend. And so, they were Indignation.

Now that Indignation had a name, they needed more members. How many people do you need to make a band? If you were a punk band, perhaps three would do: guitar, bass and drums, with someone also shouldering vocal duties. But this is hardcore, and almost every hardcore band needs a dedicated singer, an energetic person with a long mic cord running around the room, moshing across the stage, engaging the crowd, even baiting them. The frontman (or frontwoman)—the brains of the enterprise, lyrics-wise. Well, not exactly the brains of the enterprise, sometimes. Ryan had started some lyrics himself, and would be OK with corralling an uninspired singer if they found a guy with the right voice, the right look, the right energy. Either way, right now it was just him and

Lost Indignation

Matt, and they needed a singer and a bassist before they could really be considered a band.

The first step was to post a flyer at local record stores, like Mad Platters and Record Stop. Ryan asked Matt to use his own phone number, since Eckley would have recognized Ryan's if he saw it, and it was Ryan's idea to say they were only looking for a bassist, in order to make them appear a more established band, rather than merely half a band. They would worry about a singer after that. Ryan also suspected that they might get a lot more inquiries for a singer, since you didn't need to have as much prior experience or own any gear. And once they had a third member of the band, this guy might know someone too.

It was a simple quarter page flyer, done in black sharpie and photocopied at the library. INDIGNATION in all caps at the top of the page, and then some tabs to pull at the bottom with Matt's contact info.

Hardcore band looking for bassist. We practice in Yonkers. Call Matt at 793-0481. Influences: Warzone, Breakdown, Bad Brains, Token Entry, Agnostic Front, Negative Approach, Rest in Pieces, Supertouch, Sick of it All, Cause for Alarm.

They posted the first flyer at Mad Platters on a Sunday, among the amalgam of existing advertisements for bands, guitars for sale, or drum lessons available, then headed up Central Ave. to drop another at Record Stop and Stanley's, the skate shop. Ryan couldn't wait to check on the results of their flyers but also knew he would be disappointed if he went back too early and none of the tabs had been removed. Also, weren't interested parties supposed to be calling? As they approached the weekend, Matt reported having received no phone calls so far.

By Saturday, Ryan was itching to go back and check on their flyers and convinced Matt to meet him at Record Stop. He had skated over from the Hartsdale train station and was waiting outside when Matt's mom dropped him off in their Buick station wagon. He slapped Matt a high five and they headed into the store. The ad was still there, but only one of the tabs had been removed.

"It's still up!" Ryan savored the thrill of seeing his own ad just hanging there at a record store, as if he hadn't put it there a few days prior. After looking around the store for anything interesting that had arrived since their last visit, he and Matt headed outside.

"Hey, are you the guys from Indignation?" The question had been posed by a short Black punk rock kid with a chain around his waist and a scruffy jacket.

"Yeah, we are," Ryan answered after a second, having forgotten that Matt was wearing a homemade Indignation shirt. It was still unnatural

Becky McAuley

but gratifying to be referred to as a member of a band. "You saw the ad inside?"

The kid nodded. "I'm Eric. I listen to more punk than hardcore, but I play bass."

"That works, since we need a bass player. Where are you from?" Ryan asked, thinking he was going to say Yonkers or White Plains and ready to let Matt give him directions to his house, perhaps from one of the buses that ran along Central Ave.

"Fucking Eastchester!" Eric exploded, surprising them all. "I'm the only Black kid in Eastchester! Can you believe it?" He shook his head scornfully. "We moved up here last summer, for my mom's job and 'cause she wanted to get us out of the city. But it sucks. Not only am I the only Black kid, I'm the only punk rock kid in the whole school. Why couldn't we have moved anywhere else but fucking Eastchester!"

Matt and Ryan looked at each other. There were a handful of Black kids at Fordham Prep and of course numerous people of color at Roosevelt High School. But Ryan realized that neither he nor Matt had probably ever thought about what it must be like to be the only Black kid in your class, your town, your school. He also had a feeling that he and Matt were simultaneously having the same thought—that while this kid might not be able to play any Token Entry songs in a tryout because he was coming from a different subset of punk, he would be more likely than either of them to personify the name of their band, based on his everyday tribulations.

It was Matt who spoke first. "That must suck, dude," he commiserated. "Anyway, are you psyched for WrestleMania tomorrow?"

It turned out that Eric was a natural fit for the band. He came over the next day for a tryout, early enough in the day so as not to interfere with WrestleMania. His straightforward style of playing didn't bring much to their songwriting process, but his energy and enthusiasm were contagious. Ryan had a feeling that this was the first time he'd played his bass around other people since moving to Westchester, or perhaps had anyone to hang out with at all—that he had been shut out without any real friends for most of the school year. Eric filled them in while hanging out in Matt's living room after the practice. His mom, who was Black, had taken a position in admissions at the College of New Rochelle. After exploring where the Cliftons should live, she found out that a friend of a friend who lived in a garden apartment complex in Eastchester was looking to sublet their apartment for a surprisingly reasonable rate. His dad, who was white, was a freelance photographer who could ostensibly live and work anywhere. Between the lake across the street, the well regarded Eastchester schools, and the preferential rent, the Cliftons had taken the sublet without even looking at other neighborhoods where Eric might have felt more at home. Had his parents not realized what the next three years would be like for their son, or how much more racist the rest of Eastchester would be compared to the relatively idealist Interlaken community?

"The lake isn't so bad," Eric conceded. "There's a bunch of hippies who run the events there, and they're all OK. And there are some cool places to skate by the garages and stuff. But then I got to school," he shook his head ruefully. "Everyone is the fucking same! I have no one to hang out with. At first I went back to the city every weekend. But then I sort of gave up. It's just two more years," he added, as if attempting to convince himself. "And then I can go wherever I want." Ryan hoped that Indignation might provide sufficient distraction so that Eric wouldn't spend so much time missing the city. He was also intrigued by Eric having a whole other circle of city friends who might be able to get them booked on NYC shows, though Eric had insinuated that his city punk friends might think of Ryan and Matt as suburban jocks, so he didn't bring it up again.

So, bass was handled. But the fact that they had no singer was now stressing Ryan out. Eckley didn't play bass, and if he had found out about the band, there was only so much he could do about that vacant position. But Ryan could see Eckley fancying himself as a singer. He certainly had the magnetism and hardcore knowledge. His singing voice was neither great nor terrible, based on what Ryan had witnessed from the two of them yelling along to their favorite songs at home or at shows. And yet Ryan just couldn't see him in the band. Halfway through history class one day, he started thinking of reasons why:

1. They liked different types of hardcore. Eckley was more into sounds that reflected his metal roots, like the Crumbsuckers and the Cro-Mags. Ryan gravitated more towards straightforward bands like Breakdown. He also loved stuff like 7 Seconds, Dag Nasty, and Supertouch that Eckley actively disliked, though he wasn't going in those directions for this band.

2. Because Ryan was always the one with the interests and Eckley was the ringleader, making things happen. But for once he didn't want a ringleader—he wanted to shape the direction of the band himself (though of course with equal input from Eric and Matt, neither of whom had an overbearing personality like Eckley).

3. If some nameless, faceless singer joined later, this guy would still hopefully sing all the lyrics that Ryan had already written. Ryan knew that not only would David never sing someone else's lyrics, but it would also be too personal for his best friend to be singing his own songs.

So Ryan had all these arguments rehearsed, but he still figured he shouldn't shout about Indignation until they were a little further along. If

Eckley found out, they'd cross that bridge when they came to it.

Matt's parents were also surprisingly supportive of the fact that their basement had become the site of multiple band practices per week. Perhaps they realized that it was better to have Matt under their watchful eye at home, playing loud music of questionable quality, than out skating, slamdancing, or staging wrestling stunts. Mr. Zimmer worked in the city and wasn't home from work when practice wrapped up; but if Mrs. Zimmer, who got home earlier from her job with the Yonkers school district, had ventured into the basement, perhaps she would have been slightly less horrified by the quality of songs they were starting to produce. In addition to the first few songs that Ryan had brought to practice, they had written some new ones featuring mosh parts that worked with Matt's drumming style (spending a lot of time on the toms while being a little shakier with fast parts on the hi-hat). They were not exactly the next NYC Mayhem, but Matt did a decent job of emulating some of the drum parts on *My Rage*, which had been one of Ryan's favorite Rest in Pieces albums since it had come out the year before.

Now that they had a bassist, all they needed was a singer. Who did they know who could sing? Ryan thought of Andrew Rompanelli, but reckoned he might not so easily relinquish his post as the observer behind the video camera, which was his preferred role at shows. Plus, recruiting a mutual friend might further incur the wrath of Eckley.

By the same token, Warren Yatrofsky was probably also off limits. Warren was a fat, pale, sarcastic kid who lived with his mom on Lockwood Ave. in Yonkers. Until recently, Ryan and David had considered him merely a peripheral acquaintance, someone they would say what's up to at shows or at the record store but weren't going out of their way to nurture a friendship with, outside of those circumstances. But Yatrofsky had proved himself a true and loyal friend in an unexpected way last summer. They had run into him while skating at the library on a blindingly bright Saturday in August and followed him back towards his mom's apartment, in order to skate some massive hill of the type that was ubiquitous in western Yonkers. They'd gotten off the 8 bus early to buy Italian ices at Morandini's and were walking along Lockwood Ave., passing the tattoo shop, when a white Monte Carlo full of guidos rolled up next to them and stopped at a red light.

"FAAAAAGS," the driver squalled. "I'm talking to you! You look so fucking GAY! Why don't you fags take your skateboards and shove them up each other's ass?" he taunted, his henchmen cackling in the background.

Ryan, wary and aware this wasn't their part of town, hoped to shake them off and keep walking, but Eckley, of course, took the bait and more words were exchanged. Suddenly, Warren snuck up and slugged the guy through the driver's side window, and before he could react, they

Lost Indignation

all ran like hell. A few minutes later, once they confirmed they weren't being followed and the danger had passed, they all doubled over, laughing and whooping at their narrow escape. "Yo, that was sick, dude!" Eckley exclaimed, slapping Warren a high five.

"Warren Yatrofsky! Coming through in the clutch!" Ryan grinned. Warren looked nonchalant: how many dudes like that had he had to fight off over the years, while Ryan was living his not exactly popular but not exactly unpopular under-the-radar existence over in Crestwood? But Ryan could tell Warren was pleased and gratified to be praised by someone as cool as David Eckley.

After that, Warren was hailed enthusiastically whenever they encountered him, and David had called to offer him a ride to see Token Entry and Wide Awake at the Anthrax the following Friday. (Technically, Mr. Eckley was the one doing the driving, but it beat taking two trains.) Afterwards, they still didn't hang out frequently, as Warren went to public school and lived further west, but the incident with the guidos had earned their respect. And while it might be useful to have a guy in your band who could fight, Ryan hoped they wouldn't have to deploy that skill too often and mentally crossed him off the list along with Rompanelli. Not only might engaging him piss off Eckley, but Warren might also be of better use in the pit as the kind of guy who would represent for Indignation. If they didn't find someone soon, they'd post another ad.

The Easter holidays came early that year, and sure enough, the cold weather had returned. For once, Ryan was excited to be staying home. He couldn't wait to meet Liz Zimmer at Matt's family's Seder, and was hoping that she might even have some leads on a singer for Indignation. Confirming a vocalist was proving to be less seamless than recruiting Eric: he had been the first bass player who inquired and had been a fit right away. But they had already tried out two singers in the past week, while everyone was out of school for spring break, and neither was going to work. One was a kid Matt knew from school, who had a terrible voice, no sense of timing, and no background in hardcore whatsoever. There was also John H. from Port Chester, whom Ryan and David had met at a show at the Anthrax, and who had (Ryan recently remembered) scribbled down his phone number on some flyer. John was excited to try out, and he hadn't been terrible, but he was a sophomore like Matt and didn't drive, so Ryan was worried about the logistics for regular practices. And while it was true that he wasn't bad, he also wasn't great. Was it wrong that Ryan secretly wanted someone, well, *cool*, to front Indignation? Or at least someone with a modicum of stage presence?

Passover started at sundown on Good Friday that year. Ryan wasn't sure if it always lined up like that, but his dad had taken a half-day off work and dropped him at the Zimmers' in the early evening. Ryan didn't even have a chance to prepare: Liz was the one who answered the door when he rang the bell. With short dark hair and cheekbones sharper than the break on a Ron Guidry slider, Liz had rendered Ryan momentarily speechless, and he realized he had been missing a key piece of information. Of course Matt hadn't mentioned that his cousin happened to be gorgeous, since she was his cousin! All Ryan had known was that she was a cool older girl who liked good bands!

Ryan recovered and greeted her, then high-fived Matt, who had appeared behind her, and introduced himself to Marshall and Alex, Matt's friends from school. Their incessant chatter and Liz's good-natured retorts brought him back to the reality that he better not be intimidated by Liz and, instead, use tonight to learn from her as much as he could. He was going to be out of his element enough already following along at a Jewish Seder, whatever that entailed.

Apparently it involved Matt's twin sisters alternating reading the Four Questions (despite assorted bickering, as Jen was seven minutes older than Jamie), and various prayers and songs, with momentary breaks during which you were then allowed to eat a small portion of exactly one symbolic dish. He was glad he'd had a snack before he came. When the wine was poured, Ryan politely declined, as he'd started claiming straight edge last year, and he noticed Matt did the same. Was Matt straight edge now too? Eric wasn't, but Ryan was glad to know he was not the only edge kid in the band. Eckley was currently straight edge too, though Ryan had doubts about how long that would last. He certainly didn't have the same negative examples at home, as Ryan was trying to avoid becoming like his parents, who both smoked cigarettes and drank more than ever.

As the ceremony of the Seder progressed into dinner itself, Liz ended up being surprisingly easy to talk to, because she was so far out of his league that it wasn't even worth being nervous. It was also increasingly apparent that Liz was an oddball just like them, if a gorgeous oddball. Clad in an oversize purple sweater, leggings, and yellow heels, Liz baited her dad with contrary political opinions, humored Matt's sisters and her grandmother, and took the side of Matt's friend Alex in some wrestling-related debate that had broken out near the end of the meal.

Following the dinner, Matt and Liz were tasked with washing the dishes and Ryan stuck around to help, after Marshall and Alex had been picked up by Marshall's stentorian Jamaican mom. Liz, having shed the purple sweater and yellow shoes, was down to a white tank top and leggings and Ryan was trying not to stare. Nevertheless, he was glad for an opportunity to talk to her about hardcore, rather than just making conversation among a Seder table full of adults, and was encouraged when she remembered the existence of Indignation and asked about the progress of the band.

Lost Indignation

"We tried out these two singers last week, and they were both wrong," Matt explained.

"But in different ways," Ryan clarified. He was glad that Matt hadn't been attached to settling for John H. either.

"Did you think about putting up a flyer at Some Records?" Liz interjected. It was a thrilling thought.

"That's a good idea, though would anyone want to come up here to play with us? And it would be easier to practice if we got someone from up here. I mean, we could do another flyer at Record Stop, but I don't want to take another chance of David seeing it."

"Who's this David, and why don't you want him in your band?" Ryan experienced the disconcerting sensation of the full force of Liz's attention.

"He's my best friend, but I just don't want to be in a band with him for some reason. Like he would take it over and turn it into his thing, you know?"

"As opposed to our thing that we already got going," Matt echoed, zealously attacking a leftover unleavened brownie.

"Exactly," Ryan continued. "Me and Matt and Eric, none of us knew each other beforehand. We're all from different worlds, but we're having a good time writing these songs so far. If David joined, everything would be different."

"I get it," Liz concurred while meticulously drying a mixing bowl. "So, not David. Who else do you know who has the qualities of a good frontman?"

"*You* could sing!" Matt interjected, in possession of what he believed to be a spontaneous and excellent idea.

"*Me!?* Are you serious? You've heard my singing voice. Approximately two hours ago during 'Dayenu.' I'm shocked I didn't shatter any glasses."

"A lot of people would come to our shows," Matt noted shrewdly.

"You know I don't need any more people paying attention to me." It was true—and it was how Matt had started going to shows in the first place. Liz had briefly dated a kid from Hartsdale who introduced her to hardcore; she quickly jettisoned the guy but had fallen in love with the music. Soon after, she brought Matt to a Murphy's Law gig at the Anthrax, mainly to have someone to talk to and act as a male shield to repel uninvited conversation. Matt had realized later that absolutely none of her friends must have been available that day or interested in the assignment, but he had been incredibly flattered to be requisitioned by his older cousin as her plus-one.

"Maybe I could ask my friend Dion," Liz mused. "I don't think he's ever sung in a band before, but I can see him having the right stage presence."

"Is he into hardcore?" Ryan quickly asked.

"You think I'd refer someone who wasn't? Yeah, he likes the good stuff, though he came from the metal side of things. I mean, didn't most of us?" Liz flashed an unintentionally heart-stopping smile. Ryan could only hope that this Dion character would look half as good in a white tank top as Liz Zimmer.

Liz's friend Dion was indeed interested in the band, and Matt organized the logistics of inviting him for a tryout. The following Wednesday afternoon, Ryan and Eric assembled at Matt's, playing *Pro Wrestling* on Nintendo while awaiting the arrival of Dion. The doorbell rang. Matt's sister Jen dashed into the living room. "There's a man here to see you!" she exclaimed. "All of you," she clarified. They filed towards the front door, Matt quickly turning off the Nintendo, erasing the first occasion in which Ryan was actually beating him.

Standing on the doorstep was a full-grown man with a shaved head and a day or two's worth of stubble, wearing jeans, work boots, and indeed a white tank top—though one that was quite different from Liz's alluring garment. This guy had to be at least in his early 20s, if not older. Matt seemed frozen at the apparent age of Liz's purported pal, so Ryan pushed past and introduced himself.

"Are you Dion?"

"That's me, Dion Carina." He grinned and grabbed Ryan's hand in a bone-crushing handshake. Luckily Mr. Marnell had taught him a thing or two about shaking hands, and when he held his own, Dion seemed to regard him with new clarity.

"I'm Ryan. I play guitar. This is Liz's cousin Matt"—he gestured to Matt, who looked like he was getting used to the idea of Dion—"and Eric," he indicated with a head nod. Eric had crept up behind them, waved a hello, and turned to lead the way to the basement.

"That's a sick album, dude!" Dion gestured to Eric's painstakingly recreated back patch on his jean jacket featuring the Cause for Alarm riot cops logo, which had become visible as he turned. Ryan congratulated himself for his stroke of genius. At their first practice with Eric, Ryan had brought him a dub of the Cause for Alarm s/t 7". He'd thought about covering "United Races," now that their band included an Irish kid, a Black kid, and a Jew. But his ulterior motive was to introduce more hardcore bands into the life of Eric Clifton—especially those of a punk-adjacent style that might appeal to him—and influence his songwriting as a result. Sure enough, Cause for Alarm went over big with Eric, as did the Warzone *Lower East Side Crew* 7" he'd included soon after. And Eric had indeed liked CFA so much that he'd soon drawn the 7" cover featuring the riot cops onto the back of his jean jacket.

Lost Indignation

Dion followed Eric down to the basement, chatting merrily about some incident with the cops at some bar in the Bronx (how old *was* this guy, Ryan wondered?) and expressing a general fuck-the-cops sentiment, which you didn't need to say twice to a Black punk rock kid in 1988. Eric countered with some Lower East Side anecdote that caused Dion to unleash his staccato hyena cackle for the first time in their presence. Ryan was enjoying this, and thought it would be nice for Eric to come out of his shell a bit. After all, he and Ryan and Matt had some things in common, but Eric was more of the third wheel to Ryan and Matt, the original members and genesis of the band. Eric already seemed more at ease around Dion than he and Matt were, and based on the story currently unfolding, Dion was more familiar with the city and could probably understand Eric in a way they could not.

He and Matt hung back at the top of the stairs. "What do you think of this guy so far?" Matt asked, looking worried.

"Let's see what he's like on the mic," Ryan responded, descending to the basement. But his mind was already made up. He had a feeling that having Dion's comic presence would take the pressure off in terms of being a serious band. Though conversely, he knew they'd also be taken more seriously with Dion involved.

Eric was setting up, still chatting to Dion. Ryan waited for a break in the action so they could get started and found one when the others heard Matt's footsteps on the stairs.

"So, uh, here's our setup." Matt gestured around the basement and moved past the three of them to settle behind the drums. "We'll just run through some songs so you can check it out? And then if you like it, we can go back through them again to try you out."

"Only some of our songs have lyrics," Ryan clarified. "Well, most of them do, but of course you'd be welcome to change some stuff," he added diplomatically. (Not too much, he hoped.)

"That's cool, that's cool," Dion affirmed. "I don't mind hearing what you already got. Lyrics aren't really my thing." He flashed his trademark grin. Matt looked mildly alarmed, and tried to convey a glance to Ryan like, what's the point of a frontman who doesn't write lyrics? In return, Ryan gave him a head tilt that was meant to signify, don't worry, I got this, I already wrote the lyrics anyway.

And so they got down to it. "What do you want to start with, the 'Indignation' song?" Ryan asked the others. They agreed. The unofficial Indignation theme song, in which a bunch of words rhymed with Indignation, was the perfect start to the set.

"Indignation" the song was followed by one called "Not Ready," which indeed was not totally ready, and another one with no lyrics but had a great mosh part at the end. Eric and Matt were ripping through songs with unusual urgency. Maybe they were trying to put on a show for Dion. Then again, this was the first real practice in which they had amalgamated their current batch of songs into anything resembling a live set. By the time they hit "Put It Down," which was a surreptitious straight edge song that Ryan had written from the perspective of wishing his mom wouldn't drink so much, he was practically moshing with his guitar while shouting the rudimentary lyrics.

"So, what did you think?" Matt asked, breathless, after they had made it through their four existing originals.

"I think it's fucking SICK! I'm in!" Dion grinned. "Do you have the words written down somewhere so I could learn them?"

"I hadn't even thought of that," Ryan admitted. "I'll write them out for you and put a copy in the mail? Or else bring it to you the next time I see you."

"What do you think of the style?" Eric inquired slyly from behind his bass. "Is it too hardcore for you? It was almost too hardcore for me."

"It's hardcore, all right," Dion agreed. "But I can get down with that. It will for sure get people going in the pit!"

Ryan briefly gloried in the idea of people moshing for his band, then asked the question that he bet they all wanted to know the answer to. "Are you sure you want to hang out with a bunch of kids?" he blurted. "I mean, we're all still in high school."

Dion let fly another cackle. "Hey, I'm supposed to be in school too! Dropped out last year. I'd be graduating in a couple months." Ok, so he wasn't as old as he looked. "I work construction now," he continued, "and I'm trying to get a little acting work." He assumed a contemplative expression, resting his chin on his hand, before bursting into laughter again. He certainly did have the magnetism that Liz had mentioned, and Ryan was optimistic about how this would go over with a crowd. He could also see Dion making short work of hecklers and engaging the crowd in the type of playful banter that he had noticed was essential to a live show.

"Yo, can I smoke in here?" Dion had a cigarette halfway to his mouth.

"Uhh ... let's take a break and go outside," Matt hedged, bounding out from behind the drum set and up the stairs before Dion got any ideas.

After a short break, they reconvened in the basement. "OK, let's try a cover," Ryan suggested. "What are some songs you know?" After the initial spate of sloppy cover jamming in their first practice, he and Matt had subsequently played around with the Agnostic Front song "With Time," which complemented Matt's drumming style but might be too esoteric for a tryout song. Neither of the singers they had previously tried out had made it to the cover stage: Matt's school friend wouldn't have known any hardcore lyrics, and they'd had him and John H. just try to yell stuff over

Lost Indignation

some of their originals.

Dion looked uncomfortable. "Oh, play any old hardcore shit and I'll figure it out."

"What about ... do you know the words to 'Ready to Fight?' 'Friend or Foe?'" Ryan tried to think of the easiest songs to cover that he'd be able to play by ear and that Matt and Eric were also likely to know.

"I know the songs, just ..." he trailed off.

"Not the words?" Eric added helpfully.

"Don't worry about it," Ryan assured him. "We'll just play and you sing the ones you know. What's easier for you two?"

"Let's do 'Friend or Foe,'" Eric decided. Matt nodded from behind the drums. It was hard to think of a simpler hardcore song. Ryan worked out the chords, and they began. Dion hardly knew any of the words to the fast part, but he sounded good on the chorus. Unleashing his gravelly growl as he stomped around the Zimmers' basement, yelling the lines from the chorus.

"So, how'd I do?" he inquired after they'd made it through the song.

"Your voice fits our music pretty well," Ryan allowed. He could imagine their own songs sounding extra hard once imbued with Dion's vocals.

"I've never actually sung in a band, though," Dion continued. "I always thought it would be cool!"

"Hey, none of us have played in a band either," Matt chimed in. Eric shot him a look. "Well, except for Eric. In the *city*." Eric gave him the finger.

They ended up going back through their originals one more time, with Ryan telling Dion to "just yell stuff" to get a feel for their tunes and taping it all on Matt's boombox. This turned out way better than in either of the prior tryouts. Dion was a natural!

As Ryan snuck looks at Dion, he got the feeling he was inexplicably familiar. "I know I've seen this guy before," Ryan murmured to Matt as they were packing up, while Dion was upstairs in the bathroom. But where? He was more of a peripheral hardcore kid, and while they could have encountered him at the Anthrax, or even at CBGB's, it was unlikely. Hanging out at Mont Olympus, their favorite diner? Outside of the Nathan's arcade on Central Ave.? No, Ryan had the eerie feeling he'd seen him onstage in a similar capacity. Though he said he'd never sung for a hardcore band ...

Suddenly, it came to him. This was the guy who had gotten kicked out of the talent show and, subsequently, Annunciation School! In the fall of 1983, when Ryan and David had been in seventh grade, there had been a disruption at the annual talent show. This new kid from the

Bronx, some eighth-grader who looked like an adult, had gotten onstage and proceeded to break into a filthy parody song, during which he was swiftly removed from the evening's competition and then expelled from the school itself. Ryan had forgotten his name and hadn't seen him again till today; but he was the stuff of local legend, at least for kids around their age at Annunciation. That settled it. They had to have this guy in the band! Ryan imagined David's reaction to picking this infamous frontman and experienced a twinge of guilt. At some point he was going to have to tell David about everything. Just not for a few more practices, till Dion was wholly embedded in the band.

When the tryout had reached a logical terminus, they packed up their instruments and headed upstairs. Dion was outside smoking one last cigarette when Matt, Ryan, and Eric convened to discuss the results of the tryout, and Ryan filled the others in on his recollection of the talent show. On the strength of Ryan's argument that this guy *had* to be their singer, the other two agreed. Eric looked happier than Matt had ever seen him, and while Matt didn't seem 100% convinced, he seemed excited about the prospect of having finally found a singer. They trooped outside to share the verdict with Dion. He was in! Indignation had a singer. Now they were, at least in Ryan's eyes, truly a real band.

Before heading home, Ryan dubbed a few extra copies of the recorded section of their practice. And after writing out a more legible version of the existing Indignation lyrics at home, he dropped a copy of the tape and lyrics in the mail to the address that Dion had provided—on Primrose Avenue in Mount Vernon, where he had mentioned renting a room from a nearly deaf old lady. That setup sounded conducive to blasting hardcore in his room, depending on the proximity of other renters.

"Almost everyone I hang out with during the week is *old*," Dion groused the following week. They were playing *Zelda* after their second practice as a full band. It was a Thursday, and Eckley had a game. "After work, I go to the bar by the racetrack ..." Who *is* this guy? Ryan wondered. His dad? Mr. Marnell was known to stop after work and have a beer or three, but he usually frequented Clanton's or the Wretched Spaniel on Tuckahoe Road. He didn't hang out at Goose Bruno's, the bar on Yonkers Ave. to which Dion was referring, though Ryan had been past there once or twice. He had no trouble imagining how Dion got served, as he looked so much older than 18.

"What about Liz?" Matt commented slyly. Ryan wondered if that was part of Matt's unease around Dion, in being protective of his cousin in case Dion had designs on her.

"Liz Zimmer! Such a cool girl! Your cousin has really got her shit together. But yeah, besides her, Tommy, Angela ... pretty much all my friends are old. Dudes I know from work and shit. So it's fun to play video

Lost Indignation

games. And play in a band!" Yes, playing in Indignation was turning out to be more fun than Ryan had imagined, at least so far.

One issue that became apparent was Dion's inability to pronounce certain words in the lyrics that Ryan had already written. Ryan acknowledged that he had included some big words that didn't appear in the lyrics of the average hardcore band and wasn't expecting Dion to know what all of them meant, but he could have at least tried to pronounce them correctly. But even that was a struggle. "We don't need all those words," Ryan hastily agreed, mentally scrambling to edit "castigate" out of "Put It Down" after Dion kept pronouncing it "cas-TI-gi-ate" and stretching it to four syllables. Dion stomping around was the main thing they needed to look like a real band.

Such a real band, in fact, that it was only a matter of time before Eckley found out about its existence. Indignation couldn't stay secret forever: the whole point of having a band was playing shows, and if you were playing shows, you needed to tell your friends to come see you play. Plus, Ryan hoped they would be able to record a demo sometime in the next few months, though he would need to save up after a summer of work to afford the recording.

A few weeks later, on a Saturday afternoon, Ryan and David were hurrying back to the Marnells' house after skating home from Tuckahoe, as Ryan urgently needed to use the bathroom. He flung open the front door and ran upstairs, shouting a hello to his mom, who was in the living room. He didn't hear Eckley come up the stairs, so he assumed he was still on the first floor talking to Mrs. Marnell. But a few minutes later, when Ryan emerged, he was alarmed to find Eckley already in his room, looking through a pile of tapes on the dresser with a strange expression on his face. Afterwards, Ryan wished he could rewind, like a tape, to the moment right before David read what was on the label.

"Indignation practice tape," Eckley read slowly. "Where'd you get this? Who's Indignation? I've never heard of them." He held it up, then set it back down on Ryan's dresser.

"It's mine."

"I know it's yours—it's in your room." Eckley looked annoyed.

"No, I mean ..." Ryan trailed off. "It's my band."

"What the fuck do you mean it's your ... Oh." They looked at each other. Ryan could see him trying to work out how this all could have happened so quickly. The sad truth was they hadn't been spending as much time together, and David wouldn't have suspected anything for months, if not for finding this tape.

"I was worried that if I started a band without you, you would be mad because you'd want to play in it too," Ryan said in a rush. "And that if I asked you to join, then it wouldn't be my thing anymore, that you'd want to take it in a different direction. And that you might not have time. We just started practicing last month, and you've been busy with baseball. I'm sure you understand," he added without conviction.

Eckley's eyes glittered strangely. "What makes you think I'd even want to be in your band?" he retorted.

"I ..." This had never occurred to Ryan. Wouldn't Eckley just want to be in his band because they were best friends?

"Joke's on you because now you have to rely on other people," Eckley continued.

"What do you mean?"

"I'd rather be known ... for something else," Eckley continued slowly, almost as if he was working it out for himself. There were bright spots on his cheeks, what he and David called "British mad" when it frequently befell Mr. Eckley, but this was the first time in a while that Ryan had seen it in David's face.

"Something else, like what, like a different band?"

"No, just a project where I wouldn't have to rely on other people," he snapped. "Like you."

"Dude, that's fucked up," Ryan was now getting upset too.

"Last thing," Eckley continued, "No one's going to believe you wrote all those songs, and frankly, I don't either."

Before Ryan could even ponder this disconcerting turn of events (who the hell else would have written the songs, if not him, if he was the one who started the band? And how could Eckley be sure Ryan hadn't written them, if he hadn't even heard the tape?) Eckley was gone, marching down the hall, stomping down the stairs and straight out the front door, an unfortunate rewind of the path he and Ryan had just traveled only minutes earlier. Ryan heard the front door slam and darted to his window in time to see Eckley stride across the street, not even checking for cars, then stomp up the steps to his front porch and into his house.

Ryan stood at the window in shock. He couldn't believe how the day had gone awry and that this was how David had found out. He had been hoping to break the news himself in a more positive context, like "Hey, I started a band and we're playing this show next month, you need to come see us!" There seemed to be no way to salvage the situation now.

Ryan paced around his room for a bit, and as he flung himself down on his bed, the copy of *Breakfast of Champions* on his nightstand caught his eye. He had just finished reading it a few days before and had been considering naming their newest song—the one that didn't have any words yet—"Now It Can Be Told." Ironically, the phrase took on a new meaning now that Eckley knew about the band. Grabbing a pencil and notebook off his desk, he started to write:

Lost Indignation

I don't care what you know
We are here and it's our show
You don't like it? I won't weep
You don't like it? Won't lose sleep

Now, it can be told
We're the ones who broke the mold
Won't turn back I'm in too deep
I'm not losing any sleep

Ryan wasn't sure if they needed a second verse or not, but he was envisioning Dion yelling "I'm not losing any sleep!" repeatedly over the breakdown at the end, which was the best part of the song. He hoped Dion wouldn't mind that he'd written the lyrics to this one too. Now that they had a real singer, he was paying more attention to the fact that what he was writing would be sung by another person, which meant Dion would have to at least be somewhat down with the message therein.

After writing the song, Ryan felt a little calmer, though still full of dread about how this would impact his friendship with Eckley. He went downstairs to say hi to his mom, and then picked up the phone to call Matt. Miraculously, the Zimmer phone line was free, and Matt was home, which was less surprising.

"So I've got good news and bad news," Ryan began when he got Matt on the line. "The bad news is that David found out about Indignation. The good news is I wrote the words to that new song ..."

On Sunday afternoon, Ryan looked out the window and did a double take. Eckley was sitting in his yard, on the side closest to the Marnells' house, with two of the hottest girls he had ever seen. They appeared to be having some sort of picnic, with a blanket and an elaborate display of sandwiches, and Eckley was playing the guitar for them. Ryan opened the window and heard faint strains of what sounded like a Dag Nasty song reimagined by David Eckley. Ryan fumed. Eckley didn't even like Dag Nasty! He couldn't tell if the girls were digging it or not; he was too far away. Maybe they were just enjoying their hangout with a good-looking guy who played guitar.

Looking again, he recognized one of the girls as Amanda Andolina, who was notorious for being one of the hottest girls that belonged to Lake Isle Country Club. Amanda Andolina, hanging out here, on his street, with David Eckley! He wanted to call someone and tell them, but there was no one who wouldn't also ask why he, Ryan Marnell, was not out there himself. And worse yet, someone like Dion Carina would just ... show up.

Ryan stewed in his room for the rest of the day. He didn't join his mom downstairs to watch the Yankees and was considering whether he would even come downstairs for dinner. But he didn't want to alarm his parents, and theirs wasn't the sort of family where you sulked and missed dinner. Then, around 6:00, the doorbell rang. He heard his dad answer the door and invite someone in. Ryan scrambled down the stairs to find David Eckley in the kitchen, holding two trays of food, smiling like nothing had happened. Ryan's parents, having no idea of yesterday's spat, were thanking him for bringing over the leftovers. His mom even invited David to stay for dinner, but luckily he declined.

David turned to Ryan, who hadn't said a word since his arrival. "Wished you could have come over earlier! See you tomorrow morning." There wasn't a trace of sarcasm or malice in his expression. Was David going to let this go so easily? And to do that, had he only needed to remind Ryan of the difference between them and assert his dominance in their friendship? Ryan might be alone in his room playing guitar, but Eckley was the one using his guitar-playing to lure local girls into hanging out with him.

After this incident, things seemed to go back to normal in the friendship of Ryan Marnell and David Eckley, at least on the surface. But something had irrevocably changed. Luckily, Eckley was soon busy with some projects of his own.

Eckley had been training to become a lifeguard and had gotten the last of his certifications just before turning 17 in May. This coming summer, he would be lifeguarding at the Lake Isle pool in Eastchester, where the Eckleys were members. Apparently one of his fellow rookie lifeguards was a Hackley girl named Madeline Terepka, and David couldn't stop talking about her. What intrigued Ryan most about the famous Madeline was that she was really fucking mean—yet Eckley loved it! When Ryan finally met her, once she and David were officially dating, he was more than ready to corroborate that assessment. Sure, she looked great, but otherwise why would you want to spend time with a person like that? He was also a little creeped out by the fact that she looked like a hot girl version of David Eckley. Ryan was glad to have his new friends in Indignation to fill up some of the spaces in which he might otherwise have been forced to interact with Madeline. And when he someday found himself a girlfriend, he hoped she would be nicer than the object of Eckley's affections.

The lifeguard gig had started in May, as Lake Isle prepared to open for Memorial Day, but luckily Ryan had also lined up a summer job. He would be working in the stockroom of an art supply store on Central Ave. Not only was Ryan grateful to be working indoors, with regular hours and an employee discount on art supplies, but he was also excited to have secured steady employment so he could save up for Indignation-related costs. Ryan loved drawing and painting as much as he loved music. His art had taken a backseat to music lately, especially during the birth of Indignation, but he figured that eventually, music would provide opportunities to draw flyers and cover art, either for his own band or others. Overall, this gig was infinitely preferable to his "job" last summer, when he and Eckley had spent weeks cleaning out some old guy's garage down the block, only to be rewarded with $30 each at the end of their hard work.

So it didn't bother him to constantly have to hear about Eckley's gig and girl. And more importantly, now that Eckley knew about Indignation, and they had a full lineup and set list, there was little to keep them from starting to play shows.

Becky McAuley

Chapter 4
2017

When Mo started going to hardcore shows in 2002, she was keenly cognizant of having missed the opportunity to see Warzone play live. Ray "Raybeez" Barbieri, their legendary frontman, had died five years earlier, but everyone slightly older at shows and on message boards had caught them once or twice while they were still around. Now it was 2017, and there was an entire generation of hardcore kids born too late to have seen Warzone, but no one had forgotten their music or missed the opportunity to honor Ray each anniversary of his death. In 2007, Mo and Pat had gone to the 10-year anniversary show at the Wreck Room in Bushwick, where 10 different bands played at least one Warzone cover as part of their sets. This was a novel and exciting concept at the time, but there were only about 100 people there, and overall it was just another fun local show.

This time around, there was an outdoor show in Tompkins Square Park to honor the 20th anniversary. It was almost like the sequel to the Dr. Know benefit that had taken place in the park the summer before, where 2000 people had shown up. For the Raybeez show, there would be four normal bands and then a Warzone set featuring different guest vocalists for every song. As a Warzone enthusiast, Mo was psyched—not just about that set, but about the whole concept, especially since the Dr. Know show had been so much fun the year prior.

It was a great day for an outdoor show, sunny, around 60 degrees, and imbued with the sweet sadness of the last baseball game of the regular season. At least this year the Yankees were assured a Wild Card berth and knew that they would be facing the Twins at home on Tuesday (unlike in 2015, when they had backed into the playoffs while Mo and Pat were on their way to see Leeway and Everybody Gets Hurt at the Bowery Electric).

As the McGraw-Catalano alliance was not known for getting anywhere on time, they missed Regulate, but otherwise caught the rest of the show. Tompkins Square Park was a convenient place for large shows in that you could see the action from most parts of the park without having to be near the stage or packed into a sweaty club. It also made it easier to move around and have conversations with people you haven't seen in ages while actually being able to hear them.

After the four openers came the headliner that everyone had been waiting for: a full slate of Warzone songs with guest vocalists paying tribute to Raybeez. The lineup included most NYHC luminaries, from Killing Time's Anthony Comunale doing "Fuck Your Attitude" to District 9's Puerto Rican Myke being tapped for "Escape From Your Society." Bob Riley from Stigmata, owner of the elusive first Merauder demo, did a great

Becky McAuley

rendition of "Real Enemy," a song by The Business that Warzone used to cover. Mo and Pat had been watching quietly from about a hundred feet from the stage, a few rows behind the outer reaches of the pit, until Mike Scondotto hit the stage to sing "In The Mirror," which was Mo's favorite Warzone song. For various parts of the set, much of the crowd had been singing along from wherever they were located, including people far back beyond Pat and Mo. But "In the Mirror" was not inspiring the same enthusiasm in their region of the park.

Peeved by the lack of reaction in their vicinity, Mo leapt onto Pat's back at the start of the breakdown. "Go!" she hissed. Pat looked back at her, then understood and charged forward towards the pit. This would be right around the time during the live version on *Old School to New School* when Ray yelled "Let me see you fucking move!" As always, Mo marveled at people's willingness to get out of Pat's way as he barreled unstoppably towards the stage. Once they got closer to the action, Mo jumped off so they could both dance, and they stayed up front to sing along for the rest of the set, which lasted just two more songs: "As One," arguably Warzone's most popular track, and a cover of 7 Seconds's "Young 'Til I Die," which featured all the guest vocalists. There were at least 30 people on stage, and hundreds more in front of it. It was an apropos end to one of the best sets she'd ever seen, outdoors or otherwise.

The show was over but it was still early, with late September sunlight slanting through the park, and a jovial mood prevailed. Mo wasn't ready to go home, and a lot of other people weren't either. While perusing the Warzone construction gloves for sale, Mo wondered if they would encounter Tony Gerson before departing. She hadn't seen him yet today, but knew from Instagram that he was here somewhere. Instead, another Anthony soon walked past: Anthony Comunale from Killing Time. Before Mo could react, Pat gave her a look and flagged him down. Mo could only surmise that he had meant for her to ask about Indignation.

"Hey, Anthony," Pat called, putting his outside voice to good use. "My wife's got a question for you." He gave Mo a good natured push into the path of the frontman.

"Hey, what's up?" Mo had never spoken to Comunale, though she knew some of the other Killing Time guys in passing. "Do you remember anything about an old Westchester band called Indignation?"

Comunale considered his small inquisitor. "Indignation? I think Raw Deal played with them once, but I didn't watch their set."

Mo nodded. "That's what I've been hearing, that no one actually saw them ..."

Comunale looked like he was about to add something, but someone was trying to get his attention for a group picture, and he excused himself. A few seconds later, Mo realized she had missed an opportunity.

"Ah, I forgot I had my location scouting cards! In case he thinks of anyone else I should talk to!" It was too late now, but at least she remembered she had them for future conversations.

Mo and Pat ping-ponged into different conversations as they kept running into friends, acquaintances, or friends of acquaintances. Warren Yatrofsky swooped by, took a selfie with Pat, and disappeared back into the throng. A few minutes later, Mo was heatedly defending at least one-third of the tracks on Token Entry's *Weight of the World* to a peripheral friend of Pat's whom she had met various times at shows like this.

"I mean "Revolution" isn't even the best song, much less the only good one on that album," Mo argued. "And "Doing It Again" is a top tier Token Entry song, not just for that era."

"It's Dr. Know's favorite Token Entry song," said a voice behind her.

Mo turned around to pinpoint her interlocutor. It wasn't anyone she recognized—a shorter guy, darkly handsome with close cropped hair, likely in his early to mid-40s. One of the hundreds, if not thousands, of older hardcore dudes who showed up for the big shows, or for a friend's band, and then disappeared back into the world of jobs, families, and far-flung suburbs. This guy seemed to exhibit less wear and tear than the average hardcore kid who had pursued years of hard living in the form of various substances.

"That's right! I was so surprised when they played it at his benefit, but it made sense when they explained it," Mo replied. "They definitely didn't play it at the Superbowl. Or that show in Asbury Park in 2008."

"You went to that? The one that had to get moved from the Stone Pony?"

"Yup, I was there! What a weird show." While sometimes reserved in interactions with strangers, Mo conversely felt instantly comfortable with random people she encountered at shows and could prattle on about a variety of hardcore topics without knowing the identity of her conversation partner. Mo would sometimes later find out that she had been talking to, say, a founding member of Rejuvenate. But other times it was just some 45-year-old straight edge guy on vacation from California.

Tony Gerson stumbled into her line of sight. "What's up?" She hugged him hello. "I just saw Comunale go by, and I asked him about some old band whose demo I'm looking for. But I can't believe I forgot to give him my new business cards in case he finds someone who has it!" Mo lamented. "Look at this." She shoved one in Gerson's face, and he took it. "Pat made them for me, since I'm so fucking paranoid about trespassing. So we can claim we're location scouts," Mo explained. "Do you think they look convincing? Jesus, I'm such a dork."

"You should ask this guy," Tony responded, pointing towards the dark-haired guy with whom she had been discussing Token Entry. "He's a detective. My go-to for legal shit, and not-so-legal shit." The guy in question didn't look enthused about this description.

"If you saw someone trespassing and they gave you this business card, would you think they were there for legitimate business purposes?" She handed him one of the cards.

"Hmm." The Token Entry fan scrutinized the proffered item before passing it back. "Does this remove my doubt? Not particularly, since you're still not supposed to be there. I'm Anthony," he extended his hand.

"Oh, word? You're the third Anthony that I've talked to in the last five minutes. I'm Mo. And thanks for looking at my cards."

"No problem," Anthony grinned. "Are you a Supremes fan?"

Mo was about to respond in the affirmative when her quarry was promptly tackled by some bald dude and carried off into another photo op or conversation.

Soon after, she and Pat said their goodbyes to the remaining populace and departed. As they strode along the path towards Avenue A, Mo felt a profound sense of well-being in the fading daylight. Another fun park show, and she wasn't nearly as sweaty as at the end of the Dr. Know benefit last year. Besides the Warzone set, she'd gotten to see Tony Gerson, had asked Anthony Comunale about Indignation, and gotten to talk to some random dude about Token Entry.

Only later, Mo would wonder if she should have asked him about Indignation too.

After the park show, a cold. Of course Mo and Pat both caught it, as was the general pattern of Mo catching a cold at work, and despite her best efforts, infecting Pat a day or two later. She actually had no idea where this one came from, but they both started feeling sick on the Monday after the show. Outdoor hardcore shows were less of a confluence of germs than those held in close quarters, and it hadn't been particularly cold or damp on Sunday. Still, they both seemed to always get sick around this time of year, which made for a gloomy start to October, especially in years when the Yankees were not in the playoffs. This year they were playing the Twins in the Wild Card game on Tuesday, which Mo was only somewhat worried about. The Yankees tended to demolish the Twins in their near-annual playoff matchups, but Mo worried a little about everything, warranted or otherwise.

Fast forward to Tuesday. Sniffling but rationalizing spicy food as medically necessary, Mo had dipped out to pick up Indian food in Tuckahoe and grabbed Pat at the train a few stops early. She then dropped a very anxious Pat at home with the food, as the Twins had taken an early

Lost Indignation

3-0 lead and Severino was already out of the game. After finding parking, she was walking back up the hill on Overlook Street when Didi Gregorius hit a three-run bomb to tie it. It had been a high-scoring contest ever since, though the Yankees were maintaining a narrow lead after the Twins had come back again to tie the score at four all. Between this being the first game of the playoffs and her being sick, there was no fucking way she was getting any work done tonight. Tomorrow was Wednesday and she had been planning to attend an afternoon colloquium, but might skip it, and she didn't have anything due till Thursday, which, so far, was part of a story about an unhinged knitting umpire who murdered a crazed fan with a knitting needle after a road game. (Mo was counting on no one in the class to have read Robertson Davies.) Meanwhile, the similarly named David Robertson was holding the Twins at four runs after the departure of Chad Green. Not that Mo or Pat were relaxed about the rest of the game, since if the Yankees lost, their postseason would be over. The playoffs, she realized, could end up affecting her evening productivity, especially if the Yankees continued to advance. Though if they made it to future rounds of postseason play, it would be a good problem to have.

Another good problem to have: needing a distraction that was less taxing than attempting to do homework. In the worst stretches of 2014-16, she could easily have still been at work at 10 p.m.—like the day she missed Derek Jeter's final hit in Yankee Stadium—or on the way home. Perhaps this was the perfect time to start researching individual members of Indignation! Max Malkin had mentioned them each by name, or partial names, when they had met on the night of the ill-fated video sale. Not that she remembered all the names he had reeled off—but wait! Hadn't Pat recorded the entire thing?

Mo bounded into the living room and CC looked up, affronted. She couldn't believe she had forgotten about this until now.

"I can't believe I forgot about the recording!"

"The recording of what?" Pat was totally absorbed in the game.

"The recording! Of when we met Max Malkin in the park and bought the tape!"

"Oh yeah! I'll find it and send it to you right now."

"Thanks, my love." Mo petted CC and paused like she was about to sneeze, reining it in for the sake of not scaring the cat. Neither Brett nor CC was fond of sneezes.

"OK, I emailed it to you," Pat reported a few minutes later. Mo scurried back down the hall to pull up the audio the next time there was a break between innings or a pitching change.

During each commercial break that signaled the end of an inning or the arrival of a new pitcher, Mo listened to more of the conversation with Max Malkin, mostly to write down the names of each band member, but also to glean any other useful clues. The only person for whom Malkin had mentioned a last name was Matt Zimmer, the drummer, who apparently hadn't even played on the demo. As the only member that had been mentioned by his first and last name, Mo would start with him.

There were probably a ton of Matt Zimmers though. Of course the dude had one of the most generic possible names. Not that she knew the last names of the other members—for all she knew, theirs could have been equally bland and ubiquitous.

First Mo tried Facebook, but there weren't any Matt Zimmers that popped up in her search that had mutual friends, or ones that looked obviously like a member of an old hardcore band. The results were the same on Instagram, though his profile was much less likely to be under his real name there.

LinkedIn was her favorite stalking platform for work, and she loved it in a half-sarcastic, half-genuine way. She loathed the people who posted serious businessy articles and self-aggrandizing updates or listed their title as "visionary" or some shit, but did relish using it to research journalists for work, and the updates from the news feed on people's job changes were frequently useful for the database. She also enjoyed sending longshot friend requests to assorted hardcore celebrities such as Josh Loucka from Shift. There was something humorous in the juxtaposition between the intended purpose of the site and the reasons she most enjoyed using it.

Mo typed "Matt Zimmer" into the LinkedIn search bar. Oof— there were 60+ Matt Zimmers on LinkedIn. Assuming he had stayed in the New York area, she narrowed the search by "Greater New York City Area" then started reading down the page. Accountant, media planner, consultant ... hang on. There was a Matt Zimmer who worked for the WWE! Hadn't Malkin said something about this guy being a wrestling fan? Heart hammering, she opened the tab for his profile. He was a third level connection, which meant they didn't have any mutual LinkedIn friends, just a friend of a friend somewhere. Nevertheless, Mo was able to see some of the info on his profile, if not everything. He had been working as a Senior Corporate Recruiter at WWE in Stamford, CT since 2014, so it was lucky that he had shown up in the Greater NYC Area search. Further down the page, it said he had graduated from Rutgers in 1994, which was roughly the right age range for someone who had played in a band in the late '80s. In his generic LinkedIn thumbnail pic, he looked like a friendly guy, or at least not someone outright hostile. Mo clicked to request a connection, since she didn't have a premium account for work anymore and wouldn't have been able to send him a free message otherwise. In the box to personalize the request, she wrote:

"Hi! Are you the Matt Zimmer who played in a band called

Lost Indignation

Indignation in the 1980s? If so, would you be able to tell me more about the band? Apologies if I have the wrong person."
Sent.

She didn't have to wait long for a reply, which arrived a few minutes later, along with a notification about having a new LinkedIn connection. Mo realized she was lucky this guy was a recruiter, as he probably checked his LinkedIn messages much more frequently than the average person who was either not attempting to change jobs or using the site as a tool for their own work.

"Hi Maureen, that's me! Wow, I don't even want to ask how you found me, but I'd be happy to speak to you about Indignation."

She already liked this guy, who seemed much friendlier than Max Malkin.

"Amazing! I would love to hear more about the band. Let me know some times that are convenient for you, and if you would prefer to connect by phone or meet in person if you are still in Westchester. Thank you!" Mo typed back, presuming that he lived somewhere nearby if he worked in Stamford. She would try not to get too excited, in case this dude was either freaked out by her suggestion of a face-to-face conversation or if his second reply didn't arrive as quickly as his initial message.

It was now after 11 p.m., and after the Yankees had scored one more insurance run in the seventh inning, Mo felt safe going to bed. With a 8-4 victory over the Twins, there would be more Yankees baseball to distract her later in the week.

Mo was at work the next morning, trying not to sneeze on Drew Flowers and opening LinkedIn to investigate the fate of a design journalist whose email had bounced back, when she saw the notification about another new message. It was from Matt Zimmer.

"Are you free this Saturday a.m.? My daughter has a dance lesson in Mamaroneck."

"Yes!! Saturday works for me," Mo started to type. Oh crap. Saturday was Pat's birthday, and she wasn't sure how he wanted to celebrate. Though she assumed that spending the morning in Mamaroneck to talk about Indignation wasn't high on the list. Oh well, it didn't hurt to ask. She would present it as: if they got this over with, she might finally stop talking about Indignation, rather than talking about them more, which Pat would immediately, correctly identify as the actual result.

"We usually are, but it's my husband's birthday, so I'll have to ask him," she hit reply, then started mentally composing a Gchat to Pat to present this unique opportunity.

"Bring him too!" Matt replied a few minutes later.

Technically, that had been the plan all along, re: the whole meeting strange dudes from the internet thing, even if they were meeting

Becky McAuley

in a public place while his daughter was at dance class, but at least now Mo didn't have to broach the subject of her and Pat working as a team.

They decided to meet at Cafe Mozart in Mamaroneck, which was right down the street from Zimmer's daughter's dance studio. Mo and Pat had also met with their wedding DJ there, back in 2013.

"Stick with me, baby, and you'll just have to keep meeting strange men from the internet at Cafe Mozart," Mo joked on Thursday night.

"I look forward to it," Pat acquiesced.

On Friday evening, Mo was still at work when Pat texted that Don ZT was on his way to drop off the videotape. He'd had a chance to fuck around with the audio levels, and while his edited version was a digital file that had been sent to Pat via Dropbox, the Indignation tape would now also be back under their roof. Mo hoped the thing wasn't cursed. At least they didn't have to track down a VCR again to watch Don's new digital version, since she wanted to watch it before meeting Matt Zimmer tomorrow.

Mo hastened to wrap up her Friday night tasks and jetted out of Colette's townhouse in time to catch the 9 p.m. train. By the time she had scaled the stairs to their third-floor apartment, Pat had already set up the Chromecast to stream it to the TV. The Yankees were still battling the Indians in extra innings in Game 2 of the ALDS, so there was no way she was starting the Indignation tape (or pseudo-Indignation tape) till that was over, even though they no longer had cable and were listening to the game on the radio.

Unfortunately, the Yankees lost in extra innings, five hours after the game had begun. At least now that the game was over, Mo was able to turn her attention to the tape.

Don had sent two separate files: one long video file of the entire tape, digitized but unaltered, and then one of just the third band, in which he had attempted to improve the audio. They watched a bit of the Raw Deal set, then skipped ahead to the start of the second band, the bathing suit guys at the Scarsdale Pool. Even though Don hadn't done any work on this set, this time Mo could hear the singer say "We're the Merkles ..." and then some other dude in the crowd yell "Merkle's Boner!" Mo was surprised there hadn't been more bands called Merkle's Boner, or Snodgrass's Muff. Ska'd-grass's Muff? That was a ska band waiting to happen.

Mo paused the unedited file to switch to the cleaned-up set of the third band. Kids milled around up front before their set, and Mo heard the singer say:

"Yo, what's up?! We're Power Structure, we're all here today for a good cause, so move the fuck up!"

"Did you hear that!" she shrieked and whirled around. Pat wasn't at his desk, and was down the hall feeding the cats.

Power Structure. So this was definitely not Indignation! Either way, Mo still felt compelled to watch the rest of their set, if only to hear what else the singer mentioned between bands. The Power Structure guys were a generic-looking bunch of tanned white kids with short hair. The singer had his shirt off. Again she watched kids mosh for the intro, then saw their level of excitement subsequently abate during the next few songs, which still sounded crappy despite the improved audio quality.

Finally they reached the next round of banter between songs.

"Shoutout to Bad Tactic for the amp, Indignation—"

Mo slammed her finger onto the pause button on her phone, then edged back a few seconds.

"—for the amp, Indignation—" a couple people clapped— "Breakdown, and all the other bands playing today."

OK, this was more definitive proof that the third band was not Indignation! But not only was this more evidence of the existence of Indignation, it also sounded like they had played this same show. Had Malkin lied about them appearing on this tape, or had their set once followed Power Structure's? And had the tape been damaged accidentally, or had someone recorded over it on purpose? Don had mentioned that he couldn't get anything off the tape after the third band, but he had included the same few seconds of the band following Power Structure. Mo scrutinized the brief clip for clues, in case this was Indignation, and made a note to ask Matt Zimmer tomorrow. It was disappointing to confirm that Indignation was not the third band, but she was glad to have gleaned more proof of their existence. And having never heard their songs, she could still hope that they were substantially better than Power Structure.

By Saturday, both Mo and Pat's colds had abated, which was fortuitous as it would not do to show up and start sneezing on a member of Indignation. "Happy birthday, my love!" Mo brought him an iced coffee, which he had technically made the night before. She felt a little bad disrupting his Saturday a.m. birthday scene, but after meeting Zimmer at noon, they would have the whole rest of the day to enjoy.

Mo chortled when, after brushing her teeth and heading back down the hall, Pat walked out of their room wearing a checkered shirt almost identical to Mo's, and similar Dunks too.

"Oh man! We shouldn't show up and be totally matching! I'll change."

"No, you look cute, and I can wear the Soriano." Pat removed his button down outer layer to reveal the Alfonso Soriano t-shirt underneath.

Mo was already sweating as she prowled the apartment in her shirt and jeans, gathering her stuff for the Zimmer meeting. It was unusually hot for the first Saturday in October, to the point where she was contemplating turning on the air conditioner.

"Thank you for agreeing to do this," she offered as they walked to the car.

"There are a lot of other things I'd rather be doing on my birthday, but making my wife happy is always a good way to spend it," Pat reasoned. "Plus, I knew if we waited another week to meet him, you wouldn't stop talking about it all week."

Zimmer had beaten them to Cafe Mozart and secured a table. Mo recognized him from his LinkedIn picture, which was more honest than most. He looked like the ultimate dad, with thinning dark hair, a polo shirt, and khaki shorts. Mo had never seen a picture of Indignation but imagined he had looked quite different as a teenage drummer. She tried to remember what the drummer looked like in the video, as one more clue that it wasn't the same band, before remembering that it was now resolved that the third band on the tape was Power Structure, not Indignation. As they ordered coffee and muffins, she reminded herself to ask Matt about Power Structure at some point in today's conversation.

"Thank you for meeting with us! I can't believe I found a member of Indignation on LinkedIn."

Matt laughed. "This is the first time in at least twenty-five years that someone has referred to me as a member of Indignation. And I was going to be here anyway. My daughter has dance right down the street on Saturdays, and it doesn't make sense for me to go home and back while she's there. We live over in Harrison."

"Well, I'm glad it worked out to meet us here. I love this place. We had a bunch of meetings with our wedding DJ here too. To talk about what not to play at our wedding. Anyway ... I had never heard of you guys until I bought this videotape that Indignation was supposed to be on. And now I'm not sure if your set is even on the tape, but I want to know more about the band, and I'm trying to find the demo."

"There's not that much to tell. We were a band for about six months in 1988, and we only played three shows. We had a demo tape, but there weren't that many copies."

"But I hear you didn't play on the demo."

"Yeah, I decided last minute to go to this wrestling event upstate, so they found some guy to fill in. They didn't want to push back the recording, since they had already paid the deposit and wanted to have tapes in time for our CBGB's show, which we didn't end up playing. We actually broke up on the way to the show!"

"By any chance do you still have a copy of the demo? Or mp3s?"

"Mp3s!" Matt seemed to find this hilarious. "If that tape still exists anywhere, I doubt anyone bothered to digitize it! I only had a few copies since I wasn't part of the recording. I gave some to my friends, and I have no idea what happened to mine."

"I'm hoping to find one somewhere. I'd love to hear it, now that I know it exists. What were the rest of the guys in the band like?"

"Ryan Marnell, the guitarist, he died a few years ago. We started the band together. And we found this singer, Dion Carina, who was friends with my cousin. He was a real individual. And didn't fit in with a bunch of high school kids."

"Yeah, I heard about him." Mo didn't elaborate on the rest of the conversation with Sydenstricker, as she wanted to see what Matt would reveal without her interjecting what she already knew.

"I think he lives in Florida now. He never liked me very much. About as much as Ryan's best friend David Eckley, this guy who always wanted to be in our band and wasn't a big fan of me either. And the bassist Eric was a punk rock kid who moved out west somewhere. So I guess I'm the only Indignation member left in the New York area."

"Then I'm extra glad I found you. Do you keep in touch with either Dion or Eric?"

"No, I wasn't close with either of them, and as I said, Dion was no big fan of mine. Ryan was the only one I really hung out with. And I lost touch with him a few years later."

"Is there anyone else you can think of that I should ask about Indignation? Who might either have the demo or know someone who does?"

"You could ask Christine, Ryan's old girlfriend. I didn't know her well. She was from Dobbs Ferry. My cousin Liz lived in White Plains but was friends with these girls from the Rivertowns. We used to go skate there sometimes, at this old building down by the river. I wasn't there the day she met Ryan, though. He went over with Dion to drop off some flyers for our first show, which was a battle of the bands at a park in Sleepy Hollow."

Mo looked intrigued. "Wait, which building in Dobbs? Was it the one at the bottom of the long driveway that looks possibly haunted?"

"Yeah, how did you know?"

"I used to work there!" Mo exclaimed. "I mean it *looked* like the kind of place where local kids would hang out and skate at, but I never actually saw anyone there. Little did I know there was hardcore history involved."

"Hardcore history might be a stretch. So Ryan met Christine when they were handing off the flyers. She and her friends came to our first show, and they started dating a few months later. She was a nice girl, and she really helped Ryan after the band broke up. I don't know what he expected from us, but he wanted a lot more than playing three shows, recording a demo, and then breaking up before we played CB's. He was hoping that would be the first of a lot of New York shows, or a tour or whatever. It was me and him from the beginning, but he was the one with the vision. So he was pretty bummed. Christine helped get him back on track and even convinced him to go to college. He was in school for a bit but something must have happened since then I heard he was in a psych hospital and they broke up. And then he was harder to get in touch with after that."

"Damn." Mo was unprepared for the dark turn the conversation had taken and was trying to remember every detail without taking notes. She didn't want to be that asshole whipping out a pen and notepad to write down the details of this guy's psychotic break. "I know he died young, but I don't know much about him otherwise. I'm glad he had Christine though. Do you happen to know her last name? In case I want to track her down and ask about Indignation."

"Something Italian. And she was from Dobbs Ferry. I can't imagine it would be too hard to find her."

Pat laughed. "Do you have any idea how many Italian people are from Dobbs Ferry?"

"You're right," Matt conceded. "Though at least it's not that big of a town."

"By any chance do you remember a guy named Max Malkin? That's the guy who sold us the video."

"I don't remember anyone by that name, but I didn't know those other Crestwood guys."

"Do you remember anyone who used to bring a video camera to shows?"

Zimmer's brow furrowed. "Yes, but his name was Andy? Maybe Max was someone who traded tapes with Andy and that's how he got a hold of that set."

"He definitely said he shot that video ... anyway! He said that Indignation was supposed to be the third band on the tape ... but when I got to that section, the third band was really bad."

"Sounds like us!" Matt chuckled.

"No, it wasn't, since our friend cleaned up the tape, and now we can hear that it's a band called Power Structure. Did you know them?"

"Oh yeah, Power Structure. They were from further north—Peekskill area. I didn't know them well, but we played some shows with them. Nice dudes, but you're right, they weren't very good."

"Hmm ... the day this video was shot—I wonder if you guys were supposed to be on the tape too? After their set, there's about fifteen minutes where nothing happens, and then about two seconds of another band. Could that have been Indignation? Did they ever play before you on a show? Or right after you?"

Matt considered. "Yeah, they were around longer, and got us our first show. But I do remember that at this one benefit show, they played before us, since they were sharing gear with another band. Though Dion claimed they didn't want to play after us since we would have blown them out of the water. That show was the best one we ever played," Matt reminisced. "All our friends were there, and people were going nuts. And we didn't realize it at the time, but it ended up being our last show."

"So maybe that short clip is you guys. The only thing I could hear is a lyric that sounds like 'My only,' and then some dude stagedives and knocks everything over and the tape cuts out again."

Matt's face lit up. "My only crime was having too good of a time! That was from our song 'Religious Instruction.' Oh man! It was the only song that Dion helped write the lyrics to. Ryan wrote most of the other ones."

"Well, for the one second I heard, that song sounded pretty good," Mo ventured cautiously. "Like when I heard Power Structure, I was like what the fuck, is this Indignation? But hearing the clip of the other band, which I guess *is* you guys, makes me want to hear more of those songs, or I guess, your songs." Any band could sound good in a split-second clip, but she was still intrigued.

"Yeah, I guess some of our stuff wasn't so bad. Like it's nothing that I ever tried to go back and listen to. If I had, maybe I would have noticed sooner that I have no idea what happened to my tape. But kids were into it at the time. And people probably would have liked us if we kept going."

"Well I definitely want to hear more. What did the rest of your songs sound like?"

"Like a generic late '80s hardcore band? Not as good as Breakdown, but in that style. Ryan realized early on that I was better at playing on the toms than fast parts on a cymbal, so we had stuff that was like ... imagine the Side By Side song 'Backfire.' Or we used to fuck around in practice with covering the Agnostic Front song 'With Time,' since it was one that we could actually play."

"'With Time' is def one of my favorite AF songs," Mo chimed in, with Pat nodding emphatically in the background. "So this really makes me want to hear the rest of your songs. Or even the rest of one song."

"Even if I don't have the tape, I've got a bunch of stuff from that era. I did save all my flyers from when I was going to shows in high school, and stuff my cousin gave me, and then when I was in college. I went to Rutgers and saw a bunch of punk shows in basements in New Brunswick."

"Nice, I'm from New Jersey and have heard a lot about basement shows back then!" Mo didn't mention that she already knew he went to Rutgers from his LinkedIn. "If you ever dig up those flyers, I'd love to see them."

"I've been meaning to get everything out, now that my kids are old enough to look at them and see what their dad was doing back then. And I'm sure my wife wants me to get rid of some of that stuff! I'll look this weekend, and if you give me your address, I'll send you copies of anything cool."

"That would be great." Mo pulled a notebook out of her purse to write down their address on Overlook Street, and half-considered giving him a location scouting card. "Is your cousin Liz still interested in hardcore? Do you think she has any of this stuff either?"

"She's a lawyer and lives in DC. I don't think she's paid any attention to anything hardcore-wise since at least the mid '90s, but I can ask her if she still has the demo."

"How old were you guys when all this was happening?"

"I had just turned sixteen, Ryan was seventeen, Dion was eighteen but looked twenty-five, and I think Eric was around my age too. 1988! Almost thirty years ago! I can't believe it."

"Yeah, I was two-years-old, so definitely not around while this was all going down."

After Mo had settled the check, they wrapped up their conversation while heading out into the midday sunlight on Mamaroneck Ave. "I'll send those flyers your way—and keep in touch!"

"Definitely! Thanks again for doing this. And next time I'll pick your brain for recruiting tips!"

"Happy to talk hiring and recruiting, but if you're half as good at tracking down candidates as you are at researching old hardcore bands, maybe I should be taking notes from you."

The car was on Phillips Park Road, behind their second-favorite Indian restaurant, Rani Mahal. "My love," Mo slung her arm around Pat's shoulder. "Thanks for sacrificing your birthday."

"Hey, it's only 1:15, now you have the rest of the day to make it up to me. I'm joking, I enjoyed that."

"I'm glad. Even if no one seems to have this fucking tape." Mo clicked the remote to unlock the Camry. "And at least we know the name of Ryan's best friend now—David Eckley, I think Matt said?"

Pat assented, that's what it had sounded like, either Eckley or Ackley, as in Dustin.

"Also, the reason I was asking their ages," Mo continued, "is because I'm going to go to Dobbs Ferry High School and look up Christine in the yearbooks!"

"OK, Mrs. Yearbooks ... yeah most people in Dobbs go to public school, though she could have gone to Hackley, or Maria Regina or something."

"Well, I'll start with Dobbs first, and see what happens," Mo resolved. "Plus it will probably be easier to get permission to get in there, like, as a grad student doing research. As opposed to having to dress up as a student or something." Though she could only imagine the look on Pat's face if she showed up dressed in a Catholic school uniform ready to sneak into Maria Regina.

In a fortuitous turn of events, Mo received an email from her advisor on the morning of Columbus Day stating that due to some Amtrak issue, he was late returning from Montreal, and could they push their biweekly advising session to 5 p.m., rather than the customary 3:00? Unlike many offices and schools that were closed for the holiday, CFA was open and experiencing the average hectic Monday— that is, one in which Colette had set up an avalanche of tasks for everyone over the weekend and staff were managing the fallout today. Rather than leaving at her usual time, Mo marked in the CFA internal calendar that she would be sticking around until about 3:30 before heading to campus. So she was at her desk around 1 p.m., having just eaten her peanut butter sandwich and was deep into organizing some list of additional media members for the Salon Art & Design, when Tony Gerson walked through the door of the townhouse and sat down at his old desk.

For a moment, no one noticed that anything out of the ordinary had happened—in any other year, this would have been a plausible time for Tony to return from lunch. But it wasn't any other year, it was 2017, and office manager Drew Flowers was currently at lunch himself. Mo got there first. "Hey! What the hell are you doing here? I mean, welcome!"

Tony reached across the three-foot aisle between their desks to execute a one-armed hug, waving a hello to Elvis Fregosi, who was on a conference call with Colette. Mo admired Elvis's concentration, as he was frequently on the phone at what was one of the noisiest desks in the office. "I was in town with my family for the parade, and I decided to stop by and see you all—HEY, buddy!" Pierre had just woken up and charged Tony, emitting various noises that would impede Elvis's ability to follow the conference call for a good 30 seconds.

"You picked a good day to come by," Mo looked on while Tony wrestled with the dog, "since I don't have to leave for school till after three. Usually, I'd be heading out soon and rushing to finish up."

"Yeah, I figured this might be a good day to come see everyone. Where's this guy?" He indicated Flowers's desk.

"At lunch. Though I give you full permission to take back your old desk." Tony put his feet up on the arm of Anna the bookkeeper's chair.

"So, what's new?" Mo queried, remembering she had just seen him at the park show, but they hadn't had time for a normal conversation.

"Just last week, one of my students called me a goat fucker in Spanish."

"And did they know you were familiar with being called a goat fucker in at least six languages?" Though they had occasionally annoyed each other due to the paltry buffer between the backs of their chairs (and once Pierre sat down, you couldn't move your chair at all), overall Gerson had been a devoted and entertaining desk neighbor, and the entire staff fiercely lamented his absence, in a way that, Mo realized, might not create the easiest of environments for his successor. Drew Flowers was the kind of guy you could sort of joke around with sometimes, but he and Mo didn't have the shared history of having worked together at a prior job like she and Tony did, not to mention common roots and references in hardcore, both arcane and profane. Nor could Drew match Tony's sense of humor.

Other CFA staffers were starting to return from lunch, or otherwise determining that Tony Gerson was in the house.

"Oona from Altoona! Sup B?" Tony went in for a high five. He had always enjoyed fucking with delicate Oona, and in time, she had come to enjoy his presence as well. Oona mumbled something about having just finished an event for designer Milou Sinclair during Frieze Week in London. Tony was well acquainted with Milou, as he once had to entertain her on the phone for about ten minutes when Colette was late for a conference call; much to her consternation, he had started talking about British wrestlers.

"Freeze Week?" Gerson exclaimed in mock surprise. "What's next, Gang Green Week? DYS Week?"

The jubilant reunions continued: Elvis and Colette wrapped their call, and Tony left to greet them in their office area that opened onto the garden. As Tony walked back towards Mo's desk, Colette announced that if her 1:30 meeting was early, to take them upstairs to her actual living room on the third floor and offer a coffee, as she needed a few minutes to finish something.

"Oh! While you're here," Mo turned to Tony. "If I needed to get into the Dobbs Ferry High School library to look at the yearbooks, do you know how I would do that?"

"To look at the *yearbooks*?" His tone indicated that while this might appear to be a random request, nothing was ever too random for Tony Gerson, and he was used to Mo's odd inquiries. "I thought you were going to ask me about the FedEx software."

"Oh yes, I know Drew has been having trouble with that too. Let's wait till he's back and he can show you what's wrong." Tony rolled his eyes.

"Well. If you want to see the yearbooks, you should be able to get in no problem. Just call to make an appointment, stop by the front office and they should give you a visitor's pass and let you into the library. Especially if you tell them it's for grad school." Mo did not dispute this intent.

Mo was on the verge of asking him if he knew someone named Christine, though they didn't have a lot to go on besides her first name,

Lost Indignation

when the doorbell rang—or, more accurately, pulsed its infinite bleep bleep bleep through the office phones. That must be Colette's 1:30. Mo looked at Gcal. It should be Ethan Mitchell, who worked in publishing, presumably coming to discuss the seated lunch honoring the memoir by his friend Winston Alexander. After serving in the Special Forces during Desert Storm and various covert missions afterwards, Win Alexander had ended up in New York during the second half of the '90s and become a ubiquitous regular in the type of hip clubs and restaurants frequented by edgier celebs and represented by Colette Foulard & Associates, with Ethan frequently by his side. CFA occasionally did parties or lunches for Ethan's authors, and Mo had seen something on the calendar for a Thursday in mid-December.

Tony answered the door, and Mo looked over. She presumed this was Ethan arriving, and not Winston (if he was coming too) since Winston was Black, and this was a nondescript looking white guy. Still, she was intrigued to encounter Ethan Mitchell. She remembered that he had some vague hardcore and punk connection, having played in bands in Connecticut in the '80s before moving to NYC and hosting popular punk-adjacent DJ nights in the early aughts. Ethan was one of those people who Colette represented for one-off events, but as he seemed less demanding than, say, their international fashion clients or disorganized artists, Mo had never interacted with him.

"Mr. Mitchell," Gerson intoned, solemnly pumping his hand. Mo was momentarily nonplussed. Tony Gerson knew Ethan Mitchell? Of course he did: Tony Gerson knew everyone. Doubtless they had been out drinking together once at Double Down or something. Perhaps Gerson had seen Mitchell's old band, Future Humans, back when they last played the Anthrax, a legendary club in Connecticut, though Gerson would have been approximately seven years old when Future Humans last played. It was ironic that while Tony was very much not a part of the typical CFA social world, he sometimes knew more about their clients and event attendees than the rest of the office, whose job it was to know that stuff.

After the usual exclamations about their townhouse office, Tony showed Ethan upstairs as Colette had instructed. Mo was grateful that Tony was still at the office and had slipped seamlessly back into his role of office manager and greeter, at least till Drew returned from lunch. Though she was a little jealous that Tony was escorting the one client that she might have wanted to talk to, not just because of his punk rock past, but also because of the literary angle. Mo was probably years away from ever having anything ready for publication, but it didn't hurt to nurture connections on this front and make the most of her occasional access to such worlds through CFA.

Colette soon swept upstairs, resulting in the return of Tony

Gerson, like bringing down the other end of a seesaw. Moments later, a befuddled Drew Flowers returned, followed by Anna the bookkeeper. After both caught up with Gerson and Drew got another lesson on the FedEx software, Tony headed back out to rejoin his family. Mo was glad she had seen him for the second time in a few weeks, though she hoped to run into him soon at the Thai House or Petraske's so they could catch up in a non-office environment.

Mo was still at her desk when she heard footsteps on the stairs an hour later.

"So Ethan has your card," Colette concluded as they descended. "In case he has any questions about the list." Mo, half listening, nodded as Colette and Ethan said their goodbyes, and Ethan headed out as Colette maneuvered around Pierre and back to her desk. She briefly wondered where Ethan had gotten her business card, as she didn't remember giving him one, unless Colette had a stash of them upstairs or something.

The question was answered an hour later when an email arrived from Ethan. "Hi Maureen, it was nice to meet you at Colette's today. Should I contact you on this email address if I have any questions while preparing my guest list?" Mo was confused why it had gone straight to her personal email rather than her work email, until she saw that it had been sent to mo@removethisdoubt.com.

Oh, fuck.

Gerson must have held onto her card from the park show and given it to Ethan Mitchell in place of her real business card! His idea of a practical joke could have landed her in a lot of trouble if this had happened, say, last year, though things had been better lately, and there was no guarantee that Colette would even find out.

"Hi Ethan, thank you for confirming—my best email is actually maureen@colettefoulard.com. Apologies if Tony gave you my other card. I look forward to receiving the lists for your event, and please don't hesitate to get in touch if you have any questions."

She thought about adding, "Also, just to clarify, I am not actually a location scout!" But it was already a weird situation and she should keep things as vague as possible. Lots of people at CFA had creative sidelines, though she had the misfortune of an important member of an independent publishing house now having a business card for a business that didn't exist, rather than legitimate contact info that reinforced their shared interests.

Before leaving for school, she texted Tony. "You motherfucker! Why did you give him my location scouting card!"

In a moment, she had a reply. "Because I didn't have your real card!" Flawless logic.

When Mo got home from class that Thursday, there was a large envelope on the table in the entryway where the mailman left packages that didn't fit in the actual mailboxes. Mo studied the return address: it was the flyers from Matt Zimmer! She was impressed he had turned them around so quickly and hurried upstairs to open them.

Pat arrived soon after, carrying their takeout order from Jade Garden, and Mo excitedly filled him in on the arrival of the package. After destroying some veggie dumplings and half of the scallion pancakes, Mo washed her hands to rip open the package from Zimmer.

"Hi Mo, here are the flyers, including the Indignation show that never was. Enjoy and keep in touch!" Zimmer had written on a Post-it. He had included about 15 hand-drawn flyers from the late '80s: mostly shows in New York and Connecticut, and one from a basement show in New Brunswick, NJ.

"The show that never was" was on the top of the pile. Well, the *show* had happened, just not Indignation's set. Mo scrutinized the CBGB's flyer, Pat leaning over her shoulder: October 2, 1988. Pat was about to turn six. Breakdown, Outburst, Bugout Society, Iron Fist, Indignation. What a show! Too bad Indignation hadn't played.

Mo flipped to the next flyer, which was some Rest in Pieces show in Mahopac, then a Wide Awake show at the Anthrax. The fourth flyer was for another Indignation show at a park in Sleepy Hollow. It was an outdoor show with a bunch of bands, one of which was Power Structure, and there was a note at the bottom: "For directions call Sean from Power Structure: 914-528-9574."

Mo already knew that Indignation had played some shows with Power Structure. Was it a stretch that one of their members might remember something about Indignation, or even have the demo?

Before she could chicken out or think this through, Mo retrieved her phone from her purse and dialed the number. As the phone rang, Mo put it on speakerphone. "I'm calling the guy from Power Structure!" she whispered to Pat. They looked at each other in anticipation.

The ringing stopped. "Hello?" a tired-sounding female voice answered warily.

"Hi, may I please speak with Sean?"

There was a sharp intake of breath on the other side of the phone. "Sean's been dead for 20 years!" the voice snarled, before the phone crashed down in its cradle.

There was a moment of silence, then Mo and Pat started talking at the same time.

"Well *that* didn't work out how I planned!"

"You can't just go around and ask to speak to dead people!"

"Oh, man. Fuck! That poor lady! I wonder if that was his mom?"

Mo realized that she should have specifically asked Matt Zimmer if anyone else associated with the circle of Indignation or Power Structure had died, so that she didn't accidentally call them.

Ever the archivist, Mo carefully wrote "Sean—dead for 20 years" on a turquoise Post-it and affixed it to the flyer. She could only hope that the rest of the flyers from the packet, or whatever other avenue they pursued next, might yield better results. And tomorrow morning she was going to look at the yearbooks in Dobbs Ferry.

Chapter 5
1988

On a Thursday in late June, Ryan had exciting news for the rest of Indignation. He had missed the beginning of practice due to his new job at the art supply store, but figured this announcement might offset his late arrival.

"Guess what? I got us our first show! Well, technically Power Structure did. They're playing right after us. July ninth. Clear your calendars."

Matt reacted first. "Whoa, that's awesome. Where at?"

"In a park in Sleepy Hollow. Right by the train. Some battle of the bands type thing. It's a free show," he clarified. "As in we're not getting paid."

"Where the fuck is Sleepy Hollow?" Eric made a face. Ryan realized that he had probably been hoping that their first show would be down in the city.

"It's by Tarrytown, not that you'd know where that is either. But c'mon! Where did you think our first show was going to be at, The Ritz?"

"Hey, I'm psyched," Dion drawled, "for any show. You know why? Because as the singer, I don't have to carry any equipment!" They all cracked up.

"But for real. Thanks, Brains, for getting us started here." Ryan wasn't sure how he felt about Dion calling him Brains, as in the brains of the operation, as he had recently started doing. He didn't feel that much smarter than anyone else in the band. Though maybe he, Matt and Eric were all equally smarter than Dion.

"That's kind of cool that it's outside. And nearby. And all ages? So everyone can go?" Matt was warming up to the idea.

"Yeah, it's all local bands. So not all hardcore and punk bands. But it should be fun. All our friends can come see us play!"

"Or if no one shows up, then no one will know if we suck," Eric reported sagely from the corner. Ryan threw a guitar pick at him.

But as they got closer to the show, excitement increased among all parties. This was partly due to seeing their name on a flyer for the first time, in the context of being a real band playing a show rather than half a band looking for members. Ryan had gotten the details from Sean of Power Structure and drawn something up. Once the flyer existed, the next challenge was to circulate it. They left some at Record Stop and Mad Platters and brought plenty of copies to the Anthrax for a show with a great lineup on the Friday of Fourth of July weekend: Raw Deal, Rest in Pieces, Absolution, and Sick of it All. Rest in Pieces and Raw Deal both

Becky McAuley

had members from Westchester, and maybe some of their local fans would also check out the park show. Ryan also handed off a stack to John H. to post around Port Chester. John didn't seem upset that he hadn't made the cut to sing in Indignation and was instead looking forward to the first show.

All of this was easier to execute since Ryan had turned 17 a few weeks prior, gotten his driver's license, and was now able to drive himself to shows whenever he could borrow his mom's car. This was extra fortuitous since Eckley had been working weekends, and Mr. Eckley had been their main source of rides to past shows.

While finalizing the set list, Indignation also put together a new song, the first one that Dion had taken part in writing. The song was born when Dion mentioned being kicked out of religious instruction back when he lived in the Bronx. "For what?" Eric inquired. "Cindy Adducci gave me a hand job under a desk," Dion nonchalantly replied, resulting in agog expressions from Matt and Eric. Ryan recognized a song topic when he saw one, and Matt also backed the idea, having been expelled from a religious school himself. They wrote the song on the spot, with Ryan responsible, as usual, for most of the phrasing as everyone shouted out ideas and expanded the theme from the primary incident to encompass various infractions, including Dion getting kicked out of the talent show at Annunciation. Short verse, catchy chorus: "Religious instruction, aim for disruption!" Which Ryan realized later sounded suspiciously like the pacing of Sonic Reducer; but it was too late, and wasn't all hardcore derivative in some way? Verse, chorus, verse, chorus, and then Dion practically rapping over the breakdown, which ended with a line of his own creation: "My only crime was having too good of a time!"

It was suddenly one of their best songs, and most importantly, the one on which they had collaborated the most as a band.

The day after the Fourth of July, Dion had called Ryan after work to mention he was driving over to Dobbs Ferry to drop off a stack of flyers. Liz Zimmer lived in White Plains, but she had told Dion that she would be hanging out in Dobbs Ferry that Wednesday, and Dion asked Ryan if he'd like to come along for the ride. There was this old building down by the river where kids convened to skateboard by the loading dock and smoke weed on Bare Ass Beach, a sliver of Hudson River shoreline. Ryan had heard Dion mention this area, in the context of Liz's friends from the Rivertowns, but he'd never been invited along.

Dion picked him up the next day after work in his 1977 Lincoln Continental, and they drove west on Ardsley Road towards Dobbs Ferry, blasting Leeway. Ryan realized he had hardly ever been to this corner of the county, which was north and west of his dad's shop on Saw Mill River Road. What was there to come over here for?

Lost Indignation

After passing a short stretch of downtown, they coasted down a steep drop towards the river. Dion turned right onto a long driveway that led down an even bigger hill to an old building at its base. As they got closer, Ryan saw people hanging out on the loading dock: three girls and a boy. The guy had a shaved head and was the shortest of them all, besides Liz. The most stunning of the girls was Liz, of course, but the other two weren't bad looking either: there was a freckled girl wearing a gray tank top and a girl with messy blonde hair wearing ... was that a homemade Dag Nasty shirt? She was cute, too. With someone like Liz Zimmer, Ryan couldn't look directly at her for more than a few seconds, but this blonde girl was the type of reasonably attractive that he didn't feel intimidated by and most definitely wanted to keep looking at.

Dion bounded from the car, leaving Ryan trailing behind to collect the flyers and think of what he could possibly say to the girl in the Dag Nasty shirt.

Liz handled the introductions. "This is Dion and Ryan from Indignation." (Ryan had never felt so glad to be identified as a member of a band.) "And that's Kate," Liz introduced the freckled girl, "and Christine and her cousin Anthony." Was it Ryan's imagination, or had Liz flashed him a tiny smile when clarifying that Anthony was Christine's cousin rather than boyfriend? Was he really that obvious?

"Hey, I'm Ryan. That's a cool shirt, Christine. You should come to our show on Saturday. All of you," he clarified. "I brought some flyers." He handed most of the stack to Liz, but made sure to give some to each of the assembled parties.

"I'll need someone to hang out with," he continued, "since my best friend is working and can't make it." Indeed, David wouldn't be there: he had claimed he couldn't get that Saturday off, but Ryan half wondered if he was still boycotting all things Indignation.

"Well, I'm off on Saturdays, so I should be able to go." Christine answered.

"Seriously, a show in Sleepy Hollow?" Anthony looked intrigued.

"It's not all hardcore bands," Ryan quickly qualified. "Just us and Power Structure."

"You might see history in the making," Dion intoned, mock seriously, "since it's our first show! And there's a chance for us to suck historically!" But Ryan hoped that today's meeting would indeed be historic, for other reasons, as the first time he had met Christine. During their brief meeting, he had been too chicken to ask for her number, but hoped that she would appear at the show and that he hadn't seen the last of her.

The rest of the week took forever to pass, but finally it was Saturday. Ryan had been worried about the weather, since it was an outdoor show, and they had ended up with an oppressively hot yet cloudy day, with the potential threat of rain later. His mom had acquiesced and let him borrow her car, which meant he was picking up first Eric and then Matt on his way over to the park. Dion had gotten away with bringing no passengers and no gear, like the frontman that he was.

Once they had arrived at the park and unloaded near the stage, Ryan started to relax. But while hanging out with the Power Structure guys and watching the first two bands—a punk band and a ska band, respectively—he noticed that there was hardly anyone in attendance who looked like they had come to watch Indignation. Well, there were a few people: Marshall and Alex were there, looking curious, Liz Zimmer had arrived a few minutes prior, and John H. had just been dropped off. And Dion had finally rolled up shortly before their set. The only people missing were those coming up on the Hudson Line train from Yonkers and the Rivertowns. Actually, Ryan hadn't seen a train go by in a while. Maybe there was something wrong with the trains and Christine wasn't standing him up.

When it was time to set up and play, Ryan couldn't be distracted by their potential crowd (or the lack thereof). He had to focus on the first ever Indignation set! He helped get Matt's drums onto the makeshift stage, followed by his own gear.

"Yo what's up?" Dion barked into the mic, though besides their assembled friends, most of the park wasn't listening. "This is our first show ever, so you better pay attention. We are ... IN-DIG-NA-TION!" Travis from Power Structure ran in front of the stage, attempting to start a pit as they burst into their opening track, the Indignation theme song. After the opening intro mosh, Matt took them into the fast part early, but otherwise they sounded tight.

"That's the situation—we are Indignation!" There was scattered applause, and Ryan's heart leapt as a train slowly passed the park, pulling into the station a few blocks away. Soon after they launched into their next song, tentatively titled "World v. You" ("Not in step/ with the world I see/ am I not ready for the world/ or is the world not ready for me?"), he saw the crowd of reinforcements advancing towards the show: Kate and Christine's cousin and Christine herself (!), trailed by Warren and a friend, both of whom must have gotten on further south. Damn, now they'd really need to put on a show!

A few songs later, it was over. Indignation had played a show, and they had sounded half decent, besides a few small mistakes here and there! Ryan was euphoric as they cleared their stuff offstage. After accepting congratulations from Power Structure, who was up next, he walked over to say hi to the Rivertowns contingent.

"Hey! Thank you for coming to see us—I'm so glad you made it."

Ryan was careful to address all three of them, not just Christine. "The trains are all messed up; we had to wait twenty minutes at Dobbs. If I had known, we would have tried to get Liz to give us a ride." Christine smiled at him. Today she wasn't wearing the Dag Nasty shirt, but she looked equally good in a plain black top. Ryan saw Dion give him a surreptitious thumbs-up as he headed to his car, likely to clandestinely pound a beer.

With the pressure off and their set complete, Ryan was able to enjoy Power Structure more than any time he had seen them previously, which had more to do with his nerves abating than the quality of their set. But their luck with the weather had only managed to hold out for so long: halfway through Power Structure, it finally started to rain. The stage itself was covered, but most people in attendance dashed to their cars or to other shelter options nearby. Ryan was glad that Indignation hadn't suffered such an interruption, though he felt bad for the Power Structure dudes.

After their set, once the rain had ended and the music resumed, Sean Div, the guitarist, mentioned that they had a show at the Anthrax in a few weeks that they were no longer able to play, due to Nelson, the drummer, going on vacation with his family. Would Indignation be interested in taking their spot? Hell yeah they would, especially when he found out that Raw Deal and Uppercut were the other two bands! If Ryan had been on a lineup with Raw Deal and Uppercut and a member of Indignation had gone on vacation, he would have done whatever he could to juggle their lineup and still play. Ryan couldn't wait to break the news to the rest of the band. Maybe this time, they'd be more excited in advance.

A few days after the park show, Madeline broke up with David Eckley. Ryan knew that Eckley had been hanging out with another girl from the pool, and while he didn't think he'd actually cheated on Madeline, apparently she thought so and ditched him accordingly. Ryan felt a little bad for his friend. David and Madeline were going to have to work together at Lake Isle the rest of the summer, and David was getting dumped right when Ryan had met a girl he liked. Not that anything had happened with Christine yet, or might ever.

As a gesture of goodwill, as well as to add an unexpected cover (and some length) to their set, Ryan asked Eckley if he wanted to sing a cover song at their show at the Anthrax. He had just the song in mind: the Major Lance single "Investigate." The lyrics fit Eckley's situation, if you believed his side vs. Madeline's. Mr. Eckley was a big collector of Northern Soul records, and the boys used to dance around to Major Lance when they were little. More recently, David had once remarked that it would make a good hardcore cover. Evidently unembarrassed by its similarity to his current predicament, or appreciating the symmetry, Eckley readily agreed, after Ryan had first confirmed it with the rest of the band. No one else was familiar with the song, but they liked the idea of a non-hardcore cover to make them stand out. Plus, Dion looked relieved not to have to learn more lyrics.

The show at the Anthrax (and the "Investigate" cover) went off without incident, though Indignation was a little sloppier than during their park set. Maybe they were intimidated by playing a real club. Intimidation: that was a word that they hadn't managed to work into the song where everything rhymed with Indignation, though ideally, in a lyrical context, they would have been the ones doing the intimidating. Ryan hoped they hadn't made too poor of an impression on the other bands (though there was hardly anyone inside for their set) and that their performance was good enough to lead to further Anthrax shows, or even more dates with Uppercut or Raw Deal.

Leading up to the Anthrax show, Eckley had talked of little else besides his cover song debut, but with the show over, his focus returned to one of his other new pursuits: writing graffiti. Ryan had gone with him a few times, but overall preferred to work on his art in secret at home. Eckley, however, reveled in the public-facing aspect and the idea of getting his name up wherever he could, though he had never shown much interest in art previously. After a few excursions, Ryan stopped going bombing and let Eckley and Warren Yatrofsky continue to do their thing without him.

Ryan had also taken Eckley with him to the mysterious building in Dobbs Ferry, one night after work, hoping to casually encounter Christine and her friends. There was no one around, but Eckley marveled at the tiny beach, ramshackle layout, and the abandoned trucks parked by the train tracks. Though when Eckley mused about coming back here to do a piece, Ryan worried that if he got caught, it could mess things up for all the local kids who hung out here, Christine included. Instead, he tried to steer the conversation towards praising some of Eckley's recent graffiti output by the Bronx River path.

It was a step too far when Eckley casually asked Ryan to steal him some spray paint from the art store.

"Dude! I'm not going to steal fuckin' cans from my job!"

"Well aren't you the rule-follower lately," Eckley sneered. "This is punk rock— you gotta live a little!"

"You can steal from wherever the fuck you want, just not from the store where I work, OK?" Ryan didn't add that the reason he was so concerned was that he needed to remain employed for that whole summer to save up for band stuff.

Besides Eckley trying to rope him into stealing paint, Ryan's only other worry (besides his ongoing worries about his parents and not wanting to go back to school in the fall) was that nothing had happened

Lost Indignation

yet with Christine. This was his own fault, as he'd been too nervous to ask her out, or even call her, though he had finally gotten her number from Liz. And at least Liz had confirmed, through Dion, that Christine was coming to the next Indignation show. It was a benefit show being held at the nearby Portuguese American Club in Mount Vernon at the end of August.

A punk rock girl from Mount Vernon had tragically been found murdered, and a friend from the scene was putting together a benefit show to donate the proceeds to her family. Dion had found out about it and gotten both Indignation and Power Structure onto the show, the latter as a thank you for getting them their first two shows back in July.

Ryan went all out to publicize the benefit to everyone he knew: his friends from school, kids from his neighborhood, and people he'd met through shows. He drew flyers and left them at Record Stop. He and Eric handed out flyers at the Breakdown show in Tompkins Square Park, which was fucking great and the first NYC show that Ryan had attended without Eckley, who had to work.

The Portuguese American Club was about 15 minutes from home and was also right near the Mount Vernon East train station. You could even technically walk from the end of the 2 or the 5 subway lines. Hopefully this proximity to both home and transit would attract the largest crowd that Indignation had drawn yet. Ryan debated asking Christine to hang out and flyer with him, but he still didn't have the nerve. He did, however, call her to ask if she wanted a stack of flyers to post locally. When she assented, he dropped them off to her in her front yard, then shyly jumped back into the car with his dad, who had driven him over one day after work.

The benefit was on a Saturday, and due to the amount of bands on the lineup, started at 4 p.m. Somehow, Power Structure ended up being scheduled to play before Indignation, rather than after them. Originally Power Structure was supposed to share an amp with Merkle's Boner, this surf rock band from Scarsdale, but then Merkle's Boner canceled. Either way, the lineup was set with Indignation scheduled to play only a few slots before local favorites Breakdown, who were headlining. Ryan only hoped that they could live up to this spot in the lineup. Indignation was the tightest they'd ever been and now had two shows under their belt. They hadn't been around as long as Power Structure, but Ryan was also convinced they were better, practically on par with some of the "real bands" he'd seen at recent shows. Hopefully, whoever showed up would feel the same way.

There was a strong turnout for the show due to Ryan's flyering and the equal efforts of the other bands. Ryan was relieved when his friends started to arrive, some soon after doors opened, and some closer to their set. He also noted that there were a lot more people inside as they were setting up than during Power Structure's set. He, Eckley, John H., and others had gathered near the stage for Power Structure and made sure to mosh for their intro, but the energy had gone out of the room after a few songs.

Ryan was also nervous about Indignation's own performance, as he had seen Christine walk into the room as he and Eric were starting to set up on stage. Liz Zimmer, possibly the hottest roadie that hardcore had ever encountered, was helping Matt haul his drums into the club. Dion, the typical singer, was nowhere to be found while heavy objects were being moved. Ryan forgave him when he strutted into the hall a few minutes later with a crowd of his boys who all looked hyped-up and ready to mosh. John H. and his friends were circling eagerly in front of the stage, John having stowed his glasses on an amp for safekeeping. Eckley was of course up front, leaning casually against the stage like he owned it and chatting with some guys from their neighborhood.

Once everyone was on stage and set up, Ryan tried to forget how many people he knew were out there watching, including Christine. He was glad that this was the first Indignation show that Andrew Rompanelli would be recording on video. Good old Andy had also taped the Power Structure set, at Sean's request.

Ryan turned to the rest of the band. "You ready to do this?"

"I'm always fuckin' ready," Eric replied grimly. Dion paced, and Matt clicked his sticks four times to start off the intro.

Once their set was underway, it was everything Ryan could have hoped for. Every time he looked out at the crowd it was total madness. Warren Yatrofsky was out there wrecking people, as were Sean and Travis from Power Structure. But so were the neighborhood kids that Ryan had invited, like Paul Pounsenech and Kevin Altieri, who were casual metalheads at best. Matt's friends Marshall and Alex were performing these quasi-wrestling moves, and Dion's crew, not wanting to be outdone, were also going off. A couple of Eric's friends who came up from the city had originally tried to circle pit, before defecting to the free-form mosh style that predominated. Ryan was grateful that Andrew was capturing this all on video from his perch at the side of the stage.

They let Eckley do the "Investigate" cover again, and then Dion took the mic back to cover the Bad Brains song "We Will Not." Ryan's head hurt just thinking about how long it had taken to teach Dion those lyrics, and he and Eric were both ready to jump in and sing if Dion forgot the words. The place exploded. Ryan looked around for Christine, who was standing safely on a chair in the back, and for Liz, who had run up front for the cover and knew how to handle herself in the chaos. They closed with "Religious Instruction," which was a success despite Warren diving during the breakdown and knocking half the equipment off stage. Whatever—it was the last song. The applause lingered as they started to break down their gear. Sweaty and triumphant, all members of Indignation seemed stunned by the reaction they had just received. It was the first time anyone had extensively gone off for their band.

"That was fucking great! Do you have a demo tape?" John H. had rushed the stage to reclaim his glasses, which were luckily unharmed after Warren's dive.

"Not yet! But we will soon!" That hadn't been true until he said it, but Ryan realized it was time.

Summer was almost over, along with his job at the art supply store, but Ryan presumed he had saved up enough money to record and was hoping that the other guys had done the same. Dion was the only one with a full-time job; Ryan honestly had no idea how Matt and Eric were planning to finance their portion. And the band hadn't made a ton of money from the shows so far: a free show, opening at the Anthrax, and a benefit. But he would worry about that once he had a better idea of studio costs.

Ryan had assumed they would need to find a studio in the city and was planning to ask around, until this kid J.P. happened to mention later that night that Breakdown had recorded right in Bronxville. Where the hell was there a recording studio in Bronxville? Apparently on Kraft Avenue, near the train station and right down the street from The Town Tavern, where Ryan's family had taken his grandmother for her birthday last year!

"Jeff can tell you more about it," Sydenstricker continued, as the singer of Breakdown walked past.

"Hey, great set. I had heard about you guys." Ryan was thrilled. Jeff Perlin had heard of Indignation?!

"Thanks! It's cool we got to play a show with Breakdown. You were great at Tompkins. What other shows do you have coming up?"

"We're playing CB's with Outburst in October. I can find out if there's any room on that show?"

"That would rule! Also, I want to ask you about recording at the Loft." But before he could continue, Richie Kennon came over to tell Jeff it was almost time for their set. Ryan vowed to catch up with him later in the evening.

What would have already been a successful night got even better before it was over. After the last band, as everyone was milling around and packing up their stuff, Christine came over to say goodbye. Ryan walked outside with her and around the corner of the building.

"Thanks for coming to see us play!"

"Of course. I'm glad I got to see you."

"Would you want to hang out sometime, outside of a show?" Ryan asked in a rush. He had been waiting to say these words for over a month, and they had all come out in one big mumble.

"I would love to." Christine was very close to him. Ryan wondered if she was going to kiss him right here. He put his arm out to pull her toward him, and—

"Not to break up this tender moment, but Jeff Perlin is looking for you inside." Dion had snuck up behind them and patted Ryan on the back. He looked impressed, perhaps both by the fact that the singer of Breakdown was looking for a member of Indignation and that Ryan had been about to make out with a girl, but there was also a glimmer of mischief in his eye. "Hey, Chrissy! Nice to see you."

"Hi, Dion! Great set." Christine smiled shyly as Dion moved off.

"OK, so I have to head back in." Ryan wasn't sure if he should be pissed at Dion (or Jeff), or grateful that he had stopped them from inadvertently making a spectacle outside the club. "But I'd love to see you again soon. I'll call you. Get home safe!" He saw Christine's cousin walk outside with Kate, both presumably looking for her, and was glad that things had not escalated further.

Still, Ryan was in a daze while he exchanged numbers with Jeff, packed up his gear, then pulled his mom's car up outside so that Matt could load in his drums. Dion was driving Eric home, as there was no way they would have all fit in Ryan's mom's Civic. He was going to go on a real date with Christine, a member of Breakdown wanted to get his band on a show at CBGB's, and Indignation had just played their most successful show yet.

During the following week, Ryan spent a lot of time on the phone calling The Loft about recording and then relaying information to Indignation members. Jeff Perlin had indeed called to offer a spot on the CB's show and answer Ryan's questions about recording in Bronxville. Emboldened by this introduction, Ryan had contacted the Loft, and after getting pricing and wrangling and entangling his band, had managed to secure a date and put down a deposit.

Ryan would have gladly booked a hundred recording sessions rather than making a call to Christine, but once he managed to get her on the phone, neither of them wanted to stop talking. During their first real call (rather than the short one about the flyer handoff) they ended up speaking for more than two hours, despite the protestations of various siblings. Christine was the oldest of four sisters, and they only had one phone line for the six members of her family. Ryan recognized this future complication, but welcomed the challenge and looked forward to many hours on the phone with her when he could get through.

Figuring out where to take her on their date was a whole other problem. Ryan's main issue with dating, besides working up the courage to ask someone to go on a date with him, was the type of activities people

Lost Indignation

chose for first dates. Though he would have enjoyed the dark confines of a movie theater, he didn't want to sit in silence with a girl—he wanted to be able to talk to her! His fantasies of Christine involved reading with her, somewhere very private, or taking a walk in the woods together, ideally also someplace deserted.

"Do you want to go to the library with me?" It came out sounding incredibly stupid, even though earlier on the call they had been talking about what they each liked to read. Ryan loved libraries: the tiny Crestwood Library around the block from his house, the large and colorful Will Library on Central Ave., and the Eastchester Library, where he and David liked to hang out on the second floor and silently eavesdrop on the people below. So why not take her somewhere where he was in his element? Luckily, Christine did not think his suggestion was dumb at all and readily agreed. Though Ryan realized in a panic that it was Labor Day Weekend coming up, so the libraries would be closing early on Saturday.

And so their itinerary was set: Ryan picked up Christine in his mom's car on Saturday. They walked around the Eastchester Library until it closed at 1 p.m., then headed across the street to the Odyssey diner. Ryan had picked Eastchester due to its proximity to other date activities, like the diner, and because she might enjoy eavesdropping on people while hiding on the second floor, like he and Eckley used to do. As Christine perused the biography section, he was hit with a sudden wave of joy.

Ryan kept trying to think of ways to keep this day from ending. After the Odyssey, they continued to the bike path that ran alongside the Bronx River and its eponymous parkway. Luckily Christine was so easy to talk to that there were no gaps in their conversation. As they walked towards the Abyss, she was discussing her top college choices. She was planning to apply to Bard College upstate, but would be visiting an older friend there in the fall to make sure, and to some of the "seven sisters" schools, whatever the fuck that was. Christine was also applying to SUNY Purchase, just in case. "I want to be not too far away, but far enough, you know? Since my big-ass family can drive me nuts." Ryan didn't know. He couldn't imagine how his life would be different if he'd had a brother or sister. And his parents were kind of the ideal parents for a teenager to have, in that they obviously cared about him, but didn't keep track too closely of his comings and goings.

He took a deep breath. "I'm an only child. But I almost had a little sister." He had never told this to anyone. Of course his neighborhood friends knew back then, as much as an eight-year-old can understand what's going on in someone else's house, but he had never recounted it later to someone new, and certainly not a girl he was interested in. Maybe it helped that Eckley was also an only child, so no one had ever really questioned why Ryan was too.

"She died while she was being born. And my mom couldn't have any more kids after it happened. She started drinking a lot more after that." Ryan felt his eyes tearing up. "I'm sorry; I've never really told this to anyone."

Christine looked at this boy in front of her, who was already attractive but suddenly looked really fucking hot with tears balanced on his long eyelashes, and grabbed his hand. "Don't be sorry. I want to know all about you."

Ryan squeezed her hand. "And I want to know all about you." They continued down the path, Ryan nestling closer to Christine while still holding her hand. By the time they stumbled into the Abyss, they were full-on making out. An hour later, Ryan asked Christine to be his girlfriend, and she agreed.

Now Ryan had his first real girlfriend, his band was recording a demo, and they were playing CBGB's. He and David had also just started their senior year at Fordham Prep. Everything was coming together. What could possibly go wrong?

On a Thursday night in mid-September, Ryan was sitting at the kitchen table doing his math homework when the phone rang. His dad was in the basement and his mom was passed out in front of the TV, so he grabbed it before a second ring could rouse her.

"Hello?" At first there was no reply. Then he heard Matt Zimmer whisper "Ryan?"

"Where are you?" Ryan queried.

"I'm at home. But I have to be quiet." Stupid ass mysterious Zim. Ryan sensed something was amiss.

"I just wanted to let you know I'm not coming on Saturday." When Ryan sat, stunned, Zimmer clarified, "The recording. I won't be there. I have to go to Binghamton."

"What do you mean you have to go to Binghamton?" Ryan stammered, louder than he meant to.

"This wrestling thing. It's a once in a lifetime experience. Me and Marshall and Alex are leaving tomorrow morning. My parents don't know, and I'm not going to tell them until they see the note and I'm already on the bus."

"Zim. This is crazy," Ryan was incredulous. "We started this band. Me and you. We wrote these songs. We were all psyched to record. What are you doing? Why can't you go to this wrestling thing next year?"

"It's a once in a lifetime opportunity," Zimmer repeated. "A one-time event. Giant Haystacks is coming from England! Can we just record next weekend instead?"

"But we already paid the deposit," Ryan reminded him. "Well, me and Dion did. Plus if we waited till next weekend, we'd never have time for the studio to master it and then get the masters in time to dub the tapes before the CB's show."

There was silence on the other end. Ryan wanted to reach across the mile and a half between their houses and smack him. They'd been planning this for weeks!

Ryan tried again. "Is this what's really important to you? Wrestling? Or the band? We're playing CBGB's with Outburst and Breakdown. Our NYC debut! This is our chance to get our songs into people's hands! We have to have the tapes for the show."

"Of course you guys are important to me," Zimmer quickly clarified. But when he didn't finish that thought, Ryan finished it for him. "Just not as important as wrestling. What the fuck!"

"If I don't come on Saturday, am I still in the band?" Zimmer asked timidly.

"Yes. Of course. I think so. We need you to play CB's. You little shit." Ryan couldn't believe it. "Let me talk to Dion and see if we can figure something out."

"Don't call me back at this hour," Zimmer pleaded. "Seriously. I just wanted to tell you I wasn't coming. Instead of just, like, not showing up."

"Have fun at the fucking wrestling," Ryan retorted, "and at this point, I don't care if you show up," and slammed down the receiver.

A moment later, he dialed Dion's home number. There was a 50/50 chance that Dion would be home on a Thursday night, since he had to wake up for his construction job at 5 a.m., but that didn't mean he necessarily refrained from going out during the week. As the phone rang, Ryan was already debating getting out the phone book and calling every bar within a three-mile radius of Dion's room in Mount Vernon. Mercifully, he picked up on the third ring, and Ryan quickly recounted their dilemma.

"That little shit!" Dion echoed. "This is why I shouldn't play in a band with a bunch of kids. Wrestling! You got a good head on your shoulders, Brains," Dion quickly clarified. "You wouldn't run off to Binghamton for no wrestling shit. If you disappeared, I'd just check the local libraries." Ryan mentally congratulated himself that for once, his chosen forms of recreation were being construed in a positive light.

For the next few minutes, they debated the merits of postponing the recording versus recording without Matt Zimmer. Ryan knew that they both wanted to get these songs on tape, not just to have the tapes in time for the CB's show, but to have done it, to have recorded something, like a real band. Plus, there was the deposit. Their thoughts turned to who could potentially fill in for Zimmer, either for the recording or forever afterwards.

"What about Nelson from Power Structure?" Ryan suggested.

"Nelson from Power Structure is a terrible drummer," Dion replied. "He's the number one reason they suck."

"No, the number one reason they suck is that Sean is a terrible guitarist," Ryan responded wearily.

They paused, momentarily stumped. Ryan could practically hear Dion thinking.

"I might know a guy," Dion ventured cautiously. "My boy CC. He's older, but he plays drums. Metalhead, but might be down to play hardcore. I played him our practice tape in the car one time, and he dug it."

"Did you really? And he liked it? Could you call him?" Ryan asked, grateful. He had a sudden surge of love for Dion: boastful, exuberant Dion, who was nonetheless coming through for them. Though what did it say about Indignation if Dion Carina was suddenly its second most responsible member?

"I'll try him now. Be good," Dion hung up.

Ryan knew he should stay off the line in case Dion called back, but he couldn't bear sitting at the table in a silent holding pattern. Wanting to share the indignity of what had befallen his presciently named band, he dialed Christine. Busy, of course. What if he didn't get to talk to her until after they recorded? He had been thinking of asking her to come to the studio on Saturday, but it would make him too nervous.

Restless, Ryan drummed his heels on the kitchen chair and riffled through the newspapers for the box scores and league leaders. 1988 regular season baseball was almost over. To think that when the Yankees had set up camp in Fort Lauderdale for spring training, he had never met Zimmer and Indignation didn't even exist. Though Ryan couldn't persist for too long in that line of thought, considering that Indignation might not be a band in the present, either. He buried himself in the American League pitching stats and tried to shut off his brain.

Mercifully, the phone rang again a few minutes later. It transpired that CC was indeed willing to play drums for the recording that Saturday and was available for one practice tomorrow to learn the songs. "We don't have to pay him or anything?" Ryan had asked, incredulous. The idea that an adult metalhead would spend time playing hardcore for free was beyond his grasp.

"Yeah, no, he's interested in that shit, and wants the opportunity to record for free," Dion blithely countered. The "for free" free part sunk in when Ryan realized that the recording costs would now be divided three ways instead of four, if they never ended up getting the money from Zimmer.

"Crap. Where are we going to practice with him?" Ryan realized.

They would have to somehow go through the songs with him tomorrow, and Zimmer's basement was obviously now off limits.

"Do you think your folks would let you do it at the house?"

"Maybe if we do it early enough so we don't bother our neighbors. I'll have to ask my dad. My mom won't mind." Ryan mentally scanned their basement—there should be enough room for everyone to set up, though it would be tight. Would Dion's metal friend bring his drum set? "I'll ask him now. You find out what time this guy can practice."

Four minutes later, Ryan bounded back upstairs to intercept the ringing phone. Mr. Marnell had agreed, on the condition that absolutely nothing would get broken. Ryan assured him this was more of a tryout and would be a subdued affair. Dion was back on the line confirming the good news that CC could do it, to expect everyone at the house tomorrow at 6, and that this CC guy would indeed be bringing his drums. So now only one concern remained.

"You said he's a metal guy," Ryan ventured. "Is he a longhair?" He knew it was unlikely they would be playing any shows with him, but what if they did?

"He used to have hair like, down to his ass, but he cut it for his court date," Dion replied. "Trying to get visitation with his kids." Momentarily shocked that anyone playing on the Indignation demo was old enough to have not one but multiple children, Ryan recovered and sent a silent thank you to CC's nameless progeny for unknowingly influencing their dad to tone down his metal mien (or mane).

"Dion, thank you for sorting this out." Ryan was weak with relief, though already starting to worry about a father of indeterminate age showing up at his home for practice, at whom his own parents might look askance. "Wait, can you do one more thing? I know it's late, but can you call Eric to let him know about practice tomorrow? I need to make one more call, about money stuff. Hopefully Eric can make it tomorrow too." Eric had been acting weird lately and Ryan didn't particularly want to talk to him.

"Of course, man. I'm psyched about recording, and I wasn't going to let Zim get in the way of us having tapes for CB's. Though if this takes too long on Saturday and we miss Sick of It All, I will DDT his skinny Jewish ass." Conveniently, there was a show to look forward to on Saturday night once they were done recording: Raw Deal, Sick of It All, Murphy's Law, and Maximum Penalty at Streets in New Rochelle. They had originally booked the studio till 6 p.m., but Ryan shared Dion's concern that it could run later due to the complication of having a new drummer. Hopefully CC would pick up the songs real quick tomorrow.

Ryan distractedly half-assed the remainder of his homework, slammed shut his notebook, stowed it in his backpack, and trudged upstairs. Once in his room, he flashed his lights on and off three times, his customary signal for Eckley to call him. Mr. & Mrs. Marnell were way more chill than Mr. Eckley in general and were usually still up or not awakened by the phone. David had to be looking out the window at the right time, but since both his desk and bed faced the window, he often was. Ryan walked back downstairs, and sure enough, a minute later, the phone rang. It was Eckley. "What's up?"

"We had a problem with Saturday," Ryan explained. "Zimmer called to say he was leaving town to go to some wrestling thing. But Dion found a guy to fill in on drums."

"Damn, lucky break. And fuck Matt Zimmer. I never liked that kid," Eckley pronounced.

"I know you didn't," Ryan conceded. "But yeah. The only problem is that now we're splitting the recording three ways. I might have to sell some records to cover it. But even if I do, there's no way I'd get the money in time."

"I could spot you," Eckley cautiously offered. "Or fuck it. I could even be your manager or something, right? Put in one quarter of the money and sell one quarter of the tapes?"

Ryan laughed. "Yeah, one quarter of the tapes to all the girls at Hackley and Maria Regina."

"Hey, fuck you man," Eckley replied, his tone still jovial. "I'm just trying to help."

"I know you are. And I might have to take you up on that." Ryan paused. "FUCK! Why did he pick this weekend to run off to Binghamton?"

"A few things though," Eckley continued. Ryan had a bad feeling about this. "Since I'll be there anyway on Saturday. I want to do something on your record."

"Of course," Ryan acquiesced. It had already been established that Eckley would do gang vocals, along with Andrew Rompanelli and Liz Zimmer, who was supposedly coming up from the city, where she had just started her freshman year at Columbia. "I'm glad you're coming to do the backups."

"No, not just backups. I want to do a verse or something. Or an intro or some shit."

"We'll figure it out," Ryan said evenly, but he was sweating. "Whatever you want."

"Thank you, man. It means a lot." He could practically hear Eckley smiling through the phone. But why did Ryan feel so uneasy if he was doing something nice for his friend? "I'm psyched for Saturday. Can I come to practice tomorrow?"

"Sure," Ryan assented. Though this would be the first time Eckley had ever come to Indignation practice, besides the two times they had

Lost Indignation

invited him to work on the Major Lance cover. What exactly was this CC guy going to witness tomorrow?

"Awesome. See you tomorrow a.m.?"

"For sure dude. And thanks again." Ryan hung up the phone, exhausted. He had almost forgotten they had school in the morning. Overall, it could have been worse, and he was relieved to have hung up before Eckley could have asked what he thought he was going to ask next, which was, "Can I play guitar?"

The next day, Ryan could barely concentrate in class, both due to being up late the night before and because of what was happening at his house at 6:00. While Eckley was at soccer practice, Ryan came straight home to tidy up the basement and make more space for CC's drums. Were they crazy for trying to record in less than 24 hours with a drummer that no one but Dion had met before today?

Thankfully, CC wasn't the first to arrive, as Ryan was apprehensive about making small talk with someone so different from the rest of the band. Eckley had shown up as soon as he got home in his new capacity as Indignation's quasi-manager, singer of one line or possibly a verse, and the financial backer of one quarter of the recording. Plus, Ryan knew he would never have wanted to miss a spectacle like this happening so close to home. He felt a little guilty that he had never invited Eckley to more practices at Zimmer's house.

Not knowing what to expect from CC, Ryan had envisioned someone more extreme, based on the scant facts that Dion had reported. When he arrived a few minutes before 6 p.m., he ended up being a tall, reticent, and surprisingly normal-looking guy.

"I'm Chris." He stuck out his hand.

"Dude. Thank you so much for doing this." Ryan effusively returned the handshake.

"Of course, man. I liked that practice tape that Dion played for me, and I've been wanting to check out more of that stuff. I also know those guys at the studio."

"Oh really?" Ryan was intrigued. He'd never heard of another hardcore or punk band recording at The Loft besides Breakdown. Plus this actual adult had just said he liked their practice tape!

"Yeah," Chris/CC continued. "I filled in on recording for a lot of bands, including some over there."

"Awesome. I'm glad you're familiar with the space. That makes one of us! Can we help you get the drums downstairs?" Eckley had shown up behind him and was appraising CC in his cool Eckleyan way.

Eric showed up while the three of them were getting the drums out of the car, and Dion appeared a few minutes later.

"CC! My dude! So psyched to have you in the band! Well, for two

Becky McAuley

days at least," Dion revised. Ryan had rarely seen him so animated.

"How do you two know each other?" David asked.

Dion and CC looked at each other. "We met at Allen's, in Elmsford. The music store."

"Well, outside Allen's in Elmsford," CC clarified in his quiet voice. "D played me your practice tape in the car, and I dug it."

"Thanks, man. I'm going to send you home with an old one to listen to, plus I'll make you a copy of tonight's tape when we're done." Ryan popped a TDK cassette into the boombox he had brought downstairs.

CC had a good ear and quickly picked up the songs as they ran through the five they had selected to record: the Indignation theme, "World v. You," "Put it Down," "Now it Can Be Told," and "Religious Instruction." But Ryan was just as quickly regretting their new entanglement with Eckley. Once he had offered his financial backing, this arrangement seemed to empower him to make suggestions about Indignation songs that had been written back in the era when Ryan was trying to hide the project from him altogether.

First, when they were running through "Put It Down," David critiqued the mosh part. "You could slow it down here, then do a spoken word part over it, and then one last even heavier mosh!"

"I don't want to add a whole extra section," Ryan responded peevishly, resenting the interference and concerned that Eckley was going to want to do this new spoken word part himself.

"But if you'd just let me make a few suggestions, the songs might come out even better tomorrow," Eckley reasoned.

"I thought it sounded pretty good the way you played it for me," CC interjected. Damn, maybe it would prove useful having this guy in the band, at least today and tomorrow.

That was enough to quiet Eckley, at least temporarily. But when they finished with "Put it Down" and moved on to "Now It Can Be Told," he had more ideas to share. Ryan was uneasy about Eckley digging too deep into this song and somehow realizing it had been written about him. He also just wished he'd stop with the fucking commentary.

"You should do the breakdown first, and *then* the 'I'm not losing any sleep' part—"

Ryan snapped. "Dude, stop messing with our songs!"

"I'm just saying, it would sound so much better," Eckley shot back. "And this is your chance before you record and people get to know them a certain way."

"It's not too late though, some of those Supertouch songs sound different every time we've seen them."

"Case in point, maybe you don't want to be like Supertouch," Eckley countered peevishly.

Lost Indignation

"Over my dead body will you change my fucking songs," Ryan scoffed. "Plus, we're wasting time." He gestured to CC. "This guy's here, trying to learn the songs for tomorrow, and here we are, arguing about what the songs even are!" Eric let a smile slip through above his bass.

"I'm just trying to help," Eckley replied stiffly. "Unless you don't want my help with recording either."

"No, we're good, I definitely want you to be part of this. But let's just stick with the songs as they are, OK?" Ryan pleaded. Miraculously, Eckley acquiesced, possibly because Dion looked ready to kill him. They continued, though Ryan had a feeling it was not the last he would hear on the subject of "perfecting" their song structures.

Recording went as well as Ryan could have expected under the circumstances. After CC had deftly picked up the songs at practice, he once again nailed them on Saturday, even adding some flourishes to Matt's bare bones drumming. Eric had rocked the bass parts and was his best offbeat Eric self, with no trace of the recent unease that Ryan had discerned. Dion had nailed all the lyrics and sounded fucking great, probably because he didn't have to worry about remembering the words, since he was reading them (though it helped that Ryan had excised every polysyllabic term that had tripped him up). Eckley, Andrew Rompanelli, and Warren Yatrofsky (a late addition) shouted enthusiastic gang vocals at the appropriate times. Ryan wished that Liz Zimmer had shown up, but maybe Dion had told her not to come due to her cousin being such a little shit, or maybe she hadn't shown up out of solidarity for Matt. Or maybe she just hadn't wanted to make the trip up from the city.

Even Eckley's intro hadn't come out as badly as Ryan feared. Thankfully he had abandoned the idea of doing a full verse and instead recorded a spoken word intro, like the one at the beginning of the Beyond demo, which Ryan and David had bought after the CBGB's show in March. What he eventually came up with was "Straight from New York in '88—it's not your imagination, it's INDIGNATION!" This led right into their first track. So technically that meant Eckley was the first voice you heard on the demo; he also sang the first word of their first song, but Ryan could live with that in return for his help funding the recording.

The mastered tape would be in their hands a week later, in time for them to try to dub 100 copies for the CB's show. Eric had drawn the cover art, which was the letters INDIGNATION DEMO '88 above an indignant-looking dude's head exploding. It wasn't exactly Sean Taggart, but it was fine. Ryan had wanted to do the art himself, but due to Eric's lack of enthusiasm lately, he hadn't wanted to interfere. Once he had neatly drawn the lyrics for the insert, Eric had added in the bottom right corner:

Becky McAuley

Recorded at The Loft, Bronxville, NY, 9-17-88
Dion - Vocals
Ryan - Guitar
Eric - Bass
CC - Drums

Ryan wondered if Zimmer would be galled at being left off the credits. But the wording was sufficiently ambiguous that it just listed who was there for the recording, right? Not the permanent members of the band. As far as everyone knew, Matt was still in for the CB's show. He had made it back from Binghamton in one piece, and while he was currently grounded indefinitely, he assured them that he'd somehow find a way to meet them at Ryan's house on the afternoon of Sunday, October 2nd.

It worried Ryan that they wouldn't be able to practice as a full band in the meantime, though they were busy assembling the tapes. Eric came over to fold the demo inserts, which his mom had stealthily printed in the admissions office at The College of New Rochelle, and left his bass and amp at Ryan's so that Dion could drive the equipment down to the show. Eric wouldn't be riding with them on Sunday, as he would be leading two Eastchester friends down to the city by train. (Since when did Eric have any friends in Eastchester?) But Ryan didn't argue. Bringing two more people to the show sounded like a fair trade, as long as they could fit Eric's gear in the car.

Unfortunately, they wouldn't have to save room for the one person with whom Ryan most wanted to be crammed into the backseat of a car, as Christine would be away visiting colleges that weekend. At first, Ryan had been bummed she wouldn't be able to make it, but now he could focus solely on playing the show. He wasn't sure how many NYC shows she had been to and if she could hold her own while he was doing band stuff. They didn't have any other shows lined up, but he was hoping for something soon in northern Westchester or at the Anthrax, which might be more her speed.

Ryan was still dubbing the tapes, which had been going on in real time ever since he got the masters. He spent a memorable afternoon with Eckley helping assemble the demos as Ryan dubbed them, speculating excitedly about the CBGB's show. It was almost easier, Ryan reflected, to let David feel like he was a part of the band, especially now that the songs were recorded and there was only so much he could do to interfere. Though Ryan was half-watching him to make sure he didn't include any last notations on the insert to mark himself as a member of the band.

Ryan had asked Dion to inquire if CC would be available just in case Matt disappeared again before Sunday. But CC wouldn't be around that day either, as he had some sort of engagement with his kids that weekend. So they were on their own. At least Ryan and Eric had done a mini practice in the basement the day that Eric dropped off his gear.

Despite the shadow of potential Matt-related complications, Ryan was getting excited for Sunday. They hadn't played a show since August, as all their focus had been on the recording. But as long as Zimmer showed up, they were on track for their CBGB's debut! Ryan couldn't wait to put Indignation in front of a NYC audience, especially what should be a packed house for Outburst and Breakdown, even if they were playing first out of five bands. He was confident that their live show would be on point and could result in a bunch of demo sales after their set. There was nothing left to do but wait.

On the morning of October 2nd, Ryan was awakened by a noise outside his window. He had been dreaming that he was in English class and there was a bird banging against the window of the classroom. But even after he had opened the classroom window and scared it off, the noise continued. Finally, he was roused by a repeated thunking that must have been outside of his dream. His first thought was that a real bird was attacking his window at home. Ryan scrambled out of bed and peered out the window. There was no bird. Why did he have a feeling that Matt Zimmer was somehow behind this? He didn't need any more Zimmer surprises.

Ryan looked at the clock. It was 6:47 a.m., and barely light outside. Standing there in his driveway, next to a neat stack of drums, was Matt Zimmer. He was holding a tennis ball, which would explain the noise. Ryan mimed for Matt to hold on, quickly threw on a shirt and sweatpants, and hurried down the stairs and out the front door.

"Matt fucking Zimmer. What are you doing here?" Ryan half-whispered, incredulous.

"I got grounded again. From the wrestling. So I figured it would be safest to leave before my parents woke up. And then hang out till it's time to leave for the show. I mean, even if I get grounded for a million years, it will be worth it if we get to play."

"Jesus." Ryan rubbed his eyes, oddly touched by Matt's tradeoff. At least the Zimmers didn't know where the Marnells lived. Or did they? Were they the only Marnells in the phone book? "How did you get here?"

"I found Dion at the diner at 3 a.m. I had a feeling he would be there! So we picked up my drums," Matt explained. "I've been waiting outside. I think he went home to sleep."

Ryan sighed. "That's exactly what I would still be doing right now, if you hadn't turned up at my house." There was no way he was going to be able to get back to sleep now. He turned to the drums. "Let's get these into the garage. And then we'll all go back to bed."

"No way man," Matt countered, enthusiastically gripping half the stack of drums. "What are we having for breakfast?"

Ryan had to admit that having Matt around to entertain him helped the day go by faster, when he might have otherwise been nervous about their upcoming set. Eckley joined them around noon, and Dion arrived just after 1:00 to load the car. They were hoping to leave at 1:30, to have plenty of time to drive down to the city. By 1:45, Ryan started to sense that something was wrong. They had told Eric to call when he and his friends were leaving for the train. And while he easily could have forgotten, or be willfully defying instructions like the punk rock dude he was, Ryan had a feeling that he wouldn't have skipped that logistical step on this important day.

"Dad, we're leaving. If Eric calls, can you talk to him? I'll stop on the way down to call you."

His dad roused himself from the Giants-Redskins game. "Of course. I'll let you know if I speak to him. Have fun, boys."

Ryan knew that if he had been borrowing the Civic and organizing an expedition to the city, he would have been subject to additional instructions about route and parking. But for this trip they were all wards of Dion, and Dion's car would be the one at risk of debasement and defacement on the Lower East Side.

"When was the last time anyone talked to Eric?" David inquired as Dion piloted the Continental down the ramp to the Bronx River Parkway.

"I don't know, Thursday? When we made this plan." Ryan couldn't help feeling slightly alarmed. It was he who had assured them that Eric could make his way to the show alone. Eric, the streetwise city kid who had been transplanted to Eastchester against his will. How had they come up with this plan of the rest of them all riding together? Ryan should have let Dion drive Eric and his friends and then taken Matt and Eckley in his mom's car himself. Other friends were taking the train down and meeting them at the show, like Warren and the Power Structure guys. But Ryan wasn't responsible for making sure they showed up, the way he was for Eric.

"Maybe we should give him a call one more time," Ryan ventured. "And stop before we get to the city."

"I'm hungry. Are you guys fuckin' hungry?" Dion replied. Ryan thought fast. They were approaching the last exit on the Bronx River before it merged with the Sprain Brook Parkway, and Dion's penchant for 7-Eleven hotdogs was well documented.

"Get off here," Ryan instructed. "We'll go to 7-Eleven, and I'll call Eric."

Dion nodded and headed for the exit. "Whatever you say, Brains." Eckley rolled his eyes. He always bristled at the "Brains" sobriquet.

Lost Indignation

They headed south on Midland Avenue and reached the section where it turned into Bronx River Road, a dense strip of well-kept brick apartment buildings. Ryan was familiar with this area, as there was a wine store at which his dad sometimes stopped on the way to his grandmother's apartment. Today, the apartments seemed to be disgorging every one of their inhabitants—and those inhabitants' vehicles—to Dunkin' Donuts, the laundromat, and 7-Eleven.

The Continental crawled through the parking lot, where not a single space was vacant. After one full circuit, Dion gave up and double parked on Bronx River Road. "You guys go in," he instructed. "I'll stay with the car." He handed $5 to Eckley, who he must have known would be the most responsible individual entering 7-Eleven. "Can you get me two cheeseburger hot dogs and a Jolt?"

Eckley and Zimmer headed for 7-Eleven, and Ryan approached the pay phone in front of the laundromat. Luckily he had a bunch of change with him. First he called home, where his dad verified that no, Eric had not called. Then, with trepidation, he dialed the Cliftons' number, and caught his breath when Eric himself answered.

"Eric! It's Ryan. I thought you were going to call me when you were on your way down to the show?"

"I was," Eric answered, deadpan, "but I'm not going to the show."

"Wait ... what do you mean you're not going to the show! We're playing it! Or we are if our bass player shows up." This was an eerie refraction of the Matt Zimmer call two weeks earlier, except that for once, Zimmer wasn't the problem.

"We, uh, started another band. Me and the guys I was going to come down with today. They both live in my neighborhood. Our new band is more political than the Indignation stuff." Eric tried to keep the excitement out of his voice.

"How did you ... I thought you hated everyone in Eastchester! And how the fuck did you already start a band without your bass?"

"There's some kids that skate who are actually kind of cool," Eric noted, a bit defensively. "And I was just singing for now. But I'm gonna play bass too."

"I'll be in touch about getting your bass back to you," Ryan remarked tonelessly. Fuck! They had only been around for seven months and Eric had already abandoned them for greener pastures? He was also jarred by the implication that Eric hadn't needed them as friends or bandmates as much as he had thought, that they had just been a placeholder until he found his real friends.

Ryan tried one last appeal. "OK, so you have this other band. But can't you just play one last show with us? Hell, we can come pick you up right now, I bet we can fit you in the car."

Becky McAuley

"No, I don't really want to play a show today. I want to skate and listen to Conflict," Eric replied. Ryan momentarily considered if Eric had the right idea, considering how this day was going.

Just as Ryan was wrapping up the call and steeling himself to impart the news that they were down a bass player, Eckley and Matt came careening towards him, arguing about Matt's attempt to buy Jolt with nickels.

"I had to spot him just to keep the line moving!" Eckley snorted, balancing Dion's hotdogs along with his own haul. "I am sick and tired of this piece of shit not having any cash!"

"What if I'm sick and tired of your FACE?" Zimmer replied. Eckley looked like he wanted to hit him, but was holding too many hot dogs and settled for a rancorous glare.

They made their way back to the car, Ryan trailing behind to avoid the bickering. Eckley opened the passenger door without commenting on the fact that he was usurping Ryan's seat. Matt looped around to sit behind Dion, but as soon as he sat down, his Jolt exploded all over the backseat. Ryan hadn't even reached the car but he could hear Dion's apoplectic reaction, and then—

"DON'T OPEN THAT ... door," Dion warned, but it was too late. There was a deafening crunch as the rear driver's side door was ripped off its hinges. As Matt had tried to quell the Jolt fountain and remove it from causing any more damage to Dion's back seat, a passing car had disarticulated the door.

In the confusion that followed, Dion's rage was now divided between two targets: Zimmer and the driver that had murdered his door. Ryan, watching from the sidewalk and considering making a break for the nearby Fotomat, supposed it was like a double steal in baseball, in which Dion was attempting to forcefully corral two uncooperative parties.

After Dion extracted a wad of cash and/or the insurance information from the other driver, the latter drove off, leaving behind the wreck of Indignation and Dion's car. But the removal of one antagonist merely focused his remaining anger on the situation at hand.

"I quit! I quit! This band is fucking cursed!" Dion bellowed at the top of his lungs as he launched himself up and down the sidewalk as if it were a particularly capacious stage. People were staring as they exited Dunkin' Donuts and the laundromat. Due to the combination of circumstances, Ryan knew that today was the end of Indignation. But he wished he could have played on stage alongside the animation that Dion was currently displaying over the fate of his Lincoln Continental. This was far more authentic than any version of Dion they had seen at a show or in practice. Yes, he had been a good and relatively convincing frontman. But watching him rave on the sidewalk, he looked inspired in a way that Ryan had never witnessed, and finally appropriately indignant as to befit their name.

Dion decided to drive the car home as he was only about a mile from his address on Primrose Ave. If no other pieces fell off on the Broad Street bridge or on the way up the hill to Fleetwood, it was all downhill from there. Dion agreed to hang onto Ryan's guitar and amp until he could pick up everything later that week, and promised to organize the safe return of Eric's bass gear. Ryan gave him 25 tapes to sell and distribute as he wished, now that they no longer needed them all for the show, though he was still hoping to sell some despite not playing. While there might have been some small chance of playing a show with no bassist, losing both your singer and bass player within the span of five minutes was too much to come back from.

Ryan called Reliable Taxi (an oxymoron if he'd ever heard one) to summon a cab for Matt and his drums, then fished out the scrap of paper with the CBGB's phone number to pass along the unfortunate news that Indignation would not be playing that day, or ever again. 30 minutes later, the cab appeared, and, after executing the drum transfer, Dion roared off angrily towards Broad Street, muttering ominously that he'd be in touch with Matt about the car.

"Well, I guess this is it," Ryan bravely offered, after Matt had loaded the drums and his own handful of demo tapes. He could only hope that the Zimmers would be paying for this cab ride when Matt and the drums showed up at their house, if Matt had indeed been paying for Jolt one nickel at a time.

"I guess so," Matt muttered, his head down.

"Keep in touch though! You can still write me, right? Even if you can't leave your house ever again. Plus, I know where you live. I'll come throw stuff at your window. Like this morning, but the other way around." Matt summoned a weak smile. Behind him, Eckley looked annoyed, but Ryan really was going to miss this kid, not to mention their band.

But as Ryan and David walked off together across the bridge towards the Fleetwood train station to catch the next train down to the city, Ryan felt an odd sense of closure. As they walked, it was like they were turning back into two regular hardcore kids on their way to a Sunday matinee, not one guy in a band and his best friend who had always hoped to be involved too. It was such a good feeling, in fact, that he was inclined to be a little generous. When he and David finally made it to the show, with their box of remaining tapes, Ryan explained to the promoter that there had been a car accident, and yes, everyone was fine, but no, the rest of Indignation wasn't going to make it to the show. And in that spirit of generosity, perhaps he didn't sufficiently correct the impression that Eckley had been part of Indignation too.

Becky McAuley

Interlude
2006

David walked toward where Ryan was waiting on the bridge. He was dressed for work and was technically on duty. This visit to the complex on Palisade Street served a dual purpose, as kids had been throwing objects from the bridge into the path of inbound trains. When he'd managed to get a hold of Ryan last week, and Ryan had suggested meeting here, David had readily agreed. Tonight, the area was deserted, with no one in sight besides the two of them.

"'Sup, dude." Eckley nodded as he greeted Ryan. He seemed reluctant to touch him. That was fair, Ryan allowed, as he hadn't had access to a shower for a while. Eckley held out the black bodega bag.

"I stopped at Madaba." He extracted two Arizona green teas, one for each of them, and a pack of American Spirits, handing over a cigarette and his lighter. Ryan didn't smoke much anymore and he had never liked Eckley's American Spirits, but he wasn't about to turn down a cigarette. He wondered if there was anything else in the bag, which looked like it still contained more items, if that was part of why Eckley had agreed to meet him here, and how he would react if it was. He wondered also if it was a coincidence that Eckley had mentioned Madaba and if he knew that Ryan had been kicked out of the bodega last year.

"I had to come here for work anyway," Eckley explained. "Kids have been throwing stuff off the bridge onto the tracks. No one around tonight, though."

"Not that long ago, that could have been us." Ryan's teenage escapades with Eckley by his side—almost purely as a friend, only sometimes as an adversary or rival—seemed like they had happened both approximately one hundred years ago and just last week.

Ryan envied those who had the capacity and opportunity to transform. He also wasn't convinced that the MTA was his friend's real employer. Hadn't David attempted to join the CIA only a few years prior? What if he had succeeded, and merely told Ryan he had been rejected? That would explain a lot of the strange things that had happened to Ryan over the last few years and why he had sought the protections of this building by the river. But that was not the reason they were here tonight.

"What have you been up to?" Eckley asked as he lit his cigarette.

"Just painting, mostly. I found studio space near here." He didn't mention that it was in the building they were standing next to and that he technically wasn't supposed to be there at all. Did Eckley know he'd been staying here? He wasn't sure, though that would explain some of the recent incidents. "And you?"

"You know. Working. Playing guitar. Trying to write some new stuff while I wait to hear about the reunion."

Ryan didn't know which part of that sentence to attack first, though he had sworn to himself that he was going to try to stay calm. "Writing songs? Or taking pieces of the Indignation demo again?"

"For the last time, those songs were not inspired by the Indignation demo," Eckley replied wearily.

"Are you serious? They're, like, exact copies! Just downtuned and shit." He hadn't planned to rise to the bait this early.

"Yes, there are some similarities," the thief conceded. "But nothing near an outright copy. Anything else is just you being paranoid. "In fact, how's that been going?" There was a hint of a smirk around his eyes. "I ran into Mrs. Petrillo last week. She asked what you were up to."

"So you're not living there anymore either? And things have been OK here." He didn't mention that this building was the only place he felt safe, due to its complex protections from when it had been used for military experiments before being turned into offices and artists' studios. He had given up trying to explain to his mom why he preferred staying here rather than in her spare bedroom and certainly wasn't about to explain it to Eckley. Maybe they should have met inside the building itself, rather than out here on the bridge. His recent brushes with harm had all occurred in the near vicinity: perhaps the bridge was no better.

"Anyway, those new songs aren't why we're here tonight."

Chapter 6
2017

After the excitement of the flyers arriving last night, Mo was looking forward to her yearbook mission on Friday morning. Securing access had transpired just as Tony Gerson suggested: she called the Dobbs Ferry High School office and asked if she could look at the yearbooks for a grad school project. They had confirmed she could come on Friday before work, sign in, and then head to the library. She couldn't believe it had been that easy. Sure, she hadn't been 100% truthful by claiming the yearbook access was for school, though maybe she could end up weaving this into the subject of a story.

Mo was also reveling in the Yankees coming back from being down two games to none in the ALDS to beat the Indians in the final three contests. They would be moving on to face the Astros in the ALCS on Friday. Maybe the return of the Indignation tape had somehow turned things around for them.

On Friday morning, Mo boarded a northbound Harlem Line train with Pat, getting off at Scarsdale as he stayed on to transfer at White Plains. They had debated the best route to Dobbs Ferry that wouldn't involve her car, so that she could jump on a train to work right after, and ultimately decided on the train to Scarsdale, then the 66 bus to Dobbs, rather than taking the 7 bus to Getty Square and catching the Hudson Line from there. The added benefit of this route was that she got to ride with Pat for four stops. Mo stepped off the train, clutching *A Naked Singularity* like an unwieldy stuffed animal acquired at a fair, and went to wait for the bus. The 7:50 should be arriving shortly. She had low expectations for the 66 bus, and was surprised when it appeared only a few minutes later.

When the 66 reached downtown Dobbs Ferry, Mo disembarked at the corner of Ashford Ave. and Broadway and headed for the high school. For all the time Mo had spent down by the river at her old office, she had never walked along this stretch of Broadway. As she signed in and made her way to the library, Mo was irrationally nervous. What if, after this whole elaborate plot, for which she had forsaken her Friday morning writing time, she found no trace of Christine?

Arriving in the library, Mo was directed to a shelf of yearbooks. There were no students in the library, so she sat down next to the shelf to peruse the shelf of yearbooks. Based on Matt's clues, her best guess would be that Christine would have been in the class of 1989, at Dobbs or otherwise, though if she didn't find her there, she was also going to look through both adjacent classes. (And then look into dressing up as a Maria

Becky McAuley

Regina student if necessary.) Unlike the regional suburban schools in her home area of New Jersey, Dobbs Ferry wasn't a huge district, and there were, what—probably 100 kids per class? Even if she methodically worked through one class at a time, it shouldn't take long.

In the '89 yearbook, she found the section with the seniors, ready to scrutinize anyone named Christine:

Christine Baldino? Didn't look right. Christine Iannacone? Maybe.

Mo continued to flip through the pages, going deeper into the alphabet, but she stopped as soon as she saw Christine Oronzio. A girl wearing all black peeked insouciantly through a fringe of wavy blonde hair. Even before Mo saw the Supertouch quote, she knew it had to be her.

Mo took a picture on her phone of Christine's yearbook page, though she almost wanted to make a photocopy for old time's sake, like when you found what you needed in a reference book as a kid. She texted Pat: "I think I found Christine! I'll tell you about it tonight!" then thanked the librarian and walked down the hill to the Dobbs Ferry train station, wondering if she had time to stop at Scaperrotta's for an egg sandwich on the way.

When Mo had been full time at CFA, Fridays had been notoriously the most brutal days of the week. At first, Friday nights hadn't been so bad, and staff were able to escape around the same hour as most other work days. But as things had gotten steadily busier the last 2-3 years, she, Aaron, and many others had been staying later and later, to the point where she once missed Living Laser's set at the Acheron and had stopped expecting to make it to Friday night shows since. There were no guarantees on Friday: she was usually out by 8:30, but there were other nights when she was there past 10 p.m. At least under her new schedule, Mo was paid hourly and was compensated for the extra hours, unlike all the years prior. But the downside of coming into the office on Friday afternoons, which often stretched into Friday nights, was that it was the one night of the week when she least wanted to be stuck at work.

Tonight, by 8:45, the rest of the office had cleared out and Colette had fallen asleep at her desk. Mo quickly wrapped up her final tasks, petted Pierre goodbye, sent Pat a Gchat that she was leaving (unless Colette woke up in the next 15 seconds), shut down her computer, zipped her windbreaker, shouldered her backpack, and headed out.

It was always a relief to escape the CFA realm and into the real world unscathed. As she ascended the steps out of the townhouse's sublevel, the street was mostly dark besides the construction lights in the new building next door, and there were no events tonight at their neighbor Root Studios. Mo could feel herself starting to decompress as she crossed 9th Ave. and walked east on 18th Street. There was a ghostly hoot from the

Lost Indignation

gym at the high school to her left, evidence of a sporting event underway. Otherwise, Chelsea was oddly empty. She couldn't wait to sit down on the train and read, ideally with a soup from the Hale & Hearty in Grand Central if there was time, even if soup and a giant library book were technically incompatible.

Thanks to the cooperation of the 1 train and the Shuttle, Mo made the 9:00 and was able to grab a tomato soup with time to spare. Without local stops in the Bronx, you could get from Grand Central to Fleetwood in less than 30 minutes. Disgorged at Fleetwood with hundreds of others, she made her way up the Grand Street hill and home to Overlook Street.

"So, yeah, I think I found Christine!" Mo was standing in the hallway next to their tiny kitchen, gleefully devouring a scallion pancake that Pat had inexplicably left untouched last night, while Pat made the next morning's iced coffee. Brett and CC lurked anticipatorily underfoot, aware that they were minutes away from their evening feeding. "At least I think it's her. There are only three Christines in the graduating class, and this one had "What did we learn" as her yearbook quote. I looked through everyone else. Christine Oronzio," she pronounced.

"What did you say her last name was?" Pat turned on the coffee grinder.

"ORONZIO!" she yelled over the grinder.

"One more time?"

"Oronzio," she answered when the noise had subsided. "Like that building on MacQuesten that you see from the train."

"I hope she doesn't have a sister named Dana ..." A funny expression had overtaken his face.

"Oh, shit! That girl you dated in the '90s?" Mo had heard bits and pieces about Dana, Pat's first and most erratically behaved girlfriend.

"That's her," he confirmed grimly. "And she's from Dobbs. What are the chances? Especially since Christine went to high school in Dobbs, but Dana went to Maria Regina. Dana wouldn't have even been in the Dobbs yearbook. Well, after she got kicked out."

"So what should I do, get in touch with Christine and just not even mention the Dana connection?"

"I wouldn't even bring it up. We're asking about her ex-boyfriend's band, not her sister."

"If she's related to Dana and has had to deal with her all her life, there's a decent chance she feels about her the same way you do. But yeah, hopefully it won't come up." Coffee done, Pat opened the cabinet and produced a can of wet food. Brett reared upon his hind legs in anticipation and unleashed a piteous meow.

"Though if you're looking for a way to get in touch with Christine ..." Pat sighed. "I wouldn't really want Dana to have my phone number, but for you, I'd do it."

"Actually, you might not need to talk to Dana at all. I'll ask Tony if he knows Christine." The ultimate townie, Tony Gerson was the omniscient authority on local characters and legend. Mo pulled out her phone to text him, not expecting a prompt reply. It was Friday night and he'd be watching the thus-futile Yankees contest, likely at Petraske's.

"wtf this game," she typed. "Might have found what I needed in the yearbooks—do you know a Christine Oronzio?"

A few minutes later, her phone lit up, not with a text, but with an incoming call. "Tony motherfucking Gerson," Mo heralded the caller. She could hear assorted chaos unfolding in the background, though it sounded like Tony had gone outside to smoke, rather than calling from the bar itself.

"Hey, what's up?" Tony screamed back. He seemed no drunker or less drunk than one expected under the circumstances. "Yeah, Christine? I know her. I used to work with her. At the bar."

"Wait, are you there now? Is she there now?" It was not an uneducated guess, judging from the commotion in the background.

"I'm here, Dan is here, Kenny Suaper's here, oh and Shane Perry's here! He says hi," Tony bellowed. "We've got wings, we just ordered pizza, we're doing shots of Montezuma, there's this fortune teller, psychic person, she's going to do some shit for us? But first she's watching the game. Big Didi Gregorius fan."

"And Christine?" Mo prompted.

"Christine's not here, I think she's away this week, but lemme find out." Mo could hear hollering in the background. "She'll be back on Monday."

"This Monday?" Mo replied, with a mix of excitement and alarm.

"Yup, she'll be here," he verified.

"Thank you so much. For both this and the yearbook intel. Now what are we going to do about this game?"

"Yo, FUCK Dallas Keuchel. I fuckin hate this dude."

"Same," Mo concurred. "At least Tanaka is hanging in there." It was definitely weird, this first year of playoffs since they had cut their cable over the summer in preparation for her lower income. Maybe she should have been at Petraske's with Tony Gerson and Kenny Suaper and Shane Perry, gregariously awaiting a Gregorius enthusiast to elucidate their fortunes.

Mo resolved to find Christine at the bar that Monday, partly because she couldn't wait any longer, and partly because she wasn't sure of the next day that Christine would be working. Since she met with her advisor every other Monday, there was no meeting this week, which was good, because she really needed to work on her homework for craft class tomorrow. After getting home from work mid-afternoon, she made some progress on the assignment and went running before getting showered and changed for the bar. It was still so weird and cool to be able to decide to break for exercise rather than being physically stuck in the office for 11-plus hours at a time.

Pat was working until eight that night, so Mo was planning to stop by Petraske's first, then pick him up from work. This plan was less likely to freak out Christine than if she tried to contact her in advance, or if she and Pat showed up together. Still straight edge at 31, Mo was ready to relentlessly consume caffeine to justify sitting at the bar till she caught Christine's eye, like Rollo Martins and his seven cups of coffee in *The Third Man*. It would have been nice to come by later and watch part of the game, as Game 3 of the Yankees-Astros series was starting in an hour, but Mo figured that the bar would be much more crowded during the game.

Opening the door to Petraske's, Mo saw a person she assumed could only be Christine in action behind the bar. The round-faced high-schooler with her wild hair and ironic grin in her yearbook photo had given way to a wiry woman who still looked good despite being class of '89, her dark blonde hair corralled in a ponytail, moving efficiently around the bar. She looked like ... which Philip Roth book was it, maybe *I Married a Communist*, in which there's the part about the moms and dads being in good shape due to the physical work required inside and outside their homes? Christine appeared lean in the manner of someone who had held interesting jobs and probably lived an interesting life.

Mo ordered a Coke once she had caught the eye of Presumably Christine, then paid with a five and left the change on the bar.

"Are you waiting for someone?" Christine looked quizzically at Mo, alone with her Coke at the bar.

"Yes, you actually. I think. Are you Christine?"

"That's me." Christine wore a slightly apprehensive expression as she turned to the interlocutor.

"I'm Mo. A friend of Tony Gerson." The mention of Tony elicited a corner of a smile. "He told me you were working today. I just wanted to ask you something if you had a few minutes."

"Ask away."

"So I was looking for this demo tape from a hardcore band called Indignation ..." Mo plunged right in. She realized that it had been a mistake to dress like a real person, that she should have worn her Warzone hoodie or something. "I've heard a lot about them. I bought a video from this guy online, but it had the wrong band in the live set that was supposed to be theirs. I'd love to hear the demo, or at least learn more about the guys who played on it."

Christine narrowed her eyes, her expression tinged with alarm.

"Did David put you up to this?" To the question apparent in Mo's face, she added, "My ex?"

"Who's David?" But as she uttered the words, she realized exactly which David Christine must have meant. The realization stunned her. Had Christine dated both Ryan Marnell and David Eckley or Ackley, the guy that Matt had referred to as Ryan's best friend? Did this have anything to do with the breakup of the band? No, it must have happened later, or Zimmer would have mentioned it. Worse yet, could it have anything to do with how Ryan Marnell *died*?

Christine must have deduced the gist of these assumptions from Mo's expression, as her face changed into something that appeared half wry irony and half defeat, looking suddenly much more like her younger self in the yearbook photo. She sighed. "I better tell you the whole story. Before you get any ideas about me. Or that demo. But not tonight. I'm on the clock and who knows who might come in here." As if on cue, two middle-aged men entered the bar. Christine turned to greet and serve them, effectively deflecting Mo's next question regarding if Eckley still lived in the area.

"When would be a better time for you to talk to me? Or to us, actually. My husband is helping me find this demo and I'd love to bring him along too. If you don't mind." She often felt the need to justify her and Pat as a team, when it was so evident to the two of them, if not the world.

"Are you free Saturday?" Christine asked. "I'm working this private party all day, but I should be done by eight. Or I might have to do the evening shift too, but you know, I could always call Tony Gerson."

"Saturday works for us," Mo concurred, mentally scanning their calendar and finding blessedly few obstacles besides trying to uproot Pat during a potential Game 7 of the ALCS, if the series went that long.

"How do you feel about the Thai restaurant? Would be easy since it's right upstairs."

"I fucking love Thai House," Mo responded in the affirmative. Though Pat might kill her for choosing a restaurant without a TV if the series was still going. Hopefully yellow curry would be a sufficient distraction. "So 8 p.m. on Saturday then? We don't mind waiting if you're just getting out."

"Eight should work. If I get stuck, just come in here and get me." This time, Christine smiled too. "See you Saturday then."

"Yup, see you then. It was nice to meet you." Mo hopped off her stool, added another dollar next to her Coke (only one drink, after all— Rollo and his stomach would have been jealous) and left the bar before Christine could counter this assertion.

Mo was in buoyant spirits as she exited the weird little cul-de-sac/ parking lot where Petraske's was located and walked up Saw Mill River

Road to retrieve her car. After the initial faux pas, Christine seemed willing to talk, if only to set straight any warped records and present her side of the story. Even if they didn't end up unearthing any crucial clues about Indignation or the whereabouts of the demo, Mo was sure it would be an interesting evening.

The only downside was that Thai House was closed on Mondays and Tuesdays, meaning she couldn't have grabbed takeout while she was in the neighborhood. Not that she would have been able to get hot food in Ardsley, since she also had to pick up Pat first. As she started the car, she texted him that she was on the way, but figured she'd wait till she saw him in person to break the news about their Saturday plans. "Leaving now to come get you, and I have good news and bad news about Christine!"

Good news and bad news was the theme of Mo's week. Monica was on vacation, visiting her family in Texas, so it was just Mo and Shannon holding down the database and taking things one day at a time. Tuesday was going OK so far, though there was a rumor of an urgent guest list coming their way, ideally so that they could organize it and Colette could tag her own names before a call with the client on Wednesday. Mo knew not to trust the time estimates on when they'd receive a guest list, as she had so often waited around only to get the list days later. Plus, how urgent could the list be, when the dinner wasn't until December?

Young Eef, a rapper, artist and recent multihyphenate, had been wrangled by some music world friend of Colette's to host a dinner during Art Basel. Apparently to differentiate this spectacle from the myriad other dinners taking place the Wednesday of Art Basel, the Young Eef dinner was starting at midnight. Mo was only starting to grasp the logistical challenges inherent here, the first one being which date to put on the invite: Wednesday, December 6th or Thursday, December 7th? At least that wasn't Mo's problem, though matching up the guest list with their database would be. They were expecting another list later from the painter and co-host Shaki Chamberlain, but the list from Young Eef's people was the crucial one that was supposed to arrive imminently.

Around 1:45, Mo checked in with Tati in events one more time about the list. No news. She Gchatted Shannon to make sure her other placeholder project was going well—some social media thing for Elvis involving furniture designers that were in town for ICFF. All was well. Mo hastily shut down her computer and headed briskly towards the 1 train.

As Mo was walking down Kimball Ave. to class, she got a text around 3:15 from Shannon saying she felt a migraine coming on and asking if it was OK to go home early.

"Go for it—thank you for checking and feel better!" Mo quickly replied. There would be no one from the database team in the office for the final few hours, but what could happen in a few hours?

Becky McAuley

Apparently, the damn list had arrived literally minutes after Shannon had left the building. Mo didn't see Tati's text or email until she checked her phone in the bathroom halfway through class.

"Got Eef's list! Colette wants it entered ASAP so she can code hers before tomo—can u come back tonight to finish it?"

Mo knew that something like this would happen eventually, and tonight was the first time anyone had attempted to call her back to the office. And with Tati asking, she was more inclined to acquiesce, since Tati knew her situation and wouldn't have inquired unless it was a true emergency. At least she was being summoned by a text in question form rather than a screaming voicemail from Colette. She also hadn't missed any classes yet. Kingsley Ayona, their craft class professor, was hard to read, but she suspected he'd let her head out early if necessary.

Mo checked the trains on the Metro North app. The next train was the 5:25, which meant she'd be in the office around 6:30. Fuck, this was less than ideal, but if the list only took a few hours, she might still be home at a reasonable time. She had an early 2:00 colloquium tomorrow, so she'd have time after to finish her story for Thursday's class.

Returning from the bathroom, Mo quickly caught Kingsley's attention. She figured it would be less disruptive to do it now and be a little early for the train.

"I'm sorry to ask, but there's an emergency at my office and they need me to get back down there as soon as I can. Would it be alright if I missed the rest of class?"

He looked bewildered, but grudgingly assented. Mo's professors were generally befuddled by the fact that she had a "real job" in the city, rather than someone focusing on school and patching together employment around a class schedule.

Kingsley Ayona seemed utterly unaware of sports, like most of the people on campus, since anyone with half an interest in baseball might have registered this gambit as highly suspicious and surmise that Mo was trying to get out of class to go watch Game 4 of the ALCS, which was starting at Yankee Stadium shortly. At least she'd be able to listen on the train—provided the audio was working on the At Bat app—or follow along on her phone.

At that hour, the inbound trains were relatively quiet, as she was going against the flow of people commuting home. And she still had a monthly pass, rather than paying for this second foray into the city, and *A Naked Singularity* in her backpack. Upon arriving at Grand Central, she didn't even stop to grab dinner, but headed straight for work. Maybe Colette would order them food, perhaps the ubiquitous Westville, depending how long Mo stayed.

But Colette wasn't even there: according to Aaron, who was one

Lost Indignation

of the few still at the office, she had left around 5:00 with Elvis for some new business meeting uptown and was then going straight to dinner at Vaucluse. She was going to work on the guest list late tonight when she got back, hence she wanted the client's list to be entered for her reference.

"Oh, and you missed a fight! Outside the office! It was right after Colette left, or I'm sure she would have been watching it with us from up here," Aaron recounted, as Mo had stopped upstairs to say hi while her computer was starting up.

"There was a weapon that looked like a curling iron!" Oona added breathlessly. Tony Gerson was possibly the only person in CFA history who was more familiar with weapons than curling irons, so that was one more loss not having him on staff.

"I'm sad I missed it," Mo confirmed earnestly. How much other wackiness of this ilk she had missed on recent afternoons? That was CFA and 18th Street for you: if you weren't overhearing an unbelievable exchange or vignette inside the office, there was something happening outside.

On her old schedule, Mo would have gotten a jump on the list around 3:45, when it arrived, and be nearly done by now. New Mo was getting a late start and would be lucky to even make it home before Pat. She had texted him on the way down that she was heading back to work, but he was working till 8:00 tonight and probably hadn't seen the text. After that, Blind Giants had band practice at the brutal timeslot of 10:00 to midnight, as it was the only time they could get the room at Big Cat Studios, which ensured that all of them were going to be tired as shit tomorrow.

At least Mo was alone on the first floor. There was no Drew Flowers getting in her hair, no distracting chatter in the front room, just the silent companionship of Aaron, Tati, and Oona working away above her. (Which was pretty much the best place for your work allies: working away silently on a different floor.) Mo could even listen to the game without disturbing them! It took a few tries to load the audio on At Bat, but she got it going. So far, neither team had scored.

But Mo's heart sank when she saw the list. It was 178 names, and they were mostly artists and DJs who were unlikely to already be in the database. Mo wasn't sure what was worse: a list with a bunch of DJs or graffiti writers. Both had the potential to be interesting, but when you were trying to swiftly infuse a massive list into the database, there wasn't time for tangential Googling. You also had to execute twice as many searches to make sure your intended target wasn't in there under their real name *or* their DJ or graffiti moniker. And when entering a large list, if there were, say, 250 people straight up not in the database at all, you could just format and upload the list, then tag them all later for the appropriate database group. However, this list seemed to be about half in the database and half

Becky McAuley

not, and the names were confusing enough to require multiple searches, so uploading wouldn't help.

Tonight, Mo was forgoing any extraneous googling, though she might have to find mailing addresses for hard invites later, and was whipping the DJs into the database as fast as possible.

DJ Korata, based in L.A.? Not in the database, and Mo couldn't find her real name to check if she was already in under that. Mo plugged her in with minimal info and moved on.

DJ Clay D? He had 37,500 Instagram followers and was already in the database. Mo sent a silent thank you to Monica for entering him last year and dropped him in the group.

A rapper named Oof the Scorpion? He was in there too, from being invited to the Chanel dinner during the Tribeca Film Festival, presumably in conjunction with one of the films.

DJ Carina? Mo assumed this was another woman and Googled just in case she was in the database under another name.

The Wikipedia entry for DJ Carina listed: "Dion Joseph Carina (born January 26, 1970), also known as DJ Carina, is an American record producer and DJ."

Hang on. Dion Joseph Carina!? Had she just come across the singer of Indignation on an Art Basel guest list?

Mo skimmed the article and sent herself the link to read the rest of it on the train. Everything lined up with him being the same person as Indignation member Dion Carina. Naturally, Indignation was not mentioned in the article, which noted that he had moved from New York to Miami in the early '90s and established himself in the house music scene. Born in 1970 would make him 18 in 1988. Being born in the Bronx certainly made sense. And hardcore kids had gone on to notoriety in other music scenes, from rap to metal to funk to probably also house music? Mo didn't know a lot about house music, though when she clicked on the DJ Carina Instagram, it also referenced his business, Neon Dion Customs, where he built custom BMX bikes. Mo made a note to show Pat later. Both Mo and Pat rode BMX bikes—Mo because hers was small and could fit in the back of her Camry. Then Pat got a 24" because Mo's 20" green bike looked so much fun.

So Dion Carina had been in the database all along, under his full name rather than just his DJ handle, and had been invited to Art Basel events the last three years—including the Gucci party with Spinello Projects in 2014 (Mo still had the invite on her desk at home, since it featured a black cat painted by Kris Knight) and to last year's last-minute party at the Teixeira Hotel. She hadn't thought to look for Indignation members in the database, and here they were! Or at least here was Dion: searching "Marnell" and "Zimmer" all yielded multiple results, but not the names of anyone in the band.

In the meantime, she was still trying to bang through this list as fast as possible so she could eat and get home. After the excitement of the Dion discovery, Mo was making swift progress when she heard a key in the front door. Pierre bounded past her and launched himself at the incoming Colette.

"Maureen! What are you doing here?"

"I'm still here too!" they heard Aaron call forlornly from upstairs.

"This list for the Young Eef Midnight Dinner. I came back after class since I heard it was urgent. But I'm almost done!" Mo quickly referenced the list and thankfully, that was true: she was on line 152 out of 178 names. "I'll finish up, let you know what the group is called, and then get out of here."

36 minutes later, she was finally done. Mo intercommed Colette to let her know where to find the group in the database, put everything in writing to Tati—who had gone home just before Colette arrived, with Mo's assurance the list would be done—managed not to get sucked into conversation with Colette, and bolted out the door.

Fleeing at 10:05 should put her on track for the 10:32 train home, as she was definitely taking (and expensing) a cab to Grand Central. The ride to the station was mercifully quick. All her go-to takeout spots downstairs were shuttered, but she managed to board the 10:32 with time to spare, and then ordered a salad from Pizza Pizza once her train emerged from the tunnel just before 125th Street. As the train moved north, Mo alternated between trying to stay awake and reveling in the news of potentially having located Dion Carina of Indignation. Not only did she know what he was up to in 2017, but she had his email address, which made her one step closer to being able to ask about his former band.

Ejected from the train at Fleetwood, Mo headed up the red concrete stairs by Pizza Pizza to claim her salad before they closed, then struggled up the hill to Gramatan Ave. Pat was at practice, so she was besieged by hungry cats when she unbolted the door to the apartment. Even if Pat had fed them early, they would have feigned otherwise. Mo dropped her stuff and pacified Brett and CC before attacking her salad. Yesterday she had been so focused on Christine, but just 24 hours later, she had found a whole new angle through encountering Dion's email on a guest list. While the Young Eef Midnight Dinner might be a clusterfuck, it had also provided an entirely new avenue of investigation.

Riding the momentum from completing the list (and from the Yankees coming back to beat the Astros while Mo had been working away), she sent a short email to Dion to ask if he was the same Dion Carina from Indignation. If he never replied, at least she'd have an excuse to follow up in a semi-official capacity thanks to Young Eef.

Mo didn't even have time to be nervous about seeing Christine again on Saturday. Well, she had been low-key nervous all day, while at the laundromat and riding her bike and writing, but as they walked up to the Thai House on Saturday night, Christine was already out front smoking a cigarette. It also helped that Mo and Pat had been listening to the Yankees pregame on the way over and thinking about the upcoming Game 7. But here was Christine, and there was no more time to ruminate on how their encounter might transpire. It was like being pulled into an interview at CFA without a chance to write up questions or review the person's resume. You just had to wing it.

Christine spotted them, Mo introduced Pat, and they made their way upstairs to the Thai House, which was like going to someone's house, since it was located up a set of carpeted stairs, above Petraske's.

"So first off, how did you find me?" Christine inquired, once they had settled in.

"I looked you up in the Dobbs Ferry yearbook," Mo admitted. "And there was only one Christine with Supertouch lyrics on her page, so I figured it had to be you. I could have just asked Tony Gerson in the first place. But I didn't know you two knew each other." The yearbook endeavor now seemed like a pointless detour.

"I was indeed," Christine nodded, "the Christine with the Supertouch lyrics. Man, I haven't thought about that in forever!"

"I might ask you about a lot of stuff you haven't thought about in forever," Mo eagerly replied. "We've been trying to get a copy of this Indignation demo, but I also want to know more about the band."

"So what do you want to know?"

"Oh, I have so many questions. I don't even know where to start."

Pat laughed. "You don't have to ask *all* of them," he cautioned.

"No, it's fine!" Christine looked amused.

"Okay. First off: tell me about Indignation! When did you get to know them, and how long had they been a band? I got some of this from Matt Zimmer a few weeks ago, but I want to hear your side. As the impartial observer. Or partial observer."

"So, Indignation. They were from the Crestwood area of Yonkers," Christine began. "Ryan and his friend David at least, they lived over on Crestwood Avenue. Walking distance from Mad Platters, and then eventually Rockin' Rex, though we were already in college when it opened. And not far from Record Stop either. Anyway, one day they came to Dobbs Ferry to drop off some flyers. I was over there hanging out with some friends and my cousin. He had a crush on Liz Zimmer, who was Matt's cousin and Dion's friend, and she was there too.

"That's who should have dated: Liz and Dion," Christine continued.

Lost Indignation

"But they were just friends, as far as I know. Liz was too smart for him, but Dion did have this magnetism. But anyway. So I met Ryan, and then I went to one or two of his shows. Indignation had been a band for a few months, but they hadn't played any big shows. So right around the time the school year starts, our senior year of high school, they find out they're going to be opening for Breakdown and Outburst at CB's and realize they need to get a demo out. Maybe that gave Ryan some confidence," she added, smiling, "since he finally asked me out, not just inviting me to another show. Our first date was to the Eastchester Library, of all places."

"No way. I love the Eastchester Library!"

"They did too. Ryan and David, I mean. Growing up in Crestwood, they were biking or skating distance from a bunch of different libraries. You know that second floor part in Eastchester? They used to stand there and spy on people down below. And play this game to see who could find the most fucked up thing in a book in five minutes. They both loved weird facts, conspiracies, and were always trying to one up each other on that stuff. They also liked that *Coast to Coast AM* radio show."

"Oh shit, I was all about that show when I was a kid!" Pat interjected.

"So you went to the library on your first date?"

"The library and then that diner across the street, and then we hung out outside before Ryan took me home. I think he knew he had to come up with something different, and it worked. We started officially dating pretty soon after that."

Mo hesitated to ask additional questions about their relationship, and decided to press her about Ryan and David instead.

"So Ryan and David, I know they were best friends," she started. "Why wasn't David in Indignation?"

"Good question," Christine replied. "Partly because they liked different styles of hardcore. Ryan was always more of a Token Entry and Warzone kind of guy, and David liked the more metal-influenced stuff. Later, his favorite band was Demolition Hammer. But it drove David crazy that he wasn't in the band, and he was always weird about their demo, which is why I thought he might have put you up to asking about it. To the outside world it was fine, he was their friend who was almost like their roadie or their manager. But I think Ryan wanted to do something that was totally his, since he knew David would take over.

"In most of their interests, David was always the ringleader," Christine continued. "David was more aggressive, and Ryan was shy. But Ryan was the leader musically, in that he was the one getting them into new bands and writing songs. David loved playing his guitar, but he was never a natural writer like Ryan was." Christine broke off, as the owner appeared at the table to take their order. Mo realized she hadn't even

Becky McAuley

looked at the menu, but they had been here enough that she could make a snap decision.

"I can't believe we only started looking into Indignation a few weeks ago. And I've already talked to both you and Matt Zimmer."

"Happy to help. It's fun to think back on all of this. And Matt and I are probably the only ones left in Westchester."

"About people who moved away ... did you know a kid named Max Malkin? That's who sold me the tape."

"Max Malkin ..." Christine looked thoughtful. "No, I don't recognize the name."

"He said he used to be friends with someone in the band ..." Mo pressed.

Christine shrugged. "If he was, maybe it was before or after I was hanging out with those guys. Ryan and I broke up during our sophomore year of college, and I didn't get back in touch with David until 2003. Did Max say where he was from?"

"He said he had family in Yonkers and that he was just here for a work conference."

"That's not surprising, a bunch of those guys were from that same area, though some of their friends lived further west. Probably just some guy from their neighborhood."

OK, so no one knew anything about this Max Malkin guy. Back to the main players.

"What was Ryan like?" Mo queried. "Was he straight edge?"

"He was straight edge for a while," Christine reflected. "Until college."

Pat laughed. "Typical."

"His mom was an alcoholic, and he was looking for a positive outlet that took him away from that route. Not that Indignation was a positive band," she cautioned, "though they weren't super negative either. Just the usual mad at the world shit. Like things that were obvious to them to be mad about that might not have been obvious to other people, or at least to adults. But after his dad died, Ryan started drinking. And then, sophomore year of college, he got his hands on some mushrooms and a bunch of bad stuff happened after that."

"Oh man, I could see that," Pat winced. "Do not give mushrooms to the kid with mental health issues!" Mo realized that Christine didn't know they'd already heard Zimmer mention the psych hospital, but she didn't look surprised that Mo and Pat already knew.

"Indignation had this one song that was almost a straight edge song, but people didn't realize it. It was called 'Put it Down,' and Ryan wrote it about his mom's drinking. But he couldn't be too obvious because Dion, the singer, really liked to party. But he was so dumb that he would

Lost Indignation

sing anything Ryan wrote, as long as it was too abstract for him to figure out what it was about!"

Their food soon arrived, bringing a momentary lull to the conversation.

"Anyway, Ryan and I broke up sophomore year, and after moving to the city after college, I was out in Cali for a while. I didn't come back until after 9/11. I played in a band out in L.A. but lost touch with the guys from home while I was out there."

"Nice, what do you play?" Though Mo knew even as she was asking that Christine probably—

"I played bass. I wanted to be Kim from Jawbox," she laughed.

Mo looked at Pat. "You might be talking to the two hardcore kids under thirty-five who like Jawbox. Or, uh, thirty-five and under—I forgot this guy just had a birthday. But that's awesome! Do you still play in bands?"

"Not since moving back here, and now with school and work I have such a weird schedule."

"I feel that. But at least you get to work with Tony Gerson sometimes!" Christine acknowledged that compensation.

"I should have figured that you might know Tony," Mo reflected. "Since he knows everyone! And everyone in Westchester is connected somehow."

Christine scrutinized Pat. "Actually, you look familiar too."

Pat looked shrewdly back at her. "Could it be because I used to date your sister Dana?"

Christine dissolved into laughter. "Oh my god! I'm sorry." While they had originally planned not to bring up the Dana connection, Mo was glad it was out in the open.

"Me too. I mean, both that she's your sister and that I dated her."

"Hey, I've had to deal with her more than anyone! She's part of the reason, though not the only reason, that I got interested in psychology in the first place. I'm back in school," she clarified, "getting my doctorate. Which is why I'm working downstairs." Mo wished she had asked about this earlier, rather than assuming Christine was a free spirit who was still working as a bartender.

"Oh, word? I was a psych major too," Pat replied.

Pat and Christine diverged into discussing their current jobs and the merits of various graduate programs, Christine exhorting him to get in touch when he decided to apply to grad school. Mo zoned out during the psych talk and plotted her next question.

"Oh! I figured I should ask you about Power Structure? Since we think they're the other band on the videotape? Did you know those guys?"

"They were OK. I mean, they sucked as a band, but they were nice guys! I'm sure if you found any of them, they'd be happy to talk."

"Well, we, uh, found out the hard way that Sean has been dead twenty years. After we met up with Matt Zimmer, he mailed us all these flyers. And we called the number on one of them, looking for Sean. Whoever answered was not psyched."

"You weren't far off though. I know Ryan stayed in touch with one of them. Not Sean—a guy who moved upstate? Ryan may have even lived with him, after he was staying with David for the last time."

"He was staying with David?" Mo interjected, surprised. Something about the nature of their friendship unnerved her, despite them being referred to frequently as best friends.

"It was actually one of the last times I saw him." Christine's face was hard to read. "He was living upstate before coming back to Westchester for the last few years of his life."

"Speaking of David, do you know what he's up to? And is he still involved in hardcore?"

"He's a transit cop," Christine replied.

"Of course," Pat muttered.

"He signed up after 9/11, first with the MTA, and then I assume that's what he's doing in Boston. She paused. "But first he tried to get into the CIA."

Pat laughed. "The hardcore connection, that's one strike against you."

"I don't know if that's why David got rejected. There was also something about his mom's background ... or the personality tests. I mean, they would have been right to pick up something from the personality tests, though maybe you need a personality disorder to be in the CIA. Anyway, they didn't take him, and he ended up back here. I ran into him again one night in White Plains, when both of us had just moved back to the area. It was nice to see someone I already knew from my old life."

"About your old life ... I was surprised how well my yearbook search worked out. But I'm sure there will be people who are hard to get in touch with, or information that is harder to find, if I keep looking for this tape."

"You should meet Musty then. This guy, Musty Kherlakian, was at the party today. They call him Musty because he loves old books ... volunteers at the library, the Yonkers Historical Society, you name it. Let me give you his card." She slipped it out of her pocket. Sure enough, it was emblazoned with Robert "Musty" Kherlakian, volunteer research specialist. "He told me to come see him if I needed anything for my dissertation. If it was a pickup attempt, it was the least creepy one I've ever seen."

"Musty?" Pat raised his eyebrows.

"Apparently there's an otter at the Bronx Zoo named after him.

Musty the mustelid!"

"Jesus Christ."

Mo studied Musty's card. "I'd love to meet this character, but I don't want to take this in case you need it."

"How about I take a picture?" Pat offered, and pulled out his phone.

"Good call." Mo grinned. "That way we all have access to the majesty of Musty."

"Any more questions about Ryan?"

Mo paused for a second. "This is not relevant, besides the fact that tonight is the seventh game of the ALCS ..." (Pat looked aggrieved.) "But did he like baseball?"

Christine smiled, but simultaneously looked sad. "He did. He loved the Yankees. His dad was the same kind of casual fan as my family, you know, born in the Bronx, and we follow them, but not obsessively, but his mom got him hooked."

Mo paused for a second before asking the inevitable. "And Eckley?"

"He liked the Mets! He wanted to pick his own team. His dad was a Yankee fan, fell in love with baseball when he came to America in the '60s. And he somehow picked the Yankees instead of the Miracle Mets. But his mom was from Boston and rooted for the Red Sox! She wasn't around for the 1986 World Series though. Would have been like World War III."

"My family is split too," Mo offered. "My mom is the craziest Yankees person and my Dad is the calmest and most long-suffering Phillies fan. Though my great-grandpa was a Philadelphia A's fan, but then Uncle Johnny picked the Phillies, and my grandma wanted to be like her older brother ..."

Pat shot her a look. "Let's get the check. We're treating, of course," he clarified.

"Are you sure?" Christine looked skeptical.

"Of course! Thank you for everything you told us today," Mo replied heartfeltly.

"Well in that case, let me hit the bathroom before we go." Christine headed toward the bathrooms, which were by the front desk.

They were alone. Pat grabbed Mo's diminutive digits in his larger paw as he jiggled his leg and checked the score. The Yankees were only down 1-0, though it was still only the fourth inning. The owner brought the check in a little box, on a tray with three chocolates: one Crackel and two Mr. Goodbars.

Mo retrieved the appropriate cash for the bill and tip. "When Christine said Eckley's mom wasn't around during the 1986 World Series. Where was she? He would only have been, like, fifteen."

"You'll have to ask her," said Pat meaningfully, as Christine wound her way back to them across the dining room, like a cat circumventing ankles.

"All good?" Christine inquired, moving to pick her jacket off the chair.

"Yup, we're all set," Mo reached to wriggle into her own windbreaker as the proprietor swooped by. "Though I have one more thing I need to ask you ..."

"Let's take a walk," Pat suggested. "I could use a cigar from Madaba." As a former smoker, he could still be tempted into grabbing the occasional Black & Mild or loosie when hanging out with smokers.

They headed out down the stairs, out of the dead end where Thai House was positioned above Petraske's and walked along Saw Mill River Road to the Ardsley iteration of Madaba, a chain of local bodegas.

"Where to?" Christine asked, as they exited the store, lighting a cigarette and handing the lighter to Pat for his Black & Mild.

"I know just the place," Mo replied.

"Does it have a TV?" Pat looked meaningfully toward Petraske's, though it would have been the opposite of a quiet place to continue a private conversation, especially as Christine's place of work.

Christine correctly intuited his signal. "Yeah, definitely not going back to the bar. Let's walk." Mo continued north on Saw Mill River Road, Pat and Christine smoking and trailing behind her.

The parking lot of the Ardsley Library was deserted, as were the benches by the garden and the pond. Mo always loved sitting here if she had extra time after stopping at this branch.

"More libraries!" Mo gestured to their setting. "Actually wait, are we allowed to be here at night?"

"Ok, Mrs. Intrepid Location Scout."

"Don't worry about it. If anyone comes by to check on us, I'll tell them my cousin is on the force in Dobbs. He wasn't working there yet when Ryan died. He was still NYPD at that point."

"Ryan ... passed away in Dobbs Ferry?" Mo hesitated.

"Yup. He, uh, jumped or fell from that bridge across the tracks, down by that old building on Palisade. In 2006. But they ruled it a suicide."

"Holy crap. I'm so sorry." Mo was momentarily stunned and took about five whole extra seconds to add the usual reply when anyone mentioned 145 Palisade: "I used to work in that building! Though I didn't live here yet in 2006. I moved here two years later."

"That's actually where we were hanging out the day I met Ryan. He might have been living there at the end too. I sort of lost track of him in those last few years."

There was silence as they stared out at the pond. "I'm so sorry," Mo said again. "I didn't realize he had ... died in a situation like that. I just thought he had ..."

"Passed away due to natural causes?" Christine laughed ruefully. "In his mid-thirties? He was only thirty-five, not that much older than you are now."

Mo was shaken, not just by the fact that rarely anyone guessed she was north of 30.

"Though he hadn't been himself for a long time," Christine added. Unspoken, in the next beat of silence, was the assumption that Ryan had been his true self back in the '80s when she had first known and loved him, rather than whatever happened after.

Mo decided to change the subject. "You mentioned something earlier about Eckley's mom not being around during the 1986 World Series?"

"Oh yeah, Eckley. His mom left a couple years before I first met him. As opposed to when I re-met him later. First she divorced his dad, and then ... she just kind of disappeared. Moved to DC for this job. And then they stopped hearing from her. David thinks she left the country." Christine shrugged. "I never got the impression that his mom treated him particularly well. His dad was kind of a cold British guy, but you know he loves David in his own weird way. And again, I never met his mom, but I heard she kind of fucked him up." She paused. "His stepmom's great though."

"That's good," Mo agreed. Though why was she agreeing that something was good for Eckley, who may not have been such a good guy himself? On that note, Mo took a breath and rushed headlong into her final inquiry.

"Did you ever have any reason to believe that David might have been involved in Ryan's death?"

"I wouldn't go that far," Christine said carefully, "though I also wouldn't rule it out!" She laughed in a way that Mo couldn't tell if she was being serious. "He was acting extremely odd afterwards. We were fighting all the time at that point anyway. And right after, he did something totally unforgivable; that was the last straw. I moved back to L.A., and then he moved back to Boston. But I had a feeling that was coming anyway. He needed to date someone who was going to flatter his ego. And I wanted an equal partner. So I was only going to put up with that shit for so long. Unfortunately, some of my friends saw through him way before I did."

"OK, now I really do have one more question. How did you end up with him for so long?"

Christine laughed. "It was like boiling a frog, you know? Things were so good at first. And by the time small hints started to pop up, I was already invested in the relationship. And there were good things too. He was smart, he was handsome, he took good care of me. He had a steady job, he took me on dates and on trips. In some ways he was so different from my most recent exes that it took me a while to see him for who he really was. And he was very careful not to let me see his other side right away. Though it all worked out in the end. This is really what pushed me into going back to school. More than the years of dealing with my sister. I don't want anyone else to have to go through what I was dealing with, you know?

"I want to make perfectly clear to you," she looked at each of them, "I wouldn't try to approach him. He's not a good person. Definitely some narcissistic, cluster B tendencies. Or if you do ever find him, don't mention me."

Mo looked at Pat. "Well don't say that, because this guy has never met a dangerous situation he didn't like."

"Oh Jesus," Christine threw up her hands in mock reproach, but her face was serious. "Well, I can't tell you how to conduct your investigation. I can only advise you based on my personal experience. And I'll try to think of some other people for you to talk to," she continued. "That kid Eric, the bassist, though he dropped off the face of the earth. Same with Dion, the singer, who moved away years ago. And you already talked to Matt," she enumerated.

"Sounds like we have our work cut out for us," Mo agreed, though she was thinking of the phenomenon in *Night Film* of people disappearing or moving to the ends of the earth after working on Cordova movies. Had Indignation somehow altered the courses of its members' lives, or was it merely a coincidence? One dead, two dispersed to purportedly far-flung locales, and the only normal one—the local dad, possibly not so normal back then—hadn't played on the demo?

"And I'm sure there are copies of this demo around here somewhere," Christine continued. "In parents' basements or attics. I would look at my parents' house, but my sister was always stealing my stuff, so I don't think there's much left."

"Somehow, I am not surprised," Pat concurred.

The Yankees lost, 4-0, and the Astros advanced to the World Series to face the Dodgers. But in the tale of Ryan, Christine and Eckley, it wasn't clear yet who had won.

Chapter 7
1988

Life After Indignation. It was hard to believe that the band had only been a part of Ryan's personal history for half a year, which, for a 17-year-old, still felt like forever. The weekends that he thought would have been occupied by playing shows now stretched out empty before him. At some point he needed to get his shit together and figure out what he was doing after senior year. But in the meantime, he needed to adjust to the upcoming fall being so different from what he had expected.

The Mets were playing the Dodgers in the NLCS, resulting in nonstop commentary from Eckley. Once again the Yankees had missed the playoffs. Just like Indignation, their season had ended earlier than Ryan had hoped. But the weekend after the CB's show debacle, comfort came from an unexpected source. It was Sunday afternoon. Ryan's mom was on the phone in the kitchen, and his dad was watching football in the living room. The front door opened to admit David Eckley.

"'Sup, dude?" Eckley stepped inside. "I was trying to call, but your line has been busy since like, forever."

"Yeah, my mom is on the phone." Ryan gestured toward the kitchen.

"Anyway. My dad wanted to know if you want to go to the record store with us."

Ryan was oddly touched. "Of course! Come upstairs, I just need to get ready."

David had been 13-years-old when his mom left. And for a time, after the departure of Mrs. Eckley, the only thing that provided a sense of normality to her stunned son and husband were their weekend record-shopping expeditions. Ryan was at first unsure how he should act around the Eckleys during this apocalyptic household development. He had always thought Mrs. Eckley was a little irrational and scary, but she was still his best friend's mom. So he had tried to entertain his friend while making it clear that he was willing to talk about serious shit if David preferred. One Sunday, they were hanging out in David's room when Mr. Eckley appeared.

"Come along boys, we're going to the record store." Mr. Eckley wore an odd smile, or an expression that was hoping to be a smile, while threatening to crack at any second. Evidently he had realized that the best immediate step forward was to distract himself and his son, and how better than by going record shopping?

Over the next few months, Ryan joined the Eckleys almost every Sunday. Sometimes they stayed local, going to the Sam Goody in Eastchester if

Becky McAuley

Mr. Eckley had special ordered something he wanted to pick up. Other weekends he drove them down to the city, to Academy Records, to Tower Records, or the more niche stores that corresponded with his tastes.

Mr. Eckley collected jazz and soul records, so while the stores he chose leaned in that direction, there was also always something interesting for Ryan and David to peruse. At this point, both boys were into rock and entry level metal. But Ryan would realize afterwards how the records they bought on these Sunday afternoons in 1984 had laid down the first stepping stones for his musical path later on that directly led him to punk and hardcore.

So the Eckleys including him in a record hunting expedition was one way to take Ryan's mind off of the Indignation situation. And while he didn't have the band to look forward to, he still had Christine. She knew how bummed he was about Indignation and was keen on cheering him up whenever they got together. Going to shows with Christine was also a good distraction from the fact that he was attending shows as a spectator rather than a band member. The weekend before Halloween, they went to see Supertouch at the Anthrax (without David, as he wasn't a Supertouch guy.) It was one of the best sets that Ryan had seen them play, and all the more special as it was the first time he and Christine were seeing them together. Christine was a big Supertouch fan and was even including their lyrics as her Dobbs Ferry yearbook quote.

Christine appearing in Ryan's life just before senior year was lucky for several reasons. He had no idea what the hell he wanted to do with himself after graduation, and he hadn't seriously thought about going to college. Yes, Mr. McGauskan had convinced him to take AP English that fall, but he had only acquiesced because he enjoyed reading and writing. He remembered how Andrew Rompanelli's dad got to work at ConEd super early to secure a parking space, and then passed his time reading mystery novels with a flashlight while he waited to start the work day. That wouldn't be so bad, Ryan reflected, reading a book while you waited to start work and then looking forward to reading or painting or playing the guitar when he got home. But Christine argued that he should at least try to study something that could get him a job he enjoyed. She convinced him to finally take the SAT—which, if he had done in the spring with David, he would never have met Matt Zimmer—and start looking into colleges, perhaps one where he wouldn't be too far from where she ended up.

If Ryan needed a reason to get serious about college, staying close to Christine was more than a sufficient motivator. He resolved to apply to a couple of SUNY schools, including New Paltz, which was near a few private colleges that Christine had applied to. His parents were guardedly supportive of the process, and Ryan tried not to get his hopes up in case they couldn't make it work financially. Eckley, meanwhile, had decided he

Lost Indignation

wanted to go to college in Boston, and was enthusiastically preparing his applications to multiple schools. It was an interesting choice, since Mrs. Eckley had come from Boston. Was David perhaps hoping to learn more about her family, which was just as much of an enigma as Ryan's mom's relatives in upstate New York? Ryan didn't bring up the connection and tried to be excited for his friend. The two of them would be going separate ways next year, and now Ryan had his own trajectory and goals to focus on.

While Indignation had broken up only six weeks prior, any disagreements already seemed far behind. Ryan could have just let everything go, including the unaddressed issue that he hadn't wanted to play in a band with David Eckley. But instead, he decided to bring some facetious closure to the situation.

On an unusually warm day in November, they were all hanging out at the Abyss: Ryan, David, Christine, and Christine's cousin Anthony. Anthony was a nice enough kid who obviously looked up to his cousin Christine, so Ryan was happy to include him in hangouts. This kid could be the next Matt Zimmer, indoctrinated into hardcore via a cool older cousin, though he seemed a lot quieter and saner than Matt Zimmer. But Eckley seemed oddly annoyed when Anthony hung around with them. Perhaps he was mad that he, David, was between girls, Ryan realized. Eckley hadn't dated anyone since Madeline had ditched him and been summarily dissed via the "Investigate" cover. And Ryan privately wondered if Eckley had the right temperament to have a girlfriend at all, at least at this point in his life.

Anyway, today Ryan had a surprise for everyone. After Christine and Anthony arrived at Ryan's, they met Eckley outside and the four of them set out for the Bronx River path. Leaves crunched under their feet as they walked off the trail into the Abyss. Ryan felt for the tape in the pocket of his jacket. He was waiting for the right moment to unveil it, which occurred soon after they reached their destination.

"Guess what I brought today?" He produced the Indignation tape, where three confused faces awaited it. "Remember the dinosaur? This tape is the new dinosaur."

When Ryan and David were both seven-years-old, just a few months after Ryan had moved to Crestwood Ave., he and David had gotten into a dispute over a plastic dinosaur. Somehow they had decided that if neither of them could have the dinosaur, they needed to bury it in a neutral location. This ended up being the grassy island between Crestwood and Pennsylvania Avenues.

"Except this time we're seventeen, not seven," Ryan continued. "Burying this tape marks the official end to the Indignation era. And of the two of us not playing in a band together. And it's one fewer tape that you helped finance, that now we don't have to sell!" They all laughed, though David looked slightly pained.

"You should set it on fire first," Anthony suggested.

"I'll set something on fire!" Christine had unearthed the remains of a joint from the pocket of her jacket. Anthony waved it away, as he was still straight edge, like Ryan, but Eckley looked conflicted. As of today, he was straight edge, though Ryan had a feeling that was about to change.

"What better time?" David took the joint from her outstretched hand.

"I can't believe you're breaking edge right now!" This was more than Ryan had anticipated when he brought the tape as a symbolic end to the Indignation chapter. "Just for the record, I'm not joining you." He busied himself with digging the hole for the tape.

Once Eckley got over his purported amusement over Ryan's stunt, he seemed annoyed that Christine and Anthony were witnessing this charged moment. But Ryan could tell he appreciated the sentiment. And then again, Ryan reflected, as he dropped the tape into the hole and they each took turns tossing in some dirt, like a funeral—without Christine there, David wouldn't have had the opportunity to break edge while this was happening.

"You need to mark the spot with something," Anthony suggested.

"What, in case we need to come back here and dig it up?" Ryan laughed. But Christine found a 40 bottle nearby and they buried that up to its neck, next to the Indignation tape.

"Maybe this will give you better luck for our next band! Since no offense dude, it seems like you need it," David smirked. Ryan tossed a clump of leaves at him.

If burying the tape was supposed to lay the groundwork for fortuitous future musical endeavors, it didn't work right away. Neither of them managed to assemble another band during the rest of their senior year. That spring, Eckley found out he had gotten into Boston University, his first choice, and was already making vague threats about starting a band in Boston once he was settled there and had met people in the scene.

Ryan, too, was surprisingly proud to find an acceptance letter to SUNY New Paltz in his mailbox and called Christine to celebrate the moment it had arrived. Now he just needed to figure out how he was going to pay for college, though he would get another job this summer, with no recording to save up for, and at least it was an in-state school with reasonable tuition. And while he might bring his guitar to New Paltz, he wasn't counting on finding like-minded bandmates and wasn't sure how often he would be able to get a ride to shows. More importantly, he wouldn't be too far from Christine: she was going to Bard College, which was less than an hour away.

Lost Indignation

He and David attended a few shows together that summer, like the Aaron Straw benefit at the Anthrax, but neither had a lot of time off from work and both were looking ahead to their new lives that fall. Perhaps it was fortuitous that they had become more independent of each other and that they were naturally growing apart. Ryan thought back to the time Indignation had formed just over a year ago. It was crazy that everything was so far in the past tense: those first practices with Zimmer, getting to know each other and write their songs, looking for the rest of their band members, and then cohering as a full unit. This year, he had the only new person he needed in Christine. Though Indignation ultimately hadn't turned out how he hoped, at least it had brought her into his life indirectly.

Even the video that Andrew Rompanelli had shot at the benefit show had vanished. When Ryan asked for a copy to remember Indignation's best show, Andy couldn't find either the original or the copy he had dubbed the set to. He had been hoping to lend the latter to some chick named Kara who liked Raw Deal, which was the first live set on the dubbed copy. Apparently, both Ryan and Kara were out of luck.

As summer receded, so did Ryan's thoughts of Indignation. Last fall, his priorities were recording a demo and asking out Christine. This year, his sole focus was on starting college.

His roommate at New Paltz was Nate Katinsky from Nanuet, who was temperamentally the opposite of Matt Zimmer, Ryan's other closest Jewish friend so far. Nate was studying computer science and had a keen memory for basketball stats. He was both neat and agreeable, and Ryan soon realized that he had lucked out, as roommates went. But Nate's tame existence also made Ryan miss Matt Zimmer, from his messy wall of flyers and explosion of wrestling memorabilia to his offbeat enthusiasm to his ability to just make shit happen. He and Matt had kept in touch sporadically, but he had a feeling that Matt was moving on from hardcore— that or perhaps he was never allowed out of his house again to see a live show.

Two weeks after arriving on campus, Ryan saw a kid wearing a Breakdown shirt walking past his dorm. This turned out to be Greg from Katonah, who lived in the same building as Armando, a guy from the Bronx who was into both hardcore and metal. The three kept each other informed about upcoming shows near campus. There were more nearby shows than Ryan had anticipated, including a Vision show at some bar in town right after the start of their freshman year. Greg had a car, and at first they hatched grand plans to travel in this hatchback to off-campus gigs. They undertook one adventure to the Anthrax to see Supertouch, Burn, and Sick Of It All, in a show that ended in a fight, which quashed any chance of Killing Time playing, though it was rumored they were on their way. But otherwise, Ryan wasn't leaving campus as much as he expected, as there was always something interesting happening nearby.

Eckley, too, seemed to be thriving in Boston. He had not yet realized his fantasy of starting a band, but still talked about getting one off the ground once he knew more people. To Ryan, it sounded like he had met plenty of people already, though perhaps they weren't the right type of people for Eckley to play in a band with if he wanted to maintain creative control.

Ryan didn't have any leads on potential band members either (besides Greg and Armando, neither of whom played any instruments). But he had no trouble meeting other people that he enjoyed hanging out with, like Leah from Philadelphia, who lived down the hall from Armando. Leah was a night owl and eternal pessimist who was always up for an adventure, even if she thought the adventure was likely to end badly—like going to a party at the Modena Madhouse. She was quickly becoming one of Ryan's closest friends at college, and while he was pretty sure that she wasn't interested in him romantically, that fact wasn't confirmed until a few weeks later. Ryan was mentioning Christine being up at Bard, and that they were hoping to get together soon, when Leah lamented that she was obsessed with a girl from Vassar, who she wasn't entirely sure reciprocated her feelings.

Leah also hit it off with Christine when she tagged along with Ryan, Armando, and Greg to see 24-7 Spyz in Poughkeepsie. Christine met them there and then rode back with them to spend the weekend at New Paltz, though it was a tight fit in the hatchback. Christine was received favorably by Leah and the rest of Ryan's New Paltz friends, and he glowed with pride having her with him at the show and the rest of the weekend.

It had also been easier than Ryan expected to stay straight edge in college. He had imagined facing a fair amount of pressure to drink and had prepared some acerbic retorts accordingly. But kids at New Paltz were oddly chill about Ryan's decision not to drink, as long he didn't give a shit about what *they* did.

The first time Ryan considered breaking edge was when he found out about his dad. While home for Thanksgiving, his father had broken the news that he had been diagnosed with melanoma and might not have much time left. Ryan had suspected that something had been wrong with his dad for a while, but was devastated to hear that the affliction was final and fatal. His parents seemed oddly resigned to the news and determined to make the best of the situation. And he realized how much they had sacrificed to maintain the illusion that everything was fine. Mr. Marnell kept repeating that he was so glad he'd gotten to see Ryan start college— the first one in the family—which Ryan lodged in the back of his mind as further proof that he better not fuck things up on the academic front.

So Ryan stuck close to home for the rest of Thanksgiving break.

Lost Indignation

His mom told the Eckleys that same weekend, which meant Ryan was free to talk to David about the situation. David was still his best friend, but was oddly distracted when Ryan tried to ensnare him in serious conversations. He had a feeling he would feel better talking about this to Christine or Leah or even Greg and was surprised how much things had shifted in less than a semester.

Ryan had worried that this was the last time he would see his dad alive, but Mr. Marnell was still hanging in there when he came home for winter break. Eckley also seemed less competitive and more like his old best friend after their first semesters away at school. They briefly visited on Christmas Eve, before the Marnells headed to Ryan's grandmother's apartment, but he mostly spent time with Christine in the week that followed. Though Eckley had learned of an epic party at some mansion in Scarsdale while the host's parents were out of town and was attempting to convince Ryan to accompany him.

"Sorry, dude. I'm hanging out with my dad." Mr. Marnell had been planning to take Ryan out to dinner on City Island that Saturday, the last Saturday of the year and possibly the last Saturday that they would spend together on City Island. Even if his dad hadn't been dying of cancer, Ryan would have genuinely enjoyed hanging out with him. Ryan knew it was punk rock to hate your parents, but his really weren't so bad.

On Saturday, Ryan headed to City Island with his dad as planned. They had dinner at Sammy's and then continued down the street to a bar where his dad knew the owner. As the straight edge kid, Ryan was the DD, not that his dad was supposed to be drinking on his meds. They were home before midnight, with Ryan's parents heading upstairs (his mom had fallen asleep on the couch waiting for them) but Ryan, on college kid hours, was not ready for the night to end.

An hour later, he saw a car pull up at the Eckleys' house: the Pounsenech family Oldsmobile. Ryan gave him a few minutes, then deployed their old signal of flashing his lights three times, hoping Eckley would call. He positioned himself by the kitchen phone, which rang moments later.

"How was the party?" Ryan was genuinely curious, though he wasn't jealous that he hadn't been able to attend.

"It was fucking great! You missed one hell of a night. Huge fucking house, top-shelf booze, tons of weed, I did coke for the first time—" (Eckley did sound a little animated) "— fine-ass Scarsdale and Larchmont girls, a live peacock, shit was fucking nuts."

"It sounds like it," Ryan agreed.

"And everyone was there," Eckley continued. "The host was a friend of Travis from Power Structure's cousin? So Travis and Sean were there, Andy Rompanelli, John H. broke edge—like, literally at the party.

Oh, and while Sean was making out with some unbelievably hot chick who didn't even speak English, I was doing lines with Travis, which reminded him of your old pal Dion Carina!"

"What about Dion? How's he doing? I wonder if he ever got his car fixed."

"No idea about the car. But apparently he's a massive cokehead. Him and that guy whatshisname, CC, the drummer, who's his dealer. I can't believe they were in a band with a bunch of straight edge kids!"

"Well, CC wasn't really in the band. And we weren't a straight edge band," Ryan allowed. Still, it didn't fit the Indignation narrative. What had Dion said about meeting CC in some parking lot? He had probably been buying drugs from him!

"Anyway, Travis graduated the same year as us, and got a job as a messenger down in the city. First on foot, but now he's a real bike messenger. So he's crashing with his grandmother down in Mount Vernon, since it's easier to get to the city than from Cortlandt or wherever the fuck he's from. And he starts running into Dion, who's still living in the area. He's not doing construction anymore, he was driving for Nimmo's Limos, but somehow got fired from there. Says he's been riding his bike a lot, thinking of moving to the city. Travis mentions he's working for Light Speed as a bike messenger. Dion must have applied without telling him, didn't use him as a reference or anything. Because a few weeks later, he's in the messenger center and hears a story about a guy who just started but already got let go for getting into a fight on the job. Like, literally squaring up with some dude he was delivering a package to. And guess who it was? Dion Carina!"

"Hahaha! Oh, man! Fucking Dion Carina!" Ryan tried to curtail his laughter so as not to wake up his parents. "Dude, want to come over if you're still up for a bit? We can hang out in the basement or something so I'm not tied to this phone."

"I'll be right over. And I got a surprise for you." A few minutes later, Eckley was at his door, looking slightly disheveled and holding a bag of weed.

"You can't smoke this inside!" Ryan protested, thinking back to Dion nearly lighting a cigarette in Matt Zimmer's basement. "Let's go out back." Ryan grabbed his coat and followed David through the kitchen to the back door.

"I could leave some of this for your dad," Eckley offered, once they were standing outside, far enough away from the house but not too near any of the neighbors, though all the houses were dark. "Figured he might need it."

"I can't really see my dad smoking weed, though you're right, he hasn't been eating a lot lately. But give me that," Ryan put his hand out for the joint.

"You're breaking edge?" Eckley's eyebrows were raised.

"Hey, as you once said yourself—what better time?"

Ryan discovered he liked being high, and Christine was also enthused about this development. Besides her cousin Anthony, Ryan was technically the last person in their crowd to break edge, John H. having beaten him to it by a mere number of hours. And there was something in it for Eckley too: an equally stoned companion to hang with for the rest of Christmas break. They spent the next week immersed in bad movies, laughing so hard that Ryan was glad this was going on at his house, as if they were over at David's, they might have perturbed or disturbed Mr. Eckley.

But on the Saturday before they were going back to school, they were at the Eckleys, watching some documentary about MK-Ultra. Mr. Eckley paused in the doorway.

"You boys watching this nonsense again?" He didn't wait for a response before continuing down the hall.

"I love how riled up he gets about this shit," Eckley reflected. It was a long-running debate: as a scientist and inveterate skeptic, Mr. Eckley disdained anything that couldn't be empirically proven, which only further enraptured Ryan and David. Then again, there were also theories closer to home that Mr. Eckley didn't believe. Earlier that week, David had confessed to Ryan that he thought his mom had worked for the CIA (and possibly still did). He had floated this idea to his dad, who had immediately refused to consider it. Whatever had caused her to abandon their family and then disappear from their lives, his dad wasn't convinced that it could have been brought about by a third party.

"He said that's just the way she was, that she wouldn't have needed any other motivation to move the fuck away and leave us here. Said he wished that he had figured it out sooner, but that he was glad he had met her, because then at least he had me," David explained. Ryan felt for his friend. Mrs. Eckley's behavior had always alarmed him, as she vacillated from praising David too thoroughly to punishing him too harshly. At least David was stuck with his gruff British dad.

Ryan's own father passed away about a month into his second semester. After having spent quality time with his parents over break, he was somewhat mentally prepared. He was also prepared to get shit drunk with his cousins and father's extended family after the wake, having broken edge at a fortuitous time. Eckley didn't come home from college, but the elder Eckley attended both the funeral and the wake, and Christine came home from Bard on the train. But there would be no more trains or buses in the immediate future for Ryan or Christine. Mrs. Marnell sent him back to school with her old Civic, as she was planning to trade in her

Becky McAuley

husband's work truck and then procure a newer car for herself. Not that she really went anywhere. Ryan was acutely aware, as he drove himself and Christine back to school, that his mom and Mr. Eckley were both now alone in their houses on Crestwood Avenue. His mom had warned him that she might need to sell the house, once she had a better understanding of what she could get for his dad's business. Would this be one of the last times he would drive away from it on his way back to school?

It turned out that his dad's business affairs were not in as bad shape as Ryan had assumed, based on his parents' comments and attitude in recent years. And yet his mom was still planning to sell the house, as it was too big for one person with Ryan away at school. He was surprised to hear his mom recount, with a note of pride in her voice when he was home for spring break, that she hadn't had a drink in three weeks. Through a friend, she'd started going to meetings in northwest Yonkers. She was looking at apartments over there too, by the Hudson and the Aqueduct trail, and putting their house on the market that spring. Ryan was of course happy for his mom, though it was difficult to imagine his life on Crestwood Ave. coming to an end, especially when his mom presumed he was doing well and wasn't making a permanent space for him in her new plans and new home.

But he wasn't doing well. He didn't know *what* the fuck was happening to him that spring, though he would look back wistfully at spring 1990 as his last semester before he had started hearing the voices. For the first time in his life, he had trouble sleeping. When he did manage to fall asleep, he was pursued by strange dreams, featuring ominous occurrences that bled into his waking life. Ryan had always experienced odd dreams—including the one that had named Indignation—but this was different. He tried smoking more weed in the hope that it would help him sleep better and let him avoid some of the weird shit that was happening during the day, but instead it intensified the synchronicities he encountered.

Aside from seeing things that he wasn't sure were a dream or reality, Ryan also started hearing a clicking noise periodically, as if someone was opening and closing a ballpoint pen. Where the fuck was it coming from? Was someone recording him? Was the government aware of his interest in their devious practices and had decided to monitor him accordingly? He mentioned the clicking to Leah, on the off chance she could hear it too. She could not, and gently chided him that if he was hearing things, he should probably stop smoking so much of her weed. Ryan pretended to agree and briefly reverted to smoking all her cigarettes instead.

Leah was the only one on campus that Ryan felt comfortable asking about the noises. Meanwhile, no one had the full picture about how bad things were getting in other areas. He managed to push through the rest of the semester and pass all his classes, if with desultory final grades (which

Lost Indignation

at least his dad would never know about), and soon he and Christine were both back in Westchester for the summer. It was a summer of upheaval, as his mom had managed to sell the house on Crestwood Ave. and put in an offer on an apartment in Yonkers up near the Greystone train station. Ryan was thankful that it had a small second bedroom and he'd still have his own space when he was home from school.

After years of handling the finances for his dad's business, Ryan's mom had started a bookkeeping job in White Plains, so Ryan was often alone at the apartment once the move was complete. Christine was working too, back at the day camp in Dobbs Ferry. This was the first time in years that Ryan didn't have a summer job. It wasn't that hadn't thought that far ahead—he had known he would be busy for the first few weeks helping his mom move, packing up his own bedroom, and going through his dad's stuff. Eckley was lifeguarding again, and Ryan was relieved that they'd have an excuse to avoid each other. He didn't want to draw extra attention to whatever was happening to him lately, compared to his always-perfect friend who had managed to crush his first year of college and was now settling back into a summer of lifeguarding and being a normal fucking person. Though either way, Eckley would not have been a ubiquitous part of his life like in summers past. They were no longer two hardcore kids living on Crestwood Ave., as Ryan had realized grimly while packing up the basement.

While home from Bard, Christine was keen to resume attending hardcore shows occurring in the general area, but Ryan often didn't have the heart to join her. He was now located directly between her and the city, as Greystone was two stops south of Dobbs Ferry on the Hudson Line, and at least once Christine stopped by the Marnells' new apartment on her way to a show, attempting to convince him to join her. The combination of Killing Time, Supertouch, Dmize, and Burn at CBGB's lineup in July was the most tantalizing yet and almost propelled him into the city, but ultimately he demanded Christine and Anthony go without him.

Christine was likely aware that something was wrong but afraid to press the issue. Maybe she just thought Ryan was growing out of hardcore. Or, like Ryan's mom, she suspected that he was still grieving the loss of his dad and the interruption of his old life in Crestwood. Ryan was convinced that was why his mother hadn't asked too many questions about his behavior this summer, even when he was only emerging from his tiny new bedroom on an irregular basis, and especially since his newly sober mom must have been more alert to his behavior than in years past.

Despite whatever concerns Christine may have had, Ryan was relieved that she seemed determined to maximize their time together before returning to their respective schools. So far, these moments were the highlights of his summer. She did her best to get him outside: walking on the Aqueduct trail, hanging out in her parents' backyard, smoking weed on the beach by the Hudson near the building where they'd met, and then—finally, the week before school—announcing she was planning a picnic in Untermyer Park. Otherwise, Ryan might have done little that summer besides draw, read, and watch TV. In his new darkened bedroom, the visions and noises from last semester beset him less intensely, but he worried about them re-escalating when he returned to regular student life.

But he didn't have to wait to get back to school for things to move in a disturbing direction. Christine had put a lot of planning into the Untermyer picnic, attempting to make it the high point of their summer and document it for future memory. Having gotten into photography during her first year at Bard, she had her camera with her for the occasion. As she set up her shot of Ryan and their picnic spread, the clicking of the lens provided an eerie reminder of the sounds that had been following him, and suddenly he knew. Christine had been compromised and must have placed cameras in his mom's new apartment to monitor him for the government. Fuck, what if she was taking pictures of him as part of her assignment right now?! Playing it off as a joke, he shielded his face and even pulled the corner of the picnic blanket over his head. For the rest of the evening, he tried to maintain a lighthearted mood, but he couldn't escape the weight of this discovery. He might have still loved her, but now he knew he couldn't trust her.

It was almost a relief to return to their respective schools that fall. Ryan couldn't find any evidence of cameras in his dorm or bathroom, but resolved to be on guard and to limit his phone conversations in case they were being recorded. He was once again rooming with Nate, but mostly hung out with Leah and her roommate Arianne, smoking Leah's cigarettes and Arianne's weed, sometimes the other way around. Yet no amount of weed could fix his insomnia, which returned harshly a few weeks into the new semester.

After apprenticing on someone else's radio show last year, Armando now had his own show, *Crucial BBQ*, which ran from 2-4 a.m. Ryan was often still up when it came on, or far enough from sleep that he reasoned he might as well stay up. He often slipped from his room to wander through campus listening to his portable radio or to tune in while driving the Civic along the silent upstate roads. Armando had even invited him to drop by the show sometime, but Ryan had demurred, as there was too much recording equipment and technology at the radio station for him to feel secure about its environs.

But a few weeks into his sleep tribulations, Ryan experienced a more intense version of the noises and patterns he had noticed last spring, along with accompanying instructions in his head. In an attempt to distract himself, he agreed to go see Murphy's Law play behind a beer distributor

Lost Indignation

on Main Street. It was one of the muddiest, messiest shows he had ever witnessed and indeed took his mind off his recent predicament. And yet he had only gone because the show was right there in town. The idea of traveling for a hardcore show was beyond his current capabilities. Greg had been talking about going to some Quicksand show in October, but Ryan hadn't seen as much of either him or Armando lately, as it seemed like they, like Christine, had found their place at school in a way that he had not. This semester, he had mostly been hanging out with Leah, Arianne, and Arianne's cousin Ian, who was a year ahead of them and lived off campus. And who knew where to get mushrooms.

The mushrooms were Ian's idea, but if Leah and Arianne hadn't been interested, the plan would never have made it to Ryan. But when Leah mentioned that Ian knew where to get them, Ryan was intrigued. At this point he was interested in anything that might distract him from his daily existence and/or knock his brain into a different orbit. He had never tripped before, but now was the time to try it. Due to his lack of a summer job, he was short on cash this semester, but decided to invest in the mushrooms even if he needed to sell more records to Anthony the next time he was home. Good old Anthony: selling his most crucial acquisitions to Christine's little cousin had been his main source of income this year.

The final group for Saturday's mushrooms endeavor was Ryan, Ian, Leah, Arianne, and surprisingly, Nate. Ryan wouldn't have predicted Nate would be interested, but when Leah and Arianne had stopped by their room and mentioned Saturday's activities, he wanted in. It was an ideal October day and they were planning to meet up outside around dinner time, though Ian had cautioned them not to eat beforehand, as that might dilute the strength of the product. The group had debated if they should go somewhere off campus, but ultimately decided to walk down to the woods by the pond, in order to stay close to their dorms if anything went wrong.

Just after 7:30 p.m., they assembled in a small clearing in the woods. Ryan felt a thrill of anticipation. Ian portioned out the mushrooms and then passed them around. They chewed in silence. "This tastes like shit," Nate muttered. Ryan agreed and wished he had eaten something beforehand, or at least something alongside them to make the mushrooms taste less fucking disgusting.

At first, nothing happened, but he was still enjoying chilling with everyone in the woods. Now this was more like what he had been hoping college would be like. He had friends, and that was a fact! And was so happy to be out here eating fucking mushrooms with them! He threw his arms around Leah and Arianne's shoulders and declared to them as such. That was the last thing he remembered.

Becky McAuley

Ryan struggled to open his eyes. It felt like he had slept forever. Where the fuck was he, and how had he gotten here? Once he managed to open one eye and then the other, he realized he was lying on Leah's bed, atop the covers and fully clothed. The reason for his disturbance was soon revealed: Leah and Arianne were standing over him, both looking like they had just returned from outside. Arianne was holding a chocolate muffin in a napkin, which she set down on the windowsill next to Leah's bed.

"You're awake!" Arianne exclaimed.

"Fucking finally," Leah echoed, sounding annoyed, but she looked relieved.

"We brought you a muffin since you missed breakfast. I tried waking you but you were still totally out of it. You had one hell of a night last night."

"Sorry in advance," Ryan said quickly, "since I have absolutely no recollection of whatever I did."

Leah and Arianne looked at each other, and Leah spoke first. "What's the last thing you remember?"

"Eating the mushrooms, and that I was happy to be with you guys."

"Yeah, you looked pretty happy at one point ..." Arianne ventured, before she and Leah started to deliver an alternating narration of Ryan's evening.

"We were all good up until you climbed the tree."

"And then you fell out of the tree, but you were OK." Ryan rubbed his shoulder. No wonder why he felt like he had been in the pit at CBGB's.

"You were running around talking to yourself. At one point you took off towards the road, you and Nate were yelling about some shit."

"Security drove past, they started talking to you and by the time we caught up with you, you were telling them your name was Kevin Moss."

"Kevin Maas?"

"Yeah, something like that," Arianne allowed. "Nate thought it was funny, but I didn't get it."

"He's a player on the Yankees." Ryan was surprised his face still remembered how to smile. "He might be Rookie of the Year. But I'm not sure why I decided that was my name. Some of this is starting to come back to me. I thought that guy was driving an ice cream truck?"

"That could be why you were yelling about a cherry dip. We convinced him you were OK, and then we started walking around campus. You were acting a little more normal, but still talking to yourself. We finally made it back to your room, but I think Nate was afraid to be alone with you! So we took you back here instead. Ari passed out around midnight and I wanted to go to sleep too, but you kept whispering about milkshakes. I think we went to sleep around two a.m., and only because I gave you a fucking Valium. Fuck, man, you also smoked almost all my cigarettes. You're lucky I like you." Leah pretended to punch him.

"I sure am. Hey, thank you for breakfast. And for everything," he added. "It sounds like I had an interesting night. I hope I didn't fuck up anyone else's trip."

"Well let's just say you might want to stick to weed and pills going forward. And I'm not kicking you out, but you should make sure Nate knows you're still alive."

Ryan headed back to his room, left a note for Nate, and passed the fuck out for the rest of the day. But the next afternoon, Leah caught up with him as he was heading back to his dorm from English class.

"'Sup, Lee," Ryan gave her a one-armed hug as she fell into step beside him.

"How was class?"

"It was eh. I'm still all fucked up from this weekend." It was true: the noises and visions had intensified, and he had been going to bed early and barely waking up in time for class.

"Are you OK, buddy? It sounded like you had a really bad trip. But besides the silly shit, you were talking to yourself about these noises and asking if anyone else could hear them, talking about cameras, your phone line being tapped ... is there something else going on that I should know about?"

Leah looked so concerned that Ryan was on the verge of telling her about the voices or reminding her about the cameras while they were both sober. Maybe she could help him or protect him, or least would know what he was going through. But he had a feeling she wouldn't understand. Or what if she was compromised too? "I think I just had a bad night. I'll probably feel better in a few days."

When he made it back to his room, there was a note from Nate that Christine had called. This was unusual: between photography, some poetry magazine, and her on-campus job, she was constantly occupied. It wasn't like she didn't have time for Ryan, but they had never spoken on the phone frequently at school. Ever since the day in Untermyer Park, Ryan had been extra wary of communicating with her by phone, in case the calls were being recorded for her handler, and in fact couldn't remember if he had spoken to her by phone yet during his sophomore year. He tried to remember if he'd mentioned the mushrooms in his most recent letter. Was she just calling to check on him or was there some ulterior motive: was she being manipulated to monitor him?

Ryan tried to avoid his room in case he was accidentally wrangled into speaking to Christine on a recorded line. But he came home from class on Tuesday to find yet another note from Nate that he'd missed a call from her, which was again surprising, this time because he wasn't sure that Nate was still speaking to him after an incident that morning. He composed a short and cryptic note to drop into the mail to Christine, but realized he was out of stamps. He was suddenly exhausted. He fell into bed, hoping Nate wouldn't come in and disturb him, and sank into a dreamless sleep.

When he woke up, it was dark. Nate hadn't reset the clock radio after the situation that morning, and Ryan didn't dare touch it either, so he had no idea what time it was. His dad had left him a watch, which had been his grandfather's before that, but he had kept it at his mom's apartment, thinking it was too nice to wear around campus. If Leah was home, she could tell him what time it was and give him a stamp for the letter to Christine. He felt a little bad not returning Christine's calls, but he couldn't risk it, in case she was recording his words.

Fortuitously, Leah was in, reading in her bed, and Arianne was out. "I just came over to get a stamp and see what time it was," he explained. "See if I missed dinner."

"You definitely missed dinner," Leah confirmed. "It's after 9 p.m. Do you guys seriously not have a clock over there?"

"Nate has this digital clock radio alarm thing but I ... accidentally unplugged it last night. He's pissed, we both overslept and he missed a quiz or something. And we haven't reset it yet." It hadn't been an accident: Ryan had unplugged the clock once he realized it was recording him. Concerned he had been talking in his sleep, he had pulled the plug around 3 a.m. Though he did feel bad about him missing the quiz; Nate was very particular about his GPA and shit.

"That makes sense if your sleep schedule is all fucked up. Are you sure you're all right? I've been worried about you even more than usual."

Ryan sighed and flopped onto Arianne's bed. He hated the idea of people worrying about him: that meant that someone could try to get to Leah too, or try to use her as an asset. Nevertheless, it was nice having someone right here he could talk to. "Oh Lee, what would I do without you?"

Leah rolled her eyes and grinned sardonically. "What would you do without me? Maybe you'd call your girlfriend back when she's looking for you. She called me today, too. Wanted to make sure you're OK. I honestly wasn't sure what to tell her."

Ryan sat up quickly. "She said that? And she called you here?" He didn't even know how Christine had Leah's number. Had they been talking about him?

"Yeah, she's worried about you. If she doesn't hear from you soon, she said she might come down here and check on you. I don't know what's going on with you guys, but can you just call her?"

Ryan shook his head no, but at the last minute decided to make a joke of it. "I think I've developed a phobia of the phone. After this weekend.

A side effect of the mushrooms."

"Side effect of the *mushrooms*?" It was clear Leah didn't believe him, and/or that she was losing patience. "Can you just ... fucking ..." She reached for the phone, and before Ryan consciously knew what he was doing, he had barricaded himself in Arianne's closet.

"Ryan!" He could hear Leah just on the other side of the door, which was a good sign since he didn't think the phone cord stretched that far.

"It smells kind of good in here. Can I stay here for a while? But don't call her. Please?"

"I won't call her." Leah sounded resigned. "I'm going to keep reading now, OK?"

As uncomfortable as it was on the floor of the closet, Arianne's clothes and purses did smell pretty good. Ryan must have fallen asleep again, since when he cautiously emerged, Leah's light was out and he heard her snoring. Giving up on borrowing a stamp, he slipped quietly from her room.

It was warm for New Paltz in October, but Ryan was not dressed to roam around for any significant amount of time. He decided to walk past his dorm, and if the lights were off, attempt to retrieve some warmer clothing and his portable radio. He couldn't tell if it was late enough for Nate to be asleep or if he'd get lucky and their room would again be vacant.

No lights shone in the window, so Ryan successfully retrieved the radio, his headphones, a jacket, and a sweater. The clock still stood unplugged on the nightstand, leading him to believe that Nate hadn't been there in the interim. Was Nate compromised too? He wasn't waiting around to find out, and swung back out into the night.

What the fuck time was it? Presumably after midnight, as there was hardly anyone around, though occasionally he passed a fellow student. Ryan kept his head down and kept moving, in case they were somehow surveilling him too. As he walked, Ryan pulled out the radio and tuned in to 88.7, the new frequency for campus radio station WFNP. Armando wasn't on yet, but he should be soon, especially since Ryan seemed to be missing chunks of time lately. Soon the guy before him was wrapping up and Armando was doing the intro *Crucial BBQ*. As Ryan continued to wander through campus, doubling back towards the road, he was only half paying attention until he heard his name:

"Up next is 'Backtrack,' by Killing Time. This goes out to Ryan, if you're listening!"

Ryan stood temporarily frozen. Fuck, how did Armando know he was listening, and how did he know that he had just backtracked down the path he had been walking on? Was Armando compromised too? Was the station somehow recording his thoughts? If so, he wasn't safe on campus and needed to get the fuck out of here. Moving vaguely in the direction of town, Ryan picked up his pace.

As he approached the road, a security vehicle seemed to sense his presence and pulled to a stop in front of him. Ryan couldn't avoid it without looking like he was trying to remain undetected, so he slowed down yet tried to maintain his distance from the car.

The driver looked at him quizzically. "Hello, Kevin."

"I'm not Kevin," Ryan responded automatically.

"Told me your name was Kevin on Saturday!"

"Well, it's not."

"You a student here?"

Ryan wondered what he should say. Would they be more likely to leave him alone if he was? But as he dithered, an odd look slid across the campus cop's face.

"Hey, you OK buddy? You look a little bit ..."

All at once, Ryan remembered him as the guy he had thought was the ice cream man, but it was too late. As he turned to escape, he stumbled, then scrambled to right himself. He heard doors opening behind him, then footsteps as his interlocutors sprung out of their vehicle. But it was like he was moving in slow motion, and soon they were upon him. They were trying to take him! He should have been ready for this! Whatever was about to happen to him, he knew he had to put up the fight of his life.

Chapter 8
2017

On Monday night, having momentarily escaped from homework and trying not to think about how the Americans for the Arts awards were going for the CFA team, Mo was doing abs in the living room while Pat looked on and entertained her. While enthusiastic about a variety of pursuits that would have bored most people, Mo nevertheless hated to be bored and generally read *The New Yorker* (or any equivalent magazine that could easily be bent back into one page and fit between her forearms) while planking. Today she was looking at a map of Greater Bronxville, which Pat had brought home when he did marketing for the real estate company Houlihan Lawrence.

Mo loved maps, and this was a cool one—white with green type. It went as far south as Fleetwood (Overlook Street was on there) and up through Crestwood, so Eckley and Marnell's neighborhood was included too.

"Crestwood Avenue is a long street!" she muttered, mid-plank. "I wish Christine had told us *where* on Crestwood they lived."

"You could ask her," Pat offered. "Though she might not even remember."

"True." Mo realized she couldn't even remember the street or house number of her most relevant ex. "Plus, I don't know if I should be *that* creepy."

"So you want to do things the hard way, as usual, and find it on our own?" Pat chuckled. "What's the plan, then? We just go there and walk around until we find someone who knows something?"

Mo checked her watch, hit 90 seconds, and flipped around to do that ab thing where you hold onto the couch and swing your feet up in the air.

"Remember the time you wanted to go trick-or-treating, but for me to pretend to be a kid?"

Pat's eyes widened. "Oh shit."

This had all started with Pat reminiscing about the primacy and convenience of trick-or-treating as a child in Interlaken. His family's garden apartment complex had featured both the outdoors element essential to Halloween, but also the advantage of density. From there, the initial Halloween nostalgia had morphed into a theoretical plan involving both Mo and Ally ZT posing as teenagers, fully covered in some sort of cute but all-encompassing costumes, with Pat acting as an older chaperone or less than wholesome older boyfriend.

But that was merely abstract speculation on the transgressive

Becky McAuley

aspect of Pat pretending to be an older boyfriend while Mo passed for a kid. Mo, for her part, had always shrugged off comments like when the librarian at the Will Library asked her what grade she was going into. Apparently, that's what happens when you're looking for a book from the *Face on the Milk Carton* series that is housed in a separate Summer Reading section. Mo was still unsure whether the librarian was fucking with her, as she might not look 31, but she probably looked closer to 24 than 17. Pat, for his part, hadn't missed an opportunity to repeat the grade question ever since. So it was half plausible to consider a fraudulent trick-or-treating mission, if only to fulfill their earlier discussion, or now for the unique bonus of getting to knock on people's doors, on a street where Eckley and Marnell had once lived, in what was the most socially acceptable context for this activity.

This being the week before the Vedomedy dinners, Mo had scant spare time to think about costumes or the feasibility of such a plot. They would have had to come up with Halloween costumes by Saturday anyway for their friend Vik Prasad's annual Halloween party, but as Mo and Pat were both notorious procrastinators, they usually left the selection and formulation of costumes till the day of. Some of Vik's guests came elaborately attired, but Mo's primary concern was something comfortable enough to walk around in and eat food in for a few hours. And warm enough in case the party migrated outside or if Pat dipped out to hang with the smokers.

But plotting an outfit for trick-or-treating would involve more logistical concerns, from how to convincingly impersonate someone of appropriate age to finding an ensemble that wouldn't require a jacket or a purse. Even if she had to wear a placeholder costume for the party on Saturday, she could assemble something over the weekend for Halloween, which fell on a Tuesday this year—a week from today, she realized at her desk the next morning, finalizing the export of the AFTA post-release media list. It sounded like the art awards had gone well the night before while Mo was planking away.

During any busy week at CFA, extraneous problems were always going to pop up outside of the regularly scheduled shitstorm. In PR, best laid plans often meant nothing: even if you thought you knew exactly what you were going to work on, you were frequently blindsided by something totally new and urgent that developed overnight—or during the day.

Emily Chen and CFA had recently begun working with an artist named Alex Preno, whose upcoming show, split between Fuck Gallery in New York and the Yermakat Gallery in L.A. on overlapping weeks, involved a variety of spoof magazine covers. He had selected four of these to print as actual mini magazines to be sent as invites for the show. (Thankfully they weren't using the word "zines" in the press materials—and not just because normies never knew how to pronounce "zine.") Mo knew the invites would be arriving at some point, and she and her team would have to check the addresses, but likely not until the end of the week, due to some sort of printing delay. She was also already worried about "Fuck Gallery" causing their eblasts to go directly to spam, which CFA had learned the hard way via Emily's other client Museum of Sex.

The doorbell rang. Drew went to greet the visitor and Mo kept typing, but a moment later, was jolted out of her workflow nonetheless. "Hey, can you come look at this? We got a crate full of magazines?"

"Oh crap." She wheeled around in her chair and bounded toward the door. Why had they thought these were arriving later in the week? Evidently, the boxes took up too much space to hold onto, or cover with a yoga mat, like Mo had done in an emergency last year when the Teixeira Hotel people were visiting and under the impression that all invites for an upcoming dinner had left the building. For this monumental delivery that had just arrived, Mo and co. would have to finish doing the addresses and turn everything around right away. Which would be easy for some of the "usual suspects" New York recipients, but there were a lot of L.A. people on the list who didn't often get hard mailings and had no addresses in the database.

There it was, a fucking wooden crate that they would have to break down in the street, as there would be no way to get it into the building.

"Colette Foulard & Associates?" The delivery guy looked skeptical.

"That's us," Mo assented. "I guess we'll have to take this apart outside."

Dude looked confused. "You don't have a freight elevator?"

"No, this is a townhouse. This is the only way in and out." The hardware store guys across the street were observing the proceedings, amused. Mo signed for the crate and ducked inside to round up a crew of helpers. This was far from the first time that an odd and voluminous shipment had arrived at CFA.

"A fucking freight elevator!" Mo recounted the exchange to Emily, who she had collared on her way out of the bathroom. "This is a townhouse. We're putting the boxes in the shower!" And they did—a mini assembly line of six staffers while Oona held onto Pierre.

By the time they managed to get all the boxes stacked in the shower, Mo was barely able to wrap up her most urgent unfinished tasks before checking in with Monica and Shannon on where they had gotten to on the addresses. They were done checking the New York-based media, so those could start to go out via messenger while they finished the non-NY recipients. She quickly set up the RSVP email for the Young Eef dinner (youngeef@colettefoulard.com), the list on which she had seen Dion Carina's name. After Mo's herculean list-tagging last week, Tati and Keith

Becky McAuley

had been waiting for the final Save the Date graphic.

Mo made a note to ask Keith if Dion had opened the Save the Date when the blast went out, under the guise of being curious about the accuracy of the email address for the database. As of Wednesday afternoon, he had not. The initial eblast had only been sent the day prior, but Mo was always impressed with how many people opened invites within the first 24 hours or not at all. Dion still hadn't replied to her email either, which she had sent over a week ago. And as hers was not part of an eblast and she hadn't sent it with any sort of tracking software, there was no way to see whether he had opened it. However, help was soon on the way from an unlikely source.

"Guess who follows me on Instagram now?" Pat nonchalantly mentioned after work on Wednesday, as he measured out tomorrow's beans for the coffee grinder.

"Who?" Mo was putting the rest of her pasta in the fridge. It was a tight fit having them both in the kitchen simultaneously, especially with cats underfoot.

"Dion Carina," he responded with a flourish.

"What—" Mo was agog. "WHEN DID THIS HAPPEN? And HOW?"

"This morning." Pat grinned. "I decided to do a little searching, and it turns out he's a BMX guy. I think he even restores and sells them? I commented on this picture of a PK Ripper and we started talking in the comments. And then the next thing I know, Dion Carina is following me on Instagram."

"Wait, so how do I turn that into talking to him about Indignation?" Somehow this was so much wilder than like, running into the authors of classic NYHC songs in Bronxville.

"How about I DM him right now and ask if he'd be willing to talk to my wife about his old band? But first—hang on." Pat hit start on the coffee grinder.

Mo waited until the noise subsided. "Now *this* is why I keep you around."

Pat looked facetiously offended. "And not because I'm making tomorrow's coffee?"

It turned out that Dion was free to speak the very next evening. Pat had arranged for Mo to call him at 9 p.m. on Thursday night. Not only did she appreciate the setup, she also appreciated Pat's selflessness for having to hear about Indignation yet again rather than talk to this dude about bikes.

Before dialing and settling on the couch, Mo turned out the lights in the living room. The only illumination came from the light up skulls and pumpkins glimmering in their front window overlooking Overlook Street.

"Hello?" A deep voiced guy with an unmistakable New York

inflection answered on the first ring.

"Hi, Dion? It's Mo McGraw. Calling about Indignation." Jesus, why did she always sound five years old? "I'm going to put you on speakerphone, if that's OK?

"What's up, Mo? And go ahead." That way she didn't have to wedge the phone in her shoulder, and Pat could listen in, as she'd already taken over the living room for the call.

"I still haven't heard Indignation, but I'd love to hear about your time in the band! And how you joined and everything."

"My friend Liz hooked me up with those guys. We hit it off, played a couple shows ... but I don't know if I'd want to do it again!" Dion snorted. Mo wasn't sure if she should press for more detail.

"By any chance, do you still have any copies of the demo?"

"Not anymore," Dion responded bitterly.

"What do you mean?"

"I had a few after we recorded. By the time I got down to Florida, I only had one copy left." Mo waited for him to go on.

"I used to keep it out in my workshop with my boombox and my other tapes. Out behind my house, where I work on the bikes. But then one day, late '90s, I'm in there with the garage door up, and this kid comes walking up to my shop. Sounded like he wasn't from around here. And he was like, I hear you might have a copy of the Indignation demo, because he wanted to buy it." Mo held her breath. "I'm like nah, I lost that shit years ago, even though I did still have it. Who was this dude creeping around? Something just seemed off. And he left."

"And that was it?"

"I thought so at the time. A few months later, my workshop got broken into, and at first it didn't look like anything had been taken. Not my tools, my bikes. I was even restoring an '82 RA-24. Not a scratch on it."

"Wait, a Race Inc.?" Pat piped up, positively salivating.

"Yeah, a Race Inc. But then, a few weeks later, I'm going through my demos. Looking for my Up Front tape or some shit." Mo smiled at the idea of Dion Carina being a fan of Up Front. "And I see a missing spot in the rack."

"And the Indignation tape was gone?" she encouraged.

"Yes. Fuck! But what was I going to do, report that someone stole one cassette tape? As opposed to any of the valuable shit I've got in my shop? Anyway," he concluded, "I'd stay away. The tape is cursed! The whole band is cursed!"

Mo paused. "What do you mean?"

"Everything we tried to do, it just never came out right. We had some good songs, and I wish you didn't have to take my word for it. If I had that damn tape, I'd play it for you right now! But there was always

Becky McAuley

some shit going wrong. Bunch of fucking kids and they never knew how to handle themselves. Recording almost didn't happen, the drummer disappeared and I had to call a friend to fill in. Too bad my boy couldn't do the CB's show too, he had his kid's birthday party or some shit. And then the day we were supposed to play CB's and sell those goddamn tapes we had just recorded, we can't find the bassist, and the other drummer reappears and fucks up my car! And that was the day I was like I've had it, fuck these guys, and I quit the band."

Dion was silent for a second. "Those guys were more trouble than they were worth. It was fun while it lasted, but no point in sticking around. I started another band in the city, hung out in New York for a few more years ... and then I ended up in Florida. Got into DJing and the bike stuff and ended up staying down there."

"And you ended up on my list! For the Young Eef Midnight Dinner!" Mo concluded.

"Is that how you found me? Or through the BMX shit?"

"Yes, believe it or not. I saw you in the database at work for this dinner and recognized your name. Whether you can come or not, just let us know. We just sent the save the date on Tuesday, but when I checked, you hadn't opened it."

"People send me so much shit these days, I can't keep up. Especially during Art Basel. But now that I know that one came from you, I'll see if I can make it if I'm not already booked for that night. Art Basel, man, crazy times! You ever been?"

"I have not, though my office keeps threatening to bring me. So, thank you so much for telling me about all of this!" Mo was cognizant that she should wrap up the call and not take too much of this guy's time—it wasn't like she was conducting a phone interview for her zine. "But one more thing ... what did the guy look like who asked you about the tape?"

"A straight edge kid," Dion pronounced emphatically. "Wearing some baggy ass Path of Resistance shirt. Gauged ears and shit." That didn't sound like anyone they had heard about in the Indignation saga so far.

"It's always us straight edge kids causing trouble. But thank you so much for your time. I feel like I have a much fuller picture of the band. And I'm sorry about your tape."

"Everyone in that band was always so fucking sorry. A bunch of sorry asses! And you see where it got them?" Dion laughed bitterly. Though with what Mo knew about how they ended up, she wasn't sure that she could dispute this.

"Hey, where *did* the rest of the members end up?" Mo was intrigued. "I know Ryan ... passed away like ten years ago. And we met up with Matt ..."

"Oh, how is the little fucker?" Dion inquired. "He didn't say

Lost Indignation

anything about my car door, did he? He really fucked up my car!"

"Not a word," Mo grinned. "I'll have to ask him. Do you know anything about the bassist?"

"Eric Clifton? Last I heard, he was living in Alaska, doing something with fucking plants."

"Literally or figuratively?" Mo responded, but Dion appeared to not have heard or understood.

"For real," he continued, "I wasn't jumping for joy when the tape disappeared. It was part of my history. But afterwards? I've been so much happier ever since I got that fucking thing out of my life. That shit is cursed! The whole band was cursed!"

Mo hung up the phone and looked at Pat. It reminded her of finishing up a conference call and immediately intercomming your coworker once the client was off the line, or after a phone interview with a potential hire.

"I wonder what Matt Zimmer did to Dion's car? He didn't say anything about that when we met him."

"I'm sure it wasn't one of his finest moments."

"True. But that's so creepy about the tape! I feel like we have more questions than answers. What the fuck do we do now?"

Pat smiled grimly. "What we do is get ready to ask more questions on Halloween."

Halloween: always a multi-day event in NYC, especially for Mo's colleagues in their mid-20s, where the celebrations started the weekend before and occasionally continued through the weekend after (at least in the case of some CFA party in 2012, where a hay bale had been set on fire). This year, it was also a multi-day event for Pat and Mo, between Vik's party and their upcoming Crestwood adventure. Vik lived up in Ossining, but Pat's friends from all over the outer boroughs and Lower Westchester would drive up for the occasion.

For last year's party, they had brainstormed costume ideas at Mont Olympus, their favorite diner on Central Avenue in Yonkers, before acquiring the necessary elements nearby and assembling at home. This year, with no ideas on the horizon as of Saturday morning, they decided to repeat that itinerary. The costumes would be doing double duty for Vik's party and then the Crestwood foray on Tuesday, so they would either need to pick something practical for mobility and durability, or else just assemble something as a placeholder tonight, while thinking of a better getup for Halloween itself.

Today, instead of scrutinizing the local cast of characters that advertised on Mont Olympus's paper placemats, such as Dr. Angel Hong, Mo and Pat deliberated over various costume ideas. By the time that Mo's

Becky McAuley

French toast and Pat's omelette arrived, they had decided to go with Pat as Ron Santo and Mo as the on-field cat that had menaced him during the 1969 season. This would be easy to execute, since they had reversed these roles for another Halloween party in 2015, that time with Pat as the black cat and Mo as Ron Santo. Mo still had the roll of sticky blue vinyl she had used to make the first Santo costume if she couldn't transfer the letters from her own shirt, which was still around somewhere. Pat had gray sweatpants, which would work as baseball pants. And they should be able to locate the remaining items on Central Ave. without too many stops. They found football socks at Modell's that would double as baseball socks, and Mo located a black onesie in the youth section at Kohl's, to which she could easily attach a tail. "I'll easily attach to your tail," Pat muttered, back at home, as Mo scowled over her sewing box.

The cat outfit was soon complete besides footwear. Mo ended up in black Adidas sandals, which somehow reminded her of the titular cat in *My Cat Yugoslavia*, though he was a white cat and probably too discerning for Adidas sandals. Maybe it was just the idea of a cat wearing shoes. The sandals would work for hanging out at a party, but she'd have to figure out something more robust to wear over the feet of the suit for running around Crestwood on Tuesday.

The costumes survived Saturday's festivities without incident, though Mo was still brushing unspecified chip or Cheeto dust off the cat onesie on Sunday. She was also glad that the rain had held off till this morning, as it had been pouring ever since. It was a good day to catch up on writing at home, though she did have to drop off Pat for the final Blind Giants practice before their show next Saturday. Extending the weekend's cat theme, Mo had driven him to Big Cat Studios, but was relieved that Don ZT would be taking him home after practice, so she didn't have to go back out. She felt extra guilty that everyone had to travel to practice in this weather, as Blind Giants had rescheduled from their usual Tuesday night arrangement due to the impending Halloween adventure. Pat was working 8-6 this week, which would have been a perfect week to set up practice; instead, it left him available for their Halloween mission on Tuesday.

Rain pounded the roof of the apartment. Mo wrote for a while, then took a break to do abs and eat dinner. She squeezed an applesauce pack while microwaving a burrito, looked at the weather widget on her phone. Luckily this looked like a single day deluge, and clear skies were in the forecast for Tuesday night.

"You should have turned there," Pat admonished a moment too late. It was Halloween night, and they were approaching the neighborhood of Ryan Marnell and David Eckley.

"Thanks for letting me know," Mo sarcastically replied. "It's OK—I can go around the block." She pulled over to look at the map on her phone. The neighborhood was a mess of one-ways and diagonal intersections, so her confidence may have been premature. Then again, it didn't matter where they parked, as all they had to go on was "Crestwood Ave., near the library."

After three right turns, they ended up back on Pennsylvania Avenue, at the bottom of the neighborhood. "It looks like Crestwood splits off Pennsylvania, so we might as well park down here. So no one sees us showing up in a car like I'm old enough to drive," Mo joked. She executed a quick U-turn and lined up the car between two driveways on the side of the road where cars were parked. The other side of the road was just woods and then the Bronx River Parkway.

Mo felt a thrill of apprehension as she locked the car and dunked her purse into the trunk, stowing only the essentials in the pockets under her cat costume. Even if they didn't manage to procure any vital information tonight, she would have a thorough opportunity to examine the region where Ryan Marnell had lived and played—all under the darkness of Halloween night.

The plan was to proceed like normal trick-or-treaters, and then if anyone seemed especially friendly, or looked like longtime residents, Mo would ask if they knew of a family called the Marnells, and if they still lived in the area. If the hosts gave any indication of where on Crestwood Avenue the Marnells had resided, that would narrow down the trick or treating radius.

Then, if Mo and Pat encountered the Marnells' immediate neighbors, or even the family themselves, they would figure out the best way forward, based on the receptivity of their hosts. Mo had already accidentally bothered the mom of one dead guy and wanted to ensure a more nuanced approach here. If Ryan had any siblings, for example, they might be more likely to remember specifics about his friends and who was into what types of bands, compared to older relatives.

If they found the Marnells' section of the street, perhaps they'd also ask after David Eckley. Christine's warning resounded in Mo's brain about not trying to contact him under any circumstances, though this pronouncement made the prospect all the more appealing to Pat. Mo was also hoping to find someone who knew Max Malkin, whose parents still lived in "Yonkers," but Yonkers was 20 square miles and there was no indication he had lived in the same neighborhood as Marnell and Eckley. If he had been a friend of Indignation, from the neighborhood or otherwise, no one seemed to remember him.

They had decided to start on the west side of Crestwood Avenue, walking north, and then if no sufficient information had been gleaned, walk back down and inquire at the houses on the other side. As they went,

Becky McAuley

Mo also kept an eye out for mailboxes or any other clue to the identity of each house's inhabitants. So far, as they started towards where Crestwood Avenue began, a few of the houses had mailboxes with names on them, but most only had house numbers. This was an interesting neighborhood: mostly average-sized houses with a few elegant Victorians mixed in. It was an atmospheric place to spend Halloween, Mo reflected, fighting off trepidation about who they might encounter.

Depending on the duration of each visit, Mo hoped they would also make it to the Crestwood Library, which was around the corner on Thompson Street. "Do you think they do trick-or-treating at the library?"

"What, are you obsessed with librarians asking what grade you're going into?"

They trooped up the stairs of the first house on Crestwood: a Colonial with a tidy porch enshrouded in spider and ghost decor. The house was set back from the street, so Mo had plenty of time to prepare to encounter their inhabitants. But when a middle-aged woman opened the door, Mo froze, accepted the candy, and backed out before asking any questions. Pat looked mildly annoyed, but Mo made a joke about needing to get warmed up and into character, and they continued towards a red house, its front yard bordered by a stone wall, that looked entirely too quaint for suburban Yonkers.

The owners invited them in. "Happy Halloween!" Mo began. "You wouldn't happen to know ..." but she couldn't finish the sentence.

"... how many bites did it take you to chew your fuckin arm off?" Pat supplied, after a few seconds of quizzical silence, gently placing her wrist in his mouth as he escorted her outside.

"Thanks, B." Mo offered as they hastily withdrew. "I don't know why I'm having so much more trouble asking people questions than I thought I would."

"You always have trouble asking people questions!"

"Yeah, I should have thought of that in advance."

"Well we're here now, so you need to just man the fuck up and ask people about Ryan. And don't touch your face," as Mo moved automatically to touch her face. This had been a problem on Saturday, too, resulting in repeatedly smeared whiskers.

Mo resolved to keep her paws away from her visage, and they headed for the next house, pausing to let an enthusiastic group of locals run past. There were a decent number of kids out on the street, but so far no one had looked askance at Mo and Pat in their subterfuge. The dwellings were growing closer to the street and more modest in size as they went. When the owner of the next house opened the door and held out a basket of mini Reese's, Mo pocketed the candy and silently retreated. She could tell Pat was starting to get annoyed. They had planned not just their night around this, but their entire week, but it still couldn't move her to start asking what she was here to be asking.

The next house was dark. Mo didn't even bother to take candy from the bowl outside the front door; she would leave that for the actual kids who weren't also in the market for information about an obscure late-'80s band. But before they could continue to the fifth house, Pat paused in front of some shrubbery.

"What the fuck am I wasting my time here for if you're not even going to talk to people?"

"I'm not trying to waste your time—"

"Yeah, I know you're not trying to, but you are! We came out here, got all fucking dressed up, I moved band practice, inconvenienced three other people, and you could be at home doing some homework for those classes that we're paying so much fucking money for—" oof, Mo winced— "and instead what the hell are we doing out here!"

"We're trick-or-treating," Mo hissed. "Like you always wanted to. Indignation was just what made us actually do it. So shut the fuck up and get candy with me."

"OK," Pat started walking towards the next house.

"No, not that one, there are too many people!" There was indeed a crowd of multiple families at the front door.

"For fuck's sake!" Pat exploded, startling a Hulk and a Harry Potter on their periphery. "If you're not even going to try to ask questions, I'll do it myself." He stomped off into the street towards the houses on the other side.

"No, you can't!" Mo, abashed and horror-struck, turned to follow. A full-grown adult dressed like Ron Santo asking aggressive questions on Halloween with no faux adolescent accessory in sight? She could see this ending badly.

Pat shook her off and resumed his course. He was turning around to ask if she was coming or not when Mo looked up and saw, on the porch of the house across the street, something far more chilling than any manufactured frights they had encountered thus far. She froze, then bolted instinctively back down Crestwood Avenue, Pat in pursuit once he noticed that she was gone.

In high school track, Mo's favorite event had been the 800. She would run the mile or even the dreaded two-mile when pressed into service, but the 800 was her preference and specialty. The 800 was technically a sprint, if too long to plausibly be one, which Mo realized later was the best possible training for working in public relations or trying to get to your train in Grand Central when you were forever running a few minutes late. Legs churning, cat tail streaming, she galloped down Crestwood Ave.

Pat had oscillated between managing small bookstores and real

Becky McAuley

estate marketing before the recession forced him out and into college. But in high school, he had briefly worked at Barnes & Noble. Mo had heard two stories about this experience: the time he spotted Charlie Benante perusing the music magazines, and the time he executed an enthusiastic tackle of a would-be shoplifter. (Not simultaneously.) Tonight Pat managed to replicate a gentler version of the celebrated tackle of yore, bringing Mo down on a leaf pile just past Hartmann Place.

"The fuck is the matter with you!?" he demanded. This was a common refrain in their Overlook Street home, yet not one previous uttered in a leaf pile. They stared at each other amidst the leaves, now flattened from the takedown of a 117-pound human cat. Pat looked nonplussed, his earnest face telegraphing a mix of frustration and genuine concern. That, and the complicated emotions associated with his realization that Mo looked pretty hot as a cat. "Now are you going to tell me what's going on?"

"On the porch of that house ..." Mo trailed off. "I'll tell you in the car. But we have to get out of here." She dusted herself off—outlier leaves clinging to her onesie—and started trotting south towards where they had parked. Pat, resigned, turned to follow.

Finally, they saw the Camry waiting in the distance. Mo unzipped the cat getup and dug for the clicker in the pocket of the running shirt she was wearing beneath.

"OK, now are you going to tell me what you saw in that window?" Pat inquired once they were inside the car.

Only then did Mo describe what she thought she had seen and had freaked her out so thoroughly. The man standing on the porch looked identical to what Max Malkin would look like in 30 years. But the mailbox in front read "Eckley."

On the following day, the post-Halloween hangover was palpable for many, even straight edge kids who had merely stayed up too late and been tackled into a leaf pile, protected only by a cat costume and a couple of mildly crushed Reese's. Mo now regretted having signed up for a Wednesday night colloquium, even one with an author she wanted to see, as she had devoured Lindsay Clongarden's memoir the summer before. Though she'd had no idea she would be up so late on Halloween, more due to the fear, intrigue, and rumination on the Eckley situation and less due to the length of the mission itself.

Either way, this was going to require some coffee. Thankful for the sunshine and the satisfying clonk of the CFA door behind her, she busted out into the West Chelsea afternoon, heading for the new bodega on the corner. Bodega iced coffee acquired, she dialed Pat to see if she could catch him on his afternoon break. He had already left that morning when she wrenched herself out of bed in time to gallop up the hill to the 8:05 train,

Lost Indignation

one of many CFA associates staggering in after nine post-Halloween.

"Well, there are a bunch of explanations," Pat mused as she turned north on 10th Ave., picking right up where they had left off last night.

"Each more improbable than the next," Mo groused. The list of theories they had discussed last night, of why the man in the Eckley window looked so much like Max Malkin, had grown to include:

1. Pat: Mr. Malkin, if he exists, was having an affair with Mrs. Eckley, causing him to be on the porch of the Eckley home as he was leaving. (But on *Halloween*? Mo snorted, in response to that one. Plus this guy was standing on the porch looking like he owned it. He probably did.)

2. Mo: Mr. Malkin *married* Mrs. Eckley after both couples divorced, or their partners otherwise left the picture.
Pat: Wouldn't that have been the talk of the neighborhood though? Christine would have said something when she was telling us about the street. Mrs. Malkin would have been her potential stepmother-in-law.

3. Mo: Mr. Eckley had a second secret family: the Malkins.
Pat: Same as above, though that might explain why David is so fucked up.

4. Pat: The Eckleys and Malkins are somehow related: a reasonable estimation in Westchester.
Mo: But why wouldn't Max have mentioned being, like, Eckley's cousin when we met him? Instead of just saying he was friends with Indignation? Plus, the person in the Eckley house looked *exactly like* an older Max Malkin.

5. Mo: Eckley's and Malkin's dads just look similar in the way of Brett Gardner looking like Todd Frazier.
Pat: The most plausible theory yet, provided the Malkins actually exist.

They'd stayed up till nearly 2 a.m. concocting these theories. At least they now knew the spelling of David Eckley's last name.

"I just can't believe that 'Max Malkin' might actually be David Eckley," Mo snorted, passing the coffee cart by 20th Street and ascending the metal stairs to the High Line. On top of the late night and dehydration, she was also feeling the effects of the leaf pile capture. But after thinking about the Malkin/Eckley situation all day, this was now her prevailing theory. "Like, why would he go to all that trouble and make up a whole persona just to sell me a videotape? And why did he even bring the tape to New York with him in the first place? Does he carry that shit around on every business trip to entrap gullible hardcore kids?"

"I have no fucking idea," Pat exhaled. "But I want to smack the shit out of him for coming up with some elaborate plot to trick my wife."

"I don't think I was the intended target though. We don't think he read the Warzone article in *Gratitude*; he just saw the post about Warzone and Altercation and made that comment about the riffs. And I don't think he even knew I was female until we showed up in the park. It's just like ... why make up all this ridiculous shit? Like if the Indignation songs are really that good, why not just pretend he's responsible for the Indignation songs, rather than sell people a videotape of a different band while pretending to be a different person."

"He's trying to change the perception," Pat opined. "Though now my perception is that he's a piece of shit."

"Fair," Mo agreed. "Though if he thought he's going to get away with this, he doesn't know us. Or any other hardcore kids. People love getting to the bottom of mysteries."

"That's one thing when it's twenty-year-old-you looking for some obscure New Breed band type shit, since those guys all ended up being good dudes. This guy ... I don't want you going out of your way to interact with him again."

"We are going to have to confront him at some point," Mo continued.

"Not you, though. Eckley seems dangerous. Definitely some cluster B tendencies. If anyone has to talk to him, I'll handle it."

"Thanks, my love. I never knew that being married to you could be so useful."

"Get home early tonight and I'll show you useful."

"You don't have to say get home early anymore! I'm always home early now that I have school!" There were still lapses when neither of them remembered her new schedule, which, while still arduous, was overall still too good to be true. "Though I have colloquium at 6:00 and then I need to finish my story for tomorrow." This was the story she was most excited about so far, based on an incident she had witnessed from their old apartment when she watched someone throw mysterious items into the trash. In her story, this had morphed into a narrator witnessing someone throwing away a bunch of maps and then seeking to uncover the context of their disposal.

"Yo, let me run, my fifteen minutes are almost up, and I gotta make sure Jonathan doesn't burn the place down." There were at least five kids named Jonathan at Pat's school, representing every racial group, and they were uniformly diabolical, so Mo wasn't sure which one he was referring to.

While walking home from colloquium later that night, Mo realized she had never checked out any of the Ministry of Fear material. Somehow that hadn't seemed as urgent, once they realized that the videotape didn't have any Indignation riffs to be matched up with the Ministry of Fear tunes. She resolved to look on Discogs when she got home.

After heating up some leftover pasta, Mo searched Discogs for Ministry of Fear. There were a few bands with similar names, but it was clear which one she was looking for, based on the very '90s font and cover art of their main release. There were five copies for sale of their CD, *Fear Itself*, which also had the 7" material at the end. That was convenient, since she had no idea which of their stuff was supposed to sound like the Indignation songs. What had ShadowOOT said in the original thread and PMs about the riffs? She opened a new tab and pulled up the Controlled board.

Mo clicked the link to open her private messages, but the most recent one was from a guy in the UK asking about her zines back in August. Where the hell were the initial messages with Max Malkin? Backtracking to the zine thread, she saw his initial post was now listed under "Deleted User" rather than ShadowOOT. Fuck! When had he deleted his account, apparently wiping out all their PMs along with it? Now she had no contact info for this guy and no proof that they'd ever met, besides Pat's memory and the tape. But with his account active or not, ordering the Ministry of Fear CD was the next logical step. There was one available for $8.49 (the most expensive one was $14). Mo hastily completed the order, then hurried into the living room to update Pat on the demise of ShadowOOT's account.

"That is fucking weird," Pat agreed. "I wonder when he deleted it? Right after meeting us, when he realized the tape was messed up?"

"I have no idea, though I could go back and look at when his last post was? Like even if his username doesn't exist anymore, it would still say 'Deleted User'." Though Mo knew that his last post would be the one in the zine thread and that his main purpose on the board, for whatever reason, had been to interest someone in that tape and the intersection of Indignation and Ministry of Fear. "At least I ordered the Ministry of Fear CD. Maybe that will give me some fresh inspiration for who to ask about this shit. Or about if David Eckley and Max Malkin are the same person."

"Or maybe there's someone you can ask at the benefit on Saturday."

Becky McAuley

Chapter 9
1994

Getting punched in the face was not high on the list of how David Eckley would have opted to spend a Sunday, but an oddly fortuitous blow set off a chain of events that would dominate the second half of his decade. One Sunday in November 1994, Eckley had driven up to the American Legion in Haverhill to hand out flyers at an Overcast show. His band Prior Restraint was playing a show next month at The Red Barn in North Andover, and while he wasn't familiar with the openers on the Haverhill show, it seemed like the type of kids who might want to check out his band too.

Not much had changed for Eckley after graduating from college the year before. He was still living in Boston and still singing for Prior Restraint, which had formed during his senior year. It wasn't that he was unhappy with his band or his job, but he also wasn't receiving enough recognition in either forum.

When Eckley arrived at the show in Haverhill, he realized he didn't know anyone there. His initial flyering attempts were met with ennui, or whatever the less sophisticated hardcore version of that was. At least one guy in a Bruins shirt had heard of his band, though he didn't look too excited about what he'd heard.

When the second band, Magnitude of Devastation, had started their set, it was clear that the Bruins shirt dude was there to represent for them, and/or to alienate as many people as possible while underscoring his own aggression. Eckley didn't know much about these guys, except that they were from New Hampshire (due to a comment shouted over the intro) and that they were pretty heavy. He'd moved up front toward the action, but was soon getting bumped into by this Bruins guy, either accidentally or on purpose. Who the fuck did this guy think he was, moshing repeatedly into David Eckley? Two could play this game: the next time this guy came his way, he shoved him just a little harder than usual, then burst into the pit himself. This lasted about five seconds until he felt a foot meet his back. As he turned around, the Bruins guy and some longhaired dude began dragging him outside.

Just after they passed through the door into the parking lot, the longhaired guy let go of him, and Eckley felt a fist connect with his nose as he fell to the ground. By the time he got up, the Bruins shirt dude was already walking away, back inside to watch the rest of the Magnitude of Devastation set, which Eckley would have also liked to do if he hadn't just been moshed and punched.

"Don't try and come around our shows if you can't handle how we dance!" his assailant yelled over his shoulder. "And by the way," he added almost as an afterthought, "your band fuckin' sucks!"

Sputtering and stunned, Eckley continued to slink toward the car. Safely inside, he locked the doors and patted his bloody nose with a Dunkin' Donuts napkin as he turned the key in the ignition. His nose felt potentially broken, but he wasn't going to stop and check until he put some distance between his nose and the show.

But as he retreated down Route 93 to the city, he realized the dude was right. Prior Restraint wasn't very good. Not that it was his fault. In his next project he'd need to ensure greater creative control. Eckley had the soul of a frontman, but he was also a guitar player. Maybe he needed to contribute more in this area, give the guys something better to go on so they didn't end up derided in a third-rate suburb.

It should be easy enough to gently dissolve the band. Their guitarist was graduating from Suffolk in the spring, and the bassist never seemed to have time to practice. Were the rest of the guys as over it as he was? If not, he just needed to make them believe they had adopted that stance independently.

Waking up for work on Monday, Eckley hoped the swelling had subsided, but it still looked like he'd been punched in the face. Eckley was working an uninspiring business development role at this internet company in the Back Bay, attempting to do as little work as possible while waiting for something more exciting to happen. But he still attempted to cultivate a smooth professional persona and ingratiate himself with his superiors. As his nose didn't look so professional today, he opted for his regular glasses rather than contacts, which didn't entirely mask the problem but made it slightly less visible.

"Damn!" the office manager exclaimed when Eckley staggered in. What happened to you?

"Boxing," he heard himself answer. "I won't be going back."

As he had predicted, the rest of the guys from Prior Restraint didn't put up much resistance when he suggested taking a break and made up an excuse of why they would have to drop off the North Andover show. There was no use exposing themselves to potential further violence or ridicule in case the Magnitude of Devastation entourage returned to the Red Barn. So there were already thoughts brewing in the brain of David Eckley regarding his next project when he ran into Mark Ledesma.

The Saturday before Thanksgiving, Eckley was walking out of Lodato's Pizza in Allston, having just finished a few slices, when he saw a familiar figure coming towards the shop. It was that guy Mark who worked at the Newbury Comics in Harvard Square. Eckley recognized his jacket and unruly dark hair and remembered that he had once seen him playing bass in some band a few years back. In a split-second decision, Eckley abruptly changed course, retreated into Lodato's, and rejoined the back of the line, so that when Mark opened the door moments later, he was waiting in line behind David Eckley.

Eckley turned to greet his calculatedly proximate line neighbor. "Hey, you're Mark, right? I'm David. I remember seeing you play in ... Disregard, at Bunratty's." Whew. Disregard. The name had come to him just in time.

"Hey, you sure did!" Ledesma looked pleased to be remembered.

"Are you still playing shows?" Eckley figured the answer would be no, but that it would be a good segue to his next question.

"Nah, we broke up in April."

"Ah that sucks, dude. I'm actually in the process of starting something new. You play bass, right?"

"Yup. Bass and a little guitar."

They had reached the counter. Thankfully, the guy taking his order did not remark on Eckley's double dinner.

While waiting for and then eating their pizza, Eckley and Mark continued to chat about their respective recent musical experiences. Mark was disillusioned by much about his experience in Disregard, from the singer's flakiness to the guitar player's lack of commitment to the drummer playing in two other bands. That all sounded fine to Eckley, who was also hoping to start a more serious project, featuring only competent and dedicated musicians.

"I've been working on some songs," Eckley commented offhandedly as they were throwing away their trash. "I'm heading home to New York for Thanksgiving, but we should get together when I'm back in town."

"For sure," Mark looked excited about this prospect. "I'm glad I ran into you."

"Yeah, what a coincidence," Eckley marveled, reveling in the fact that no one could disprove this characterization.

But his triumphant recollections of the encounter started to dissipate when he acknowledged that he would now have to come up with the songs he had mentioned. Eckley considered himself a talented guitarist, but he wanted something compelling with which to ensnare Mark Ledesma and future members. So far he hadn't had much time to think, due to the busy short work week and traveling home for Thanksgiving.

Mr. Eckley, being British, had never been into the American holiday, but now that he was married to Jean, it was more of a celebratory occasion. David's new stepmom was a kind, effervescent nurse who was about ten years younger than his dad. David wanted to love his stepmother, and he supposed he was beginning to, as much as he was capable of loving anybody. He recognized how much happier they were together than his parents had ever been, at least when he had been old enough to notice. Still, he tried to think about the situation as little as possible, so as not to dwell on Jean's attempts to replace (or not replace) his mom. Then again, he tried to think about his mom as little as possible too.

On Friday morning, Jean had started gently joking about some of their plans for the house. Unlike many empty nesters who would have considered downsizing—at least before climbing multiple flights of stairs became impractical—they were incrementally but steadily optimizing their space, from painting to redecorating to replanting the backyard. In the spirit of these modifications, Jean had brought up moving his stuff out of his childhood bedroom and upstairs to the little room on the third floor which was a rarely used storage room, across the hall from his dad's study. "Of course, I wouldn't have done it without asking you," she cajoled, "but you don't come to visit us very often, and your room would make such a lovely guest room."

"I don't need to come *visit*, it's still my own fucking *house*," Eckley had wanted to snarl, or maybe retort that there was nothing wrong with turning the other extra second floor bedroom into a guest room, but he played along. He had assumed that his room overlooking the street would be his forever, but he tried to hide his discomfort and acquiesced to the plan. He'd still have a place to sleep and to keep his childhood things, and Jean was right—he did come home less often. Better to keep the peace and keep himself in a position of power to object to more egregious changes in the future.

Eckley was in town through Sunday, so he'd have plenty of time to start moving his things to the third floor, and Jean and his dad could do the rest. He wasn't worried about them moving stuff like his old clothes or furniture, but wanted to make sure that they didn't toss any of his musical ephemera. He had only taken so much with him to Boston, due to the size of his dorm freshman year. So there was still a prodigious stash of cool shit remaining in his old bedroom in Crestwood. Some of it would never have a place in his Boston life, like the Power Structure demo, or the obsessive letters from Allison Syzmanski, one of the many girls who had been in love with him in high school, but there was probably—

He opened a shoebox, and froze. Inside the box were nine copies of the Indignation demo tape.

Eckley plucked a copy out of the box and shoved it greedily into his old cassette player. How could he have forgotten that these tapes were still here? Ryan had given him about 25 tapes in return for his help in financing the recording last minute after that stupid fucking Matt Zimmer kid didn't show up, but since then he had sold or given away the others, including the one that he had brought with him to Boston University. During his years in college, Eckley had moved on from secretly wishing he was a member of Indignation to meeting the right people (and his own band members) and playing in various bands. Hardcore had moved on,

Lost Indignation

too, from straightforward bands like Indignation to the metal influence that was way more interesting to David Eckley.

Eckley smiled as his youthful intro at the start of the tape led into the Indignation theme song. He had forgotten how good these songs were, though not so good that anyone else was likely to remember them, especially in Boston, where no one had heard of Indignation. And not so good that they couldn't be subtly modified into a heavier style. Here, in this box, was the genesis for the material he would show to Ledesma when he was back in town.

If the Marnells still lived across the street, David would have worried that Ryan would somehow know what he was up to, but Ryan's mom had moved away between their freshman and sophomore years of college, and he hadn't seen Ryan since last year. Whatever. It wasn't his fault that Ryan hadn't let him in the band and hadn't tried harder to re-form Indignation (with Eckley as part of the new lineup) after three members quit. They could have done so much more with these songs, resulting in recognition for everyone, yet Indignation ended up just another forgotten band. All the better for Eckley, who could now give these songs the second life they deserved and position himself as their rightful author.

To ensure that their origin remained obscure, he granted the others a watery grave in the Bronx River the next day, after packing one tape to bring back to Boston. And when Jean asked if he'd moved everything he wanted to his new room upstairs, he was able to confirm that he had.

Things began to take shape in early '95, when Eckley met up to jam with Mark Ledesma in his basement. Mark liked the songs and expressed interest in assembling the rest of a band.

"Now we just need a guitarist!"

"You wouldn't want to play guitar?" Ledesma clarified. Eckley in fact had been bringing his guitar to demonstrate the songs.

"Nah. I mean of course I want to help write the songs and shit, and I could do both until we get someone on guitar. I'm just better as a singer."

While they may have still needed a full-time guitarist, at least Ledesma had a lead on a drummer, which was always the most difficult band component to acquire.

"I know this drummer who swims—this guy Bill. He quit smoking weed when he had a kid, and he still drinks, but you know what he does now? He goes swimming! He's probably in better shape than any of us." Mark laughed. "And it sounds like he's bored and wants to play in a band again."

"I like the idea of this swimming drummer," Eckley replied. "Sounds like he knows how to stay out of trouble." Except for the kid part, he almost added. He also doubted that anyone in hardcore was in better shape than himself.

Becky McAuley

Mark had also heard of a friend of a friend who might also be interested in playing guitar, this guy Tyler Vossen, who Eckley also knew peripherally, but they weren't sure about him.

"That guy Tyler," Mark cautioned, "He's a good guitarist, but he's had some drug problems in the past. I think he's straight edge now though."

"I don't know about the drug thing, if I want that in the band. Or a straight edge kid!"

"Hey, he's been doing really well lately. I just wanted you to know the full picture. Maybe we should have him try out and see what we think?"

So Tyler Vossen was invited to practice, after talking it over with Bill, who had turned out to be a perfect fit. Not only was he professional and even-tempered to the point of being almost alarmingly calm (maybe it was the swimming), but he was also a hard-hitting drummer and technically adept. His own personal listening veered more towards the metal side of things, but that was what they needed for this project, rather than some youth crew kid who couldn't rock a double bass pedal.

Vossen was a shy, prickly, occasionally funny dude. At first Eckley couldn't get a read on him, as he was mostly quiet and serious, but would occasionally interject such a cranky comment or hilarious quip that would bust them all up into laughter. He was working at a grocery store and seemed to be taking care of himself. Eckley was relieved that he also didn't appear to be one of those showy straight edge kids, just quietly committed to his new sober life (though he did refer to himself as straight edge).

Most importantly, Vossen was a good guitarist and easy to collaborate with. He was open to other people's ideas and able to build on them, and they all voted to let him join this band, still unnamed. Eckley carefully introduced some old Indignation riffs in their new downtuned form, and Vossen expanded on them to create full songs. Eckley soon realized that he liked having this guy around, to the point where when his current roommate decided to move out, he asked Vossen if he was interested in taking the room.

Vossen had mentioned his lease was ending and agreed to move in. Eckley would have preferred to have Mark Ledesma as a roommate, who was more easygoing and fun, but he lived in Mission Hill with three other guys and seemed happy with that arrangement. Also, living with Tyler would allow Eckley to keep an eye on him, not precisely due to the fear that he would break edge and relapse, but also to ensure that he was making the type of choices that would result in being a reliable member of the band.

And Vossen ended up being a pretty good roommate who stayed in his room and kept to himself. But Eckley couldn't figure out why they had so far managed to live in the same home without discord, though

Lost Indignation

at practice he and Vossen were the ones most likely to clash. Perhaps it was because Bill and Mark were such laid back guys, or because Eckley and Vossen were most susceptible to creative disagreements during the writing process, since they were both guitarists trying to shape the musical direction of the band. Eckley was keenly aware that he should back off in most creative disagreements, besides the ones where Indignation riffs were involved, for the sake of the long-term life of the project.

For that reason, he tried to delicately introduce a potential name for the band. Eckley wanted them to be called Ministry of Fear, after the Graham Greene book. Mr. Eckley was a big Graham Greene guy, and Eckley the younger had sort of inherited his proclivities. Though he often insinuated he'd read more Graham Greene than he actually had, when Ryan had been the one who read the books and tried to sell Eckley on the plots.

Bill initially thought it was too close to the band Ministry, but then acquiesced. Mark claimed he was on board too, as he said it sounded fucking cool and fit their direction as a band, though he joked that he might withdraw support if he came up with anything better. Vossen, for whatever reason, didn't like it, though all his one-word band name ideas were terrible. So they became Ministry of Fear, mostly because no one could come up with anything else that stuck and they wanted to get a demo out and start playing shows. That was the advantage of being the smartest person in the band, Eckley reflected: you could end up getting your way if no one else had the ingenuity to find another solution.

But being the smartest guy in the band didn't prevent everyone else from doing stupid shit that could still fuck things up for all of you.

* * *

In the aftermath of what would have been their first New York show, Eckley wondered if he could have done anything differently. Or was it fate intervening to make sure no one in New York heard them play, unlikely as it would have been for anyone to recognize the original Indignation material underneath their songs? Either way, there was nothing he could do now, besides think back over every detail of what was supposed to be their NYC debut.

It was October 1998, and they were on their way to New York to play a Sunday matinee at the Wetlands with All Out War, Fahrenheit 451, and a few other local bands. James from Self Alarm had gotten them on the show, to return the favor after Eckley had gotten him a show in Boston in July. Eckley couldn't wait to introduce New York to Ministry of Fear via a Sunday matinee at the Wetlands, one of the best clubs for hardcore shows in New York at the time.

Becky McAuley

Ledesma was driving. You would think he would be a more aggressive driver, being a native Masshole and all, but he was always fucking cautious, and this trip seemed to be driving with even more care than usual. Vossen, after breaking edge last year and briefly backsliding into addiction, claimed to have touched no substances for two weeks, which might have been true, based on his exceedingly bad temper during the ride so far. And Bill Cole, the swimming drummer, just sat in the back and slept, as usual. Not a bad travel companion to have, Eckley conceded, as Bill was currently the only one in the band not driving him crazy.

Over the last few years, Ministry of Fear had made serious strides as a band. Once they'd solidified their lineup, recruiting Vossen and then finding and ejecting a troublesome second guitarist, the writing process had taken off. First, they'd released a four song demo in the fall of '95. The two best demo songs, Eckley pretended not to realize, were reworked Indignation songs, just downtuned for contemporary taste and embellished with additional guitar work. It was oddly exhilarating to be like hey guys, check out this riff I came up with, when the riff in question was in fact just an Indignation song he'd reworked the night before. Eckley always made sure to ration the "discovery" of these riffs to always have something to fall back on if their writing process got stuck later.

Consequently, only two songs on the demo were based on tracks from the Indignation demo. And when it came time to record their 7", *Suspension of Disbelief*, another Indignation tune slipped in, but with its riffs broken apart as the foundation for two new tracks in addition to the two demo songs that were re-recorded for the 7". This left only two songs from the Indignation demo yet to pilfer, though he thought there might be more that had remained unrecorded but had been captured on that videotape that he'd liberated from Andrew Rompanelli's collection. But when he'd recently tried to rewatch it, he couldn't find their set from that benefit show in Mount Vernon, which he swore was on there, and the sound quality was so bad that he was unsure how much he could have gleaned anyway. At the spot where he thought Indignation would be, there was a Power Structure set—was he remembering wrong and Indignation had played after them? He hadn't had a chance to study it further, as Vossen had walked into the apartment while he was fast-forwarding, and he wouldn't have wanted to un-pause it on a song that sounded exactly like one of their new tunes.

The Indignation-based songs were a hit and carried the rest of the demo as a respectable first release, garnering good reviews in a bunch of zines, including the holy grail that was *In Effect* Fanzine. On the strength of the demo and then the 7", Ministry of Fear had gotten booked for an assortment of Boston-area shows, then started venturing further into Connecticut, Rhode Island, New Hampshire, and Western Mass. They played Albany and Portland, central New Jersey, and Sea Sea's near Scranton, PA. There were plans to go to Canada. Eckley wondered how soon they'd be ready for a real tour and if all of them would be able to get off from work at the same time. He and Bill were the only ones with reliable Monday-Friday schedules: Ledesma worked in a restaurant and Vossen always seemed to be bouncing from one job to another and doing the bare minimum to make rent. And Bill had his family commitments, on top of his day job as a union ironworker. At least Eckley and the others were blessedly unencumbered in that regard. So far, they had managed to practice regularly and to get together early in '98 to record *Fear Itself*, their debut LP. Eckley hoped they'd continue to play more out-of-state shows to showcase that record and the three-way split they released with Self Alarm and Ashamed of Mistake a few months prior. The split featured one of the tunes from the new LP: of course the one based on the last available Indignation foundation, though their CD version of the full-length also had the 7" at the end.

When they got offered the matinee at the Wetlands, Eckley decided that was an opportunity they couldn't pass up. They'd played Long Island earlier in the year with Self Alarm and Home 33, but had never taken the stage in NYC proper. Eckley wanted today's show to be extra special, even if it was shaping up to be anything but.

Eckley wondered if Ryan Marnell would be there, then tried to banish the thought from his mind. After all, Marnell hadn't turned up at the Fateful Encounter show in Port Chester last month, where Eckley was just along for the road trip, though he'd heard that Marnell had been sighted at another 7 Willow Street show, trying to sell paintings out of his car or some shit. Apparently he'd moved on from hardcore and was trying to make it as an artist, if "trying to make it" was how one could describe his onetime best friend, who had experienced mental illness setbacks over the last few years and had even been homeless at one point. David had tried to keep his distance, both due to Ryan's erratic behavior the last few times he'd seen him and, lately, to put some space between the Ministry of Fear songs and the guy whose riffs he had lifted (no—had *perfected*). He had unconsciously and then consciously avoided agreeing to a Ministry of Fear show in the New York area, perhaps concerned that Ryan would be there and hear the similarities for himself. Though he acquiesced to the Long Island show earlier that summer, as Eckley figured there was less of a risk of running into anyone who knew the songs.

Finally, they were pulling up in front of the Wetlands, the charm of each other's company having long since worn off during the ride. Ledesma ejected the remaining members, their merch and their gear, and pulled around the corner to look for parking. Eckley and the others headed towards the side door, where James had mentioned they would load in.

But as they were hauling their stuff, Vossen managed to bump into a guy who was heading out the door.

"Gotta watch yourself there, dude," sniped the dude who Vossen had nearly bodied with a box of merch. He had short brown hair and an earring and didn't look particularly welcoming.

Vossen, being Vossen, came back at him with some smart-ass comment that immediately solidified the guy's malevolent cast of eye.

"He didn't mean anything by it," Eckley automatically interjected.

"Or what if I fucking did?" Vossen snarled. Jesus, this was exactly what they needed as their very first interaction at the club. Eckley's heart sank further when, after they had finished loading in, he saw Vossen's antagonist sit down behind the merch table for Unknown Quantity, the band who was scheduled to play right after Ministry of Fear.

"Fuck, I think that was one of the guys from Unknown Quantity," he muttered at Vossen as he hustled him towards the downstairs bar. What if Ministry of Fear had to set up their merch right next to them? How the fuck had they gotten off on the wrong foot so quickly?

Downstairs, they found and greeted James from Self Alarm. Eckley was relieved that Vossen decided to have a beer. The dude seemed to be in a different stage of recovery nearly every week, but Eckley didn't give a shit about his recovery and it would be easier for everyone today if Vossen would lighten up a little. They were still at the bar with James when the first band, Starve, went on upstairs. Eckley realized he should mention what had happened upstairs, to gauge what type of trouble they had just made for themselves.

"What's the deal with these Unknown Quantity guys?"

"What do you mean?" James looked concerned.

"This guy here," Eckley indicated Vossen, who was now on his second beer, "got in a very slight spat with a dude who plays in Unknown Quantity. Or is one of their boys at least."

"Shit, which one of them did he piss off? I mean you don't want to mess with any of them, but they're varying degrees of fucked up. The drummer's alright, but he's a black belt in something. Nick, the guitarist, is the craziest dude in that band. He once threw Vito from Ashamed of Mistake into the Long Island Sound! At this show out in Throggs Neck ... anyway. The bassist is OK. And Jason," he angled his head at a gigantic bald guy making his way towards the stairs, "he's basically harmless. Though I still wouldn't want to cross any of those dudes. Which one did he manage to piss off?"

"Uhh, it was a short guy with brown hair, and an earring?" Eckley verified, praying this was the unnamed drummer or bassist, only somewhat mollified by one of the largest humans he'd ever seen being pronounced as relatively harmless.

Lost Indignation

"That's Nick all right," James verified, looking grave. "I'll see what I can do to sort things out," and hurried off.

The next few minutes passed without incident. Eckley found himself caught up in conversation with a Connecticut guy he knew from going to shows at the Anthrax, and then this girl who was trying to tell him about some band photography project she was doing at NYU. While wrapping up the discussion with the NYU girl, just after Starve's set finished upstairs, he saw, lumbering past and significantly more jacked than when he had last encountered him, his old Yonkers friend Warren Yatrofsky. Warren was almost 10 years older than when Eckley had last seen him, but looked double that.

"Warren!" Eckley reached out and tapped him as he went by. After a second, Warren's face lit up and he pulled David into a bro hug.

"David Eckley! Holy shit. How you been?"

"Things are good, I'm in Boston, and my band is playing here today! Ministry of Fear," David specified, in case Warren didn't know. Damn, it felt good to say that his band was playing a show in New York.

"Good shit. Did you catch Starve? They're fucking sick!"

"Nah, we were actually just loading in." And accidentally riling up Unknown Quantity, he almost added.

James's band was up next. Eckley wondered when he'd have a chance to talk to Nick, hopefully before Ministry of Fear's set, in case the dude realized who they were. He looked over at Vossen, who was still at the bar with Mark Ledesma (who was now talking to the NYU girl) a few seats away. Somewhat convinced that Vossen was in good hands, he finished his beer and went upstairs to watch Self Alarm.

But a few songs later, Ledesma was at his elbow. "Yo, Vossen is trying to get weed. I just heard him ask a high school kid if he had any! Some kid who looks like he's not even old enough to be in the club!"

"Jesus. Can he just fucking hang in there for a few more hours until we play? And not start any more shit?"

"What else did he do?"

"Talked shit to one of the dudes in Unknown Quantity, who's playing right after us. So I'm hoping we can keep him away from them and their table. Where did we end up setting up?"

"Uh, right next to Unknown Quantity?" Mark grinned. "Bill's over there now. I'll tell him to keep an eye on things."

What happened next appeared to play out in slow motion. Mark was walking towards the merch tables, but making intermittent progress through the crowd while avoiding the obstacle of the pit. Bill was at the MOF table, but with his head turned the other direction, talking to one of the guys from Starve. There was no one at the Unknown Quantity table, which was to their table's right. At that moment, Vossen, who had apparently snuck upstairs, reached down to grab something from the floor between the two tables. He was unzipping a pocket of a backpack before Eckley realized that he had never seen the bag before, that it was not something that Vossen had brought with them on the trip, and—

A flurry of action erupted in front of the merch area. Nick, the guy with the earring, had appeared out of nowhere, ripped the backpack out of Vossen's grip, and lit him up with a series of quick jabs. Eckley halfheartedly attempted to intervene, without putting himself at too much risk. He didn't want to end up like the day he had gotten punched at the Magnitude of Devastation show. Things were supposed to be different with Ministry of Fear! He grabbed Mark's arm as he moved toward the action, hoping to extricate them both.

Suddenly, a familiar face loomed over them: Warren Yatrofsky. "Get your boy out of here and settle this outside. We don't have enough clubs left to let you assholes ruin this," he gruffly instructed, yoking up Vossen and hustling him out toward the street. Eckley had a wild hope that he would be able to mediate the situation once they had escaped the club.

Their ragged procession made its way outside: Yatrofsky, Vossen, Eckley, Ledesma, with half of Unknown Quantity in pursuit. Nick was still jawing and trying to get at Vossen, undeterred by the bulk of Yatrofsky. Eckley's heart sank. Everyone who was anyone in NYHC seemed to be assembled outside the show. If they escaped grievous harm from Unknown Quantity, he might still expire due to sheer embarrassment.

After conferring with Warren, who apparently knew the Unknown Quantity dudes too, Jason rushed in, towering over both his band and Eckley's. "OK, you can't pull this shit here, first disrespecting my bro and then trying to steal his shit. You have two options: let Nick get in a few clear shots at your boy, which will end with all of you getting your asses kicked, or get him in the van, get him the fuck home, and drop off the show."

Fuck! So much for their NYC debut. It was immediately clear that they would have to cut their losses and leave. James ran outside as soon as the Self Alarm set was over, having seen the situation develop from the stage and having shortened their set due to the kerfuffle. He looked stressed and apologetic, in tacit acknowledgement that the situation was now out of his hands.

Eckley tried one more option. "I'd kick his ass myself if we could still get to play!"

"That's not happening," James said quickly. "I'm sorry it worked out like this, but it's best for you guys to get out of here now in one piece. These guys are from the Bronx, they are crazy fucking dudes. You do not want to mess with them." Eckley didn't mention that Vossen had already messed with them and rued his fatal miscalculation in inciting the ire of a

Bronx band.

Once Vossen had been shunted into the van, Eckley instructed Mark to stand by and make sure he didn't pull any shit, then returned to the club with James and Bill to pick up their stuff. He couldn't decide which role would have put himself in a worse light: staying back at the van with Vossen like a little bitch, or having to return shamefacedly to the club to retrieve their gear. He picked the latter, mostly for a last chance to talk to James and try to patch things up. He couldn't believe that this dude had gone out of his way to book them in New York and then Vossen had ruined it all. Luckily James seemed to understand that things like this happened at hardcore shows, and the show would proceed smoothly once Ministry of Fear had been excised from the lineup, which would now skip right from Self Alarm to Unknown Quantity, as if MOF had never been there at all.

After getting everything out of the club and back into the van, Eckley steeled himself for a silent ride home. He was hoping to go the entire way without speaking to Vossen, if possible. "I'll drive," he spat. Ledesma hopped gratefully out of the driver's seat and circled around to the passenger side. Vossen was in the back with Bill, looking worse for wear after the confrontation. Perhaps it was fortuitous, Eckley realized, that they hadn't brought along any friends to see them play. Though perhaps with a bigger crew, they could have overwhelmed Unknown Quantity and stayed on the show.

After some initial consultations about directions, they drove up Hudson Street in silence. It wasn't until they were on the Cross Bronx Expressway that Vossen asked the question on everyone's mind.

"Are we still a band?" No apology, nothing. Just: "Are we still a band?"

"I don't fucking know!" Eckley exploded, thumping his fist on the steering wheel. "We'll talk about it when we're back." Since fuck, unlike Mark and Bill, he was stuck with Vossen at home too. They would have plenty of time to discuss at home, if Eckley didn't beat the shit out of him first.

"Why the hell did you do that? Try to get into that guy's bag? After you already started shit with him earlier?"

"First off, I wasn't sure whose backpack it was. I knew it was one of those Unknown Quantity dudes, and fuck those dudes anyway. Also, I thought he might have some weed," he added defiantly.

"And you thought the best place to get weed was taking it from a guy you had already pissed off? Who was playing a set right after us? We're not in Boston, we don't know who's who, you can't just go around doing shit like that!"

Vossen didn't even respond or defend himself. Despite his posturing, Eckley was sure he knew he had fucked up.

Becky McAuley

Hours later, they arrived at Mark's house in silence, dropped their stuff in his basement, then split off to their own individual routes home. Vossen was riding with Eckley, who continued the silent treatment until they were looking for parking.

"I think you need to move out. If you tried to steal that guy's weed, how do I know you're not going to steal my shit?"

Vossen protested that he would never steal from Eckley, had never stolen from him in the three years they had been living together, and that it was different trying to take something from a random backpack at an out of town show. But eventually he agreed to move. Last Eckley heard, he was living with that kid Kyle from Fateful Encounter in Mission Hill, though he wasn't going out of his way to ask about Vossen's personal life when he saw him at practice.

And so Ministry of Fear was saved by David Eckley putting some space between himself and Tyler Vossen. They played a couple shows in early '99, but were mostly gearing up for their first real tour in March, a week and a half to Florida and back with Fateful Encounter.

It was a miracle how everything had come together, that they'd all managed to take off from work at the same time and then patch together a decent string of dates. Eckley had handled most of the booking himself and had done a damn good job of it. Conspicuously, (or not so conspicuously, he hoped) there was no New York show.

By sharing gear, they managed to get both bands into one van, though it was a tight fit. Eckley was glad that neither band had a second guitarist and that everyone from his band got along with the Fateful Encounter guys. He could only hope they could say the same by the end of tour.

Most of the FE dudes were pretty chill, particularly Jon Marasco, the singer, and Kevin Brubaker, the guitarist, who were both in their mid-20s. Dave Park, the bassist, was a Korean guy from North Jersey who was going to school at Northeastern. He was an enthusiastic kid who talked more than Jon and Kevin combined, but was easy to get along with overall. Dave loved Brawl Park, that band from Brockton, and while Eckley referred to him as "The Other David," everyone else called him "Brawl," "Brawl Park," or simply "BP."

The drummer, "Wild" Kyle Raubvogel, was another story. Wild Kyle was the original connection between the two bands, as well as Vossen's new roommate. He was one of those straight edge kids who was so unpredictable that you couldn't imagine his behavior if enhanced by any additional substances. There were in fact various rumors that Wild Kyle was *off* his meds, but playing drums for hours a day seemed to keep him somewhat in check. He was a good drummer, if more erratic than

Lost Indignation

the metronomic, heavy hitting Bill Cole, and hopefully his exuberance wouldn't overwhelm what was otherwise a mature group on this tour, compared to the average eight hardcore kids who could be packed into a van.

Their first show was at a VFW hall in northern New Jersey, and they were lucky to crash with the guy who booked the show. From there they headed to a bar called the Crooked Krishna, outside of DC, which was run by a disgruntled former Shelter roadie. Eckley vaguely remembered a story about this guy stiffing Andrew Rompanelli in a video trade, but wasn't about to bring that up on this dude's home turf, especially after the debacle in New York last year. So far, everyone had been remarkably well behaved, Vossen included.

After the Crooked Krishna, they continued to Richmond to play with Striking Distance at Twisters, then to North Carolina. They played a crappy show in Jacksonville, FL that almost no one attended, then rolled into Miami for a Wednesday night show at a bar called Cappy's where they got a surprisingly strong response. And since they made it from Jacksonville to Miami in five hours, they had time to explore the city, skate, and get food before the show. Mark Ledesma spoke Spanish, which ended up being useful in Miami. Eckley only knew a little Portuguese from his mom, and it wouldn't have helped here anyway, or anywhere, unless Ministry of Fear ended up touring in Brazil or Portugal, either of which would be super sick. He tried to put her out of his mind, the way he did whenever he thought about his mom.

There was one part of his past that he wasn't trying to put out of his mind: a casual side quest to reacquire any copies of the Indignation demo still within the possession of Dion Carina. Eckley had it on good authority that Dion Carina had been, if not quite chased out of New York earlier in the decade, then perhaps strongly encouraged to relocate after getting too involved with a girlfriend of one of the Sunset Skins. Last he'd heard, Dion had pivoted to the house music scene and was working as a DJ and restorer of BMX bikes. The bike part was the only thing that surprised Eckley, who had thought he was more of a car guy. And if he still had any copies of the Indignation demo, Eckley was prepared to reacquire and then destroy them accordingly, to sever one more connection between the two bands.

None of the Ministry of Fear or Fateful Encounter guys had any idea who Dion Carina was, but Eckley waited until they were in Miami to mention the errand. Before leaving for tour, he had tried to look up Dion's address on the internet, but gave up when he couldn't easily track it down. The morning after their Miami show, when they were still crashing at the house of Joey from Blackmail Note, Eckley asked to see the phone book. Sure enough, there he was, under Dion Carina. Eckley almost couldn't believe it was that easy. Perhaps Dion's New York problems hadn't followed him to Miami. Well, here was one New York problem who was about to follow him.

Half the guys were hanging out and skating outside, the other half lounging in Joey's kitchen. The only person missing was Mark Ledesma, who had hit it off with some local scenester the night before and crashed at her house per a special invitation. Accounting for a few extra minutes to pick up Mark, they still had a few hours left before they needed to get on the road to Tampa. Eckley realized that he should offhandedly suggest a stop on the way out of town. He asked Joey if he could jump on his computer, then dialed up Dion's address on MapQuest. After picking up Mark, it would only take them about 20 minutes out of their way.

Having rounded up both bands and said their goodbyes, they settled into the van. They reacquired Mark, who looked dazed but ecstatic, and Eckley introduced the idea of their next stop. He had made sure he was in the driver's seat this a.m. "So I heard this guy in Miami might have this demo tape I need," he began nonchalantly. "But I don't want him to know it's me. Rival collector thing, you know? I wouldn't want him to charge me an arm and a leg. So it would be great if one of you could, ah, just go ask him if he still has it. And see if he'll sell it to you. He doesn't even need to know that I'm involved."

"If I do it, what's in it for me?" Wild Kyle piped up from behind him.

"I'll buy you dinner. The next two days. And if he sells you the tape for less than $20, you can keep the change. Deal?"

It was a deal. At the next red light, Eckley passed him a $20 bill.

"Wait, what's the name of the band?"

Eckley hesitated. "Indignation."

A few minutes later, the van was creeping down Dion's block. Eckley parked a few houses before Dion's and directed Kyle to the appropriate dwelling, a ranch house with a garage in the back. Kyle hopped out blithely to execute his mission, but a few minutes later, he was back empty handed.

"What happened?"

Kyle shrugged. "Said he didn't have it anymore." But he had a strange look on his face and Eckley had a feeling he wasn't telling the whole story.

Halfway to Miami, they were stopped at a gas station when Eckley resolved to find out what had really transpired.

"What the hell happened back at Dion's?" he sat down next to Kyle, who was sitting on the curb drinking Surge, which was one of his primary food groups.

"So I go in there, ask him about the demo, and he says he doesn't have it," Kyle began, mirroring his earlier story. "But I could tell he was

Lost Indignation

lying. And I looked up, and right behind him there's this boombox and a bunch of demo tapes and one of the cases said 'Indignation.'"

"No shit," Eckley marveled, wishing that Kyle hadn't given up so easily. "And you wait until now to tell me this?"

"The whole thing was weird. I saw the tape, it was right there, and he either knew that I could see it and didn't give a fuck, or didn't realize. And I didn't think I could grab it and get out of there alive." This was saying a lot, coming from Kyle, who had won various improbable fights despite weighing approximately 140 pounds and being consistently hampered by huge pants. "At least now we know it's there, and what his setup looks like."

"Indeed we do," Eckley agreed. But through the whole second half of tour, through Tampa and Atlanta and Blacksburg, VA (another surprisingly fun show on the campus of Virginia Tech) and Sea Sea's in PA, he couldn't stop thinking about Dion and the tape. Why had he lied about it when the tape was right there? And how could Eckley somehow get it out of his garage forever?

It turned out that one member of Ministry of Fear would be in Miami more than anyone had anticipated. Mark Ledesma, who had no shortage of girls hanging around him in Boston and never seemed to be looking for anything serious, had fallen hard for Zoe Goodman of Miami. A month after meeting her on tour, he had already flown back down to see her and couldn't stop talking about her at practice. Eckley was concerned about their ability to play upcoming shows if Mark was going to put all his time off work towards visiting Zoe, and he hoped the relationship would reach a natural conclusion. But in June, when Mark was still lamenting not having the money to fly down more often, Eckley seized this opportunity.

"Hey, the next time you go," he offered, "I'll pay for your flight, and you only need to do one thing for me while you're there."

Ledesma readily agreed to the strange condition of his trip. Eckley lied and said he was planning to sell the tape to some guy in Germany for an incredible sum, hence the flight offer, but when Ledesma did manage to come back with the demo—"I had to wait all day, but the second he stepped out of the garage, I ran in, snagged it, then booked the fuck out of there"—it offered only temporary relief. What would Dion do when he discovered the demo was missing? And how many more copies were out there, in the hands of people still listening to hardcore in 1999 who might connect the dots? On hardcorewebsite.net, he made a fake username and put out an ambiguous call for copies, buying up one from some guy in Astoria, but the post didn't yield any others.

And while the Miami Indignation heist had been a success, he couldn't ignore that things were intensifying between Mark and Zoe. So when Mark announced one day at band practice that he was moving,

Eckley's heart sank, but he was hardly surprised. He had been hoping that if things got serious, Zoe would move to Boston, as hardcore kids loved to move to Boston from other places. (And then maybe Eckley could someday fuck her too, as she was pretty hot.) But Mark was moving in with Zoe instead. He was tired of the cold weather and the cost of living. Her uncle owned a bunch of restaurants and was getting him a job. He and Zoe were getting an apartment together and a dog. Eckley tried to see Life of Agony-loving, all-black-wearing Mark Ledesma in Miami, and failed. Hopefully he'd be back soon, if they hadn't already moved on.

Ministry of Fear had a month or two to find a new bassist, as they had shows booked for later that fall, but nothing right away. Eckley's first choice was Dave Park. While slightly annoying in an almost Matt Zimmer way, he was an adept bassist and if Eckley had put up with him for an entire tour, he should be able to handle playing in a band with him. But Dave was moving too—to Brooklyn for a new job in Manhattan, Kevin mournfully recounted when Eckley called to ask for Dave's number. So now Fateful Encounter was down a bassist too. Kevin could probably have filled in on bass for MOF himself, but didn't want to commit to a second band while his own was also in turmoil.

After a few unsuccessful tryouts, with no leads on a bassist, Eckley decided to take matters into his own hands. He bought a cheap bass and resolved to learn the Ministry of Fear songs. If worst came to worst, they could play as a three-piece, with him singing and playing bass simultaneously. This worked out OK in practice, but did not go over well when they tried it live at a show with Ten Yard Fight at a church on Tremont Street. It wasn't their crowd, but Eckley also knew they could have delivered a more engaging performance if he had been running around with the microphone where he belonged.

After the show, no one seemed interested in organizing their next practice. Not only had they lost their bassist, they had also lost their practice spot in Mark's basement and were now practicing at a studio in Allston. Bill was always at one of his kids' sporting events, and Eckley had vague unconfirmed suspicions that Vossen had resumed his relationship with harder drugs. Were things coming to an end for Ministry of Fear?

With the understanding that this could be their last show, Eckley set out to get Ministry of Fear onto a show with Bane and Reach the Sky at the Palladium in Worcester. After successfully inserting MOF onto the lineup, they managed a few practices and played the show as a three-piece. Kids were dancing and trying to sing along even though Eckley was stuck behind his bass. It wasn't the end he would have predicted, but who knew if it was really the end anyway?

And then it wasn't the end, after all: Eckley managed to get Ministry of Fear onto the Back to School Jam lineup in fall 2000, a show of sufficient import that Mark (and Zoe) flew home for the occasion. Despite hardly practicing with Mark, it was the best they had sounded since he had left the band. Eckley could deal with this being their actual last show, rather than limping along playing a show a year whenever Mark returned to Boston.

After Back to School Jam, Eckley didn't hear from Vossen for months, though what he did hear, he didn't like. Vossen had moved back to his hometown in Western Mass and had slid back into addiction. Probably just as well that the band was on hiatus. Eckley tried to occupy himself with girls and friends and work, but he felt oddly empty not playing in a band. He was also hesitant to start something else, in case Mark moved back or he couldn't find band members as cooperative as his incumbents. If he did ever start a new band, he would want Bill on drums for sure. In the meantime, he tried to put both Bill Cole and Tyler Vossen out of his mind while waiting for something to change. David Eckley was not the type of person who waited for change; rather, he was the one who took things into his own hands and/or influenced the decisions of others to reflect his own (superior) reasoning. So he had been in an odd state of inertia when his phone rang in November 2001.

Tyler Vossen was on the line, apologizing for his recent absence. Eckley had indeed called him drunk a few weeks ago, wanting to talk about band stuff and temporarily forgetting about Vossen's addiction. While he had never drunk-dialed a girl, apparently he had drunk-dialed a band member, and cringed at the recollection. Vossen admitted his recent relapse after the breakup of the band and the death of his uncle, but said he'd been clean for two months now. That's why he was calling, he explained: he needed to get away from another relative who was a bad influence, rather than being forced to spend the upcoming holiday with this person and the equally dismal remainder of his family.

"Can I stay with you for a bit? Or just over Thanksgiving? I don't want to be home while my cousin is here."

Eckley hesitated. It was true he was going out of town for six days, so it wouldn't be like having a guest underfoot. Vossen had been a good roommate when they lived together in the '90s. And he was still the best guitarist that Eckley had ever worked with and amenable to implementing someone else's ideas. Two very important characteristics if you wanted to control the songwriting process. In the end, he gave in.

Thanksgiving was the first time that Eckley would be home since 9/11. Just 20 miles north of Ground Zero, his childhood neighborhood of Crestwood had not been spared the effects of that day. A guy over on Read Avenue had died in the towers, and his dad and Jean's neighbor, in the house that had once belonged to the Marnell family, had narrowly missed going to work that day when he remembered he had a doctor's appointment. As Eckley drove up Crestwood Ave., American flags adorned almost every home, including his own. It had also been a strange year for baseball, with the World Series going into November after the brief pause in the season. Like every time that the Yankees were in the World Series (besides last year, when they played his Mets), Eckley almost wished he could root for them, just to antagonize Red Sox fans, but at least took solace in reminding people of the Mets' 1986 victory whenever possible.

Eckley had taken off work on both Tuesday and Wednesday and was looking forward to going out on Wednesday night, as was his custom, to catch up with old friends who were in town. Paul Pounsenech was usually good for a couple of drinks, but this year was in Pennsylvania with his new girlfriend's family. On Tuesday night, he was helping Jean wash the dishes when the phone rang. It was Ryan Marnell, asking if he wanted to meet up the next day. How had he even known to reach him here, Eckley wondered, before realizing that Ryan probably didn't have his number in Boston, much less his new cell phone number. Ryan sounded more lucid than the last time Eckley had seen him, and after a moment of hesitation he agreed.

"Where do you want to meet?" Eckley was expecting him to pick something like the Piper's Kilt or the Eastchester Inn, but he suggested the Wretched Spaniel of all places, over on Tuckahoe Road. Jesus, the Wretched Spaniel! That was the type of bar their dads would have hung out in, if Mr. Eckley had hung out in working class bars and if Mr. Marnell had still been alive. Then again, David and Ryan weren't so young anymore. Maybe after 30, you were destined to frequent the Wretched Spaniel.

"David Motherfucking Eckley! It's so good to see you." Ryan had beaten him to the bar on Wednesday. While heavier than when David had last seen him, he seemed surprisingly alert and coherent, two things that had eluded him during their last encounter.

"And you, buddy." They embraced. "You look good!"

"I've been on these new meds. Things have been a lot better." Ryan looked relieved, and a bit more like his old self.

"I'm glad to hear that, bro," Eckley concurred. "How's your mom doing?"

"She's good," Ryan nodded. "I'll tell her you said hi. Hey, look what I just found in her storage space! I can't believe they were there all along. I figured I'd bring you one since you lost yours." He pulled a tape out of his jacket pocket. It was the Indignation demo.

Eckley took the tape and held it carefully in his hand. "Whoa, thanks dude. That means a lot, considering its history." He grinned, trying not to reveal his distress at the tape coming back to him once again in these circumstances. He had indeed mentioned to Ryan that he had misplaced

Lost Indignation

his last copy, back when there was more at stake.

"We already tried to bury it once, but it just keeps coming back!" Ryan laughed. He really did seem much better.

"You said it, my friend. We can drink to that!"

So the Indignation demo traveled to Boston. When Eckley got home at the end of the weekend, the tape was still in his pocket when he hung his jacket in the closet. And when the weather abruptly turned colder, his lighter coat stayed there, with the tape in its pocket, unattended.

Vossen had been at Eckley's apartment when he got home at the end of the weekend and was still there a few weeks later. Eckley had half-heartedly suggested a few times that perhaps it was time to leave, but overall Vossen had been an ideal guest, quiet and clean and unobtrusive, so he wasn't pushing the issue. These days, Eckley often stayed late at work using the high-speed internet to download music while working on his application to join the CIA, which was his new obsession ever since 9/11 and the demise of Ministry of Fear. All interactions with his guest had been amicable, so Eckley was surprised when he came home one Wednesday and opened the door. Vossen was sitting on the couch with a copy of the Indignation demo on the coffee table in front of him.

Tyler Vossen considered himself a relatively honest person. Besides the incident with the weed and backpack back in New York, he didn't make a habit of going through people's stuff. And he had never taken anything from Eckley when they were roommates. But this week he was a little short on cash. He didn't want to ask Eckley for money directly, but maybe there was something in a pocket of one of his jackets that he would never miss.

Instead, when he reached into the pocket of Eckley's tan jacket, his fingers closed around a cassette tape. Vossen drew it out inquisitively. It looked like a demo tape from a band called Indignation. Rudimentary cover art in black and white. Thing looked old. Out of curiosity, Vossen brought it over to Eckley's stereo in the living room and popped it into the tape deck.

Listening to this tape, he was glad he was totally sober, since there were moments when you could have mistaken it for Ministry of Fear in an alternate universe. Some of the songs had an eerie similarity, with the only different bits sounding like something that had been intentionally changed. These guys were pretty good, in a bare bones, old school style: definitely less metal than MOF. He carefully removed the insert and lyric sheet, searching for info about the band. No David Eckley listed as the guitarist, or anywhere in the lineup. Who the hell were these Indignation guys, why was the tape in Eckley's pocket, and why did the songs sound so much like Ministry of Fear? Then again, technically Ministry of Fear sounded like this other band, since it said the demo was recorded in 1988.

Vossen didn't have all the facts here, but he had the undeniable feeling that he'd been tricked, that Eckley hadn't written their early songs after all, and that he needed to know more about this demo to satisfy his creative curiosity—and, if necessary, call out his host for ripping off some other band's shit. Though if Eckley admitted to it, that could just stay between the two of them. No need to tarnish their songs to anyone outside of the band.

Eckley arrived home from work, clutching his mail and some groceries, always feeling a little off in the week leading up to his mom's birthday, when he saw Vossen sitting in the living room, a demo tape on the coffee table in front of him. At first he didn't even realize what tape it was, though he should have been paying more attention.

"Who the hell is Indignation?" Vossen's voice suddenly cut through his reverie. "I was listening to the tape. They kind of sound like us."

"The fuck you talking about?" Eckley snapped to attention. "Have you been going through my shit?"

"Found it on the floor of the closet," Vossen replied casually. "While I was hanging up my coat." Eckley knew he was lying, though he wasn't 100% certain. He scrambled to remember the chain of events after he and the Indignation demo had made it back to Boston. Had he ever taken it out of his pocket after the night he met up with Ryan? Had Vossen really found it on the floor of the closet, or had he been digging in Eckley's jacket pockets for cash? The differences were immaterial: either way this guy had been prowling in Eckley's belongings, and he needed to regain control of both the tape and this conversation.

"Whatever, dude. But you don't need to worry about that demo." He sighed. "I should have told you this a long time ago, but those songs inspired some of our stuff. I actually wrote the songs on that Indignation demo, and then sort of reworked them for Ministry of Fear. I wasn't credited on the demo, but none of those dudes are in hardcore anymore, so they didn't care if I wanted to reuse them. I didn't want to tell you guys, since I wanted our band to be our new thing. Not just an extension of Indignation."

"Sounds to me like you stole this band's songs and didn't want us to know you hadn't written them yourself," Vossen countered aggressively. "Which is kind of fucked up."

"I shouldn't have to prove anything to you, but aren't you giving me the benefit of the doubt? You're my friend, and you're living in my fucking home. We've known each other almost seven years."

"Maybe I don't know you as well as I thought," Vossen remarked sagely. "But I guess it's just a tape, right? And it's not like these guys are hunting us down for using their riffs? 'Cause it's like, if you did do it, I

Lost Indignation

wouldn't care. I just want to know."

Yes, Eckley acknowledged, it was just a tape. And no, he wasn't going to admit to anything.

When Tyler Vossen overdosed and died the week before Christmas, people in the scene were sad but not surprised. Guy had gotten back into heroin, they'd heard, which would have happened at some point, possibly even sooner if the singer of Ministry of Fear, his old band, hadn't given him a place to stay to try and get his life back on track. They'd heard he'd been having a hard time, trying to stay away from bad influences in his family during the holidays. Sucks that things had to turn out like this for Vossen, but they'd seen it happen too often over the years, and lots of people in hardcore had gone before their time.

And David Eckley played his part. Not just in the role of the grieving friend and band member, reminiscing with the others, getting shit drunk with Bill and Kevin and Kyle (who had broken edge in October) and stirring halfhearted talk of a benefit show. But also as the catalyst, by purchasing the heroin from a friend of a friend, which had then found its way into the same jacket pocket where Vossen had found the Indignation demo. Apparently, the next time Vossen looked in the pockets, to see if there was anything he'd missed, he'd found something even more enticing than an '80s hardcore demo. Not that Eckley was sure what had happened, since he hadn't been home at the time. Obviously, it was a tragedy that couldn't have been avoided. Nothing to do with him! Though he may have added a little something extra before slipping the bag into the pocket. And when his lease was up at the end of the year, he chose not to re-sign, closing his Boston chapter behind him.

Becky McAuley

Chapter 10
2017

The "Saturday" event that Pat had referenced was the annual benefit for Steven Reyer, held on McLean Ave. Steven was a ConEd worker, married with three children, who had been killed by a wrong-way driver on an entrance ramp to the Bronx River Parkway in 2013. To honor his memory, and ensure his family's financial security, friends and coworkers had organized annual benefit shows since his passing. Previous iterations were hosted at Rory Dolan's: all-you-can-eat, all-you-can-drink affairs that featured curious accounting and offered a few punk-adjacent live bands. At one point, Steven Reyer had been a peripheral hardcore kid. He was also the source of the hardcore pestilence that attached itself to the ConEd workforce: first Miles Wong, guitarist in Pat's band, Blind Giants, then Don and Ally ZT, then a horde of less reliable others. This year's benefit featured the best lineup yet: a ska band, an oi band, and right in the middle of the ska-oi sandwich, the Blind Giants reunion.

The end of Mo's work week had been a frenzied muddle of tagging lists, exporting lists, and messengering invites for Vedomedy. Colette was aggressively trying to raise the attendance for Saturday's closing party, though Mo predicted they would be well over capacity, as 600 people had already RSVP'd. With three seated dinners on Wednesday, Thursday, and Friday, a panel discussion, and the closing party Saturday, the marathon of Vedomedy events was finally almost over. The dinners had caused so much stress and strife among staff and invoked blatant apathy from nearly every media member that Aaron had tried to entice. So Mo was surprised when a former CFA colleague Gchatted on Thursday to mention that her new artist client had enjoyed the dinner and wanted to get on the list for additional Art Basel parties.

"That's awesome! I'm glad she had a good time," Mo typed with a straight face. "If she's free the Wednesday of Basel, I can probably get her on the list for this midnight dinner." Probably get her on the list! CFA was still dramatically short on RSVPs, and Colette was planning to tag a list of additions next week once Vedomedy was over.

The Friday night dinner and panel discussion loomed, and Mo suspected that Saturday's closing party would not be free of incident. Elaborate Freddy, the breakdancer, rappers—not Young Eef, unfortunately otherwise engaged—and protesters were expected, the latter due to Andres Serrano's "Fish Christ" installation. Were they protesting the profusion of tropical fish, scattered about the property in bespoke tanks, in a statement about cruelty to fish? Or were the protesters primed on Serrano's body of work and the fact that this one involved fish consuming representations of Christ? Due to the potential security threat, the cops had been warned in advance, a private security firm had been engaged, and Keith had been identified as the police contact on the staffing chart.

"But cops hate me!" Keith protested during the staffing meeting for Saturday.

"I can't believe I'm missing this spectacle," Mo lamented as she eavesdropped on the meeting. "Not that I ever work events."

"It's not too late," Aaron reminded her tetchily. "We could still staff you."

"No, I have this ... benefit dinner thing. In the suburbs." No one at work needed to know Pat was in a band, much less a hardcore band.

Mo hadn't seen Blind Giants play, so her knowledge was limited to local lore, studying their lone vinyl release and the crappy practice tape Pat had unearthed. She knew they were fast, raw and simplistic—closer to a hybrid of Negative Approach and early Wrecking Crew than the heavier '90s vibe that permeated Pat's personal taste—and that Pat had been an absolute maniac on stage. Though that had been the younger, lithe-er and looser-limbed Pat, an effortless executor of cartwheels, a rangy blur in a Yankee cap and oversize white tee. There was no consensus on whether Blind Giants had actually been any good. An occasional old head might speak their praises (usually one who enjoyed Awkward Thought), but mostly people seemed to have shown up to see what Pat would do next: jumping off speakers dressed as a giant tampon at the Garfield VFW, or headwalking while playing an inflatable saxophone to a Fishbone cover.

The Blind Giants set would follow openers Darryl Skaberry, a local ska outfit featuring Darryl Daniels, a SHARP skin and ConEd guy, on the mic. Pat had known Darryl for years and supported some of his previous musical forays, but privately referred to this latest endeavor as a "third-rate Inspector 7." Nothing But Trouble, an oi band, would finish things off. They featured one more ConEd guy on drums, though guitarist and last week's party host Vik Prasad practiced criminal law.

After being held at Rory Dolan's for years, the annual benefit had relocated to an upstart competitor down the block known as Donovan's. There were rumors that the organizers had gotten an insanely good deal on liquor and other necessities, but some apprehension remained among both the attendees and those playing, as this place was yet untested. The older, gentler incarnation of Pat Catalano was unlikely to break anything on purpose, but the same could not necessarily be said about the crowd. Mo had heard there were mirrors that lined one whole wall of the club, which was not always compatible with bands that inspired flailing appendages. Though there would likely be scant moshing at tonight's festivities, which was more in the vein of a sit-down benefit, populated by 30- and 40-somethings with more of a propensity for drinking than dancing.

Lost Indignation

And even if this was a tame show overall, how would the venue react to the sheer amount that each attendee might drink when presented with an open bar? Mo would likely be the only straight edge kid in attendance, joined by a handful of people in recovery, but there was a decided lack of moderate drinkers among the ranks of hardcore kids, not to mention ConEd personnel. Hardcore kids didn't really go in much for moderation on anything, except for in that Uppercut song.

"I am not even fucking with McLean on a Saturday night," Mo announced, easing the Camry into a spot between two driveways on Woodlawn Avenue, just across from Tara's Corner Deli. She was well versed in the local parking challenges from her haircuts at Elektra's, and usually parked in a residential neighborhood at the top of the hill rather than trying her luck down on McLean Avenue.

The venue was brightly lit, sparing Mo her the usual anxiety of walking into a dark club and not knowing anyone or not being able to see the people you did know. Ally ZT ran up and hugged her, then went back to assist her brother with his drums. Don was the unlucky soul who had been coerced into playing drums for Blind Giants as a teen and was now busy hauling assorted gear into the club.

The front half of the room held enough round tables to sit a hundred people or more, with room for a small makeshift stage behind the dinner area. As rumored, Mo noted the wall of mirrors along the entire left side of the room. There were two bars, one along the non-mirrored wall and the other near the front. Mo imagined they would be stretched to capacity and hoped the wall of mirrors would withstand the crowd.

At the front bar, Mo asked for a Shirley Temple, and was told there was no grenadine, an inauspicious sign for any new establishment. "An auspicious sign"—is that what Max Malkin, aka David Eckley, said that day back at the park? Mo grabbed a Coke and headed back to their table. She waved hi to Tony Gerson, separated by a clump of guys wearing flight jackets, as the room filled up and things started to get underway.

It was fortuitous that Darryl Skaberry was opening. Being a ska band, they had the most members and would take the longest to set up. Darryl was an engaging frontman, but there was only so much he could do with the material. Plus, he had to depend on eight other people for the execution. Mo conceded that the band was well suited to a sit-down environment—or at least moreso than the rest of tonight's bands. In situations where everyone was sitting rather than leaping up to mosh or singing along, it wasn't as obvious when people didn't visibly dig a band's set. Mo made a mental note to debut her own future musical endeavors in front of a seated crowd.

Darryl and co. finished their set about 30 minutes later to somewhere between polite and hearty applause. It was approaching 9

Becky McAuley

p.m., and Blind Giants was up next. Pat handed her his keys and glasses, and went to set up, like a less risky version of heading off into the pit. Gary and Miles tuned their respective instruments while Don testily shuffled his drums. They had been unable to engage the original bassist and had temporarily requisitioned Gary Muttley, who had now played bass for approximately 30-50 bands.

Blind Giants opened their set with "Free (but Cursed)" from the *Sudden Onset Aggression* comp, which had also featured Awkward Thought and a previously unreleased Starve track. It was a curious choice for an opener, as not many people knew the song or owned the comp, but Mo had once heard Pat remark about not opening with a song that people would be upset if they had missed, especially at a show where people might still be at the bar or smoking outside between sets. It had therefore become their habitual first tune.

After the comp song came "To Life," the first song on the 7". The recorded version opened with a clip from *Blacula*, from one of the scenes where he's at the club and the Hues Corporation is doing their thing. "But enough about death—here's to life!" was immediately followed by the ubiquitous four stick clicks that preceded the song.

So far, the crowd seemed livelier than during the Darryl set, and people continued to stand up and get closer to the action as Blind Giants moved onto the next track. "War of Attrition" and "Fake Ideas" were followed by "Trade Secrets," which opened with light-hearted riffing on assorted minor fraud and "trade secrets" at an establishment loosely based on a bookstore where Pat was once employed (not the same bookstore at which he had tackled the shoplifter.) The second chorus led into one of the only slow breakdowns in the Blind Giants catalog—more in the vein of Next Step Up than one of those fast Warzone style breakdowns that was closer to their usual thing. Mo turned a clinical eye toward the potential pit, curious who if anyone among the quadragenarian throng would take the bait. Sure enough, Warren Yatrofsky charged into the crowd and a handful of young enthusiasts burst forth to flail about in his wake. How old was Warren Yatrofsky anyway? He had to be at least 45. Now there was someone she hadn't yet thought to ask about Indignation. Mo resolved to corral him later in the evening.

Up next was an Eastchester-specific spoof on Suicidal Tendencies's "Institutionalized," played over Breakdown's "Pipe Dream" on repeat, with Pat railing about how all he wanted was one jelly donut from Galloway's, a legendary bakery on Harney Road. The jelly donut escapades were followed by "Foresight" and "Conflict of Interest": "It's a conflict of interest, but my interest is conflict!" Mo knew this was the last original, as they were ending their set with a cover of Operation Ivy's "Caution," which engendered an appropriate crowd reaction, but not one that endangered the mirrors. (Perhaps it was wise that they hadn't covered Warzone's "In the Mirror.")

Mo had swarmed forward along with Ally and the others during the Op Ivy cover, but retreated at the end of the set to allow the usual handshakes, hellos, congratulations, and space for the band to start breaking down their gear. Even though Mo hadn't been the one on stage, she still felt like her events were over at a track meet, and now they could just relax and enjoy themselves. Nothing But Trouble was in the process of setting up. They were one of those bands that Mo had often heard about but rarely seen play, and she always forgot that she knew so many of the members. Here she hadn't seen Vik since his last Halloween party, and now she was seeing him and his wife two weekends in a row! And this time she had the advantage of not being dressed as a cat.

Like Blind Giants, Nothing But Trouble was no longer an active band, and their material was long out of print, though a copy or two was probably lurking in John Franko's distro. Mo always forgot how good they were, like a Westchester version of the Wretched Ones, though their big song always reminded her of the Bruisers song "American Night." With their working-man songs featuring catchy, easy-to-remember choruses, they got the most singalong action of the night (or at least sway-along with your arm around the singer and your nearest neighbor).

They closed with a cover of the Misfits' "Attitude." Mo looked around for Tony Gerson, trying to catch his eye, as they had once joked that this song was about a former coworker and had in fact matched up various hardcore, punk, and oi tunes to the deficiencies of various colleagues past and present. She would have thought Shane Perry would be here too, but maybe he had an acting gig or was out driving his cab. About half the crowd was on its feet, encircling the band, in that state between moshing and standing, that in-between when everyone is participating but there isn't really a pit. The popularity of covers may have been on the wane in hardcore overall, but they were alive and well at this show.

Mo was glad they had served coffee after dinner and that she'd been drinking Cokes steadily through the evening. Though all three bands' sets were over, this party wasn't ending any time soon. After a few impromptu speeches and the results of an earlier raffle, most people were still hanging out at the tables or the bar, less out of a sense of not wanting to go home, like at the Raybeez show, but from wanting to make the most of their time visiting with friends they saw far too infrequently.

From the look of the remaining patrons, the cash bar (and open bar) had executed one hell of a haul, and not only would Steven Reyer's children be set for college tuition, but also for a variety of advanced degrees. Mo looked around for Pat, who had wandered off, and instead spotted Warren Yatrofsky. He was one of those older Westchester dudes that she always saw around but didn't know that well. She had never had a conversation with him without Pat present, during which he and Pat usually communicated via insult.

There were many options when your name was Warren: Warren Sidemyhead, Warren Peace, Warren Semble—but he always just went by Warren Yatrofsky. She could only imagine his tolerance and how much he would have had to drink to make him look that unsteady in his black running shoes.

"Yeah, what's up hon?" he mumbled.

Mo leaned in closer. "Do you remember someone named David Eckley?"

Warren narrowed his already half-mast eyes. "What did you want with a guy like David Eckley?"

"Just to ask him something about an old band," Mo demurred.

"He was just here ..." Warren gestured toward the street.

"WHAT!?" yelped Mo, destabilizing two tipsy blondes behind them.

"Not tonight, at that fall fair thing on McLean back in September."

"Ah, you got me," Mo admitted, relieved. "I thought you meant he was here tonight. Though I was here that day too! Getting my hair cut down the street!" Fuck! Her only consolation about Eckley having been so close by was that at that point, she hadn't known he was the target or the problem: she had still known the tape seller only by his sobriquet Max Malkin.

"Nah, but he's here once in a while. If you want to talk to him, he'll be at the Wretched Spaniel. Every year. Night before Thanksgiving. In town to visit family," Yatrofsky mumbled. "Father still lives over in Crestwood. He comes every year." Mo thought of Mr. Eckley on the porch on Halloween.

Warren affixed her with his bleary stare. "You should really come out that night. Straight edge kid like you, you could even drive me home!"

"That sounds more up Pat's alley than mine. Well, not the driving. But maybe you'll see us there," Mo acquiesced. The only time she'd ever been to the Wretched Spaniel outside of its occasional hardcore shows was for a friend's comedy night, but she could only imagine the flavor of the regular patrons. But yes, more of a job for Pat, assuming he was willing to risk his safety and accost the famous Eckley on behalf of his wife's schemes.

Pat soon rematerialized and they left Warren to it, assuring them he was not yet done and did not need a ride home tonight. There were so few people left in the club that they didn't really have to execute an Irish goodbye, or a Jewish goodbye. Mo often joked about how the conflicting hereditary goodbye styles had made her wholly indecisive about how to exit any gathering. Maybe that was the root of her indecision about everything in general.

"That was fun." Pat threw an arm around her pencil skirted waist as they walked up the hill towards the car.

"It was a great night. Hey, can I wear this?" Pat, drunk and impervious to the cold, wasn't even wearing his hoodie, which Mo swiftly co-opted from where it was draped over his shoulder.

"I was talking to Warren Yatrofsky," she began. "And guess who will supposedly be at the Wretched Spaniel the night before Thanksgiving? David fucking Eckley."

"No shit."

"Imagine if we went to the Wretched Spaniel and asked him about Indignation!" She paused. "Or, say, you and some friends, without me in the way, went to ask him about Indignation?"

Pat squeezed her shoulders. "As much as I love having you around … you're right, maybe it's better if you're not there, if shit gets interesting?"

"Oh man," Mo grinned. "What exactly did I just suggest?"

The next day, once Mo had picked up their breakfast at Gramatan Hot Bagel, she wondered how things had gone at the Vedomedy closing party. For most CFA events, she could either search for news coverage the next morning or pull up Instagram to see which celebrities were featured on the CFA feed, before getting the full report from her coworkers. But for this one, she didn't even have to Google or go to Instagram. It was right there on Page Six's Twitter:

Guppies Gone Wild: Fish Christ Riot in Chelsea
"It was full scale madness at the Vedomedy Gallery closing party last night in Chelsea. The tropical fish, part of the Andres Serrano *Fish Christ* installation, made it clear they weren't finn-ished on the dance floor when they burst out of their tanks during an encore by breakdancer Elaborate Freddy. The fish were rescued by publicists onsite from the Colette Foulard Agency, who provided temporary refuge in the bespoke bathtubs with Bottega Veneta accessories, three of which will adorn each Vedomedy property, slated to be completed in 2019. Each unit will also feature two private swimming pools, for the east and west exposure …"

Mo stared. Holy crap. She couldn't have imagined that while wrangling the likes of Warren Yatrofsky, Aaron and the others had been wrangling fish! And while this sounded like a catastrophe at the time, was it finally the spark they needed to get anyone to write about fucking Vedomedy?

By Sunday morning, it was all over the news: Page Six, *Vogue. com*, *the Observer*, and that was just the beginning. Mo's heart went out to

Becky McAuley

whichever CFA staffers or interns were going to have to clip this avalanche of articles next week. There were going to be more clips than the time that Amanda Bynes was spotted at Number 8!

Some accused the fish liberation of being a stunt, to which Colette darkly hinted that on the contrary, perhaps the party had been sabotaged by protesters or competitors. A seismologist was called in, alongside a fish psychic and a Feng Shui expert. "A *fish psychic?*" Pat echoed, eyebrows raised from here to Peekskill as Mo recounted the details. Yes, Colette's dog psychic (technically Pierre's dog psychic) had a connection to the fish psychic and had put her in touch. "I guess she's an expert in ... are you ready? ... that school of thought."

CFA events often featured a certain amount of chaos, from an almost-riot during a surprise performance by Ghost Pool at an art installation, to the fish foofaraw on Saturday. Luckily it was the type of excitement that made its way to the gossip columns and made Colette's parties even more legendary, rather than dissuading future attendees.

"Hey, did you ever realize that you might be the common denominator in all these events?" Pat suggested jokingly, as Mo recounted the increasingly ridiculous aftermath of the fish incident (the fin-cident?). "Between this, the show, and the Harry Potter riot at your old job, maybe you're the disturbance!"

"Disturbing the peace, Gut Instinct style," Mo mused. "Or disturbing the ... Pisces?" Pat threw an empty paper towel roll at her. "Except I can't be blamed for the fish one, since I wasn't there. I was busy trying to ask Warren Yatrofsky about Indignation, so technically, that's his alibi too."

Mo wasn't exactly regretting asking Pat to intercept Eckley at the Wretched Spaniel, though she soon realized the plan had escaped her control. As she observed the unmitigated zeal with which Pat was preparing for the event, she wondered if it was precisely the element of danger that had ignited his enthusiasm. Perhaps he and the friends who were joining all missed the sort of unpredictability that had featured more prominently in their younger escapades, before they had shifted into more staid lives. While excited that the fervor for this Indignation-adjacent project had extended to Pat's friend group, Mo had to let go of the trajectory of the proceedings, hope that everybody had a good time, that nobody got hurt, and that the posse ended up with some relevant information. What if David Eckley didn't even show up this year? At least they would all have enjoyed a night out together at the bar. Or what if he did, and was actually as dangerous as Christine had suggested?

Vik Prasad had confirmed he was available, and Pat was still deciding if he should involve Don ZT. He had asked Shane Perry, who was

Lost Indignation

a maybe, as he would be driving his cab on what was one of the busiest nights of the year for transporting drunk people from the bar to their ancestral homes.

While Pat preparing to encounter Eckley was a logical next step, the investigation on Mo's side had reached a natural lull. And no matter how busy she was with work and school, her brain still always needed additional projects. One last member of Indignation remained unaccounted for: Eric Clifton! Now that they had his full name from Dion, perhaps she would pursue him next.

Inspiration struck from an unlikely source, amid what was shaping up to be one of the most hectic weeks in CFA history, which was saying a lot, because every week was busy at CFA. Vedomedy was over, and then soon the Salon Art & Design was finished too. But in their wake, the office had collectively realized that there were now only a few weeks left before Art Basel: one full week, a short week for Thanksgiving, and then, mercifully—for the first time since 2012—a last full week in between Thanksgiving and the fair. It was going to be weird as fuck not being there at night during Art Basel this year, but Mo was intensely thankful to avoid those evenings in the office for the first time since she had joined CFA in 2011.

On Monday, Oona, while hopping next to Mo's desk waiting to pee, had made an offhand comment to Aaron about researching the history of high-end terrariums. Mo's ears perked up. She was always intrigued by clients that weren't just another art fair, design firm, or hotel.

"What's this about terrariums?" Mo inquired while furiously editing a list of additions for the Young Eef dinner. Attendance still hadn't reached their expectations, probably because it was a fucking midnight dinner. At least there was one fewer undecided person to chase down for a yes or no: Dion Carina had indeed declined due to another DJ engagement.

"Adina Carthage. She's a potential client; we met her at Salon. She invented some type of terrarium called the Carthaginian Case? So we're doing some research for the proposal," Oona imparted in her inimitable manner.

"Very cool. Carthaginian Cases sound hard as fuck, almost like the Pentagon Papers or something."

Terrariums. What had Dion said about Eric, that he was "living in Alaska, doing something with fucking plants"? What kind of plants would he be growing in Alaska? Could he be dealing with terrariums? It was one more thing to Google, a more specific piece of information to narrow the results where previous searches had failed.

When Mo floated the theory to Pat that night, she was met with an unexpected torrent of information. Though she should have known to expect it by now, as Pat knew so much shit about so much random shit, and his many pockets of fascination had been gleaned and nurtured through late night Wikipedia binges. The initial mention of Alaska and terrariums turned into an enthusiastic monologue about why, in fact, Alaska was the perfect place for terrariums. Even if they were totally off-base, and Eric was working with plants in a different context, Mo now knew a lot more about terrariums.

The next day, while waiting for Colette to get off a call, Mo tried Googling Eric again. The Carthaginian Cases had imbued her with fresh inspiration, and now, any research on the subject, or research on the type of media who covered terrariums, could be considered work related. She tried "eric clifton AND alaska AND terrarium." No results with "Eric Clifton," but there was a popular terrarium night at a coffee shop in Anchorage, in partnership with a local bespoke terrarium company. Extra Terrariums were apparently known for making outer space plantscapes—like the surface of Mars, but with plants. Or fucking plants, as per Dion. Mo searched Extra Terrariums and found their website and Facebook links. Fuck, she needed to get back to work, even if she couldn't start anything detailed since Colette would inevitably be ready to summon Mo and Elvis to the delayed meeting as soon as she immersed herself in another project. What had started as a momentary diversion into the world of terrariums had turned into the usual endless chain of Googling.

Mo clicked on the bio section of the terrarium site. "Eric and Lucy founded Extra Terrariums in 2014 after moving to Anchorage from San Francisco." Frustratingly, the bio did not include their last names, but went on to describe their background in tattooing and transition to creating art with plants. Hang on. Hadn't Matt mentioned something about Eric moving out west? She Googled "Eric Lucy AND Extra Terrariums" and found an article in the *Anchorage Daily News* about a recent terrarium night at the coffee shop. There was a picture showing a heavily tattooed Black guy with a heavily tattooed Asian woman posing behind one of the outer space terrariums. Could this really be Eric Clifton? There was only one way to find out. Mo tabbed back to the Contact Us section and copied the info for future research, just as Elvis stuck his head around the corner to say Colette was ready for them.

An hour later, while hustling along 18th Street in her grandfather's scarf and furry earflap Knicks hat, Mo dialed the number on the Extra Terrariums site. It rang through to voicemail, so she left a message without going into too much detail. It was probably best that no one had answered, as she needed to move as fast as possible, along with cooperation from the 1 train and the shuttle, to make the 2:25 train. And so that she could wear gloves on both hands rather than holding the phone. Somehow it was already really fucking cold, and it was barely mid-November!

But after dashing onto the 1 train, then galloping for the shuttle, and now moving through Grand Central at a pace somewhere between a trot and a run, Mo was anything but cold. Why was it that whenever she was most behind schedule, the train she needed was departing from a track on the other side of the terminal? As she steamed towards track 16 in her Jordan I's, probably the fastest she'd run since Halloween night, she felt her phone start buzzing in her purse. She had a minute and a half to go, so she'd make the train even if she took time to answer. She whipped the phone out of her bag. It was a 907 area code ... oh shit, 907 was Alaska (the state, not the rapper) and this looked like the same number she had just dialed.

"Hello?" Mo slowed to a walk and tried not to sound too out of breath as she turned into the doorway for track 16.

"Is this Mo McGraw?" Mo verified that this was indeed Mo McGraw.

"This is Eric, up at Extra Terrariums." Guy made "up" sound like he was calling from White Plains or something, rather than Alaska. "I got your message. I'm not sure why the hell anyone cares about Indignation in 2017, but I can try to answer your questions."

Mo nearly floated down the ramp to the train. "Amazing! I'm glad I found the right person. I'm about to get on a train. But I would love to speak with you at any time that is convenient. I get out of class at 5:30 east coast time."

"How about later today, around 9:00 your time? Want to do this on Skype so you can see the terrariums?"

Mo was touched. "Sure, I would love to see them! My Skype name is mo dot mcgraw dot 914."

"Moe—with an 'e'?"

"No 'e.'" "McGraw ... and then 914. Like ... you know."

Mo unearthed her ancient Netbook, from before she had a desktop computer, and made sure she had Skype installed before Eric was expected to call that evening. She was sitting on the couch at 9 p.m., making sure there wasn't too much living room mess visible behind her, when Eric's Skype call came through.

"Hi, Eric—how's it going?"

"What's up, Mo?" Eric adjusted the camera. He looked a bit like the rapper Omega Jackson. "Do you want to see the terrariums before we get started?"

"I'd love to!" They had looked intriguing on the website, and she also wanted to be polite and show interest in his craft.

Eric had picked up his phone or laptop and was walking around so she could see the works in progress. Mo was glad she had elected to Skype. The terrariums were awesome. There was nothing natural about the backgrounds, which featured disconcertingly bright colors designed to mimic the terrain of imaginary distant planets and moons, but with real plants mixed in.

"Is that Ganymede?" asked Pat, leaning in over Mo's shoulder to get a better look. She knew he wasn't talking about Kurtis Blow's nemesis in "Way Out West."

"Hell yeah it is."

"Damn, those are cool. If you ever need terrarium public relations, my office is signing our first terrarium client! Anyway, before we get to Indignation ... what's it like living in Alaska?"

"Well, I've only been up here a few years and mostly stayed in the city. Our little community in Anchorage, it's a bunch of outcasts. For people who never fit in anywhere. Are you familiar with the concept of marginal man?" Eric asked.

"Yeah, like the band! And the idea of being from two cultures and not fitting into either of them? I was reading this article in my college's alumni magazine"— Pat groaned, as he had already heard this six times— "about this guy who went to my school and saved the dad of that guy from Marginal Man the band during some battle in World War II. So technically that guy is responsible for the band existing, a little bit. And yet Inouye's son still didn't fit in either culture, you know? After his dad and this medic guy went through all of that."

Eric laughed ruefully. "Try being a half Black punk rock kid ... In *Eastchester* in the '80s! My mom got a job up there and we moved to Interlaken because she knew someone there that we could sublet from—"

"Wait, did you say you grew up in Interlaken?" Pat tuned in.

"I only lived there for three years," Eric clarified. "I lived in the city as a kid and I moved right back after high school. Three years in Eastchester was more than enough!"

"When did you move there? My family was there from '89 through the mid '90s."

"In '87. Had to go from the East Village to Eastchester High School! It got better though once I met other kids into skateboarding. Did you know Jesse Gordon-Thomas? Darren Dosta?"

"Oh man, Darren Dosta used to babysit me!" Pat laughed. "He was either the worst babysitter or the best babysitter, depending on my perspective vs. my mom's perspective."

"It all depends on perspective," Eric remarked sagely. "Like, I didn't realize it at the time, but my mom was doing the best thing for us. My dad was a drug addict ..."

"Mine too," Pat muttered.

"And she thought moving up to the suburbs might be good for him ..."

"Yes, because that worked out *so* well for my dad ..."

Lost Indignation

Eric grimaced. "I know, right? But her heart was in the right place. Change of environment for all of us without moving us up to bumfuck middle of nowhere. Which, coincidentally (he spread his arms) is exactly where I ended up."

"So, uh, how *did* you end up in Alaska?" Mo ventured.

"It was my girlfriend's idea. We were both tattooing at the time in San Francisco but ready to get out of the city and do something different. She had started working on these terrariums, and then we ended up moving up north and starting our own thing."

"That's punk rock right there, DIY, controlling your own destiny," Mo nodded.

"Yeah, and that's sort of what happened with Indignation." Mo leaned closer. "I had answered this ad at Record Stop and joined the band. They didn't have a singer yet, but Matt and Ryan had already written most of the songs. We ended up getting a singer, playing a couple shows. We even recorded something; it started to get real. And then a bunch of us quit on the same day." Eric laughed. "For different reasons. I just wanted to hang out with my new friends once I had someone else who was willing to listen to me. I was a punk rock kid, wanted to do a political band, and Indignation wanted to play generic hardcore."

"I've heard," Mo concurred, "about their style, and everyone quitting on the same day."

"Who told you that?"

"Dion Carina! Well, first we talked to Matt and he didn't say anything about ripping the door off Dion's car. And then I talked to Dion and he told me the rest of the story."

"I wasn't even there for the door thing. I was on the phone with Ryan, telling him I quit! But Dion was always cool to me, and he told me all about it."

"But you were still in the band when they recorded?" Mo pressed on, "and if so, you wouldn't happen to still have your copy of the demo, right? You're my last hope."

"Yeah, I recorded with them, but no more demo. My mom got rid of that stuff after I moved to the West Coast. I took the bare minimum with me since I wasn't sure how long I was going to be living out there."

"Oh man, no one seems to have this shit," Mo lamented. "Anything would do at this point. Demo, live set, or whatever."

"You should talk to this guy Andrew, he might still have a video," Eric suggested.

"What's his name?" Mo scrabbled for her pen.

"Andrew Rompanelli. I'll send you a link to his profile, he hit me up on Facebook a few years ago about a trade for some Bay Area band. He taped a bunch of shows back in the day, and I think he shot at least one of ours."

"Nice, I hope it's better than the other tape this dude tried to sell me. You couldn't even hear anything till our friend cleaned up the audio. And then it turned out to be some other band followed by like one second of an Indignation set. But I'd love to get in touch with Andrew."

"Yeah, look him up on Facebook." A phone rang in the background, and Mo realized that in Alaska, it was still afternoon.

Eric walked away from the screen. "I have to take this. It's the person we're doing the *Cannibal Holocaust* terrarium for."

"Thank you for speaking to me! And I loved seeing the terrariums."

"Any time. Good luck with the tape and let me know if you have any more questions." Eric waved and ended the call.

"So Andrew Rompanelli," Mo reflected. "Is he next on my list?" Though why did she suspect the tape that Eric mentioned was the same flawed and unfortunate slab that she already owned?

"Just do me a favor," Pat replied. "Next time, don't go off on any tangents about stuff you read in the *Alumni Weekly*."

The next day, Eric sent a link to Rompanelli's Facebook profile, and Mo shot him an exploratory message about the video. In retrospect, hadn't Matt mentioned someone named Andy too? But as of two days later, the message was still unread. Maybe the guy didn't check Facebook very often? At least she had the link to his profile. They had only one mutual friend: J.P. Sydenstricker. If he didn't get back to her soon, she'd ask Sydenstricker if he had other contact info.

Somehow, after a long week of craziness at both their jobs, Mo and Pat made it to the weekend. Saturday dawned with the customary breakfast sandwich and couch relaxation, but soon segued into productivity, as Pat was preparing to host a game night for the first time in months. This resulted in the type of cleaning that most people do as regular maintenance, but always threw Mo and Pat into a flurry when they were about to host other humans.

Mo was donating her desk chair for the evening, as it was the least cat-haired seat in the house for Don ZT. He was somewhat allergic to cats but usually did OK for a few hours unless Brett and CC decided to personally menace him. Pat still hadn't asked him about coming on Wednesday. They had been weighing his spontaneous personality against his tech knowledge in case they needed to get into Eckley's phone, but then Mo remembered that Christine had said that Eckley loved Demolition Hammer, and Don did too. A ready-made conversation topic in case other avenues failed! Pat resolved to invite him and knew he would be down to attend, unless he was otherwise engaged.

On Sunday afternoon, Mo saw a new Facebook message from Andrew Rompanelli. "Hi, that does sound like my tape. Could you take a

Lost Indignation

short video of your screen and send it to me, like the beginning of the Power Structure set? Should be able to tell from where I was filming, though I can't imagine there are too many other videos of Power Structure!" Little did this guy know they'd had the whole thing digitized, and she wouldn't have to take a video on her phone! Mo asked for his email address so that she could send him the cleaned up file of the whole Power Structure set, along with the entire run of the tape, and offered to give back the original VHS if it was his. Only after hitting Send did she realize she'd now exchanged multiple messages with this guy without even asking about Indignation. Though this situation was now bigger than the Indignation tape: if the Power Structure video had been shot by Andrew Rompanelli and not by Max Malkin/David Eckley, that would trap him in another lie.

Rompanelli provided his email address and said he'd be happy to have the original tape back in his collection, if it was indeed his, and perhaps he could trade something to Mo in return. She knew exactly what to ask for. "You wouldn't still have an Indignation demo tape?"

"No, that disappeared right around the same time as your video! And I swore I had filmed them too, but I can't find that either. Thought I put it on the tape you have. Maybe they played after Power Structure? I wonder what happened to it?" Somehow, this had been the exact answer Mo was expecting.

Becky McAuley

Chapter 11
2003

On a cold night in January 2003, Christine Oronzio was on yet another first date. This time she was at the Black Bear in White Plains with some doofus named Justin or Dustin. Like so many of her other first dates lately, Justin/Dustin was going on about the need to invade Iraq, a position that would render a second date unlikely. Christine's eyes glazed over and she picked at her onion rings. Probably best to say nothing at all, rather than trying to engage. Then again, this guy was lamer than the last one, and the sooner she conjured a vituperative rebuttal, the sooner she could be home in her pajamas. She opened her mouth to respond.

"C-O! What did we learn?!"

Christine looked up, attempting to place the dude with short dark hair and intense blue eyes who was striding towards their table. It was that guy David, Ryan's best friend and old neighbor.

"David Eckley?" she ventured. Up close, he didn't look that much different than he had back then. The intervening years had agreed with him, as he was even more handsome now than when she had first met him in 1988. Then again, back when she had known him, he was merely Ryan's best friend, and she hadn't ever looked at him the way she was looking at him now.

"You got it!" Eckley pulled up a chair next to their table, Justin/Dustin shrinking in horror. Christine was so grateful for David's appearance that she tried to treat him extra warmly, as an old friend whose reappearance was most welcome, especially if it put a merciful end to the disappointing date. Eckley, to his credit, played along. A few minutes later, Justin or Dustin had left the premises, throwing $10 on the table, disgusted or dejected or both.

Christine turned to Eckley and raised her eyebrows. She wasn't outright flirting with him, but dropped the friend act and rewarded him with a coy smile. "So, do you do that professionally?"

Eckley smiled in return. "Only when my services are required."

"Well, you got here at the right time. Can I buy you a drink?"

"I was just going to ask you that same question." He signaled the waiter.

"What have you been up to?" Christine asked, once their beers had arrived.

"I decided to come back to the city after 9/11. I wanted to be able to do some good. I just started training to be an MTA police officer."

"Same for me, about coming back to the city after 9/11. My dad, he was in the North Tower. And afterwards he was having anxiety so bad that he couldn't go to work. He's doing a little better now. But when he was out of work, my mom started thinking about selling the house. Which would have been a huge project. Especially because my sister is still living there! Dana, the youngest, she moved back in. She and my mom fight nonstop! So all of this was going on just when I was starting to think about moving back east, or trying someplace new. But my parents called and asked me to think about coming home. So here I am," she finished lamely. "Why am I even telling you all this stuff?"

"Well, I never knew a lot about you. Besides being Ryan's girlfriend. And that you were from Dobbs, had a big family. And that you liked Supertouch."

"I'm impressed you remembered that part. I wouldn't have pegged you as a Supertouch fan."

"Oh, I'm not," Eckley conceded. "I just remembered that you liked them." That was her first mistake, Christine would think later. Never date a hardcore kid who didn't like Supertouch.

And yet, that night, there was no need for hesitation or to ponder red flags. The conversation flowed naturally and encouraged the spark between them. Soon they had moved on from the Black Bear to Gryphon's, then to the Haunted Frog, and then finally for pizza at Nicky's. Christine leaned a little closer to Eckley each time they stepped out into the cold to continue their Saturday night. He looked so good in his hat and scarf, and Christine was struck by how easy it was to be with him. It wasn't like getting to know a new person—it was getting reacquainted with someone she already sort of knew but had never looked at before in this light.

In the 12 years since she and Ryan had broken up, Christine had pursued a variety of relationships, but only two serious ones: her ex after college, when she was living in the East Village, and a situation that had deteriorated in L.A. a few years prior. Most recently she had been living in Oakland with some super hot 25-year-old who absolutely did not have his life together, before being called home after 9/11. She wasn't looking for anything serious and was mostly going on dates in White Plains for something to do. Also to feel less disconnected in Westchester, which seemed so different in her early 30s than when she had spent the first half of her life here.

Christine had always been averse to settling down—well, besides that ancient era when she thought that she and Ryan Marnell might be together forever—but would it be so bad to spend time with someone like this, who she felt like she already knew, rather than continually attempting to meet new people who were invariably a disappointment? As the night continued, she half-hoped this wouldn't be the last she saw of this David Eckley guy, that it would be more than just an upgrade from an otherwise unsatisfying date in White Plains.

Lost Indignation

They ended up at a shitty bar in Hastings, not far from Christine's new, also shitty, studio apartment. She had just moved there in September, after spending a few months with her family. It was fortuitous she had found the apartment when she did, as she and Dana might have killed each other spending another week under the same roof. She and David stayed up until 5 a.m., making full use of her own place. But it wasn't until she woke up the next morning, David still asleep beside her, that she felt the weight of what she had done. This guy sleeping beside her was Ryan Marnell's best friend! Yes, they had broken up over 12 years ago, which also wasn't her idea, and yes, he had rebuffed any further attempts to reconnect until she had stopped trying sometime in the early '90s. But how long did you have to wait to date your ex's best friend, or was that off limits forever? She hoped Ryan would never find out about last night's adventure, which would probably be a one-off anyway.

But over the next few months, they continued to see each other sporadically. David worked nights, and Christine's ongoing anxiety about dating her ex's best friend kept her from seeking him out more often. Yet she always picked up when he called, or replied when he sent her a text (texting!—now that was a new way to communicate with someone you were interested in). And while forcing the doubts into the back of her mind, Christine continued to warm to having him around. It was nice to date someone who acted like an adult, who was smarter and more polished than the type of guys she usually went for, yet rooted in the same subculture and could understand that aspect of her life.

One day in June, David had taken her to Untermyer Park for a picnic, and they got onto the topic of the past bands they had played in. Christine had pretended to be thrilled with the picnic plan and didn't reveal the source of her angst: that she had done the same thing with Ryan 13 years ago. It was one of the last times she had seen him in person, and he had never quite seemed the same afterwards. He had reacted oddly when she tried to take his picture, despite having various cute pictures of them together from the two prior years of their relationship. Well, she didn't have to worry about that today when she pulled out her new digital camera. David loved the camera and knew he looked great in pictures (and out of them).

Early in their relationship, David had mentioned that he had been in a band called Ministry of Fear, but it hadn't come up again until today, when Christine had mentioned she had played in a band while living in L.A.

"I didn't know you were in a band!" David seemed surprised.

"Yeah, I played bass!" Christine didn't add why she had picked bass over guitar, the summer before her junior year in college: she hadn't wanted to play the same instrument as Ryan, so that on the off chance they got back together, they could potentially play music with one another.

"Where were you a few years ago, when our bass player moved to Florida?"

"I was out in L.A., so I wouldn't have been that helpful. Was that what happened to Ministry of Fear?" So far in their relationship, if you could call it that, Christine had avoided too many personal questions, as David often responded with strangely evasive answers.

"Yeah, after Mark moved away, it just sort of ... fell apart. They weren't as committed as I was. And it was my band, but I didn't want to replace too many people."

"Did you ever think about starting something new down here?"

"Not really. It would be like starting over. I mean, I'd write all the songs anyway, but I'd need to find other people to play them."

"There's always me," Christine joked.

"What kind of band were you in?"

"Kind of like Jawbox or Shift. So probably not your style." David allowed that no, neither Jawbox nor Shift were his style. "It never went anywhere, though I structured my whole life around band stuff and shows while I was in L.A. I had all these shitty jobs so that I could be available to play shows, or take time off if we ever got organized enough to tour. I guess that's how I ended up where I am now." Christine had been temping in the Flatiron District ever since she had moved back. She was a quick study at the miscellaneous office tasks the marketing company threw at her—from proofreading to data entry—though as a psych major, she felt like she could be using her brain on something more difficult or meaningful.

"That's true for me too, though," David said slowly. Christine wasn't used to hearing him speak introspectively about himself. "I wonder what I would be doing now if I had gotten a more serious job in the '90s, rather than focusing on band stuff."

"Well aren't we quite a pair." Christine draped her arm around his shoulder. More than ever, she was glad that he had found her that night in White Plains. Lately she had barely thought about Ryan Marnell. And the next morning, when David asked her to be his girlfriend, she hesitated only for a second.

When they first reconnected, Eckley had been living off Katonah Avenue in the Bronx with a couple of roommates, but later that year, he got his own place in Yonkers, near the intersection of Midland Avenue and Mile Square Road. The new apartment was in the private home of an old lady named Mrs. Petrillo, though it was a decent-sized one-bedroom with its own entrance and had access to her yard on that side of the house. Christine had visited a few times, though they still mostly went to her studio out of habit. But for some reason in early 2004, Eckley was suddenly evasive about letting her come over.

Lost Indignation

Christine tried to get to the root of his recalcitrance, but none of his answers made sense. He insinuated that she got a little too loud during certain activities, or that Mrs. Petrillo didn't like him having visitors. They were both over 30: Eckley should be allowed to have visitors! And his landlady hadn't raised these objections right away. Christine hoped that she could eventually outlast the issue if the landlord became hard of hearing, though based on the reports from Eckley, her hearing must have been unusually acute for a 79-year-old.

It was one of the first nice Saturdays in March, and Christine had made up her mind to surprise David at his apartment. He had worked until early that morning, and had indicated that he didn't want her to come over before he had to leave for work again late in the afternoon, but she was hoping he might feel differently when he saw what she was wearing under her favorite jeans and spring jacket. Ever since they had reconnected last year, the physical aspect had been one of the most crucial parts of their relationship. Christine sometimes still couldn't believe how good David Eckley still looked at 32, while she herself was cognizant of no longer being as young as she had once been. David could have been dating younger girls, as she sometimes jokingly reminded him, but she also tried to remind him of her own unique and superior experience in a variety of areas.

With the sun shining and RJD2 blasting from her unrolled window, she was about to turn from Mile Square Road onto Kingston Avenue, Eckley's street, when she saw Ryan Marnell walking towards her. Was it really Ryan? He had shaggy hair and a beard now, rather than the youth crew fade he had sported when they dated, but it was definitely him. She beeped. He jumped, and she immediately felt bad; she pulled up beside him and lifted her sunglasses so he could see who it was.

"Ryan! Remember me?"

"How could I possibly forget?" Ryan's expression was hard to read. Why did she think he would be happy to see her?

"What are you doing over here?" Christine realized that before spotting Ryan, she wasn't even sure if he still lived in Westchester.

"I'm staying with someone up the street," Ryan explained.

"Oh really? I have a friend who lives around here too."

"I'm actually looking for a new place," he added. "Bit of a nightmare situation. Hey, who's your friend?"

"Oh, you wouldn't know them," Christine answered after a pause. "But I'll walk with you for a bit." She pulled her car over into an open parking spot. All the better to surprise David if he didn't see her drive up.

Suddenly shy, she and Ryan walked in silence, until he stopped in front of ... wait, wasn't that David's house?

That question was answered when their mutual "friend" stepped out of the side door, wearing a hoodie and jeans, probably on the way to the bodega for cigarettes. Christine briefly froze, then tried to continue nonchalantly down the block, but Ryan had already seen David, and turned toward her with a look that was equal parts pain and incredulity.

"What the FUCK!" Ryan looked utterly devastated. "Is THIS your friend!?"

"I was just trying not to hurt your feelings!" Christine said quickly. Knowing David Eckley, she had an idea of how this could escalate.

"Obviously you don't give a fuck about my feelings," Ryan shot back.

"You're right, bro," Eckley deadpanned, having arrived between them. God, he was so hot in his bodega outfit with his hood up, even if Christine had a feeling he was about to cause irreparable damage to at least one relationship. "If she cared about your feelings, then she wouldn't be riding my DICK!"

It was then when Ryan began to sing. "Oh, baby you ... you got what I need ... but you say he's just a friend, but you say he's JUST A FRIEND ..."

Christine looked around. If Mrs. Petrillo and her equivalents weren't spying on them before, they would be now.

Abruptly, Ryan turned around and stomped past Eckley towards the house, continuing to sing as he went. Christine stood frozen in the yard. But David just shrugged. "Want anything from the bodega?" Stricken, she shook her head no, and he ambled off towards Mile Square Road.

Christine remained in the yard, abandoned by both her former and current boyfriends. She didn't know what the fuck to do. Get back in her car and drive away from this drama she had inadvertently created? Christine didn't consider herself a dramatic person, at least compared to her youngest sister, but she had blundered into concocting some here. And she wanted to stay and confirm that Ryan was OK. She had no idea what his mental state had been like in the past decade, but he had been in the hospital when they broke up—or when he flatly demanded a breakup and she valiantly resisted.

She was on the verge of either venturing toward the house to check on him or attempting to intercept Eckley on his way back, when they both reappeared: Eckley with his cigarettes, planting his hand onto Christine's ass as she squirmed away in shame; Ryan bursting out of the door, carrying a box and two duffle bags and still singing Biz Markie. They watched him stomp towards an ancient Honda Civic parked up the street (oh my god, Christine realized, the very same car where she had administered his first blowjob, not to bring more history into the situation), deposit the bags, and march back into the house. Was he living with Eckley, and now moving out, all because of her? She turned to him for an explanation.

Lost Indignation

But Eckley just shrugged. "Now you see why I couldn't have you over? I was just trying to give a friend a place to crash. But you couldn't stay away. You naughty girl." He slid up next to her again, evidently enjoying the scenario of being the dominant male and victorious recipient of Christine's affections. But Christine felt no affection, just guilt and horror. Yes, she had picked David Eckley, but she didn't want to rub it in Ryan's face and wanted to be as respectful as possible to her ex. And she was frankly alarmed that this incident had brought out an opposite reaction from her current partner.

Ryan went past them again, determinedly lugging what looked like an easel and some canvasses. Christine wondered what he had been painting, and then if she would ever see him again. She wanted to leave, but also worried about what would happen if she left him alone with Eckley. So she stayed until the end: she and Eckley standing awkwardly in the yard while Ryan removed his remaining personal effects—singing all the while—then slammed the door to his Civic without looking back.

"Trust me, that was going to fall apart sooner or later," Eckley reflected the next morning. They were at the Raceway Diner after he had gotten home from his overnight shift. "I was doing him a favor by letting him stay here. But Ryan's just the latest person I couldn't save from themselves. Who knows where he's gonna go now." Christine had heard about Eckley trying to keep people out of trouble, including his old roommate in Boston who had died of a heroin overdose, and the guilt he experienced when he couldn't sufficiently intercede. Maybe that's why he had been drawn to changing careers once he had moved back to New York. But she had difficulty consigning this Ryan situation to the same category as an example of Eckley's failed altruism when he had been so evidently gleeful as the winner of Christine's affection. You should be able to be happy being a winner, she reflected as her eggs arrived, without stomping on the loser.

"And you shouldn't feel any guilt about this either," Eckley continued, as if reading her thoughts. "What you and Ryan had—that was a kid's relationship. You were able to grow up and move on; I don't see why he can't too. And you should see what he's been like for the last decade. Couldn't keep a band together, couldn't keep a job or an apartment. You're lucky you ended up with me." He grabbed her hand across the table and kissed it as she reached for her fork. Though whether it had been luck or merely fate that had brought David into her life, she wasn't so sure.

Eckley had also mentioned that when he was choosing a new career, becoming a transit cop had been his second choice after he was rejected by the CIA. He didn't talk about it often, but she sensed that he was still bitter about having been eliminated from the selection process, though being a former hardcore kid probably had something to do with it, so she had urged him not to take it personally. It could also have something to do with a theory that Eckley had let slip one night: he thought his mom had been in the CIA. No, he didn't have any definitive proof, besides her abject secrecy and the odd trajectory of her government-adjacent career. Mrs. Eckley had left when David was 13, so he had now lived longer without her than with her. And he blamed her for all sorts of things: that she had vacillated between treating him like the greatest thing in the world and a piece of shit, and that she was also the source of his trust and abandonment issues. Though Christine had her bachelor's in psychology and was starting to consider going for her master's, she didn't feel qualified to comment and instead encouraged him to seek professional help, a suggestion he always rebuffed.

But overall, for David and Christine, the good moments outweighed the bad. Christine could only hope that wherever he was, the same was true for Ryan Marnell.

* * *

When Ryan had moved in with David Eckley, things were looking up. He had been painting and painting and painting, storing the overflow in his old bedroom at his mom's apartment, though at some point, he was going to run out of space. Well, maybe in his future home he'd have more room. He had chosen not to renew the lease for his attic apartment on Villa Ave. in Yonkers since his rent was being raised and his landlady was nosy as fuck. First she hadn't let him bring his cat, Vivian, who was now living happily with Ryan's mom. That should have been a sign of things to come. Next, she was constantly complaining about the smell of paint, since he didn't have a separate studio space anymore, everything having gotten so much more expensive in Westchester lately.

He had been working at this warehouse on MacQuesten Parkway in Mount Vernon, but had gotten let go just after giving up the lease on his apartment. The only explanation was that they had found someone who could do his job both cheaper and better. A normal left-leaning person might have blamed management for wanting to pay another worker less, and a normal right-leaning person might have blamed an immigrant for taking his job. But Ryan, who didn't trust the government in any form whatsoever, knew that neither factor was the real reason he had been let go. Of course the CIA didn't want him to have a job! They must have been deliberately influencing his performance the entire time he was there. Anyway, he was glad the job was over, as he hated working down the block from that business with the Oronzio sign. The owner was Christine's dad's cousin, but in the world of Ryan Marnell, it primarily served to remind him of his ex, whom he had never really gotten over, although they hadn't spoken in a decade.

Ryan hadn't had a girlfriend since Christine, nor had he been adept at maintaining close friendships. In the '90s he had started a band called True Bug with Travis Suslak from Power Structure, but then Travis had moved upstate. His friend Leah from college called once a year or so, but she was working as a rabbi outside of Philly. After his grandmother had died, he had stopped hearing from his cousins. Really the only person that Ryan was consistently in touch with was his mother. So he had blithely declined the opportunity to renew his lease, and now, without a job, there were very few people he could call for a place to crash. His last resort would be to stay with his mom in northwest Yonkers. She had a two-bedroom apartment, and he'd get to be reunited with Vivian, but the second bedroom was tiny, and Ryan would feel like he was in her space. (His mom's, not the cat's.) Plus, he wouldn't have any room to paint, since the bedroom was already full of his existing work.

But there was always his old friend David Eckley. He and David had kept in touch on and off through the last decade before they had caught up more thoroughly the night before Thanksgiving in 2001, when Eckley was still living in Boston. Soon after, Ryan had run into him at the Rambling House in Woodlawn. Eckley was back in New York, living with roommates a few blocks away, and had given Ryan his new number. They had seen each other sporadically the last few years, and when Ryan saw him at Burke's a few weeks before he was supposed to move, he thanked the voices that had told him to walk to the bar that day. Turned out Eckley had moved out of Woodlawn to his own place near Mile Square Road and hesitantly agreed to letting Ryan crash there, with only one condition: "Don't tell anyone you're staying with me."

It was easy moving in with David, since Ryan was just moving into his living room and didn't have much space to bring anything. Ryan barely owned any furniture, mostly just CDs, records, clothes, and his painting things. Anything else he was keeping he stashed at his already overflowing bedroom at his mom's. Vivian would be thrilled by all the new hiding places he was creating for her.

Things were OK at first, since David was hardly ever home. He worked nights, and when he wasn't at work, he often wasn't in the apartment. But once Ryan had been installed at David's for a few weeks, a new problem presented itself. The apartment was in a private home in Yonkers and had its own entrance, but anyone could see him coming and going up the driveway. Ryan soon realized that while he may have kept his promise about not telling anyone he was living with Eckley, his nosy landlady and her equally perspicacious neighbors were more than aware of his appearance in the neighborhood. Fuck! Somehow he had gone from one overly-observant landlady to another.

Becky McAuley

At first, he couldn't tell if Mrs. Petrillo was markedly malevolent or merely meddlesome. She had asked him a variety of pointed questions about what he was doing there and how he spent his time. Ryan had rapidly mumbled answers: that he was just briefly staying with Eckley, and no, he was not planning to take up residence in the apartment. Not only did she seem unconvinced, but Ryan swore that she had subsequently recruited various cronies to track his every move.

So he wasn't surprised to realize that the neighbors were also controlling his thoughts. He didn't reveal *that* part to Eckley, just that there seemed to be an unusual amount of eyes on him lately, or on their apartment in general.

"I'm telling you—she's not spying on you. Though to be fair, you've been acting really fucking weird."

"Forget I said anything." He should have known that David wouldn't have been sympathetic, that perhaps David was even behind the increased surveillance! He still didn't believe that David had been rejected from the CIA, even if he was purportedly working as a transit cop. Or that even if he wasn't the source of the watching, he didn't seem affected by it. David was there so little and never seemed to bring friends or girls to the house. Ryan had a feeling he might have a girlfriend somewhere, as he'd heard him on the phone occasionally, but the calls always seemed to arrive on Eckley's cell, rather than the landline.

The situation reached a breaking point one Saturday in March, though not in a way that Ryan expected. He was walking back down Mile Square Road when someone honked at him from a passing car. Ryan immediately recognized Christine behind the wheel, listening to some great song that would remain stuck in his head for at least a year. She was as gorgeous as ever, inadvertently dazzling him when she flipped up her sunglasses. Ryan realized that the sunglasses move was probably to ensure he recognized her, but he would have recognized her anywhere. That didn't mean that he knew how to feel about her sudden appearance. Of course he had been thinking of her on and off since they had broken up in 1990, wondering if he had correctly concluded she had been compromised. But if he had known he was going to re-encounter her, he would have preferred more warning, and for the reunion not to be taking place where his movements were monitored and his thoughts possibly at risk. Though he was intrigued to learn she also had a friend in the neighborhood and was on the verge of asking if this person was experiencing similar issues when she got out of the car to walk with him.

As they meandered down Kingston Avenue, Ryan tried to think of something to say that would compress all his feelings from the last decade into one cogent and persuasive statement, but the voices were fucking with him again. They had reached David's house before he was able to speak.

Lost Indignation

Ryan stopped, about to indicate that this was where he was staying, that it was nice to have seen her, and they should keep in touch after he moved, when David walked outside. Christine paused, looked horrified and tried to play it off by continuing down the road. But Ryan's mind, while taxed by the interference of his neighbors, was still able to put two and two together as soon as he saw Christine's reaction to him seeing her and David in the same place.

He couldn't remember exactly what had followed, except that his suspicious were confirmed and that he had been propelled into the house as if by an otherworldly force to get his stuff and get the fuck out of there. At one point, he found himself singing "Just a Friend," louder than he'd sung anything since the backing vocals for the Indignation demo. If the old ladies on the street hadn't had suspicions about him before, they certainly would now. But that was OK; he was getting the fuck out of here and away from the reaches of the mind control (he hoped). The Christine thing hurt, but maybe it was the push he needed to get away from the surveillance. And she and Eckley fucking deserved each other.

At least he didn't have a lot of stuff to move. In retrospect, he should have pulled the car up into the driveway, but he wanted to avoid any further confrontation with Eckley. What if his neighbors somehow engineered it for Eckley to throw himself under the car? Christine would never forgive him for running over her new boyfriend. So he awkwardly shuffled his belongings out to the Civic, parked on the street a few houses down, and managed to get it all in a few trips. Sweat pouring down his forehead, Ryan closed the car door for the last time on Kingston Avenue. Now that he was done, where should he go?

There were so few people he could call, but that wasn't a problem, as he felt like driving for hours. Wait—hadn't Travis from Power Structure moved somewhere up near Albany and told him to call if he was ever in the area? Well, tonight he was going to be in the area. He wished he had Travis's number on him, then laughed aloud when he remembered he had everything he owned in the car! Before he got too far up the Thruway, he pulled over at the rest stop in Ardsley to find the box that contained his notebook of contact information. Travis sounded surprised to hear from him, but confirmed he'd be around that night and that Ryan was welcome to come by.

After playing in bands that had shared a stage in the '80s, Ryan and Travis had teamed up in True Bug in the '90s. Travis was the only person in Power Structure who could play his instrument somewhat proficiently, so Ryan felt lucky to have secured his bass playing talents. They had started as a Helmet rip-off, for which Ryan had initially had high hopes, but soon fell apart after issues with the singer and drummer. After the breakup of True Bug, Ryan had mostly withdrawn from hardcore to focus on art, and though he had been to a few shows in the '90s at 7 Willow Street and The Low Down, he hadn't followed hardcore closely after that.

Travis had been Ryan's main link to contemporary hardcore and enjoyed keeping him apprised on developments involving former Indignation members. Around the time True Bug had formed, good old Dion Carina had been singing in a new band called Behold the Mind. He had moved to Brooklyn, run afoul of some notorious locals after getting too cozy with one's girlfriend, and then relocated to Florida. Ryan was relieved to learn that he wasn't the only member of his old band who had made a total mess of things.

Thanks to the clear directions he had been provided, Ryan was turning into Travis's driveway just over two hours later. His former bassist met him at the door.

"Yo! Thanks so much for letting me come stay."

"Don't worry about it, dude. I was just playing *Soulcalibur*."

For a few minutes they sat in silence, occasionally punctuated by Travis rebuking the game. "What the fuck—I blocked that!" Ryan realized that at some point he was going to have to explain why he was here, even if Travis had not yet asked outright.

"So I was living with David Eckley, remember him? And first I had some issues with his neighbors, who are all these nosy old Yonkers ladies—"

"I know just the type," Travis concurred.

"And then I can tell he's dating someone, but I'd never met her. Until tonight, when he shows up at the house with my ex Christine! I was living there for months and had no idea. So that was it. I just moved all my shit out and got in the car."

"Fuck! That sucks, dude. But wow, David Eckley, I haven't thought about him in forever. What's he up to, besides dating your ex?"

"He went to school up in Boston, played in some bands, and then moved back down to New York after 9/11."

"What bands was he in? He wasn't in Indignation with you, right?"

"No, he was never in Indignation. Ministry of Fear was the one you've probably heard of? I think they put out a record." Not that Ryan heard of them either until Eckley had recently mentioned them.

"Oh shit, I have their CD. They were pretty good. I saw them at the Saratoga Youth Center with Dying Breed."

David's band being "pretty good" brought no comfort to Ryan, though he was intrigued. "Are they really? I've never actually heard them."

"Are you serious dude? You were so tight back in the day. Though if he's banging your ex then maybe you're not that close." Ryan winced, but he couldn't argue with that logic.

"Here, let me finish whipping Heihachi's ass and then I'll put on the 7" songs at the end of their CD. It's my favorite of their stuff."

Travis soon went to fetch the CD and skipped to the 7" material. As soon as Ryan heard the main riff of the first track, he knew something was wrong.

"What the fuck! These are my songs!"

"What do you mean?" Travis looked unsettled by the direction this night had taken.

"That's from 'Put It Down!' The Indignation song! They just ... turned it into something else." It was fucking disorienting hearing this recycled Indignation tune as the basis for this downtuned, more metallic track.

"Should we listen to the rest of it? Hopefully it's a coincidence?" They sat in silence through the rest of the demo, punctuated by Ryan's exclamations each time he recognized another Indignation riff. It was a four song 7"; he recognized Indignation in at least half the songs, and another on the full length.

"I can't believe this shit." What the hell was going on here? Just a few hours ago, Ryan had been likely living in the same house as a copy of this CD, as he was sure David must have at least one copy lying around, thoroughly unaware that David Eckley had stolen both his songs and his ex-girlfriend.

"And I mean, like, how did no one notice? And why the fuck did Eckley think he could get away with this?" How did *you* not notice, Ryan almost wanted to ask, as Travis would have remembered the Indignation songs, right? Though the realization hit him that their demo had been recorded over 15 years ago and hardly anyone was likely to remember. One of the many pieces of his life that hadn't worked out as he had intended.

"Perhaps I wasn't wrong," Travis reiterated, "that this guy ain't much of a friend."

At least the Indignation revelation resulted in Travis becoming an extra generous host, as he was soon offering Ryan some weed and Vicodin alongside their beers. A few hours later, the day's events still stung, but Ryan was feeling slightly less, well, indignant.

"Fuck, man. I'm gonna need to figure out a place to stay."

"You can crash here for a while. I don't mind. And this area isn't expensive." Ryan was surprised to hear how little Travis was paying for this house, which had one bedroom and a moldy bathroom, but still. "If you ended up wanting to stick around, I'm sure you could find an apartment. And there are some good shows in Albany."

"I haven't even been going to shows," Ryan admitted. "I just need a place to live. And to paint."

"You still doing the art thing?"

"Yeah, man. When I can. And my mom's family is from somewhere not that far from here. Not that I know any of them," Ryan realized. Had that been an unconscious plan to drive up here, or just a coincidence? His mom never talked about her family and she never came up to visit. His dad's family had all seemed normal, so maybe someone on his mom's side was the key to the issues he was experiencing.

"If you're looking for work, there's someone else up here that you know," Travis continued. "Guy that played drums for Indignation? He's an arborist, he's got his own company over in Stephentown."

"Matt *Zimmer*?" Ryan asked. He couldn't imagine Zimmer as a tree man in upstate New York, unless he was recruiting lumberjacks to turn them into wrestlers or something.

"No, Chris—that guy who filled in on the demo. You guys were right not to use Nelson!" He laughed.

Ryan had almost forgotten about CC, the friend of Dion's who had swooped in at the last minute to record with them. In their brief interactions, he had seemed like a quiet, chill dude. He vaguely remembered something about CC being a drug dealer, but that was a decade and a half ago, and there would have been plenty of time for him to reinvent himself. Ryan didn't know anything about trees, besides smoking them sometimes, but perhaps this dude wouldn't be a bad guy to work for. He thanked Travis for the tip and vowed to get in touch.

On Monday morning, after Travis had left for work, Ryan had called the number for Double C Trees that was listed in his host's phone book. He was surprised that CC remembered him and invited him over to chat that afternoon. And while CC didn't have any openings on his staff, he knew a guy who ran a print shop whose new guy had just quit. Did Ryan perhaps have any experience in that line of work? In fact, he did: he had briefly worked at a print shop in Mamaroneck before quitting when he became convinced that a frequent customer was reading his mind. But his boss had liked him, and it transpired that he was willing to give him a reference. A week later, after typing up his (only slightly falsified) resume on Travis's computer, Ryan had a job.

And soon he had a tiny apartment above a garage out on Zief Lane, a dirt road a few minutes' drive from the print shop. There was no kitchen, and it had a shared bathroom downstairs in the garage, but it was affordable and had good light for painting. Ryan had called his mom to let her know he had moved upstate, and she sent him some money to put towards the security deposit. This part of the state was fucking beautiful, and that, plus the fact that he hardly knew anybody and didn't have much else to do, just let him paint and paint and paint. After a few months, he was running out of space for all his work and started paying $10 a month for a storage unit on Route 22 in Stephentown. And sometimes, he even managed to forget the whole sorry tale of David Eckley and his incursion onto Indignation.

But this idyllic time lasted under a year: in December, the owner of the print shop informed Ryan he was selling and moving to North Carolina. Ryan's role was eliminated during the transfer, but at least he had been working for long enough in a real W-2 job and was able to get unemployment for the first time in years. He knew he was supposed to be looking for jobs, and he did, halfheartedly, but there wasn't much in the area. Maybe he needed to move back to Westchester. He didn't want to give up this apartment, which was the cheapest place he'd lived in forever, but the lease was up in April and he would run out of money if he didn't find a job soon, as his unemployment was about to run out. What he really needed was some money to paint (and a place to paint) without having to work full-time. And how the hell was he supposed to manage that?

The answer would appear, once again, in the form of David Eckley.

* * *

After Ryan was out of the picture, Christine slowly forgave Eckley for how he had rubbed the relationship in the face of his friend. They enjoyed the rest of 2004 together, even though Christine was alarmed that she couldn't get him to vote for John Kerry that fall. It was OK that they were so different, right? Overall, Christine enjoyed that David liked to have his way and be in control. She had always been independent, but was also indecisive and liked to let things take their course. That had been the problem with Slow Blink, her band back in L.A.—that it was her and three other equally passive dudes, none of them ambitious enough to take things to the next level or the certainty that that's where they belonged.

Besides the Ryan thing, the next major fight between Christine and David occurred when Arup, her old drummer from Slow Blink, was visiting from L.A. in February 2005. Arup was one of her closest guy friends and no one to worry about, she tried to indirectly reassure David (without implying that he *was* worrying); he had seemed a little snappish about Christine going down to the city to hang out with some guy. Arup didn't even date white girls! Or hook up with them, as far as Christine knew, though she was now a few years removed from being an endless ear for his dating shenanigans. Nevertheless, she was sure that David would have tried to tag along if he wasn't working that night. He had come over for a few hours that afternoon before work and before Christine was heading down to the city.

She met Arup at Washington Square Park, and they walked over to Red Bamboo. After migrating east to Double Down after dinner, Arup proposed continuing to Williamsburg to hang out with his hosts. They took the J train to Marcy Ave. and were soon screaming Bold lyrics while drinking Sparks in Arup's friend's living room, before venturing outside with assorted roommates and guests to play wiffleball in the street. "I HOPE that's a wiffleball," some passerby remarked acidly, after one of Christine's line drives ventured a bit too near his car, which busted them all up into hysterics. Somehow, "I HOPE that's a wiffleball," was the funniest thing she'd heard all night, including Arup's impression of Matt from Bold. Fuck, the wiffleball had been a great idea! They used to play sometimes in parking lots in L.A., but this was the first time she'd played in the middle of the street in Brooklyn. Christine was down to her sweater, with her coat, hoodie and purse draped over a nearby iron railing. She was glad she had worn her Adidas shell toes, which she had chosen to pacify Eckley that she wasn't trying to look attractive, instead of her high heeled boots, which wouldn't have worked for wiffleball.

Fuck. She had barely thought about her boyfriend all night, while enjoying the New York version of the type of silliness she and Arup used to get up to in L.A.. What the hell time was it? Christine retreated to claim her purse from the railing and pulled out her flip phone. 1:27 a.m.! And her phone was almost dead. There was no guarantee that she would make it to Grand Central for the last train home to Westchester. She could ride all the way home on the subway and take a cab home to Hastings from the end of the 1 or the 4 train, but why deal with all of that when she could stay out all night and take the first train home in the morning? She and Eckley had made vague plans for him to stop by her apartment again when his shift ended early that morning, but she was having too much fun in Brooklyn. She used the last of her battery to leave him a rambling voicemail about the wiffleball and missing the last train and that she would be back at her apartment in the morning if he still wanted to come by and spank her with a wiffleball bat—which suddenly seemed like a great idea ("Hey, can I borrow this?" No, it unfortunately transpired that she could not, "Though I'm sure you can get one at any fine local sports emporium or minimart!" Arup yelled into the phone as he carried her off over his shoulder, Christine shrieking that she was leaving a voicemail). Once the message was complete, she turned off the phone to save the last modicum of battery and headed to the bodega with the others to re-up on the Sparks and continue their night.

When Christine finally arrived home the next morning, sweaty and disheveled and still drunk, Eckley was at her apartment, and he was livid. Any fantasies she may have harbored about making things up to him once she was a little cleaner and then going to the diner for breakfast were immediately quashed by his disproportionately disturbing reaction to her night out. First he accused her of fucking Arup.

"We were playing wiffleball! With three other people!"

Lost Indignation

"Oh, so did you fuck them too?"

"You know I wouldn't do that, plus we were listening to Bold, and I don't think it's possible for anything sexy to happen while listening to Bold!" Somehow that was even funnier than "I HOPE that's a wiffleball," though unfortunately only to Christine. Her laughter didn't make a dent in David's cold fury. After continuing to scream for about 20 minutes about how he couldn't trust her, he launched himself out of the apartment, slamming the door behind him. Christine sank onto the bed, exhausted and disappointed. So much for the leftover good mood from the night before.

After four days of silence, during which Christine had tried tentatively reaching out, but only once, Eckley reappeared at her apartment with flowers and a duffle bag. He swore that he missed her and that he would never blow up at her again the way he had Sunday morning. Christine, in turn, apologized for not communicating better on Saturday and not acknowledging his feelings.

"And I think you need to go to therapy," she added. "I know that you have trust issues based on stuff that has happened to you in the past, and I understand if that still has an impact on you, but you can't take it out on me." When she had brought this up previously, David had flatly resisted, but this time he tearfully vowed to find a therapist.

Apologies accepted, Eckley gestured to the duffle bag. Inside was a wiffle ball bat, along with a change of clothes and his MTAPD uniform. "I was thinking we should move in together," Eckley explained. "If we have more time together, I wouldn't worry so much about you going out with your friends in the city. But first we better test out that wiffleball bat you were talking about."

"It's not a bad idea, moving in together. I'll think about it, though I like having my own place. You know I just renewed my lease in December, and this apartment is too small for two of us. But you're right, I'm not going to move in with a guy who doesn't own a wiffleball bat. Let me just change into my ... uniform. So you can punish me for Saturday."

For the next few months, Eckley reverted to treating Christine respectively and attentively, and his eruption in February seemed to recede as an anomaly. He would occasionally mention the idea of living together, and Christine was slowly warming up to the idea. With Easter approaching, she decided to invite him to Easter dinner with her family. Her parents were still living in their house in Dobbs Ferry, though Dana had moved in with two roommates in West Harrison. Eckley had met her parents and her other sisters Stephanie and Marie in the past, and of course her cousin Anthony knew him from back in the day, but this would be the first time she was inviting him for a family holiday, as the kind of guy she was considering keeping around. She supposed he was, for now, if not long term. It wasn't that she had tried to keep him from her family; afterwards, she realized that may not have been a bad idea.

Eckley charmed Christine's various assembled family members throughout the Easter meal. Anthony was working down in the city, which she realized was fortuitous: he was her only relative who had never seemed impressed with Eckley, and had, in fact, expressed outright dismay when Christine had finally admitted she was dating Ryan's best friend. True, David had been more dismissive of Anthony back in the '80s, unlike Ryan, who had always been genuinely kind to her cousin. And there was of course the real cop vs. transit cop rivalry, as Anthony was currently working for the NYPD (though he was disillusioned by their recent tactics and hoping to transfer closer to home in the next couple of years, or quit policing entirely). Still, it unnerved her that her quiet, observant, heart-of-gold cousin seemed to straight-up dislike her boyfriend. Besides his trust issues, abandonment issues, and overconfidence in himself, was there something else about Eckley that she should be worried about?

Christine would have been able to answer her own question if she had walked into the kitchen at just the right time. Eckley had volunteered to help with the dishes, with Christine vowing to join him in just a few more minutes (she was looking at old photos with her dad). Dana had gone out the front door for a cigarette, but moments later, she silently let herself in through the kitchen and slipped something into his pocket, casually brushing his back with one of her huge tits. David, with his hands in the water, couldn't even react before she disappeared the way she came. For the rest of the visit, he tried to avoid interacting with the 25-year-old Dana, and especially avoided looking at her big blue eyes and distracting body. But once he had dropped Christine off at her apartment, he couldn't wait any longer, pulling into the Hastings High School parking lot to jerk off to thoughts of Dana, exploding almost immediately into a Dunkin' Donuts napkin. God, Dana was so hot! Why couldn't Christine be her twin, both age-wise and tits-wise? With that taken care of, he reached into his pocket to see what she had put there, though he was pretty sure he knew. It was her cell phone number.

If David Eckley was acting at all unusual over the next few months, Christine wouldn't have attributed it to the fact that her boyfriend had started fucking her youngest sister. Instead, she was prepared to chalk up his jumpiness to the return of Ryan Marnell. Ryan had been living upstate, but was now back in Westchester. Was David not planning to mention this to her at all? She wouldn't even have found out if she hadn't seen his phone ringing one day, the screen indicating "Ryan cell," before Eckley snatched it up and took the phone into the bathroom with him, closing the door. When Christine asked him about it, Eckley was oddly evasive, just mentioning that he had run into Ryan at Dunkin' Donuts. Though he soon changed most of the contacts in his phone so they were listed under just the first letters of their names.

But Ryan being back in town potentially influenced a larger change in their lives. A few weeks later, Christine's landlord informed her that he was hoping to start renovations on the building, if they could come to an agreement to end her lease. As soon as David heard that she might have to move, he started talking nonstop about moving in together and getting out of his lease with Mrs. Petrillo. And when she saw the apartment that a friend of Eckley's dad was subletting in Hastings, she was down. It was a garden apartment on Broadway, walking distance to the train and the Aqueduct trail, and a big one-bedroom where they would both have their own space. They were finally moving in together, but at least it would (sort of) be on her own terms.

Christine wondered if David's alacrity was partly because he didn't want Ryan to know where he lived. But why would that be? Ryan Marnell was the furthest thing from a threat. She knew David had been in touch with him, but for some reason, he seemed like he didn't want her to know about it. Every time she heard him conducting a hushed phone conversation in the other room, she assumed it was with Ryan. There was no way she could have known that David was sometimes talking to her sister instead.

In October, Christine had to get some document notarized for her car title and decided to bring them to the guy that her dad always used, an architect who was also a notary and whose office was in that building down by the river in Dobbs Ferry. She had been surprised at first that their old hangout was now an office building, though it was nearly as dilapidated as she remembered it, and the small offices and artists' studios looked mostly occupied. She was walking out of the building towards her car when she saw Ryan Marnell sitting on a bench by the pond.

"Hey, Ryan?" This time she approached with more caution than when she had accidentally surprised him last spring. But Ryan held up his hand, either waving her over or at least not waving her away.

"How have you been? I was just getting some stuff notarized by the architect here."

"Oh, Stefan? He's a nice guy. I work in the building sometimes," Ryan replied, but didn't elaborate.

"Isn't that wild, that there are businesses here now? Real adult people working here rather than just kids hanging out?" Referring, without meaning to, to the fact they had met in this very parking lot. Christine still remembered almost every moment of that first interaction, but didn't want to remind herself how different that Ryan had been from the one sitting next to her now. That Ryan, with his whole life ahead of him, brandishing the flyer to his band's first show. That Ryan, who was actively trying to impress her, rather than merely tolerating her questions now.

Nevertheless, Christine was seized by a wild hope and started to ask him one last question that she'd wanted to articulate for years. "Ryan, did you ever wish that—" she started, at the exact same time as he said:

"This is the only place I feel safe."

"Oh." Christine supposed that negated the rest of what she had been planning to say.

"Don't tell him you saw me here," he continued sharply.

"Don't tell who?" But she realized there could be only one person to whom Ryan was referring: David Eckley. What did it mean that they were each avoiding each other?

"But I do have one more question for you," Ryan continued. Christine wondered if he was finally going to ask her—

"... what was the song you were playing in the car when you saw me last year?"

* * *

One Monday night in August 2006, as she was falling asleep, Christine thought suddenly of Ryan. She was alone in the apartment in Hastings, with Eckley at work. She wondered how Ryan was doing, if he was still hanging out at that building in Dobbs. Maybe she should go over there with a burned copy of the RJD2 CD, even if he had brushed her off when she first offered. But the thought faded as she drifted into sleep. The next day, she had a vague feeling that something was wrong but couldn't put her finger on why she felt sad.

On Wednesday morning, when Christine woke up for work, David was sitting at the kitchen table. Today was his day off, but he was usually still asleep at this hour due to his schedule working nights.

"Babe, there's something I need to tell you," he started, his face oddly blank. "Before you find out from the newspaper."

"What are you talking about?" Christine was immediately alarmed.

"On Monday night, when I was at work, this guy got hit by a train ... and I just found out that it was Ryan."

"Oh my God." Afterwards, Christine wasn't sure who had started crying first, as their grief seemed unstoppable and instantaneous, or at least hers was.

Somehow they had migrated from the kitchen into their bed. It was, Christine noted grimly, not only the first time they'd had sex in a while, but also the first time when Ryan was no longer alive, no longer a shadow in the back of their relationship. With every thrust she could almost imagine herself saying, "He's gone, he's gone, you won."

But any feelings of reconciliation had evaporated in the days leading up to the funeral and wake. David was particularly prickly on the subject of Ryan's funeral and couldn't understand why Christine wanted to attend. "The wake, yes, I can understand, but the funeral?"

"Who knows how many friends he even has left?" She muttered between her tears. "I think it makes sense for me to go with you."

"Well first of all, you weren't his friend," David countered. "I was his best friend, and you're my girlfriend. And that's how you should be seeing this."

"That is so unfair," Christine choked back. "I've known for years that you never think of anyone besides yourself, but—" she had a half second to dodge before Eckley's fist smashed the wall behind her head.

"Goddamnit, this is not the week to pull this shit!"

"And it's never OK to treat me like this," Christine replied calmly. "Luckily, I was just leaving." She picked up her purse and stalked out the door to the Hastings farmers market before he could object.

Sometimes on Saturday mornings when David got home from work, he stayed up late to have breakfast with her, which at one point had been some of their happiest times together. Lately, she'd either been feigning sleep when he got home or making sure she was already out of the apartment. It had been a mistake to be here at all, and now she'd have to stay away for as long as her farmer's market haul could handle. And after the Ryan-related events were over, she knew she had to start thinking about leaving for good. While she and David hadn't been getting along for a while, today was the first time he'd tried to hit her, though she was sure it wouldn't be the last. If her family was OK without her on the East Coast, then there was nothing stopping her from moving back out west. She had eventually traded the lame temp job for a permanent but equally lame job in Tarrytown, but it was nothing that couldn't be severed with two weeks' notice. And while she had a feeling that David wouldn't let her go so easily, perhaps they were sufficiently sick of each other that he would see it was for the best to go their separate ways.

The wake was on Sunday in Eastchester, with the funeral to be held on Monday at Annunciation Church back in Crestwood. David was working Sunday night, but Christine assumed he would put in an appearance with her on Sunday afternoon, even though he was also going to the funeral on Monday. (Whether she would be joining him was still up for debate.) But on Sunday, when she went into the bedroom to check on him and suggest they should start getting ready, he looked incapacitated and exhausted. "Can you please just go without me?"

"Are you sure?" Christine wavered. While it might look odd for her to show up without Ryan's childhood best friend, she wouldn't mind getting to visit with old friends without David there, provided that any others came. Liz Zimmer was down in DC, and their old friend Kate was living with her family in Connecticut and couldn't make it either. Christine hadn't been in touch with any of Ryan's own friends in years. She hoped there would be a decent showing, but somehow doubted it.

"I'm sure. Just go." She graced his forehead with a kiss, then continued getting ready. Usually David was a huge fan of the black summer dress she was wearing to the wake, but her ensemble elicited not one compliment as she assembled it under his distracted gaze.

Christine grabbed her sunglasses and transferred her things to her grandmother's black purse. "I'll tell everyone you said hi, and I won't stay long."

As Christine parked on Main Street and walked down the hill towards the funeral home, she felt like an echo of her former self arriving at a hardcore show alone. Though luckily, back then, she'd rarely had to do that, as her cousin Anthony had been so willing to tag along even when Liz and Kate weren't around. She had thought about calling Anthony to come with her today, but he was probably working, and she wouldn't have wanted to explain the situation with David. Anthony had never trusted the guy, and he had been right all along, she conceded. He had a good heart, her cousin, and she knew that when she eventually broke the news about breaking up with David, he wouldn't try to say "I told you so" and would just be happy she was safe.

While the wake wasn't crowded, there was a decent smattering of people in attendance to pay their respects to Ryan. Christine was crushed into a hug by Warren Yatrofsky, who looked significantly older than when she had last seen him, and she nodded to one of the guys who she thought had played in Power Structure. Aside from Sean Div, the one that had died in the '90s, she could never remember the rest of their names.

"Christine?" She turned. It was Ryan's friend Leah Sheftel from New Paltz, her wild black hair now carefully cropped. Christine had been briefly concerned about Ryan's closest college friend being female, until she found out that Leah was in love with a girl at Vassar, which is how she had ended up at New Paltz in the first place. They had only met a few times, and the last time they had seen each other was in the hospital with Ryan, 26 years before.

"Leah! Wow. I wasn't sure how many people knew about Ryan or that his mom would know how to get in touch with."

"I gave her my number in 1990," Leah recounted, "and told her to call me if anything happened to him. Which she has, a few times since. But nothing like this. She asked me to do the eulogy," Leah smiled wickedly. "I wonder if it's the kind of church that would mind that there's a lesbian

Lost Indignation

rabbi involved?"

Christine smiled. "If they do, fuck 'em." As she looked around for any old people she might have scandalized, Christine wondered why no one had asked David to say something at the service tomorrow. Or had he declined and thought it not worth even mentioning to her? He had been acting so strangely that she was glad Leah was in charge, and it was fitting for a lesbian rabbi to honor the offbeat life of Ryan Marnell.

After catching up with Leah, Christine spotted Mrs. Marnell between condolences and stepped over to greet her.

"Mrs. Marnell? I don't know if you remember me ..." Which was a cover for if Mrs. Marnell did remember her, and not fondly.

"Christine!" Mrs. Marnell beamed a smile at her and hugged her hello. "Of course I remember you. But please, call me Eileen." Christine was glad that the news of her treachery had apparently not reached her.

"I was so sorry to hear about Ryan. "And I can't imagine what you must be going through. But I'm just glad I got to be part of his life." It was true: now that he was gone, there were fewer painful moments of wondering what he was doing, and it was easier to just remember the past.

"It's been a very hard week," Eileen confided. "Much worse than when Dennis died ..." She paused, acknowledging that Christine had been at that service too. "In some ways, I'm glad to know he's not in pain. All those years I worried about him, not knowing how he was feeling, or where he was living ..." Her voice broke, then she steadied herself. Christine wondered how many people had let her share her true feelings about Ryan's death and was glad she could provide a sympathetic ear.

"Honestly, one thing that bothers me," Eileen continued, "is that they're saying that he did this himself. I'm sure it was an accident. But I couldn't convince them to change it on the official report," she added sadly. "There's a difference, you know, about where he'll go after this? But no one wanted to listen to me."

"Oh, Eileen, I'm so sorry, I didn't even think of that." Christine felt even worse for Mrs. Marnell. "He died in Dobbs Ferry, right?" She tried to think if she knew anyone in the police department there. The old friends of her dad's were probably long gone.

"Yes, he'd been living over there for a bit ... at one point he was staying with me, but then he said he felt safer there ..." Eileen looked like she was about to lose it, but stayed on track. "And I know he didn't want to die, at least that day" she continued, stronger now, "since when they found him, he didn't have his watch. His dad's watch—well his grandfather's. He had managed to keep it through all the tough times. He must have put it away somewhere if he knew he was going to be doing something messy or risky. Maybe he took it off to paint ... I haven't had the heart to go through his car yet."

"Well, whatever the police report says, I'm sure he'll go to a good place," Christine replied. His mom squeezed her hand.

"So he was still painting, then? Right up until the accident?" Christine tried to steer the conversation in a more productive direction.

"Yes, he painted so much the last few years, and he was going to have something in a show in Hastings ... they're all over my apartment. I should give you one, to remember him by, if you'd like."

"I'd love that." Christine was touched. She would love to have a painting of Ryan's, though how would she explain it to David, or move it across the country, if that was still her next step?

"Write your phone number in the guest book ..." Eileen gestured to the front of the room, then caught the eye of an elderly couple moving towards her. "It was so nice to see you, Christine, and please do keep in touch." Christine vowed to do just that, and stepped away to let Mrs. Marnell greet other guests.

Christine stayed at the wake for longer than she had planned, though as she walked outside and checked her watch, there were still a few hours left before David had to leave for work. Before leaving town, she texted him to ask if he wanted anything from Burrito Poblano, which was just over the border in Tuckahoe and possibly the village's next-most-famous export after its eponymous marble, but he didn't respond. Could he be asleep, or did he just not want to hear from her? What if there was something actually wrong with him, related or unrelated to his grief about Ryan's death? Christine denied her own burrito craving and decided to head straight home to check on him. "Nevermind about the burritos. See you soon!" she texted, before starting the car.

As Christine drove west on Tuckahoe Road, listening to Jawbox's "Dreamless," she became increasingly convinced there was something amiss with David in general. She gunned it up the roller coaster hills on Roberts Avenue before turning on Broadway towards their apartment in Hastings. They had been subletting from that friend of Eckley's dad since they moved in together last year, but Christine loved the apartment and had wished the arrangement was permanent, back when she wasn't thinking about upending their life together.

Turning into the parking lot, Christine saw a car that looked like her sister Dana's, though there were a lot of gray Mitsubishi Eclipses around, and what would Dana be doing here without her? She found a spot and hurried up the path towards their apartment, but before opening the door to her common entrance, she froze. There were two voices coming from her bedroom window, two people that Christine knew well.

Dumping her purse in the flowerbed outside the window, Christine ripped the screen from the window frame and cleared the sill out of sheer adrenaline, just in time to see Eckley pulling the sheet over himself and her sister scrambling off the bed, her stupid tramp stamp catching the late afternoon light.

"You know it's not my fault," Eckley reflected calmly, looking surprisingly dignified (and still, heartbreakingly attractive). "This was all her idea. Plus, she's so much younger and hotter than you."

Afterwards, she would think of how when Ryan used to mosh at the Anthrax, he often remembered none of the band's set, only that he had been in constant motion. Christine entered a similar fugue state: smashing a lamp on David as he tried to hold her off, Dana scrambling to retreat; screaming at them to get the fuck out, that she never wanted to see either of them again; hitting David again and again with their bedside phone, once she'd decimated the lamp and alarm clock. By the time she could have gotten a clear shot at her sister, Dana was long gone.

Christine wanted to smash David's stupid face, but when she rampaged into the closet where he kept a mini workbench with his tools neatly hanging from pegboard, she couldn't find the hammer. Only years later did she recall this detail and read anything more into it than her inability to use it on her now-ex boyfriend.

What did she learn, David had asked her back in 2003? Not much, apparently, if she was still willing to trust her sister and David Eckley. As she paced around the bedroom, David having heeded her exhortations to get the fuck out, grabbing his work clothes and scrambling out the door to change who knows where, likely at the gym, but possibly at Dana's apartment (Christine didn't even want to *think* about how many times he'd been to Dana's apartment or that when their parents were helping her sister with her rent out of the goodness of their hearts, they were partially financing the love nest of David Eckley), her mind was suddenly clear. Of course she wouldn't go to the funeral with him. And she'd quit her job and move back out west, after getting tested for every STD known to man.

At least, stuck in her usual inertia, she hadn't started a master's program in New York. And now this horrible scene and its fallout provided an ironclad reason to break up with David, and maybe he wouldn't try to chase her, or hurt her, when she tried to leave. They'd been growing apart for a while, but how much of that was due the ministrations of Dana? Christine didn't want to find out. She had always been amenable to fresh starts. Within a month she'd be back in L.A., though soon she'd learn through his Myspace location that David had moved too: back to Boston. They were all gone from Westchester now: Christine, David, and Ryan Marnell.

Becky McAuley

Chapter 12
2005

When Ryan first moved back to Westchester, he was staying with his mom, but quickly recognized this was not sustainable. He needed a space of his own, mostly to paint, but also to live without his mom incessantly asking him questions. It was different than when he had been a kid back on Crestwood Avenue. Here, there was hardly enough space for both of them, even with his mom at work during the day, though Vivian was happy he was back. It was similar to the situation he had been facing a few years prior, yet more dire since he had been so productive during the past year.

A few weeks after his return, Ryan was driving around Dobbs Ferry when he decided to venture down the driveway to that old building by the river where he had first met Christine. It was no longer abandoned and had been converted to offices and artists' studios. The front door was open, and he walked right in, nodding at a friendly UPS guy with a hand truck full of packages. While exploring the third floor, he passed the open door of a studio and looked inside. He wondered how expensive it was to rent space here. But he didn't have to ponder for long: the artist in question came hustling back from the bathroom. With little prodding, he launched into an account of how he had come to have a studio here, along with the history of various past incarnations of the building. Apparently, it had been a bible factory, a brewery, and—more recently—had housed a branch of the Office of Naval Research. "There's almost no cell service in this place, since the walls are so thick," his conversation partner continued. "Along with all sorts of other irregularities due to its former lives."

"It does sound like it's had an interesting history," Ryan acknowledged. Though he was intrigued not by the traditional history aspects, but rather by the types of protections that might be in place if government research had been conducted here. Would the thickness of the walls, or whatever was blocking the cell phone service, also prevent outsiders from reading his thoughts?

45 minutes later, Ryan finally got to mention that he, too, was an artist. Joel, the keeper of the studio, seemed like a chatty, lonely old guy, and invited Ryan to stop by the space any time. Ryan wasn't a big fan of people, but he recognized this invitation as the first foothold to securing a place in this strange building. So he returned a few times to visit, and Joel complimented his work when Ryan brought a painting to work on in the fourth floor breezeway.

Soon, Joel was inviting Ryan to use the space when he wasn't around. He was going to the Catskills in July, and he wouldn't mind having someone stop by to check on things. "And there are so many other spots here that I'm sure you could find a quiet place to work," Joel continued. "The roof, the abandoned bathroom on the fourth floor, hell there are multiple abandoned bathrooms in this place. You didn't hear this from me, but you probably don't even need to rent space here to work here, you get the idea?"

Ryan did get the idea. He took Joel up on the offer to use his space while he was away that summer and used that time to get familiar with every inch of the building that he hoped would be his new home. And it was true that when he was in here, the voices didn't seem to bother him as much. It was the best he'd felt in years, his time upstate included. And when Joel returned, he seemed legitimately impressed with the work that Ryan had created while he was away and promised to talk to some people about Ryan's output. He told him to keep the set of keys he had loaned him and to use the space any time it was free (with the implication that he didn't want company while he was working). It was the perfect arrangement, in that Ryan could leave some things in Joel's studio, but he preferred working in some of the other corners of the building. He had discovered that he could hide other personal items in the ceiling of one of the basement bathrooms and had started sleeping in Joel's studio too, crashing on an inflatable mattress that he kept in his car. When was the last time he had felt as alive as he did now, painting at night on the tiny open section of the roof or waking up on the floor of the studio around 6 a.m., the first light finding its way in through the windows? Possibly not since Indignation.

Somehow, everything always led back to Indignation.

One afternoon in May, soon after the discovery of the space in Dobbs, Ryan had seen Eckley coming out of the Dunkin' Donuts on Odell Terrace in northwest Yonkers, not far from his mom's apartment. Instinctively, he slid down lower into his car. He knew he should confront his former friend, but he wasn't ready. Instead, he made a note to hang out here more often until he encountered him again. But two weeks passed, and he hadn't seen Eckley. And as the interval increased, the more he craved the opportunity to confront him. But when they were face to face, what would he even say? Ryan cringed thinking back to when he had bestowed his extra copy of the demo on Eckley in 2001, after Eckley claimed to have lost his. Obviously that had been a lie, unless he'd lost it right after ripping off all the songs!

When he did finally spot him again at Dunkin', Ryan waited until David was exiting with his coffee, then popped out of own car, keys in hand, to make it look like he had just arrived.

"Dave! What's up dude?" Ryan was glad Eckley didn't drop his coffee, though that might have served him right. They continued converging, though at a slower pace than Eckley had been moving previously. Ryan was glad he had caught him by surprise.

"Ryan Marnell," Eckley greeted him warily. "Where have you been hiding?"

Hiding? He hadn't been hiding. "I've been living upstate," Ryan explained. "I just got back to Westchester, so I've been staying with my mom, she still lives around here. Are you over here now too?"

"I'm sometimes in the area," Eckley responded evasively. Ryan wondered if that meant he was still with Christine, who was from Dobbs Ferry and could easily still live in one of the Rivertowns.

"You remember Travis, from Power Structure? I hung out with him a few times when I was living up by Albany." Ryan didn't mention that he had fled to Travis's house specifically on the night of the painful interaction with Eckley and Christine last March, that Travis was the reason he had signed a lease up there in the first place. "He said he saw Ministry of Fear play once in Saratoga. He really dug you guys." Eckley didn't react, but he looked slightly on edge, like he was seeing Ryan for the first time since he had exited the Civic. "So he played your CD for me."

"And?" Eckley seemed compelled to seek some sort of feedback. "What did you think?"

"I thought some of those songs on the 7" sounded a lot like Indignation. Could be a total coincidence." He tried his best to keep his voice light.

"Definitely a coincidence," Eckley agreed. "I didn't even play guitar in that band. I just sang. I don't know if Tyler, the guitarist, ever heard your tape."

"But you wouldn't want anyone to get the wrong idea, right? Has anyone else ever actually said this to your face, or just me?"

"Just you," Eckley responded, now more weary than wary. "I have to get home. But I'm glad I ran into you." He nestled the coffee in the crook of his arm and extricated his wallet with his free hand. "I've been meaning to get in touch with you, and make sure you were OK. Think of this as me giving you your security deposit back." He drew out five twenties, and handed them to Ryan, who hated himself as his hands closed around them; neither of them acknowledged that there had been no security deposit when they lived together, as Ryan hadn't been paying rent.

"You're still at the same cell number?" Ryan admitted he was. "I'll give you a call sometime, we can catch up somewhere better than Dunkin'. Dinner's on me. I owe you that, after last year."

"Are you—" Ryan couldn't bear to ask the question, or hear the answer if David was still dating Christine.

"Nothing has changed," Eckley replied breezily. "Anyway, I'm glad I ran into you!" Ryan wondered if he could say the same. He continued across the parking lot, $100 richer, though no closer to getting Eckley to admit the truth regarding Ministry of Fear.

Ryan didn't expect to hear from Eckley, if at all, but a few weeks later, he discovered he had missed a call from him, presumably while he was painting in one of the upstairs bathrooms in Dobbs, which had surprisingly good light and little traffic. Ryan didn't mind the building's lack of service, since no one ever called him, and he considered it a positive if it kept people from finding him. When he returned the call a few hours later, he was equally surprised that David answered on the fourth ring, and, after hearing a door close behind him, suggested they meet for dinner.

They went to Silvio's, which was on South Broadway in Yonkers, in what ended up being the first of multiple dinners there. David always paid, and though Ryan didn't bring up the demo again, there was a tacit understanding that these dinners existed so that Ryan would not mention the demo again. He also made sure to get picked up and dropped off at his mom's, since Eckley already had the address from back in college.

Not only did they not talk about the demo, but David seemed to make a point not to mention Christine either. Ryan was always a little edgy during these dinners, trying to determine if the omissions were because they had broken up or because Eckley was, for some reason, sparing his feelings. Not that he'd given a shit about Ryan's feelings when stealing his songs or his girl in the first place.

During one of the dinners that fall, a woman who seemed to know Eckley from work stopped by their table. "And how's Christine?" she asked innocently after a few pleasantries.

"Doing well. I'll let her know you say hi," he responded charmingly and disarmingly before changing the subject. Within a few minutes, their visitor and her husband had left the restaurant. Ryan slumped in his chair, unable to even finish his penne vodka. He had held out hope that Christine and Eckley might have somehow broken up, but of course they were still together. It was he, Ryan, who was the broken one. And the only advantage he held over Eckley in any area—that he was the true author of those Indignation songs—he couldn't even get his friend to acknowledge. Eckley seemed to accurately intuit his despondency and was quiet on the ride home. As Ryan got out of the car outside his mom's building and they exchanged their goodbyes, they both knew they weren't going to do this again.

So when Ryan saw Christine coming out of the building in October, he wasn't surprised if David had somehow figured out where he lived and sent her to check on him, if David could no longer keep tabs himself over dinner. But he had been getting so much good work done here, and couldn't let her scare him off when he had too much to lose. So as much as he wanted to keep looking at her forever, he tried to keep the conversation short. But he had to ask her about that song that she had been playing last year.

"Smoke & Mirrors." It was a song by someone called RJD2, off his *Deadringer* CD. Christine offered to burn it for him, but Ryan brusquely declined. "I'm not sure when I'm going to see you again," he remarked as he hastily retreated.

But over a year after first associating the song with Christine, he couldn't get it out of his head, and a few weeks after seeing her at the pond, he asked some kid at work if he might be able to get him a burned copy. Ryan had started filling in on busy days at a screen printing company that operated out of the basement of the building. He had met the owner while walking back from the bathroom with a jar of brushes, and if the guy thought Ryan was an artist and a legitimate tenant of the building, he wasn't going to correct that impression. It was perfect fucking timing since he really needed the money. He couldn't hit up Eckley anymore, and even without rent, he still needed to eat and pay his cell phone bill. And his car was less reliable these days, due to its near-antique status. Ryan couldn't imagine what would happen if he no longer had the car as a home base for when he wasn't supposed to be in Joel's studio. Hopefully if it broke down, it would do so right here, in the parking lot of the building.

Lots of people in the building seemed to know each other, and after a few months of helping out at the screen printing place, Ryan also started picking up occasional shipping work at a book company on the third floor, through this kid Tony at the screen printing place. Ryan vaguely thought he might be a hardcore kid based on the style of the t-shirts he wore to work, but he didn't recognize the names of the bands. When Ryan asked, Tony was able to get RJD2 mp3s and burned him the CD for $5. And once Ryan had it in his Discman, he listened to little else for the rest of 2005 and into 2006.

Ryan didn't know what type of music this was considered, besides the fact that it was fucking great. Had he felt this way about a record since he first heard Supertouch or Helmet or 3's *Dark Days Coming*? How would he find more of it? He wished he had someone to talk to about this stuff, but his confidence and clear thoughts dissipated every time he left the sanctuary of the building. And who did he even know who was familiar with this style of music, besides Christine? One way or another, his thoughts always led back to Christine. He tried not to think about her, but she kept coming back to him in dreams. Whenever that happened, he tried to get it down on paper, in images or words, and then distract himself with something else. He had recently gotten a Yonkers library card, once his driver's license and cell phone bill were both under his mom's address, and started putting copious quantities of books on hold at the Dobbs Ferry library. It was a warm place to read on his days off, though after an hour or so he always gravitated back to his newfound home.

And so a lonely but somewhat sufficiently sheltered Ryan made it through the winter in Dobbs Ferry. The heat in the building was unreliable, and on the coldest days, he sometimes ended up going to his mom's, which she and Vivian enjoyed. He spent a week with Viv while his mom was in Florida with a friend from AA, but didn't want to be underfoot when she came back. He was excited for the start of baseball: the Yankees had signed Johnny Damon over the offseason, and he was expecting good things from Robinson Cano.

One afternoon in July, with no plan in mind, Ryan decided to make his way down to the city. His car had been acting up, so after confirming he had enough loose change to buy a MetroCard at Madaba, he took the old-school and cheapest route to Manhattan: catching the bus up on Broadway and then transferring to the 1 train at Van Cortlandt Park. But by the time he got off at Christopher Street, he realized he was going to Generation Records. Though he hadn't attended many shows in the past decade, he had remained tangentially interested in hardcore. Maybe he could pick up some flyers for upcoming shows or dig around in the used CDs downstairs.

There were a few people browsing the bins upstairs, but Ryan headed straight to the basement when he arrived. He had just turned the corner towards the racks of used CDs when he heard someone say "Ryan?" Looking up, he saw his old friend John H. from Port Chester.

"What's up, buddy? Holy shit—it's been a long time. What have you been up to?" Ryan hadn't seen John in at least 15 years, though he had looked for him when he went to a handful of shows at 7 Willow Street in the '90s. In contrast to Ryan's shaggy hair and beard, John was still sporting a shaved head. He didn't look so different from his teenage youth crew self.

"I moved down to Brooklyn, and I'm becoming a yoga teacher. I've been working here part-time while I get that going." John certainly looked like he'd been taking care of himself.

"Good for you. I've just been painting. Kind of fell out of touch with hardcore. But I figured I'd come down and pick up a couple flyers, see what I'm missing."

"Bro! It's a crazy time for hardcore. Tons of reunions. The Crumbsuckers are playing, and Outburst at the end of August. And they're having all these CBGB's farewell shows since no one is sure when it's gonna close." CB's was closing? That was news to Ryan. "You can catch them on the livestream online even if you can't make it ... oh, and online, that's where the real action is these days—on the message boards. The Bridge 9 board, hardcorewebsite, people are always talking about reunions, asking if old bands are gonna reunite, and looking for old demo tapes and shit. Can you believe that someone was asking about the Power Structure demo?"

"Oh man! Good dudes, but that demo ... not something I'd go looking for in 2006." Ryan didn't mention that he had stayed with Travis somewhat recently, and that, in fact, Travis was the one who had put him onto the fact that Eckley had stolen his riffs. Realizing an opportunity, he tried to keep his tone lighthearted. "Do you ever see anything on the message board about a band called Ministry of Fear?" He wasn't sure if John would recognize the name or know that they were Eckley's band.

"You know what, I just saw a thread about them on B9 ... Boston band, right? Which makes sense, since it's a Boston board. I think someone was saying they might do a reunion."

"How do I get on this message board? Actually, fuck it, I don't even have a computer."

"You could get online at the library or something ... here, I'll write it down for you." John picked up a flyer for an upcoming Subzero show and wrote out the URL.

After a few more minutes of conversation and checking out the used CDs, Ryan walked back towards the train. It was 4:17, the Dobbs Ferry library was open late on Wednesdays, and he didn't want to wait to look up this message board. And yet, to avoid paying for a Metro North ticket, he went back the slow route he had come, then headed straight to the library once he was off the bus, his heart thudding as he sat down at a computer and signed in.

Having navigated to the message board, Ryan figured out how to search by keyword and soon located the Ministry of Fear thread. People complimenting the 7", people reminiscing about seeing them in Worcester, in Maine, and at Back to School Jam. An apparent fan being summoned to the thread by another poster and typing in capital letters about the breakdown in "Suspension of Disbelief," which Ryan thought he remembered from Travis's house to be the part Eckley had stolen from "Put it Down."

Ryan had seen enough. Disgusted, he signed off and walked out to Main Street. It was a beautiful evening in Dobbs Ferry, with another hour or two before the sun would set over the Palisades. One of the only good things in his life right now was going down to the river to watch these sunsets. He just wished he had someone to appreciate them with, someone like Christine.

He had been thinking about her more than ever, and was keenly aware that if he called Eckley right now and Eckley was home, she would be right there, potentially listening to their conversation. He didn't want her to feel sorry for him, that was for sure. Christine was never going to be impressed by a semi-homeless artist who lived in his car down by the river and was being monitored by the CIA. No, these days she was interested in the kind of guy who was a real fucking person with a job as a fucking transit cop. A guy whose band was reminisced about on the internet and might even do a reunion. He knew that eventually he needed to confront Eckley about this reunion idea, before it became a reality and Eckley played those Indignation songs on stage *again*, but he had to figure out what to say.

When he dialed Eckley later that night, the call rang through to voicemail. Maybe he was at work: Ryan thought he worked nights, but wasn't sure of his schedule. When he tried again a few days later, this time David answered, but seemed oddly evasive. "I've got a lot going on right now, but let's meet up soon," he assured him. Ryan didn't even get to bring up the reunion before Eckley had hung up on him.

But miraculously, later that week Ryan had some potential good news of his own. One afternoon when he walked into the studio, Joel was there with a woman named Lisa who was organizing a gallery show in Hastings that fall. He encouraged Ryan to show her a couple of canvases that he had left in a corner of Joel's studio, and Lisa was impressed. The show had something to do with trains or transit, so Ryan mentioned hurriedly that he had just started a Metro North painting. This was not strictly true—he had only done sketches, but he was electrified by the idea of someone from a gallery displaying a modicum of interest in his work. This tenuous connection was enough to knock Ministry of Fear right out of his mind for the next few weeks, as he did little else but work on the train painting. He was already indebted to Joel, and could this be the big break he needed?

Ryan was so focused that it took him another few weeks to make it back to the library and check the Bridge 9 board. When the page loaded, he was briefly sidetracked by a flyer for an upcoming Outburst reunion at CBGB's. Outburst, the very band that Indignation had almost played with on the day of their untimely breakup. Should he try to attend the reunion? Could he even afford it? Maybe the book company would have some extra work for him, or he could borrow money from his mom.

Clicking out of the Outburst thread and scrolling to page two, he was soon confronted by another thread about Ministry of Fear. A poster named "brendan v," whom Ryan thought he remembered from his last visit to the board, seemed to be the main instigator of MOF adulation, but a couple other kids were joining in. And then—Ryan caught his breath— the username "mercenaryaggression" with a Mr. Met avatar replied, "reunion def happening soon, just gotta get a few pieces in place!" That had to be fucking Eckley, due to the combination of a Demolition Hammer reference, the Mets, and most specifically, the Ministry of Fear inside knowledge. Was he just one of the pieces, Ryan wondered, who had to be put into place so that Eckley could move forward with his plan?

Like most nights, Ryan had the studio to himself once Joel had gone home, but he couldn't focus as Eckley's words reverberated in his head. After a few more unproductive changes to his Metro North project, he grabbed his cell phone and walked down to the railroad bridge. Who knew if Eckley would even pick up the phone.

Eckley answered on the second ring, and after the barest preliminaries, Ryan cut straight to the purpose of his call. "I wanted to ask you about something I saw online. Is it true that a Ministry of Fear reunion might happen?" Ryan tried to keep his voice steady and not betray his rage or apprehension.

"Oh yeah, I've been meaning to talk to you about that," came Eckley's casual reply.

"You have?" Ryan was caught off guard.

"Yeah, once I started putting something together, I realized you might be able to help me with something. Actually, there's something in it for both of us."

Ryan wasn't sure how to respond. What could Eckley mean? Was he planning to pay him off again or could it be something even better, like the chance to play some Indignation songs onstage at a reunion? He hadn't played his guitar in years, though it was still at his mom's. But before he got too far ahead of himself, would he even want to share a stage with Eckley? He had to regain control of the conversation.

"What were you thinking?" Ryan finally replied.

"I'd love to tell you about it in person. I'm still working nights, but let's get up soon, and I'll fill you in?"

Ryan agreed. He was glad Eckley wasn't making specific plans to meet right away, since he needed time to get ready for whatever he might propose. And when they hung up the phone with nothing confirmed, he felt a hint of hope for whatever Eckley might tell him. Was it possible that things might be looking up in more than one area of his life?

But any optimism from the Eckley conversation and the art show news soon dissipated due to the disconcerting events that transpired in the following weeks. Ryan had walked up the hill to the library to check for additional news about Ministry of Fear, and swore that someone was following him down Palisade Street on his walk home. It was a blue car that he didn't recognize, but he had the distinct impression that it was driving slower than usual and waiting to see where he was going. He darted towards the driveway for his building, hoping that the car would continue on Palisade, and for a minute he thought they had, until he saw it turning in behind him. Diving behind some sort of electrical station halfway down the hill, he watched the car continue down towards the building, then waited until it returned up the driveway. Had they known to look for him here, or was it merely a coincidence? In the world of Ryan Marnell, there were no coincidences.

On the Wednesday after the incident with the car, Ryan was supposed to meet his mom for lunch at her apartment. It was an ideal summer day, and since his car had been increasingly unreliable, he decided to walk to Yonkers and then take the bus or the train home. It was only four miles to his mom's, and maybe he would even stop at Lisa's gallery in Hastings on the way home. Ryan had been working up to visiting in person, despite Lisa insisting he should drop by any time. Not only did he feel off balance and uncertain whenever he was outside the protections of this building, but the potential of her showing his work felt like it could evaporate at any time. What if she was able to access his thoughts and didn't like what she found there?

The day was free of excessive humidity and Ryan scaled the hill with ease as he walked into town to catch the Aqueduct trail at Chestnut Street. At least he didn't have to pass Christine's childhood home, which was just a few more houses past where the trail cut across Chestnut. Ryan had no idea if her parents still lived there, as he hadn't been there since the summer before his sophomore year. Sometimes he wondered how he had stayed in this town at all. Trying his best to forget Christine, he strode into the woods, following the path towards Hastings.

Ryan was waiting at one of the street crossings to the next section of the path and had just ascertained that there was no traffic coming in either direction as he stepped into the road. He had nearly made it across when a white SUV parked nearby was suddenly in motion and heading straight for him. One moment the car had been stationary, and in the next, it was upon him. Ryan managed to fling himself backwards into the street to avoid being struck. He wasn't sure how long he lay there afterwards before picking himself up to get out of the intersection. By then, the vehicle was long gone. Ryan looked around, but no one else seemed to have witnessed the incident, and if they had, how could he know they hadn't been part of orchestrating it? While he had moved so fast that he didn't have a clear memory of exactly what happened, he was sure that the driver had looked at him directly while accelerating, leaving no doubt about his intent.

Though shaken up and bruised, he knew he needed to get to his destination as quickly as possible, and continued down the path at the closest thing to a run. Whoever was trying to kill him must have known he would be heading through Hastings, or perhaps his whole route and destination. Had they somehow found about the gallery opportunity and thought he was heading straight there? Had they put the idea in his head to try to walk there in the first place? And was the whole art show a setup?

Ryan didn't know what to think, and tried to act normal at lunch. Though when his mom correctly surmised something was wrong, he gave her a hurried summary of the incident, then took the train straight home from Greystone to Dobbs Ferry. For the next few days, he ventured outside the protections of the building as infrequently as possible, subsisting mainly on snacks from the vending machine in the lobby. He didn't want to risk encountering any more assassins or leaving his mind open to extraneous voices or ideas from outside these walls. The situation was obviously escalating, and Ryan felt powerless in the face of his pursuers' machinations. But how to address what was happening to him and convey to anyone who discovered his death that he wished to keep on living, and did not wish to die?

The answer came to him one night while he was listening to *Coast to Coast AM* in his car. The episode was on mind harassment, and Ryan realized he had experienced some of the phenomena being discussed on the show. He had never called in to *Coast to Coast* before, but this was his chance, not only to discuss his symptoms, but as some sort of record of the fact he was here and how he had lived. He wouldn't disclose his real name. But how to make it clear that it was him, to anyone who might be listening now or in the future? In the end, he gave the name of a fellow protagonist dodging death: Arthur Rowe from the Graham Greene novel *The Ministry of Fear*.

Ryan had also started a new painting that was more text-based than his previous work. He was pretty satisfied with how it had come out and had hid it for safekeeping in the ceiling of the basement bathroom until he could bring it to his mom's. If they managed to finish him off, let this be another record of his present state. He had just walked down to BA Beach when his phone rang. Somehow, he knew it would be David.

"Hey, are you doing anything next Monday?" Ryan responded that he was not.

"Great, I'll be working, but I'm local now. Where do you want to meet?"

Ryan hesitated. Due to all the weird stuff happening lately, he was loath to draw Eckley down to the river, though maybe he was safer on his own territory. Sometimes at night as he stood on the bridge, a smattering of lights burned in the building behind him. Other artists working late, perhaps, and more than once he had the uncanny feeling that the building, and/or the artists, were protecting him.

"Do you remember that building down by the river in Dobbs? Let's meet on the bridge over the train tracks." Strange that Ryan would even have to frame the location to someone with "do you remember." When compared to its significance in his own life, how could he have possibly forgotten?

And then they were on the bridge, and Ryan had no time to second-guess his plan.

"Anyway, those new songs aren't why we're here tonight." Eckley gestured to the bag. "I have something that might help you get on board with the idea of a Ministry of Fear reunion. It will be easier for everyone if it works out. Plus, because I'm such a good friend and wanted to help you."

"As opposed to you being here because you stole my songs and my tapes and my girlfriend and then tried to undermine every ounce of my fucking sanity? And now you feel a tiny sliver of guilt and want to make amends?"

The tight smile never left Eckley's face. "Yes, I'm dating Christine, but the rest is bullshit. The Ministry of Fear stuff was all me. And if every riff of every hardcore song had to be original, hardcore would be long fucking extinct. Any similarity is just a coincidence. And let's be honest, I'm not responsible for whatever the fuck happened to your mind. That was all you."

"That's what you want people to think. And you've never had trouble convincing people to believe you. Except this time, I'm not going to let you get away with that shit. You know I've had some problems the last few years, things that affected my clarity of mind. But at least I figured it out when I did."

"The last few years? You mean all the way back to when you wouldn't let me in your band? Worried I was going to steal the spotlight? And when you had that breakdown in college and pushed away Christine, who might be the best thing to happen to either of us?"

Ryan stared at him malevolently. He wanted to fucking kill him. "Enough about Christine. And I'm not even going to get into the people you've had following me lately. Back to the fucking songs. I can't believe it took me so long to put this together. You took my songs, almost note for note. It's so obvious that anyone who gets their hands on your stuff and the Indignation material will hear the same thing."

Eckley persisted with his eerie calm. "No one is following you, and no one is getting their hands on the Indignation material. I fulfilled my duties as an executive producer long ago in making sure those songs get the audience they deserve ... which is no audience at all."

"C'mon, you know those songs are still out there somewhere. It's 2006, everything is being put on the internet. Kids live for that shit. People are all about reunions right now! John H. told me some guy was even looking for the Power Structure demo. Fucking Power Structure!"

"Pretty hard to do a reunion without a key member." Eckley smiled inscrutably. "Well for some bands, at least. And besides, timing in hardcore is everything. As you are aware, Ministry of Fear is going to play again sometime soon. Putting Indignation back together after that would be lame as shit. Who would believe you had come up with those songs first, instead of the other way around?"

"This is ridiculous," Ryan muttered. "What's in it for me if I let your Ministry of Fear reunion happen, which by the way no one will give a shit about anyway? With no one the wiser about where you got those songs?"

"You would have found there's a lot in it for you if you had just shut the fuck up and minded your own business," Eckley snarled. "But it's too late for that now. You already tried to blackmail me. Which puts me in an unusual position, as someone in law enforcement capitulating to a local degenerate due to some misunderstanding from twenty years ago. But you are, after all, my oldest friend. And we can't let creative differences come between us. So one last time, I brought you what you asked for." He reached into the bag.

"But I don't want your money anymore," Ryan countered bravely. "I want to tell the world what happened. And I want you to publicly apologize. And then you can do your stupid—"

"Apologize?" Eckley's eyes popped. "Tell the world? The world doesn't even know you exist anymore," Eckley hissed. "Which one of us has been playing in bands the last fifteen years? Not you!"

"But I'm the only one who knows the truth!" Ryan protested.

Apparently Eckley didn't care about the truth, or Ryan's version of it: before Ryan could react, Eckley whipped a hammer out of the Madaba bag and smashed him in the temple.

"You can't do this ..." he tried to say, but he couldn't speak.

As Ryan crumpled against the fence on the north side of the bridge, Eckley grabbed him by the throat, hit him again a few more times for good measure, ripped his watch from his wrist, then slammed his body up against the side of the bridge. That was the last thing Ryan remembered, as Eckley started to push him over the railing.

"But who are they going to believe," said the person who had already tried to rewrite history, as the body had started to fall. "You, or me?"

Becky McAuley

Chapter 13
2017

While CFA was fortunate to have an extra week between Thanksgiving and Art Basel this year, the Wednesday before Thanksgiving was still traditionally a wild day at the office. There was no colloquium that Wednesday, so Mo was going in for a full day, with the expectation that she wouldn't be able to see Pat off before the Wretched Spaniel expedition. As it worked out, he wasn't coming home first anyway. Vik was planning to pick him up from work on the way down to the bar, and then they would stop at Carlo's for dinner. Mo was mildly jealous of the Carlo's visit, as it was a decent Italian restaurant down the street from the Wretched Spaniel. But she would still be at work and didn't want to crash the party.

"So the final lineup," Pat was outlining on Tuesday, "is me, Vik, and Don. Shane's still a maybe, he might stop by, but he'll be driving the cab."

"That sounds like a good crew," Mo concurred. "And of course Warren Yatrofsky." Warren's presence could go either way, due to his allegiance to both parties, but he would be useful in identifying Eckley and providing a natural bridge for their target to start drinking with the interlopers.

"And I'll try not to worry about you," Mo continued, "since it's my fault you're going there in the first place."

"You better not," Pat laughed. "You did start this shit."

Mo had been expecting an exceedingly late night pre-Basel, but by 8:15 pm that Wednesday, things were surprisingly under control. After executing a final check-in with Colette, she managed to grab a soup and still catch the 9:00 train home. Just as it was weird yet cool to be less integral to this year's Basel prep, it was enjoyable but strange to be home alone with Brett and CC, as Pat was usually around in the evenings these days.

By 10:45, Mo had fed the cats, locked the deadbolt, and climbed into bed with a back issue of *People Magazine*, fully intending to stand up in a minute to brush her teeth and turn off the rest of the lights. She wondered how things were going at the Wretched Spaniel, and if Eckley had arrived. Would Pat tell her if he had? She had last heard from him when they were leaving Carlo's for the bar.

Mo realized she had been reading the same sentence over and over concerning some country singer's divorce. Her eyelids were drooping. CC repositioned himself in the crook of her knees. She would hate to move him. But she was going to stand up in one more minute ...

Hours later, she awoke, the reading lamp still on. What the fuck time was it? Mo looked around. No sign of Pat. She scrambled to check the time: it was 4:26 a.m.! Didn't the bars close at 4:00? Even if they had stayed till closing, which would have been almost eight hours after they arrived, wouldn't Pat be home by now? What the hell had happened? Heart hammering, she texted "my love where are you and are you ok?" Not that this might result in immediate relief if his phone had died during the long evening.

But 30 seconds later, she had a response. "All good lady! Almost home, we're just grabbing some food and then Vik is gonna drop us off."

"Omg I'm glad," Mo texted back. "See you soon, can't wait to hear about your night!!" She reclaimed *People Magazine* from where it had fallen next to the bed, as there was no way she was going back to sleep before he was home. At her feet, CC stirred. He often slept in their bed all night, with Brett nearby on the windowsill or laundry basket. Just what she needed: to jumpstart their crepuscular clock. They'd be begging for food even sooner than their usual overtures at 5:45.

At 4:47, Mo heard a key turn in the lock, then Pat's size 13 feet stumble in and the deadbolt turn behind him.

"Hey! How did it go?" Mo whispered. Thanksgiving might be the rare occasion when the entire Boxhill family downstairs was still asleep at this predawn hour.

"It was interesting. Everyone's OK, I met David Eckley, he's real, I almost hit him, but he tripped on a sculpture and passed out. And then we went to White Castle. I'll tell you the rest in the morning."

"You can't just leave me hanging on that note!" Also why the fuck were there sculptures at the Wretched Spaniel?

"Just go back to sleep. And I'm going to feed the cats so they don't keep us up." A moment later, she heard the unmistakable sound of dry food being poured into ceramic cat bowls, and then satisfied chomping as Pat climbed into bed.

It only seemed like a few minutes later when Mo awoke to someone knocking on the door. Thoroughly disoriented, she bolted upright, convinced she was late for work, only to remember it was Thanksgiving Day, and the bedside clock showed 9:38 a.m. Her second thought was that it must be David Eckley. She gently but urgently pummeled Pat in case he was needed as backup.

The memories of last night's description of events came flooding back. "Didn't you say something about a sculpture?" Mo asked groggily. (*Something About a Sculpture:* the alternate title of that Mark Harris book.) She flopped out of bed, threw on a Warzone hoodie and basketball shorts, and crept to the front door, which was across the hall from their bedroom.

Mo peered through the peephole. It was not David Eckley, but

Lost Indignation

merely Shane Perry. Mo had a vague recollection that he was potentially involved in last night, but wasn't sure if he'd been able to make it due to driving his cab.

"Who is it?" Pat called from across the hall.

"It's Shane Perry!" Mo stage whispered in reply.

"Giuseppe McCleary?" Pat replied. Mo, thoroughly confused, responded by unbolting the door.

"Hey Shane! So good to see you! What's up?"

"Maureen McGraw!" Shane, who always called her by her full name, enveloped her in a bony embrace. "I'm here with a gift for you. Well more of a loan, really," he clarified, Mo still nonplussed. "The phone and wallet of a man you might know as ... David Eckley?" He presented them with a flourish.

Mo stood, frozen in front of the proffered objects before gingerly accepting them, as one might accept a mutilated bird from a proud pet. "How did you ..."

"I just offered to plug in the phone for him and never gave it back!" Shane chuckled. "He was so drunk, he had no idea where he lived. After driving all around Yonkers and Eastchester, I asked him for his wallet. First to make sure the man could pay me, second to see if he had any form of ID. He's a Masshole though, according to his license," he clarified offhandedly, as Mo's heart thudded at the idea of having Eckley's home address. "Finally, after a stop at 7-Eleven on Garth Road, he was able to remember where his father lives. The whole thing took over an hour. You bet I extracted an appropriate tip."

"Wow," Mo was dumbstruck, not only from the sudden appearance and this tale, but from the fact that if Eckley had been this drunk, who knew what he had revealed to Pat, Shane and the others. "It sounds like you guys had quite a night! Thank you for dealing with him and bringing this over. Though what happens if he gets in touch with you to get his stuff back?"

"Well it's in your hands now!" Shane continued merrily. "But just for a bit. I'm picking up at Galloway's. I'll be back in forty-five minutes, an hour tops. Gives you time to do what you need to do." He winked at Pat, who had just emerged from the bedroom, and moved toward the door. "Oh, and you don't have to worry about him calling right away. He thinks my name is Giuseppe McCleary, so he'll be looking for a cab company or driver under that name."

Mo teetered on requesting the backstory here, but decided to roll with it. "Shane, for real, thank you for doing this. And being part of this adventure."

Shane shrugged. "Any time! It was the most fun I've had on Thanksgiving eve since 2003. I was in Dobbs Ferry that night too. Back in a bit." He ducked out and closed the door behind him. Mo continued to stand in the hall and slowly turned to face Pat, who stood in the doorway of their room behind her. "What's this about Dobbs Ferry? I thought you were at the Wretched Spaniel."

"Hang on." Pat hustled toward the living room. "We only have forty-five minutes, or probably more like an hour, depending on how the line is at Galloway's. Which, on Thanksgiving morning, will be long, but still. I've been doing some research, but I gotta install this shit." He handed Mo the wallet and scrutinized the phone.

Mo finally snapped to the reality of the situation. "OMG, I can't believe we have David Eckley's phone in our house! What if it rings?"

"I'll say "This is Max Malkin," Pat replied without missing a beat, as he headed back towards the kitchen to start making coffee. Mo hadn't thought to make the iced coffee last night, but she also hadn't anticipated such an exciting start to their morning.

"How do you have his PIN?" Mo followed him from the kitchen to the living room.

"Don watched him put it in a bunch of times last night. That was the original plan, to get my hands on his phone long enough to install something. But I didn't have a chance. Once he was out cold, I checked his phone, but it was dead. So I'm glad this worked out." Coffee started, Pat alighted back at his desk, exuding intense concentration.

"What are you trying to do? Can I at least like, look at his texts or something?"

Pat looked up. "If this works, we'll be able to see all of his texts for the foreseeable future. Don't expect him to say anything related to Ryan, or anything else particularly incriminating, but I'm sure he'll say something useful, one way or another."

Pat had soon successfully installed the app, which would capture Eckley's future incoming texts, and they transitioned to saving his existing texts, which only went back a few weeks. Unfortunately, most of the contacts in his phone were entered only under their first initial, so while they would be able to glean some context from the recent texts, it would be difficult to decipher the identities of his conversation partners.

The most recent texts were from the following:

> An unread text from someone just listed as M: "miss yr face. come to the yellow marble with me and el on sat?"

> A flurry of texts from A: "hey dude any news on the reunion?"
> "See anyone last night who could fill in?"

"let's meet up when ur back - sunday?" None of these
had received a reply.

"What reunion is he recruiting for?" Mo said slowly. "If it's
Ministry of Fear, why would he be looking for band members down here?
And why does this other guy seem more interested than Eckley?"
  "I have no fucking idea." Pat pulled up the next set of texts,
which were from someone named D, beseeching Eckley to meet her (Mo
presumed it was a her) after the bar, wondering where he was, and going
into detail about what she would do to him if he showed up as promised.
  "Damn, sounds like you cockblocked David Eckley by taking up
his whole night!" From the string of texts, it appeared that Eckley had
initially promised to meet up with this D after stopping by the bar, but
had been at the Wretched Spaniel much longer than expected after he was
unwittingly ensnared by Pat's conglomerate.
  Pat checked the missed calls. Eckley's phone had 11 missed calls
from D's number between 11:49 p.m. and when the phone had died. Sounds
like this D person had really looked forward to their rendezvous, and then
intently attempted to hunt him down when he hadn't showed. Considering
the amount of time Don ZT had been looking at Eckley's phone with him,
it was kind of amazing he hadn't seen at least one of these calls come in. Or
maybe he had.
  Pat rechecked D's number and stared at the texts. There was
something unsettlingly familiar about the number and text phrasing, and
he reached the same conclusion right when Mo asked:
  "You don't think there's any way that D could be ... Dana?"
  "Oh shit—I think that might have been her number! If she still
has the same one." But was it possible that Eckley could have dated one
Oronzio sister and then later hooked up with another? Or could a Dana
dalliance be what Christine was referring to when she mentioned David
doing something unforgivable?
  "That would add another layer to the Christine and David story,"
Mo mused.
  As Pat finished with the phone, Mo gingerly examined Eckley's
wallet. The picture on his driver's license was intense and unnerving.
And although he was groomed quite differently than when they had
encountered him in the park, it was almost definitely the same person. Mo
took a picture of his ID, then continued to poke through the wallet. There
were a few credit cards, a debit card, and a MBTA ID.
  Wrenching her attention away from the wallet, Mo consulted her
watch. "I still need to hear about last night! And get ready for Thanksgiving."
She needed to leave for her Aunt Ray's in just over an hour, and true to
form, she still hadn't packed.

Mo continued examining the contents of Eckley's wallet. "Why does he have a library card signed by ... Ty ... V-something?"

Pat shrugged. "How would I know? A third alias? How many names does this guy have?"

"Actually, hold on." When people at work asked Mo what her superpower was, she answered that it was the ability to recognize a name if she had seen it before. Not necessarily putting faces to names, or remembering faces, that was more of Pat's thing. But she was good at remembering a name in written form, which had served her well at both the book distributor job and at CFA with both the database and resumes. She trotted down the hall to retrieve the Ministry of Fear CD from where she had left it with other recently acquired CDs that were not yet filed alphabetically.

Ministry of Fear is:
David Eckley - Throat
Tyler Vossen - Guitar
Mark Ledesma - Bass
Bill Cole - Drums

"I thought I had seen those initials recently! Tyler Vossen is a guy from Ministry of Fear. We'll have to Google him later, see what he's up to. Or wait, are there any texts from him?"

Pat confirmed there were no texts from anyone in the phone as T, or B. And while the M in Eckley's texts seemed more like a female friend from the "miss your face" phrasing, it could have potentially been this Mark guy from the band.

"OK, so we'll have to keep an eye on those developing situations. But holy shit. I can't believe you got his phone. Well, you and Shane." Shane/Giuseppe indeed reappeared minutes later to reclaim Eckley's items, thus ending their stay in the McGraw-Catalano household. "So now are you going to tell me about last night?

"You keep getting ready. If we run out of time, I'll tell you on the phone tonight!" This was a significant offer, since Pat hated talking on the phone, though Mo did usually call him to say goodnight when she was out of town.

"Or you can tell me while I'm getting ready!"

"Trust me, I know your packing style—I don't want to distract you." Mo's packing style generally meant swerving from room to room, getting distracted from whatever she had been doing in the prior location, and forgetting at least one crucial item after her initial departure. At least she was coming home tomorrow afternoon, as she and Pat had tickets to Killing Time and Outburst at Brooklyn Bazaar. So she only had to pack for

Lost Indignation

one night.

As accurately assessed by Pat, Mo had barely finished getting ready in time to pick up her brother Max in Washington Heights and head to Pennsylvania. Pat agreed to call later and impart the full story of the night with Eckley.

After Thanksgiving dinner, Mo's mom and Aunt Ray were drinking coffee in the kitchen with Grandpa Joe and Grandma Rose, and her dad and Max were watching a movie. Mo realized she should seize this opportunity to call Pat while she had a room to herself upstairs, which was not the easiest feat with seven people staying in a three-bedroom house. She texted him to check if it was a good time to call.

"Give me five minutes. I'm trying to wake up my sister, and then I'll go downstairs." At his grandmother's apartment on Garth Road, there was often a natural lull between dinner and when Pat, his mom, and his sister would go over to his mom's cousin's place in Interlaken for the unofficial after party and dessert. Except half the time they didn't make it, if everyone ended up taking an impromptu nap after dinner.

Mo climbed the stairs to the guest room she was sharing with Max. In a prior era when Max was much smaller, Mo had usually slept in the real bed and Max in the trundle bed. Now that he was nine inches taller than Mo, he got the real bed and Mo the trundle. She turned off the light for maximum atmospheric effect and sat down on the bed.

Pat answered on the first ring.

"How was your Thanksgiving?"

"It was good, but I don't want to talk about Thanksgiving! I want to hear about last night!"

The night in question had started off according to plan. Vik had picked up Pat from work and driven him down to Yonkers so they could eat at Carlo's before meeting the others at the Wretched Spaniel around 9:00. It was odd being at Carlo's in this context: Pat was usually here with his mom's family, after they had first come here for his uncle's birthday a few years back. Pat barely knew the Italian side of his family, as he hadn't seen his dad or any of the Catalanos since 1988, but his mom's Irish family sure loved Italian food. He and Mo had also eaten there occasionally or picked up takeout. The sausage and peppers were fucking dope, and Mo liked some pasta dish with broccoli and garlic.

This part of the night felt almost normal: him and Vik going out for a meal before the main event. Outside of the benefit show, the annual Halloween party, and the occasional confluence at The Bayou among large groups, Pat couldn't remember the last time he had straight up chilled with Vik. Whatever happened after, it was nice to catch up about work, TV shows, and the Dungeons & Dragons game they never seemed to get off the ground. It was hard to believe they weren't just heading home to their respective wives afterwards, rather than heading a few hundred yards down the road to ... do what exactly? Act a part in one of Mo's schemes come to life? It was almost like they were hunting a fictional character, the type of thing Mo would have made up as a kid—wish hard enough and your stories involving Playmobil characters or baseball cards would become a reality. But Yatrofsky had verified that Eckley was real. And the more that Pat learned about Indignation and Ministry of Fear, the more bizarre the situation became. At this point he wanted to get to the bottom of things as much as Mo did. And in return for Eckley's initial deceit, they would hopefully extract something to help illuminate the story of Indignation. Or get some form of revenge for Eckley attempting to trick Pat and his wife with a false moniker.

Don and potentially Shane were just in it for some entertainment, a night out at the bar, and the possibility of witnessing (or participating in) some Boston herb getting his ass beat. Pat had only imparted the barest skeleton of the story: that a dude from Boston who had ripped off Mo in a trade would be home in Yonkers for Thanksgiving and was likely to make an appearance at the bar. That was enough to secure the involvement of his associates.

Vik was the only one who had gotten more of the story at dinner: that there might be no need for violence, that perhaps they would only end up sticking close enough to get this Eckley guy drunk, get some more info about him, and hey, if they got the chance, sneak a parental monitoring app onto his phone so Pat could read his future texts. Pat knew this form of technological subterfuge would appeal to Vik, who practiced criminal law but had a keen layman's interest in cybersecurity. And yet there was a similar excitement in the air that reminded him of going to a show as a teenager, the ever-present adrenaline of knowing something might happen.

They walked out of Carlo's and into the parking lot in the back of the building—the same parking lot, in fact, where *In Effect* had interviewed Tony Pradlik from Rockin' Rex, as Mo had recently reminded Pat after re-reading the interview.

"Should we even move the car?" Carlo's was almost next to the Wretched Spaniel, but their buildings had different parking lots and entrances.

"Might as well," Vik shrugged. Pat had a feeling they were both thinking the same thing, that it was better to have the car nearby in case they needed to leave quickly.

The Wretched Spaniel's parking lot was packed, not quite the level of crowds associated with the rare hardcore show there, but crowded nonetheless. Vik snagged a spot in front of the pizza place just as a customer was departing.

Vik checked his phone as he locked the car. "ZT should be here any minute. His sister is dropping him off."

The bar was relatively full, as one would expect for the night before Thanksgiving. Pat didn't see Warren Yatrofsky, or David Eckley, but it was still early. In the meantime, he resolved to merely enjoy himself while watching for their arrivals.

"'Sup, homie?" Pat went in for a hug and patted Don ZT on the back when he appeared. "Where's your sister?"

"She just dropped me off. She was going over to the Eastchester Inn."

Pat nodded. "I think my sister is there too. I hope she's not coming back for you, as this might be a long night. Our guy isn't even here yet."

"I'm not worried." Don had a mischievous grin and Pat could tell he was looking forward to his role in enticing Eckley into conversation, ideally about Demolition Hammer or similarly obscure metal bands, and then inciting additional mayhem if required.

Warren Yatrofsky was next to arrive, with a couple other Yonkers guys that Pat knew peripherally from Smokey Tooth-era shows but were another sub-generation older than him. Yatrofsky was in his element with this type of crowd. How on earth had he ever started hanging out with David Eckley? Pat had to keep reminding himself that Yatrofsky was technically a neutral party in this situation if he was drinking with Eckley on an annual basis. Though when it came down to it, Pat and Warren had been on the same side in every fight over the last 20 years.

Warren and his friends were posted up along the bar, but Vik had managed to secure a table further in the back, near the pool table. Pat was coming back from the bathroom when he heard a familiar phrase.

"An auspicious sign," someone was saying to a hulking blond guy that Pat didn't know. He subtly glanced over at the speaker while continuing to his table. He had to look closely, but it was almost definitely David Eckley. Though he looked much different tonight: his hair was short, jaw recently shaved, and the glasses were nowhere in sight. In a button down shirt, dark jeans, and Air Max 90s, he looked much fresher and more put together than when they had met him in the park. Almost as if he was a totally different person, though Pat wasn't fooled. He had likely arrived within the last few minutes, but hadn't attracted their attention until that particular auspicious utterance—the same phrase he'd used back in the park about having the same name as Mo's brother.

"He's here" Pat muttered to Vik after returning to the table.

"Which one?"

"Guy in the button down, over near the bar? Looks like a prick?"

Becky McAuley

Pat realized he wasn't surprised that Eckley looked more respectable than anyone here besides Vik. Why did Eckley even come here at Thanksgiving? He didn't fit in with this crowd, which was mostly local degenerates and skewed older when not hosting hardcore shows.

"Word, we'll keep an eye on him. How do you want to handle this?"

"I'll introduce myself at some point, and then depending how that goes, we'll take it from there." Pat was honestly unsure how quickly this could turn from being faux buddy-buddy with the dude, to shaming him about the tape, to the potential for actual retribution.

A few minutes later, while Yatrofsky was outside for a cigarette, Pat moved down the bar towards Eckley. How should he address him? As Max? Or acknowledge he knew that his name was David? Pat couldn't well pass himself off as a stranger. Not having the benefit of a disguise that day in the park, he himself looked exactly the same as the day they'd met, if more winterized.

Pat saw Eckley handing over his credit card to start a tab. He lurked nearby until Eckley, startled, turned and noticed Pat behind him.

"Hey, what's up?" Pat began jocularly. "I checked out that Ministry of Fear stuff since we last saw you. Kind of reminded me of Demolition Hammer." Though technically true, it wasn't necessarily meant as a compliment, but Pat figured it was best to lead off with flattery. Then again, Eckley didn't know that Pat knew that Ministry of Fear was his own band.

Eckley looked wary. He must have recognized Pat, but gave nothing else away.

"But why'd you sell my girl the wrong tape though?" Pat continued. "Or why did Max sell my girl the wrong tape?

"What do you mean?" Eckley replied. He seemed more alarmed about the tape than the moniker-related deception.

"There's no Indignation set anywhere on it," Pat continued, more belligerently. "Well, maybe there's about half a second of an Indignation set. You told us they were the third band, which ended up being some shitty band called Power Structure, which we only figured out when my boy over here remastered the tape." He nodded at ZT, who had materialized by his side. "Unless they were on one of the parts of the tape that won't even play."

"Honestly, I'm sorry if the tape got messed up. I wouldn't have sold her the wrong tape on purpose," Eckley stated earnestly. Pat had an odd feeling that for some reason he was telling the truth. "The whole point was for someone to hear those Indignation songs," Eckley continued, "and realize I wrote them, once you recognize them in the Ministry of Fear riffs later on! You know, get the tape out there in time for the reunion. We're going to be playing again, sometime next year."

Pat decided to be generous, as the tape was no longer the largest issue at stake. Never mind the fact that Eckley had outed himself as a member of Ministry of Fear, rather than a purported fan. "I believe you, man. Maybe you can send us the right tape if you find it? Shit happens."

"Of course, bro. And in the meantime, how 'bout I buy you a drink? What are you drinking?"

"Jameson and ice." Actually, he was planning to drink very little tonight, keep his head about him for whatever went down, but might as well start things off right.

Eckley signaled the bartender, then handed Pat his drink once they were made.

"Tell me one thing though. Why did you introduce yourself as Max?" Or play it off like you weren't a member of your band, he almost added.

Eckley seemed caught off guard. "I always do that when I'm meeting people from the internet. For privacy concerns. Some of the people you meet through hardcore? You can never be too careful!"

"I get it, dude. To the internet!" Pat lifted his glass, even though Eckley was straight up lying to his face. Eckley followed, perhaps unsure if he was being fucked with.

After having a drink together, both gradually wandered back to their respective groups. Pat was determined to present it as a coincidence that he and his friends were also in this particular bar, on this particular night. He had also considered how to explain it to Yatrofsky. Conveniently, he didn't have to. About a half hour later, totally unaware of Pat and Eckley's first interaction, Yatrofsky caught his arm. "That's David Eckley over there," he confirmed, already a little drunk.

"Really? Why did he tell me his name was Max the first time I met him?"

Yatrofsky shrugged. "He's just a weird guy. Hey, didn't your girl want to ask him something about his band?"

"Oh yeah! I'll have to ask him tonight while we're here," Pat nonchalantly replied.

In that vein, he and the others were still hanging out at their table in the back, enjoying what looked on the surface like a regular night at the bar, yet keeping a joint eye on Eckley to ensure that he did not slip away before they could accost him for more info. Pat was trying to avoid thinking too far ahead, but knew it would look best to naturally circulate and not stick to Eckley all night. He hoped they could then re-encounter him when he was already drunk, or if that wasn't happening, perhaps help him get there, but not in a way it would appear they were influencing the course of his evening. After making initial contact, addressing the issue of the mislabeled tape, and confirming he was indeed David Eckley, what steps would lead to a more serious conversation? These things usually ended up working themselves out, following Pat's usual logic of "play it by ear."

Short of gleaning some damning information about Eckley's involvement in Ryan's death, as Christine had opaquely suggested, the other long-range goal of the evening was for Pat (or Vik) to get their hands on Eckley's phone and install the app that would gain Pat access to his future texts. But first they needed his password. At one point Vik was able to hover behind him at the bar for a few minutes undetected, but only saw him enter it enough times to get a partial read on the digits. They would have to try again later at close range.

Eckley also seemed to be bouncing back and forth between groups. Pat intuited that Eckley knew a couple of people here, but that he had no close friends in attendance, and was perhaps at the bar more out of nostalgia rather than to hang out with anyone specific, except maybe Warren Yatrofsky.

Around 11:30, a catalyst appeared in the form of Shane Perry. He had texted that he was coming after all, and while Pat was glad to have one more ally on hand, he was also curious about how the idiosyncratic Shane would stir up the proceedings. Pat had surreptitiously snapped a pic of Eckley when he learned that Shane was on the way, in case they somehow encountered each other before Pat could brief him. "This is the guy. He's sort of a tinfoil hat dude." This turned out to be a surprisingly prescient move.

Pat was on his way back from the bathroom again when the door opened, and in swept Shane. Vik turned to greet him, but Eckley was in the way. Pat moved to intercept him. But before he could introduce him, he heard:

"Giuseppe McCleary. From Italy by way of Scotland. Pleasure to meet you!" Shane intoned in a Scottish accent as he pumped Eckley's hand. Giuseppe McCleary! Christ! Shane was an actor and sometimes did accents around people he didn't know, or for customers in his cab, but Pat hadn't planned on Shane showing up in character. He was curious how it would affect tonight's proceedings. In the meantime, he was tickled that Eckley was getting a taste of his own medicine by being introduced to someone bearing a false name, and even better, from someone who didn't even know about Eckley's own similar steps toward deception. Pat lurked near the bar, attempting to look casual, to stick close and hear what would transpire.

"I'm just in the States for a few months for a role," Shane/Giuseppe was explaining. "And there's no better way to get to know the locals than by driving a cab! Got my car out front," he continued. "If you need a ride."

"That's ... good to know," Eckley allowed. Pat imagined he was wondering if this dude was even licensed to drive in America, or if he knew which side of the road to drive on.

"You know why I got the job?" Eckley didn't encourage him. "Conspiracy theories!" Shane continued gleefully. "I am a walking encyclopedia. Well, usually a driving encyclopedia. And this play's about a Scotsman. It was like it was written just for me!"

"What's it called?" Eckley looked interested despite himself, and perhaps a little alarmed.

"It's called ..." (Pat braced himself for the title—it was probably whatever Shane had been listening to on the way over, as he could tell he was making this up as he went along) *Diary of a Madman*."

"Is that about—"

Shane cut him off. "A Scottish reporter who's here to investigate one of the MK-Ultra doctors."

"Oh shit, MK-Ultra!" Eckley looked interested. "Have you read *Acid Dreams*?"

"Who do you take me for?" Shane replied, grinning. "Of course I have. And that *Wormwood* show coming out on Netflix, about Frank Olson? Can't wait."

Pat silently observed as they continued in this vein for another minute or two while moving closer to the bar, while he, Vik and Don converged from the other direction. He didn't want to miss the rest of this conversation.

"I hear the Navy used to do experiments at that building in Dobbs Ferry down by the Hudson," Eckley remarked, not realizing that he had inadvertently opened up the conversation to the group. Shane/Giuseppe wasn't listening, as Don had spotted him and was hugging him hello.

Pat closed his mouth. He had been about to interject "I think my wife used to work in that building," but at the last minute, decided to let the conversation develop organically.

"I used to write down there by the train tracks," Eckley added.

"Write what, plays?" Giuseppe asked.

"No, graffiti. Back in the '80s. I wasn't very good," Eckley stiffly clarified.

"Were any of us?" Pat chuckled. He could afford to be generous, as the subtle shift of power had not gone unnoticed, and he suspected that Eckley would be on the defensive the rest of the night.

"I heard they spotted some mutant-ass creature in the pond," Don concurred. "It was like half snake—"

"Half-shark-alligator-half-man?" Pat interjected, only half joking.

Suddenly, their conversation was the focus of that section of the bar, with everyone chiming in, friends and otherwise.

"I heard the CIA was doing some shit there."

"Nah son, I think that was DARPA."

"I heard some guy drowned in the pond when they were doing submarine testing, and his ghost still haunts the place."

"There is definitely some weird shit there. My daughter went to camp there; they put fish in the pond, like for the camp, and all the fish died."

"Yo, that pond is so deep, it connects to the Hudson or some shit? When the Army Corps of Engineers—"

"It was the Office of Naval Research," Vik pronounced from the end of the bar. "I used to work with this dude whose dad had been on one of those projects. It fucked him up for life."

Resolving the name of the agency in question did little to dampen the speculation, which continued apace. Though what had fucked him up for life, Pat wondered. Radio waves? Chemicals? High lead content in the walls? Something he had witnessed during a test or experiment?

"I'm sure he's not the only one who got all fucked up," Don chimed in. "What if people died there while they were doing research? Whole building is probably *haunted as hell!*"

"So why don't we go over there and check it out? Stir up some ghosts on ... Thanksgiving Eve? Does that exist in America, like Christmas Eve?" Shane elbowed Eckley in the ribs. Eckley looked uncomfortable.

"You mean tonight?" Eckley downed the rest of his whiskey and ordered another.

"Yes tonight! Anyway, that's the point of the play," Shane continued. "The main character, that's me, discovers some dodgy experiments going down at this facility and tries to get the truth out, but ends up being a target himself."

Eckley's face looked like he was struggling with how to respond. He turned to Vik, attempting to change the subject, perhaps assuming that Vik was the sanest one there.

"So, uh, what do you do for work these days?"

"Criminal defense attorney," Vik replied without missing a beat. "Here's my card in case you ever need it." Eckley looked unsettled, not realizing that Vik did this to pretty much everyone he met.

Following the graffiti conversation and the mass speculation about the building in Dobbs, Eckley seemed even more determined to impress them and redeem himself. Pat thought back to Christine's reference to Eckley's narcissistic streak. Could they use this knowledge to their advantage, goading him into revealing too much while trying to put himself in a better light?

At one point he observed Don talking to him about Demolition Hammer and Sepultura, decidedly from a fellow fan's perspective, and perhaps in false deference to Eckley's presumed veteran status in the hardcore and metal communities. Eckley looked oddly uncomfortable and less effusive than one might have expected, possibly due to Don pretending his phone had died, and asking him to repeatedly pull up YouTube videos on his own phone (and thus repeatedly enter his PIN).

After escaping from Don, Eckley weaved in and out of conversation with Yatrofsky, the blond guy, and others he evidently knew. But periodically he kept wandering back towards their circle, particularly to Shane. Pat didn't want to push their luck and was waiting for an opening to organically engage him in conversation. Ideally, Eckley would come back to them of his own volition. So far there hadn't been a chance to get their hands on his phone, but perhaps that would also transpire as the night wore on, and hopefully Don had gotten the PIN.

It was 1:30 a.m. The bars didn't close till 4:00, but people were slowly starting to head home. Warren Yatrofsky had said his good-byes a few minutes earlier and looked steady on his feet as he left the bar. If things did get ugly, there went the one neutral party between them and their target. Eckley himself was engaged in a halfhearted conversation with an aging rocker type but didn't look ready to call it a night.

Pat stood halfway between Eckley and Vik, trying to catch the eye of the latter, who was coolly observing the room from over by the pool table. Don was at the bar and Shane had disappeared. But as he sought Vik's gaze, Vik jerked his head meaningfully. Pat turned around to find Eckley heading his way.

"What's up?" Pat intercepted him.

Eckley looked somewhat worse for wear. "I want to show you something," he mumbled.

"Then show me," Pat thought of Mo and that Show of Force live set she used to play nonstop around the time they met, where the singer yelled something like, "You think you're so hard? Show me!" Mo and her obscure tapes, always getting them into these situations! Though this time, Pat was enjoying himself. Besides the one Jameson and a round of shots after Shane arrived, he had been drinking ginger ale, was confident he had the upper hand on Eckley in the sobriety department, and was ready for whatever the fuck this night had been building to.

"Not here," Eckley mumbled.

"Outside?" Pat clarified. Was this it? He could feel Vik watching them, ready to alert the others if necessary.

"Not here," Eckley looked around. "Have to drive. Something you got to see."

"I'd say you're in no condition to drive, buddy." Don, in no condition to drive either, appeared behind them and good-naturedly shook Eckley by the shoulder. He didn't even flinch. Was it possible he had no idea that this group could do him harm, and that, in fact, he was attempting to lure all of them offsite to an undisclosed location?

"I'll drive." Vik approached and eyeballed the group: himself, Pat, Don, and Eckley. "I can fit all of you."

"What about ..." Don had started to ask about Shane, by his actual name. Pat wasn't sure if he had even heard Shane introduce himself as Giuseppe McCleary.

Vik raised his eyebrows. "Let's wrap up and we'll figure it out." Eckley wasn't even following this conversation. Vik steered him to the bar to close their respective tabs.

Shane had reappeared and behind the pool table, talking to some old guy with a luxurious moustache, who, despite his age, nevertheless looked like he could still fight the entire bar and win. Pat headed over to extricate Shane and brief him that Eckley wanted to take them somewhere, no one knew where yet, that Vik could fit everyone in the car, but that Shane should follow surreptitiously in his cab just in case.

Tabs settled, they filed outside. During the occasional hardcore shows here, half the club would have migrated to the parking lot, but tonight, the lot was almost deserted.

Vik clicked open the car and climbed into the driver's seat. Pat offered shotgun to Eckley as the guest of honor, and he accepted. This left Pat and Don in the back, with Don behind Vik and Pat behind Eckley.

"Where to, captain?" Vik queried. As he backed out of the space, Pat saw Shane getting into his cab at the other end of the lot.

"Need to show you something," Eckley mumbled again. Was he falling asleep? Pat regretted not putting him in the back seat, where he could probably have swiped his phone and wallet without an iota of effort.

"... office of naval resource ... research," he continued. "That place in Dobbs Ferry."

Pat held his breath. What the fuck could Eckley want to show them at that building in Dobbs that would require such an elaborate mission, not to mention a two car caravan?

"Fuck yeah!" Don was on board. "I am so down to see this shit!"

"But what about ..." Eckley suddenly seemed to realize that Shane wasn't with them.

"Giuseppe's on his way," Pat quickly reassured him. "You think he's gonna miss this? It was his idea. He'll meet us there." How could he meet them there if they hadn't told him where they were going? Luckily this leap of logic went right over the head of Eckley.

"It was my idea," Eckley muttered truculently, then fell silent.

Vik turned onto Tuckahoe Road, Shane not far behind. Pat had no doubt that Shane would be able to follow them, but he texted him nonetheless: "This drunk idiot decided we are going to Dobbs after all. 145

Lost Indignation

Palisade Street." He knew the address from when Mo had worked in the building.

"How do you want to do this?" Vik conferred. They were passing Staples, heading towards the Sprain Brook Parkway.

"I'd take 87 to Ashford." It was the most direct route, rather than trying to fuck with the Saw Mill and Ravensdale Road or whatever. How was it that Eckley just expected that they knew where they were going, without giving them directions or an address?

Pat's phone buzzed. It was a text from Don beside him that just read "3287." He was momentarily confused until he realized that must be Eckley's phone PIN!

"Oh shit! You got it?" He texted back. Don nodded, and Pat fist-bumped him. Eckley was none the wiser.

Vik navigated his Acura up the thruway, past Stew Leonard's, the toll plaza, and got off exit 7 in Ardsley. They glided up Saw Mill River Road, past the ancient Carvel, and turned on Ashford Ave. Pat looked longingly in the direction of Thai House, shuttered for the night, as they crossed the bridge over the Saw Mill Parkway. Perhaps Eckley wanted to show them some graffiti thing down by the train tracks in Dobbs? He knew that Eckley had been a transit cop here before he moved back to Boston, but Eckley didn't know that Pat was aware of his occupation. It was amazing how much time they had spent researching this guy and his role in the Indignation saga, and here was in the flesh and by all indications totally unaware of any ulterior motives.

Soon they were descending the hill at 145 Palisade. The intermediate smaller parking lots on the way down the hill, once filled with rubble and decrepit cars, were freshly paved and had been demarcated into overflow parking for Mercy College, which was just up Route 9, with signs denoting the regularity of shuttle bus pickup. The place was evidently under new management from the era Mo had worked there, back when they were forever running out of heating oil. And was that a sculpture? Some sort of skeletal art thing reared up near the famous pond, and a couple of smaller, lower iterations lurked nearby.

Vik parked by the pond, and from the headlights sweeping down the hill behind them, Pat figured Shane was about to do the same. Once extricated from their various vehicles, they met at the grassy area next to the pond, near a few of the new sculptures. Eckley was stumbling around near the water, though he would occasionally attempt to wander off towards the driveway that wrapped around the south end of the building and led to the bridge over the railroad tracks. Shane, however, was enthusiastically outlining something involving the pond, and each time Eckley tried to shift the focus of their sojourn, Shane corralled and redirected him. Had he not gotten the message that Eckley wanted to show them something, or did he not realize that whatever he wanted to show them might be at a different part of the grounds?

Eckley muttered something about a bridge, and something else snapped into place for Pat, though he didn't tell Eckley what he had just deduced, and he just as quickly lost the revelation. Hopefully he would re-remember it to tell Mo in the morning.

Don walked over to Eckley, and Shane resumed whatever he had been trying to explain about the pond, whether or not the various assembled parties were paying attention.

"... then take forty paces around the pond and his ghost will appear!" Shane intoned excitedly.

"Will you shut the fuck up about forty paces around the pond!" Eckley roared. He seemed suddenly lucid, though to Pat's experienced eye, he was still extremely drunk.

"You're all so fucking stupid ... God, I'm so much smarter than all of you. I can't believe you brought me all the way here and you still weren't smart enough to figure it out!" Eckley sneered.

"Figure out what, that you make a better train pig than graffiti writer?" Pat asked sarcastically.

"How the fuck ..." Eckley seemed caught off guard that Pat knew he was a transit cop, but recovered and mumbled something that seemed to contain the words "tape," "internet," and "your wife."

"What's that about my wife?" Pat asked sharply.

"Only an idiot couldn't put together the pieces ... I gave you every clue," Eckley scoffed and slurred.

"I wouldn't flatter yourself, homie. Not that many people even give a fuck what your name is, or about your shit-ass band." The tone was calculated to taunt someone into swinging on him, in which case he would annihilate them, a frequent tactic of younger Pat.

Behind him, the mood shifted palpably, especially in Vik, who didn't trust this Eckley cat one bit. Pat was pretty sure he was carrying, but hadn't explicitly asked.

"You ain't so famous that you have to fuck with some elaborate-ass nom de plume, son," Pat continued. This was perhaps what he had wanted all night: the chance to call him out, not just to extract info.

The "son" was what got him: Eckley charged. But a clandestine sculpture lurked in his path. Tripped up by its abstract form, he slammed down hard face-first into the grass and lay still.

There was a moment of shocked silence. Pat had imagined knocking him out in various scenarios, ideally after harvesting all pertinent information, but not that it would be handled so unexpectedly and spectacularly by an inanimate object.

"Is he ... alive?" ZT ventured.

Lost Indignation

Vik took his pulse. "He's breathing, but he's out cold." He picked up the iPhone that lay on the ground beside him. "His phone's dead though."

"Well, we're not going to wait around until he wakes up, or to charge the phone. You got this, Mr. Uh, McCleary?" Pat gestured to Shane/Giuseppe. The phone, the original target of the evening, now seemed almost like an afterthought.

"I certainly do," Shane smiled devilishly.

"Let's get the fuck out of here before we get charged with desecrating a sculpture." The offending art object looked surprisingly intact after its encounter with Eckley.

Pat and Vik managed to muscle the unconscious Eckley into the backseat of Shane's cab, where he would be carted off to wherever he was staying once he regained consciousness, hopefully with no memory of what the fuck he was doing in Dobbs Ferry. Once both parties were in the cab, Pat, Don, and Vik headed back to the latter's car. As they were leaving, Pat looked around. After Eckley had been unceremoniously removed from the premises, he was officially off-duty. Thai House might not be open, but White Castle sure as shit was, and to paraphrase Prince Paul on that Run the Jewels guest spot, the night was just getting started.

Chapter 14
2017

Black Friday dawned with a flurry of excitement at Aunt Ray's. Mo would be driving back to New York by herself, as Max was riding home to NJ with their parents to visit his high school friends over the long weekend. To get home in time for Outburst, Mo needed to leave by mid-afternoon. Finally, she had said good-bye to everyone multiple times (the Jewish Goodbye outweighing the Irish Goodbye here) and was on her way, the Camry humming along the moonlike pavement of Route 380.

40 minutes later, Mo had just reached the last section of 380 where you're flying downhill as it readies to join regular old Route 80 when the opening beat of "Daytona 500" blared from her phone. As per tradition, this ringtone heralded an incoming call from Kenza, dating to the rudimentary version that Kenz had installed on Mo's flip phone just before tour in 2007 so that Mo would always know it was her. Mo pressed Answer, then hit the speakerphone button and dropped the phone in her lap.

"Kenz! How was your Thanksgiving? I'm so glad you called."

"Hello, my love." Kenza was calling from somewhere quiet. Mo did not hear any football on the other end, and her husband was an obsessive fan. "I'm actually at work right now," Kenza sighed. That explained the lack of background noise. "That's why I'm calling. Besides the fact that I wanted to say hi since I won't see you until Christmas. We're closed today, but I just came in for a few hours to get something from the archives. You know how I'm teaching this class on radio and mass persuasion? Next week we're doing conspiracy theories and radio shows—everything from Father Coughlin through Alex Jones. But I wanted to do something about *Coast to Coast AM*, too, and find them a good example of what people call in about."

"That sounds like a fun class," Mo agreed. *Coast to Coast AM—*wasn't that the show that Christine had said Eckley and Marnell had liked? She was about to mention them when she realized that Kenza would have no idea who they were.

"Anyway, there was this episode on mind harassment, voice-to-skull technology, all that stuff. And this guy calls in and starts talking about this building that sounded just like where you used to work!"

Alarm bells were going off in Mo's head. "Wait, what were they saying about the building?"

"I think he was living there ... he was talking about this building that used to be a brewery and a bible factory before it was used for military research. It had all these protections. Almost like Hogwarts." Kenza laughed. "He thought that these people had been reading his thoughts, but once he was living in the building, he felt safe, since there was all this strong stuff in the way. Poor guy. But he still thought something might happen to him, so he wanted to call into the show, almost like as a witness to what he thought was going on."

Mo was momentarily shocked into silence (a rare occurrence). She didn't even know where to start, as she realized she'd never had an in-depth conversation with Kenza about the investigation. There had been plenty of times to tell her, but somehow, every time Kenz had asked how she was doing, there were more obvious answers involving school or work or daily annoyances. There had been no room for arcane extracurriculars like exploring the history of an unloved demo tape from 1988 and the shadowy cast behind its conception and suppression. But Mo realized that even without officially chasing Marnell and Eckley, she would still have been excited by the revelation about the building.

"Oh, man. You're right, that sounds like where I used to work! The mention of the bible factory *and* the brewery really seals the deal. I need to hear this. Do you have the recording?"

"Sure, I can send you the link," Kenza affirmed. "I thought you might be interested!"

"Of course I am. I think I might know who you're talking about, the guy living there. Sort of a minor hardcore legend. He passed away a few years ago." She made no mention, however, of how she had been hunting him and how their lives had recently intersected.

Somewhere around Parsippany, her phone buzzed with a new email. It was Kenza sending the link to the show! Mo kept driving. She and Pat were constantly at war with their data plan, so she didn't want to start streaming or downloading till she got home. Though as someone who was terrible at waiting, she still thought about it every few minutes, in what amounted to a long ride home, though there was surprisingly little traffic at the George Washington Bridge.

Finally, Mo was home, and had lugged all her luggage and leftovers up to the third floor with the help of Pat, who met her on the porch. Once upstairs, after exchanging the perfunctory greetings and gropings, she recounted Kenza's discovery.

"Whoa. I'll pull it up right now." Pat walked to his computer.

"How long is it?" Mo was hoping it was just a snippet from the show, rather than the entire show itself.

"Crap, it's like two hours. I'll start listening to it now, and if I get to the Ryan part, I'll go back and we can listen together on the way to the show." Luckily this seemed like the type of topic Pat was interested in, even outside their interest in the potential caller. Mo continued unloading her food, trailed by Brett and CC.

Lost Indignation

"How's good old David Eckley? Has he said anything in his texts?"

"Not much in his texts at all ... maybe still recovering from Wednesday night."

"Or he knows we somehow have access to his phone?"

"We didn't leave a trace. I even switched the Bank of America icon onto the app I installed."

"You think of everything." Mo hadn't thought to confirm with Shane exactly where in Yonkers he had dropped off Eckley. But she would have been willing to bet everything in Eckley's wallet, plus her own, that it was at a house on Crestwood Avenue.

Pat queued up the episode while Mo was in the shower and getting ready for Outburst, then pulled it up on his phone to continue playing once they were in the car. He had been able to skip some of the special guests during the first hour, but they had just opened up the phone lines and there was still a ton of time left. So far, there was no one who remotely sounded like Ryan, though the other callers' stories about their experiences with "mind harassment" were an oddly compelling and atmospheric soundtrack as they cruised the deserted streets of western Mount Vernon towards the Bronx River Parkway.

"When is this from again?"

"August 8, 2006." Christine had mentioned that Ryan had died in 2006. If this was him on the show, Mo wondered when it had been recorded in relation to his death.

Mo was taking the route where, to avoid the traffic at the Kosciuszko Bridge, you snuck onto Greenpoint Avenue early by taking the exit for the Long Island Expressway while not actually getting on the LIE. She was just merging onto the service road when they heard George Noory say "Let's go to our wildcard line—you're up, on Coast to Coast."

"Hi George, this is ... Arthur Rowe."

"Oh my god!" Mo exclaimed.

"SHH, shut the fuck up!" Pat hissed. "Wait, hold on." He hit pause and started to laugh, so immersed in the moment that he had temporarily forgotten they weren't listening to a live broadcast. It did all seem so real, on this desolate stretch of service road, as Mo waited to turn onto Greenpoint Ave. "OK, go ahead."

"Arthur Rowe is the main dude in the book *The Ministry of Fear*! And people keep trying to kill him! Sorry, you can hit play again." Pat rewound and resumed the transmission.

"And where are you calling from?" the host prodded.

"New York State," the caller answered softly. OK, if this was Ryan, he wasn't likely to name the exact location *where* in New York he was calling from, but apparently that was sufficient.

"Arthur in New York, what's on your mind?"

"I think I've experienced mind harassment ... or I was. I was hearing voices, people trying to give me instructions. I could tell they were reading my thoughts ..." he trailed off.

"But I found myself the safest place," the caller continued. "A building with these ... protections, from when it used to be a military research facility. Before that it was a bible factory and a brewery. It's a very old building, and whatever's in the walls, it's blocking them from getting in my mind. I've been staying here on and off in a bathroom. It's spidery and half out of order, but it keeps me safe. When I'm here at least. Every time I leave the area, I swear someone is trying to finish me off. The voices come back, and one of them tried to run me over. So I wanted it on record that they might be trying to control my mind, that I might be in danger, but I'm not giving in."

"Wow." Pat hit Pause and they drove in silence as the bleak industrial landscape gave way to Greenpoint proper.

"If that was him ..." And who else could it have been? There were too many coincidences, from the Ministry of Fear references to the fact that the caller had been describing the building where Ryan had died.

"It's like three points of a triangle," Mo mused. "Or a square. A parallelogram? Eckley took you to the building in Dobbs, so something there is obviously important to him. The person we presume was Ryan was on this show, talking about what we think is the same building and its creepy bathroom. The Ministry of Fear references also tie it to them. And the show documented that Ryan was scared." But was he scared of David Eckley, or was the building in Dobbs important to both of them for two different reasons entirely?

These ruminations were cut short by finding surprisingly convenient parking and making their way towards Brooklyn Bazaar. As usual, Mo and Pat were running late, and once they got inside the show, there was still a huge line just to ascend the stairs. The second floor was so packed that they could barely get inside. Mo had been going to shows for 15 years but still never tired of the electric but disorienting feeling of walking into a dark and overcrowded club.

They had missed the first few bands, and King Nine was up next. When Mo had seen Outburst at CBGB's back in 2006, it hadn't been much more crowded than the average matinee. But tonight, it was obvious that much of the crowd was here for Outburst, and it was unlikely that she and Pat would attempt to make their way up front. Indeed, Outburst received a way more enthusiastic response than at their '06 CB's show. A significant portion of the crowd then left before Killing Time, who nonetheless played a long and inspired set for those who had been wise enough to stay.

Afterwards, much like at the park show back in September, no one seemed to want to leave. Mo hugged Sydenstricker, who had filled in for Killing Time while Rich McLoughlin was in Ireland for work, and immediately regretted it when he was entirely saturated with sweat. "Whoa!" she jumped back.

"What did you expect? I just played a show."

"Hey, Remove this Doubt!" A voice exclaimed. Mo turned. It was the guy from the park show who Tony Gerson had said was a cop. "My cousin says hi. My cousin Christine," Anthony clarified, in response to her momentary befuddlement.

"Wait ... Christine's your cousin?" Mo gasped in realization. Suddenly, two independent pieces of information came flooding back: that Christine's cousin had once had a crush on Liz Zimmer, and then later, that same night, the reference to a cousin on the force in Dobbs Ferry, who hadn't yet been working there when Ryan Marnell died. But Mo hadn't known that these two referenced cousins were the same person, or that the cousin with a crush on Liz was a hardcore kid.

"Yup, she told me someone was looking into the situation with Ryan. I didn't realize the connection until tonight and remembered the name from seeing your business card. I wasn't working in Dobbs yet when it happened, but let me know if I can help."

"Thank you. I might have some questions for you. I found out a bunch of new stuff since I talked to Christine."

"You know Anthony?" Sydenstricker sidled over, somehow even sweatier than moments earlier. "I sometimes ride bikes with this guy," he elaborated.

At the mention of bikes, Pat appeared as if by magic at Mo's elbow, resting a hirsute forearm on her shoulder and presenting an opportunity to steer the conversation back to Ryan. "This is my husband, Pat," Mo clarified, "And Pat, this is Anthony. Christine's cousin," she gave him a meaningful look. "Who's on the force in Dobbs."

Sydenstricker, oblivious to the developing situation, suddenly drew his own conclusion regarding the circle of four, registering the Westchester connection if not the familial coincidence.

"Oh, are you still looking for that Indignation demo? You should ask this guy. Except he probably doesn't have his either. No one still has it!"

"Nope," Anthony confirmed. "Sold mine back in the '90s. Couldn't believe anyone would want it. Wait, you're looking for the Indignation demo?" He shot Mo an inquisitive look.

"Long story," she demurred.

"Hey, forget the Indignation demo—we should all get together and ride bikes sometime," Pat interjected.

"What kind of bike you got?" Anthony asked Pat.

Becky McAuley

Mo turned away to let Pat continue the discussion. The more that Pat and Anthony could nerd out together about bikes, the more likely they were to see him again soon in a non-show context. Thinking quickly, she grabbed a kid passing nearby, who she knew only peripherally and had interacted with more on Instagram than in person.

"Hey, Will? This is J.P. Sydenstricker. I know you had a question about the Shock of Pain 1993 European tour?"

The kid looked starstruck. "What's up, dude," he managed. "Were you in the band for that show in Berlin when there was a riot during Leprosy Vector?"

Mo hid a smile and turned away just as Sydenstricker launched into the tale. She wandered over to the Killing Time merch and nodded a hello to John Franko behind the table. She and Pat had already hit the Outburst merch earlier in the night, surmising correctly that it might sell out. By the time she turned around to check on Will and Sydenstricker, and more importantly, her husband and Anthony, she saw Pat gesturing as if they had just exchanged contact info. Hey, if they were in touch, she didn't need to be. This was one of the many advantages of having a spouse more outgoing than herself.

As the throngs dissipated, Mo and Pat made their way downstairs to the car. "Are we still cruisin' for a Pruz-in?" Mo inquired. One of the best places to stop on the way home from shows in the city was Pruzzo's, the 24-hour deli in their old neighborhood in the Bronx. It was pretty much on the way home if you took the Hutch rather than the Bronx River Parkway, so as long as Mo wasn't too sleepy, they stopped there after most Brooklyn shows.

"Yeah, if you're not too tired. I could absolutely murder a chicken cutlet right now."

"I'm not super hungry but I might need some snacks." Even late at night, it was often hard to park by Pruzzo's, so Mo usually pulled up at a fire hydrant across the street and stayed in the car, after giving Pat an elaborate ranked list of her snack preference in case the grill was off or they didn't have a specific subspecies of Cheetos.

Mo navigated the Camry to the LIE, onto the Van Wyck, across the Whitestone Bridge, and up the Hutchinson River Parkway to the exit for their old neighborhood. They followed Westchester Avenue under the 6 train, then pulled up across the street from Pruzzo's.

"We don't have any plans tomorrow, right?" Pat asked as he was getting out of the car. Mo confirmed they did not, and assumed he was checking in terms of how excessive of a sandwich to get, depending on the next day's activities.

"That's good, because I was talking to Anthony—"

"And you're going to ride bikes with him tomorrow?"

Lost Indignation

"—No, will you ever let me finish a sentence? We're meeting him in Dobbs Ferry tomorrow to look at the building."

Despite the late night after Outburst, Mo woke up Saturday full of enthusiasm for their impending mission in Dobbs Ferry. In an echo of the Matt Zimmer coffee meeting where Mo and Pat had accidentally assembled almost identical outfits, today they both independently donned their new Outburst merch. "I mean, it's not my fault that you get dressed in the living room," Mo sniped. She had layered her new Outburst longsleeve under a puffy vest, though she might not even need the vest, as it was already 47 degrees. Pat was wearing his new Outburst shirt in the Knicks colors.

"Who knows, maybe Anthony will show up in one too? It'll be like our uniform." Pat was adjusting his royal blue and yellow Yankees hat, attempting to determine if it was a better match than a Hartford Yard Goats hat.

"Fine, I'll leave mine on too. David Eckley is about to find out the hard way that he's on thin ice!"

And so they made it out of the house by 11:37, meaning they would be almost on time to meet Anthony at noon. Mo was about to turn into the driveway down to the building in Dobbs when she noticed the parking signs everywhere and how much neater the property looked overall. Freaked out by its new orderly aspect, she managed to snag a spot on the street instead.

Pat had taken out his phone to text Anthony and let him know they had arrived when they saw him walking down the hill towards them. He greeted them and fell into step as they started down the prodigious slope towards the structure at the bottom.

"Where'd you park?"

"At work."

Mo had forgotten that the Dobbs Ferry police station was nearby on Main Street. She acknowledged that it must be nice to work right in downtown Dobbs, for the restaurants and such. "I only ever worked down here." She gestured at the building ahead of them. "At a book company on the third floor."

"Oh yeah? So you know all about this place," Anthony concluded. "It's a local legend."

"Yup, I got that idea. Christine was talking about how you all used to hang out here. She's so cool, your cousin."

"Isn't she? I was so lucky to have the Oronzios as my extended family. Her dad is my mom's older brother. I grew up in south Yonkers, but I spent a lot of time at their house in Dobbs. I even lived with them while my parents were getting divorced. That's how I got into hardcore," he reflected. "I was staying with them in the summer of '87 and all three of

Christine's little sisters were driving her crazy. The two of us would walk around town just listening to tapes on her boombox."

"Awesome. Did you go to any shows around here, or were you mostly down in the city?"

"We went down to the city sometimes, but we also went to the Anthrax, Streets in New Rochelle, whatever weird places they had Indignation shows, like some park in Sleepy Hollow, and the Portuguese American Club in Mount Vernon ..."

"We live in Mount Vernon!" Mo interjected with the same verve as Adam's convivial declaration of "we're Jewish!" in *The Autograph Man*. The Portuguese American Club was down by the Mount Vernon East train station, on the New Haven line. Had the famous missing Indignation show with Power Structure taken place a mile from her home on Overlook Street?

"Nice! I like going to Johnny's when I'm in the area. Great pizza."

"If you like pizza," Mo countered, "you should let us take you to our friend's new restaurant sometime. Pizzeria La Rosa, over in New Rochelle."

Continuing down the hill, Anthony reminisced about past local live music, from the Supremes playing in Yonkers (Mo actually knew about that one) to shows at The Low Down that he and Pat had both attended in the '90s. As they approached their destination, Mo wondered when everything here had gotten so cleaned up. The building looked freshly painted or power washed, and everything, from the parking lots to the building to the statues, seemed sleek and polished. It was obviously under different management from when she had worked here, and she felt a pang for its old incarnation. Had she fully appreciated it when she had been here, when it was still wild and decrepit, before it had been gentrified like almost every other piece of lower Westchester lately?

"What is this place now, the Grounds for Sculpture?" Mo exclaimed as they reached the bottom of the hill. She had spotted the cluster of statues, including the one that had likely tripped up Eckley. The marauding sculpture looked so innocent in the light of day. "Hey, at least today I have my location scouting cards! So we should be OK if we run into anyone."

"Or that this time you're with a Dobbs Ferry cop."

"Oh, yeah. Duh." Mo grinned.

"Detective, actually." Anthony handed his business card to each of them. "I'm now interested in a professional capacity, not just because we're looking into what happened to my cousin's ex. I'm technically off today, but it sounded like an interesting way to spend a Saturday. Though I could also be out riding bikes with this guy and J.P." He nodded to Pat. "Next week maybe?"

Lost Indignation

"Yeah, that should work."

"I'm sure you already know about this, but this story actually involves two of your cousin's exes. Since I believe Christine also went out with David Eckley." Mo added.

"Or for full disclosure, three, if we're talking multiple cousins." Pat pointed to himself. "I used to date Dana," he explained.

"Oh my God, I'm sorry. Dana! I mean I love her, she's my cousin, but ... hey at least you ended up with your lovely wife here instead. And yes, unfortunately I was aware of the David Eckley era. I never liked the guy, not even when I was sixteen-years-old and he was a friend of my cousin's boyfriend. Ryan was always nice to me, but Eckley acted like I was a nuisance hanging around. And then when Christine got together with him ... I always tried to tell her he was bad news. Unfortunately she didn't see it until it was too late. But yeah, never liked the guy, but I also never thought that ..."

"He was capable of murder?" Mo said quickly, thinking of Christine's ambiguous comment.

"We'll see about that. I'm looking forward to you showing me anything relevant here, so that I can run with it in an official capacity if I think there's something worth looking into."

"So, no pressure," Pat teased. They all laughed. Mo wondered if she should mention their suspicions that Dana was also hooking up with Eckley, but the conversation had moved on.

"OK. First things first ..." They were standing facing the building, with the pond behind them and to their right. To their left was the driveway that led around the side of the building to the bridge. "So we know Ryan fell or jumped or was pushed from the bridge, since he got hit by the train." Mo shivered. "But last night, we heard this recording of a show on *Coast to Coast AM*, from the year that he died, and I think it's him calling in. In the recording, he mentions a building that sounds like this one, and that he was staying here on and off, in a bathroom. And he introduces himself by another name, as Arthur Rowe, who's a character in the book *The Ministry of Fear*, and insinuates that someone is trying to kill him. So that if something happens to him, he wants people to know about it."

Anthony confirmed that yes, he wanted to hear that recording.

"I can send it to you," Pat confirmed. "Oh, and I actually recorded when we were here on Wednesday night too."

"What?! You didn't tell me that!" Mo was shocked that Pat had forgotten to mention this critical fact.

"Yeah, in case Eckley said anything incriminating. I haven't listened to it yet, so I don't know how it came out. But I can pull it up."

"Wait, but before you play the recording! Or as Outburst would say, 'But wait one second.' I should give Anthony the full picture. You already know about David being friends with Ryan, and I assume you picked up on the fact that David sort of wanted to be in Indignation too." Anthony nodded. "But I need to get you up to speed on the more recent part of how we even got interested in this. I'll give you the short version." Pat rolled his eyes at the idea that any Mo story could be condensed into a short version and occasionally kept her on track as she recounted to Anthony how "Max Malkin" had attempted to sell them the videotape and all the odd incidents since, including how the Wretched Spaniel hangout had migrated here on Wednesday.

"So if this guy is so invested in the Indignation story that he made up a fake name and basically a whole character—a fan of Ministry of Fear instead of a member of the band—to sell us a videotape in a park, we figured something was up. And then it's just gotten weirder from there." Mo concluded.

"And that was the short version?" Pat verified. Mo held up both middle fingers.

"Anyway, I've got the recording from Wednesday." They all fell silent and drew closer to Pat's phone. Mo realized what a weird scene they were creating for anyone who happened to come down the driveway at that moment, or look out the window if anyone was in their office or art studio on the weekend. Though she supposed it was no stranger than huddling with "Max Malkin" during the tape transaction back in September, or whatever went on here Wednesday night.

Mo faintly heard someone declaiming in a Scottish accent, which must have been Shane/Giuseppe. "Can you make it any louder?"

"Nah, that's as high as it will go. But wait, you'll be able to hear Eckley better since he's next to me. That's him, mumbling something about the—oh, shit." Pat hit Pause and moved the recording bar a few seconds back.

"Not the pond ...need to show you ... at the bridge." Pat stopped the recording again.

"What did he say about the bridge?"

"Yeah, I forgot that part. So Eckley was the one who got us over here, but when we all got here, Shane was going on about something with a ghost and the pond. And Eckley tried to break away and said something about the bridge. But then he started screaming about being smarter than us so I forgot." Pat hit Play again. This time they heard Eckley much more clearly telling everyone to shut the fuck up, that he couldn't believe they hadn't figured it out, and that he'd given them every clue. Then Eckley and Pat arguing back and forth, the word "son," and a huge crunch.

"What was that, the sculpture?" Mo looked over at it. She was still surprised it looked OK after its collision with Eckley.

"Yup, and that's the end. He tripped on the sculpture, passed out, and Shane put him in the cab," Pat recounted more for Anthony's benefit.

"What was he saying about the bridge? Do you think he was ... trying to tell all of you that he had actually pushed Ryan off the bridge or something, and everyone was too dumb to realize it?"

"When Ryan died, Christine did tell me something that afterwards struck me as odd," Anthony cut in. He had been listening in silence, first to Mo's description of recent events, and then to the tape. "She said that David knew about Ryan dying before it was in the newspaper or anything. She said he was on duty that night, as a transit cop, and that David was actually the one who found Ryan."

"Oh, man. What kind of coincidence is that? Or no coincidence at all. Should we go over to the bridge?"

"Might as well." They walked past the front entrance of the building, towards the driveway that wrapped around its southern flank and led to the one-lane bridge over the train tracks. Back when Mo had been working here, the bridge had been closed to vehicular traffic. She had only ever darted across it to take the shortcut to the Dobbs Ferry train station if she was going straight to Yankee Stadium after work, as the new Yankees station was on the Hudson line. But the bridge seemed to have been reinforced and cleaned up, like most of this area, and was apparently frequented by anyone heading to the outbuildings by Bare Ass Beach, on the shore of the Hudson.

Rounding the corner, they continued up the incline of the bridge. It was strange not only to be here for the first time in six plus years, stopping midway to check things out, rather than scurrying across to catch the 6:18 train to Yankees-153rd Street. And that the location was suddenly imbued with so much more significance.

"So this is where it happened." Mo looked down at the tracks and towards the Dobbs Ferry station. Would everything have looked more ominous the night Ryan died? Maybe not though, if he was practically living here. Maybe he had no idea he was in danger that night.

They stood in silence looking down at the tracks. "Should we check out the rest of the building? Or do you want to go down to the river first?"

Anthony grinned. "I've spent enough time on Bare Ass Beach that I don't need to go over there today. We started calling it that after my cousin's friend Liz mooned some rich people's boat." He turned around and started walking back down the slope of the bridge, towards the main building. Mo looked in the window of the artist's studio that was right by the incline of the bridge but couldn't see much besides plants. A dog barked somewhere in the building. It was hard to tell if some of these studios were a workspace, a home, or an ambiguous space in between. Maybe it hadn't been so odd that Ryan was living down here at the end.

"So, we're looking for a bathroom," Mo summarized as they

opened the front door and stepped into the lobby. "And it's probably not the one on the third floor by my old office, since there were always people coming out of the women's room due to the dance studio down the hall. And the men's room was like three doors down from the book company I worked for. But there are all sorts of weird bathrooms all over the building. There's one on the fourth floor that me and my coworker used to walk up to sometimes if we wanted extra time to talk."

"I feel like you're overthinking this," Pat admonished. "Don't think about it like what you know from working here. Or at least don't read so much into it. What's the least used part of this building or has the most unused rooms?"

"The basement."

"Then we should try that first. Also, that sounds the most spidery, if that's what he said on the show."

Rather than take the elevator one flight down, Mo led them to the stairs, which continued down to the lower floor. There was a little light in here, from the sides of the building where the hill sloped down to the tracks, but it was still creepy and basement-y. Mo knew there were some businesses down here, like a screen printing company that Tony Gerson used to work for before she met him at the book place, but there also seemed to be the most empty space, at least when she was working here. Her experience with the basement was mostly limited to walking through it with trash or helping take large shipments to the back loading dock to get picked up by UPS Freight.

They passed a room full of intense looking valves, and Pat stopped to snap a picture. What the hell would valves like that even be used for? There were so many unique aspects of this building left over from its former lives.

"I wonder if this is it?" Mo peeked her head in. Like many of the bathrooms here, there was just an open doorway, but this one was narrower than normal. She ventured inside first, with Pat and Anthony following.

All the urinals were covered by black garbage bags, and two of the three sinks. One of the toilet stalls was boarded up in a half-ass job, the floor was filthy, and part of the wall was peeling off. Still, Mo could see why Ryan could have spent time here. There was something reassuring about this strange building, even in its dank basement. It appeared that hardly anyone came here even in 2017, when much of the building had already undergone a glow-up. What must it have looked like in the mid-2000s when Ryan died?

Pat looked up to where there was a crumb of light coming in from a window near the ceiling. "He might have been living here, though I bet he was painting in a different room. There's not much light in here."

Lost Indignation

And then Mo saw the ceiling tile.

The ceiling over the sink area was high and vaulted, but the toilets were almost located in an alcove with a lower drop ceiling. One of the tiles was loose, and what looked like a piece of posterboard was sticking out of the corner of it. Mo was instantly intrigued, but were any of them tall enough to reach it? She looked at Pat, sensing he understood. And in an unintentional re-enactment of the Warzone park show two months before, where Mo had climbed onto Pat's shoulders to get up front during "In the Mirror," she once again jumped onto his back and hoisted herself up his shoulders. With Pat steadying her, she reached up to seize the poster board from the tile, managing not to shower all of them in gross ceiling dust in the process.

"Gotta work on our circus act before we take it on the road," Mo said briskly, wondering if she had just freaked out Anthony, but he looked unfazed. Pat rubbed his shoulder while Mo scrutinized the liberated object. Larger than a letter-sized paper but smaller than a poster, it was extremely dirty, but appeared to bear some sort of poem inscribed in red paint, with otherworldly roses decorating the perimeter. One she could decipher it, Mo started to read aloud, realizing in horror that some of the phrasing sounded familiar:

And if I go away
I did not wish to die
I found myself the safest place
I do not wish to die.

Holy crap. Mo was 99% sure that the *Coast to Coast AM* caller had also used the phrase "I found myself the safest place," since it was singularly odd enough to have been stuck in her head since. If they had any remaining doubts about the voice on the show being Ryan Marnell, that would be one more thing that would tie the caller to this building and this situation. Who else could have crafted this illustrated poem thing, and why would they have hidden it under the ceiling tile in a bathroom? Had it really been here for over 11 years? That was plausible, due to the shape it was in.

"'I found myself the safest place ...' that was one of the phrases the caller used on the radio show I mentioned. So unless another person was living in a bathroom here and called into *Coast to Coast AM* thinking someone was trying to kill them, that means Ryan painted this." If this was the first piece of Ryan's art they had encountered, Mo wanted to see more, since this thing was creepy as fuck. How was it possible that they had run across a Ryan Marnell original that had been in a bathroom of her former office building the entire time she was working there, and they still hadn't found the fucking Indignation demo?

"I definitely need to hear that show." Anthony looked grave.

"Could you also look up when Ryan died? Or do you remember? This show was recorded in August 2006."

"I think he died in August 2006, too. I'll check when I get back to work, and let you know."

Mo pressed on. "So do you think, after seeing all of this, that ... Ryan might not have killed himself? Or been the victim of an accident either?"

"It's certainly compelling, if circumstantial," Anthony concurred.

The unanswered question hung around all of them: if Ryan Marnell hadn't intended to kill himself, then who had?

"And what should we do with this thing? Should we take it home or leave it with you?"

"I might need this in case we reopen the investigation. But do you want to take a picture first?" Pat snapped some pictures before Anthony tucked it gently under his arm, of the main side and of something scrawled on the back that looked like "say goodbye to Liv." Mo wondered who that might be.

After ensuring that there was nothing else hidden in the bathroom that they could discern, Mo, Pat, and Anthony conducted a cursory walkthrough of the rest of the basement, then headed up to the third floor so that Mo could see what company had taken over her old office. Pat also stopped at an operational bathroom, but it was clear that their tour of the building had reached a natural end. In some ways they had found what they had been looking for—another sign that tied Ryan to the building and to the radio show. But today also raised as many questions as answers.

"Oh! You said something about selling your Indignation demo?" Mo realized she better ask Anthony this while they were walking back up the driveway. She wondered when they would see him again or how much time he would realistically be able to spend re-investigating the death of Ryan Marnell, formally or informally.

"Yes, I did. Late '90s, some guy DM's me on hardcorewebsite, asking if I had any old Westchester hardcore tapes and then asks about the Indignation demo. I was surprised someone would want it, but I agreed to sell it to him."

"Do you remember anything else about him? Unfortunately the board died a few years ago so those messages are long gone. And I assume this was before PayPal."

"I'm sure it was a well-concealed cash transaction. And the only thing I remember was the guy was from Boston."

"Fuck, that sounds like Eckley. I wonder if he was collecting all the copies to destroy them, or for some other reason?" She was wondering if they should mention to Anthony the app that they had installed on Eckley's phone, but they had reached the top of the hill.

"OK, so I'm going to head up to work and look up a few things about Ryan. But I want to hear that show, and let me know if you find anything else relevant."

"Dude, thank you so much for spending your time on this!"

Anthony shrugged. "It's the right thing to do. Plus, like you, now I want to know exactly what happened here."

And something had definitely happened here, besides the night of Ryan's death and the long ago day when he met Christine. Between Ryan's ties to the building, the voice on the radio, and Eckley's comments on Wednesday, it was clear that this complex had been a place of significance not only for Mo McGraw, but also for Ryan Marnell and David Eckley.

Sunday was the end of the holiday weekend, and it was time to get back to real life and prepare for the upcoming week of work and school. Mo realized resignedly that they needed enough stuff from Costco that it made sense to go today, and that, hopefully, people were all shopped out from Thanksgiving preparations and Black Friday. Then again, every time she thought the New Rochelle Costco would be empty, she got what was one of the last spots in the parking lot. She would venture in that direction later in the afternoon, leaving Pat at home to continue cleaning up their apartment.

In the car on the way over, she pulled up a District 9 live set on her iPod. The set was from a show at the Stone Pony in 2007 which Mo had attended. It was a soundboard recording: excellent quality with crisp vocals. The recording started part way through the song "I," the first song on the demo, with Puerto Rican Myke shouting out "Gary Muttley! Gary Muttley!," who was in District 9 at the time, and had filled in for Blind Giants at the reunion. "I" soon transitioned into "Fool," Mo's favorite D9 track out of many contenders.

Mo had been too young for District 9 in the '90s, but was lucky to have seen them at the 2006 Superbowl of Hardcore and a bunch of times in the years immediately after. "Fool" was the best kind of hardcore song, with a distinct second verse, rather than just repeating the lyrics from the first one. Who were some of the best bands with second verses? Killing Time definitely. Bad Trip? Token Entry? And then you had a rapper like Bumpy Knuckles who rightly proclaimed himself the king of the third verse. Anyway, while pondering this conundrum, she had missed almost all of "Fool," which was already up to the part about revenge and hands being bloodstained.

Bloodstained. Mo sat bolt upright, which was probably wise, as she was approaching that five-point intersection where Boulevard turned into

Kings Highway, but that wasn't the source of her shock of alertness. In the official description of events, Ryan Marnell had died on the railroad tracks, either from jumping or falling from the bridge or being hit by the train that arrived soon after. Based on what Mo and Pat had discovered in the last few days, one could also speculate that he had been thrown or pushed off the bridge by David Eckley. But what if Eckley had somehow killed him before tossing him over the railing? Would these separate injuries have been missed, due to the encounter with the train moments after? And if a murder weapon existed, even if DNA evidence was unlikely, how the hell would they locate this item? Though if they did find such a thing, it would bolster their otherwise circumstantial evidence against Eckley.

Mo called Pat once she had parked at Costco, in one of the very last rows, since this place was always a shitshow on Sundays, post-Thanksgiving or otherwise. She knew he hated extraneous phone calls, but this was too exciting for just a text.

"So, what if Ryan didn't just jump or fall or get pushed off the bridge, but was killed *before* he went over the railing?"

"Hmm." Pat was silent, and Mo was sure he was assessing this new idea. "It's not a bad theory. He wouldn't want to chance Ryan surviving the fall and crawling off the tracks before the train could come. And it's less risky than going down there to finish him off."

"Could you ask Anthony? I'm about to go into Costco. If it's not weird that we bother him about this."

"I'm on it," Pat agreed.

It transpired (during the 57 minutes while Mo was inside Costco, 18 of which she was waiting on line to check out) that Anthony was also intrigued by Mo's idea to the degree that Pat had suggested he join them at Pizzeria La Rosa later. Mo never objected to a visit to Pizzeria La Rosa, their friend Matt's new restaurant which had opened in September, besides the fact that it was literally around the corner from Costco, and she would need to drive home to unload their perishables, pick up Pat, and then drive back to New Rochelle. Maybe she'd have another epiphany while driving on Kings Highway.

"Three days in a row that we're seeing Anthony! This is becoming quite a thing," Mo remarked, as they pulled the car into the parking lot at La Rosa. She kept an eye out for cats, as there were some ferals who were known to hang out back here.

Anthony was waiting for them in the lobby when they arrived. "I didn't realize he was with you!" Matt had come out to say hi, and directed them to one of the booths near the kitchen. "I would have sent him over to look at the records until you got here." Matt knew that Mo and Pat rarely got anywhere on time, even without the Costco complication. Pat plucked an Andes mint from the bowl on the counter, as Matt walked Anthony over to the record player and La Rosa's small zine library. But their guest seemed even more taken with the old photos of New Rochelle that adorned the adjacent hallway. Mo realized it had been a good move bringing him here. Even if her theory about a David Eckley murder weapon went nowhere, Matt might have won a new customer.

Finally they were all seated. While perusing the menus, Mo was about to elaborate on her new theory. But she realized that first, they better update him on the developments with Eckley's texts, and their ensuing suspicions about Dana.

"I doubt this is even legal, but we managed to get a parental monitoring app onto Eckley's phone so that this guy gets a copy of his text threads, incoming and outgoing." She pointed to Pat. "Anyway, Eckley hasn't said anything interesting yet, and no one has sent him anything interesting either. And all his contacts are under like, one letter names in his phone. Some guy apparently wants one of his bands to do a reunion, which was a surprise to me, since I didn't think anyone cared about his bands? But there's one thing we figured out. I don't even know how to say this, since Eckley also went out with Christine, but he might also be hanging out with your cousin Dana. She's just in his phone as 'D,' but Pat thinks he recognized her number."

Anthony sighed. "I can confirm the number for you. But I had a feeling this has been going on for a while. Christine told me what happened after she and David had broken up, that Dana had something to do with it. How the hell both of my cousins got involved with this loser is beyond me."

"Well at least they didn't hang out on Wednesday! Since Eckley accidentally got drunk at the Wretched Spaniel and missed out on meeting up with her. But I don't know how often they ... visit or anything. We'll keep an eye out for his texts, in case you want to talk to her about him. Because if they see each other often, then I guess Eckley is down here more than we realized." Mo thought back to September when they were buying the tape from "Max Malkin." Had he been down here for a work conference at all? And then at the McLean fall festival two days later, when she was getting her hair cut, and Warren had mentioned later that Eckley was nearby.

"Dana's an adult. What else can I tell her besides to be careful and to call me if she's ever in trouble? Not that she ever listens to anyone."

"I'm glad you had some idea about it already. Anyway ..." Mo paused as a young waiter approached their table. "Sorry, did you have enough time to look at the menu?" After brief deliberations, they had ordered and were back on track. "What did you think of the idea that Eckley might have somehow killed Ryan before throwing him onto the tracks? And if he did use a weapon, where the hell would we even look?"

"It's an interesting idea. And if it really happened that way, I might know where to look for something."

Becky McAuley

Mo held her breath.

"If I was telling someone to look for a murder weapon, and I will indeed be getting in touch with my contact in Tuckahoe tomorrow, the first place I'd tell them to try is in the Abyss. Where I saw Ryan and David bury an Indignation tape in 1988."

Chapter 15
2011

David Eckley first met Adam Risk during '80s Night at Commonground. After moving back to Boston, Eckley started attending this type of thing, first the punk nights at Blackout Bar, and now these '80s Nights. It was almost too easy to pick up girls here, as he was so much better looking, not to mention smarter, than the competition.

Tonight, Eckley was sitting at the bar, waiting to encounter a woman up to his standards. A guy he had seen around at shows was handing out flyers to people in the vicinity, but so far had not approached Eckley. What was this dude's deal? He should have been honored to have someone like Eckley come to his shows. Eckley resolved to set him straight once he was approached. Sure enough, the dude came over with a flyer a few minutes later.

"Adam Risk," he introduced himself. "I book shows, and I just started a label. Mostly reissues, but also some new stuff."

"Are people interested in that now? I've never thought about reissuing my old band's records."

"Oh, what band were you in?" Risk looked intrigued.

"Ministry of Fear," Eckley replied, masking his irritation that this was not self-evident, that MOF was not a household name in 2011. Then again, this Adam Risk guy looked to be in his late 20s, and maybe he wasn't from Boston, or around for the glory days of Ministry of Fear. Eckley would indeed later confirm that he was from somewhere in Connecticut, and his real last name was Risskov. Harmless enough to apply one of those ubiquitous scene sobriquets, but perhaps that should have been the first clue about the risk inherent in partnering with him on any business venture.

"Word, I've heard the name," Risk uttered, partially rescuing himself. "But before my time."

"Hardcore is cyclical," Eckley replied. "Everything's your time if you bring it back to light at the right moment." And yet, he had never really considered any sort of revival for Ministry of Fear, despite what he'd told Ryan Marnell or said on the Bridge 9 board. One quarter of the original lineup was dead, and another was living in Florida. In fact, Eckley hadn't played in any bands or written any music at all since they broke up in 2000. Not during his stint in Westchester, and not more recently after moving back to Boston. Since his return, Eckley felt out of step with contemporary hardcore, which was obviously no fault of his but rather of the scene itself. He went to shows infrequently, when a band he recognized was playing, and of course frequented these sort of quasi scene nights to pick up girls.

Becky McAuley

"Well, if you guys ever think about playing again, or want to talk about a reissue, let me know," Adam handed him a flyer. "That's got my email and my Twitter."

"Thanks, I'll be in touch." But first Eckley decided to test this guy Adam Risk. After watching him interact with Serena Noble, who was a semi-ubiquitous presence at these types of things, and noticing how desperate and pathetic he looked, Eckley made up his mind to sleep with her, and in fact, briefly ended up dating her. It wasn't exactly to spite this Adam Risk character, who had offered him nothing but positive things, but perhaps to show him who still had the power. But instead of instilling a long-standing rancor between them, it somehow sealed the deal and made Adam Risk obsessed with David Eckley. The next time Eckley saw him, this time at Great Scott, Risk went out of his way to say what's up and ask if anything was happening with Ministry of Fear. Every time he encountered him in their overlapping social circles, Risk's fawning escalated, to the point where Eckley was sure they would end up working together at one point or another. It was only a question of context and what was in it for David Eckley.

The next fateful encounter at Great Scott was at British Invasion Night a few years later. Eckley was getting weary of these themed nights, but they were a good opportunity to meet people. About an hour in, Eckley spotted a heart-stoppingly beautiful girl in her late 20s who looked supremely bored. She was tall, with long brown hair and a Leeway longsleeve, surveying the scene from a table near the bar. Surprisingly, she was alone. On the strength of the Leeway longsleeve, Eckley strode over to introduce himself. He had always gone for brunettes, from Dana all the way back through Madeline Terepka and Jessica Jacobowitz (with whom he had cheated on Madeline Terepka). Christine was blonde, but she was one of the only exceptions. No wonder it was inevitable he had gotten involved with her sister. Putting the Oronzio sisters out of his mind, Eckley moved towards this girl who was in a whole different league.

"*Born to Expire* or *Desperate Measures*?" Eckley queried while sliding into a chair at her table, avoiding the cringe-factor pickup line of referencing *Open Mouth Kiss*.

"That's a hard question." She crinkled up her face. "I fucking love so many songs on *Desperate Measures*, but I gotta go with *Born to Expire* out of loyalty, since I loved it before I got a copy of *Desperate Measures*. You know how when you first get into hardcore and it seems like so much happens within like, a few months? And now it's like I've been listening to a band for two years, but I still consider them a new band." Eckley nodded, and silently congratulated himself at having selected a topic that had generated a genuine answer, rather than prompting a brusque brush-off and sending him back to the other end of the bar. He also noted that she was placing herself as a veteran hardcore participant, rather than summarily dismissing him as some creepy old guy. Not that he was creepy or old, but he was also at least a decade older than this luscious Leeway chick.

"Well, I'm glad you gave it some consideration, since I'm a *Desperate Measures* guy myself. But if you let me buy you a drink, you can present your case for *Born to Expire*." Within a few minutes of having returned with their beers, they were looking up Leeway videos together on his phone. Lindsay, her name was, had let him creep incrementally closer to her as they laughed together over the "Kingpin" video, before moving on to Life of Agony and Merauder live sets. Eckley found himself letting down his guard and just being goofy with this beautiful girl. By the time that Lindsay's friend Phoebe was done with British Invasion Night, Eckley and Lindsay weren't done with each other, and Lindsay elected to stay.

Over the next few weeks, Eckley spent more time with this woman than anyone he had dated in years. He was wholly captivated by Lindsay Vedeno from Rochester, New York, who had moved to Boston for college and never gone home. It wasn't that he hadn't wanted to date a hardcore girl previously, it had just never happened, with the exception of Christine. In the '90s they were in short supply, and the hot ones were generally already attached to some hard dude. Plus, in the wider world, there were so many other women available for David Eckley to pick from. Christine was different: she was someone he had known from his pre-Boston life. And if you were going to point to one transgressive feature about him going out with Christine, it would have been that she used to date his best friend.

Lindsay was technically his first real relationship since Christine, though he had dated a lot in the interim, Serena Noble included, though no one for longer than for a few months. Also, there was always Dana. After the explosive denouement in 2006, Eckley had sworn her off for a while as too much trouble, despite trouble being what had attracted him in the first place. But after a few years of Eckley living in Boston, with Christine out of the way in L.A., Eckley and Dana had reconnected. They met up a few times a year when both were single, and/or when Eckley was home in Yonkers for holidays, including a memorable silent backyard blowjob during an unusually warm Thanksgiving 2007. But as soon as he met Lindsay, Eckley removed Dana from his mind for the indefinite future. He didn't want her getting mixed up in what was developing organically with Lindsay.

So far, the age difference hadn't been an issue in their relationship: at 28, Lindsay was a decade and a half younger than Eckley, though he of course was in much better shape than the average 43-year-old. His only concern was that Lindsay was best friends with this guy Rob Cecil, whom

Eckley did not trust at all. Rob Cecil was supposedly dating a fat youth crew girl from Framingham, whom Lindsay of course defended with the typical magnanimity of a super hot chick, but he always picked up on a shift in Rob's mood when Lindsay was around, more so than with her other guy friends. Lindsay swore these friendships were strictly platonic, and David believed her, based on the interactions that he witnessed: most of her guy friends treated her like a cool younger sister. But there was something that rankled him about this Rob dude, maybe because he and Lindsay were so much closer in age.

Lindsay was easy to travel with, and in 2016, Eckley took her to This is Hardcore to see Integrity and Burn. It was kind of cute dating a girl who was excited about a hardcore fest as a vacation destination. By the time he was dating Christine, they weren't going to many shows, much less large festivals like this which seemed to have mushroomed over the last decade. Plus he loved being seen with Lindsay. There were way more hot girls at shows than he remembered, but she was still one of the best-looking ones there. He didn't even mind hanging out with Rob Cecil for part of the weekend, since Rob had recently moved to Philly and was otherwise out of the picture.

Eckley and Lindsay had taken off work for the next few days after the fest, and they charted a meandering route back to Boston. Eckley always enjoyed the Catskills more during the week, when there were fewer people around, and played it off like he had just discovered this bed and breakfast in Fleischmanns when, in fact, he had met up with Dana there the year prior.

As night fell, they were sitting on camping chairs back by the creek. Eckley casually steered the conversation towards things they felt guilty about. Lindsay was talking about leaving for college while her brother had been having a hard time back in Rochester and how that had affected their relationship ever since. Eckley didn't give a shit about Lindsay's brother, but managed to feign sympathy until it was his turn to speak.

"I was in this other band once, called Indignation," Eckley began offhandedly. It was important for this not to sound premeditated. Lindsay was a smart girl, and he enjoyed that her skepticism required his tales to be watertight.

"Yeah, I think you mentioned them," Lindsay echoed.

"And the guitarist killed himself," he continued. "I always felt like there was more I should have done for him."

"Oh, shit," Lindsay seemed shocked. "That's terrible. I'm so sorry. You never told me about that part." She clutched his hand.

"Well, it wasn't while the band was active. But we were still friends. I had just seen him before it happened. I wonder what I could have said or done differently." As he spun this alternate history, Eckley also tried to remember if Lindsay knew about Vossen too, so it didn't seem like a pattern that his guitarists were always dying off. Luckily he was able to maintain a calm facade under pressure; if Lindsay had picked up on any distress, she could have attributed it to his guilt over his friend.

Lindsay was sufficiently moved by this revelation, and afterward, seemed fascinated by the idea of Eckley playing in this band Indignation whose guitarist had killed himself. All the elements of that night had helped the story attain its necessary vibe, and she was even more attentive than usual the rest of their trip. Lindsay had a lively imagination and the tendency to insert herself into every story, so it was important that he had established an emotional connection with the band.

"I'll see if I can dig up any of their stuff," Eckley promised when Lindsay inquired again after their trip, simultaneously congratulating himself and trying to remember what the fuck had happened to the rest of those tapes. He would never have thrown a box of them into the Bronx River if he thought he could have used them to his advantage decades later! Previously, his goal had been to obliterate all traces of original Indignation material, back when he was first adapting it for Ministry of Fear, and then again when Ryan was trying to make trouble for him in the mid-aughts. Though instead of pretending Indignation had never existed, Eckley now realized that he could have tried to pass them off as his band all along. Inserts didn't list his name? No problem, he could have made new ones, or blithely insisted to Lindsay that DION was his graffiti name. That was his voice in the intro, after all. Who was to say that kids these days wouldn't believe he had played on the tape as well?

It compounded the mystery of Indignation that he didn't have any mp3s and the material was so hard to find, even for someone who had (in his account, at least) played in the band. He had Rompanelli's videotape in a box somewhere, but who knew if that thing even still played? At this point Eckley only owned a DVD player, so if he ever parted with the video, in the service of furthering his Indignation legacy, it would be caveat emptor for the new buyer.

Plus, by entwining himself into the story of Indignation, David no longer had to fear Lindsay connecting the dots between these riffs and the Ministry of Fear material if she did manage to hear the demo. He had played her MOF early on, and of course she had said all the right things or else he wouldn't have been dating her. Being from Rochester, she was always trying to get him to listen to her hometown favorites Borrowed Time, and Eckley had to admit the similarities between their style and his old band, though he privately deemed Ministry of Fear to be superior.

Yes, Lindsay had been good for him. But before he could casually yet calculatedly unearth any Indignation songs and use her as a conduit to spread his version of the truth to a new generation, she seemed to forget all about them, and stopped asking after their material. Lindsay's new obsession that fall were two defunct post-hardcore bands from L.A.: first Big Collapse, Josh's band after Shift, and then a lesser-known band called Slow Blink. At first he had merely tolerated the presence of Slow Blink on her speakers, both in the car and at home, until she had started telling him the story of the band. They had a girl bassist and released a few records in the late '90s but had never taken off. Eckley realized with horror why this story sounded familiar ... because they were Christine's band! What if Lindsay managed to get in touch with Christine and they somehow compared notes about him! Not that either of them should have anything unflattering to say about him, but still, he couldn't let that happen.

"Stop fucking listening to this shit!" Eckley roared one day while she was blasting *Recidivist History*, Slow Blink's full length album, for what seemed like the 50th time that month.

"What is wrong with you?"

"I'm just tired of it, OK? And it's boring! I thought you liked better music than this!"

"I like a lot of different music," Lindsay stared back at him flintily. "And who are *you* to say what I can and can't listen to? Why should I trust someone who doesn't like Eaten Alive and didn't even care that Billy Club Sandwich is back together? You are so out of touch!"

"Me? Out of touch? You're lucky I even bother getting in touch with you." Eckley marched out of Lindsay's apartment and slammed the door. It was to be one of their many fights that fall, and before Christmas, they had broken up. The feeling was mutual, though when Eckley, in a rare method of reflection a few months later, tried to reach out, Lindsay was evidently still so mad at him that she ignored every method of communication, from texting to Instagram DM. Instagram was eventually how he found out that Rob Cecil, having shed the youth crew girl, had come to Lindsay's rescue a few months later.

This ignoble conclusion aside, Lindsay had taught him more than any girl since Christine. First, she had gotten it stuck in his head that present day hardcore kids were susceptible to various retro phenomena, including bands that hadn't been popular the first time around. In fact, the more obscure, the better. Kids were now interested in various third-tier bands, like fucking Strong Mentality or even Self Alarm. Imagine how these kids might feel about Ministry of Fear, who had never quite earned the fame they deserved?

That was the catalyst for the plan he had started to put into place, once he returned to some semblance of normal. After the breakup with Lindsay, Eckley hadn't felt like himself in months. There was no desire for a rebound, and he ignored Dana's texts when he was in town for Christmas 2016. And right when things were improving, he discovered that Lindsay and Rob Cecil were now a couple, that Cecil featured prominently in all her pictures from This is Hardcore 2017, and that she had moved to Philly a few weeks later. Each development was a new blow to Eckley's psyche, particularly because they had kept things amicable and she had never blocked him on Instagram. (Not that this would have mattered, as he had also started following her from a nondescript fake account soon after they started dating, in case this eventuality did someday occur.) For most of August, he was barely able to eat and didn't set foot in the gym. He stopped cutting his hair (until he was at risk of violating policy at work) and stopped wearing his contacts. He declined all social engagements. Work kept him busy, and in his moments at home, he mostly lay in the dark watching Netflix. Until one day when he looked in the mirror near the end of August and realized he looked like a totally different person.

If Eckley attempted to convince the current crop of hardcore kids to rediscover Ministry of Fear, it could come off as forced or pretentious if he were hyping his own band. But what if he vouched for their greatness as a totally separate person, merely a fan of the band, and could convince others to join his legion? But no, even that route was too direct.

Maybe the Indignation tape was the key to Ministry of Fear's return! Eckley could claim to be the architect of the original Indignation riffs and bill them as an early version of Ministry of Fear, to pique the interest of a whole other subset of hardcore kids.

Eckley took an odd pleasure in molding himself into someone no one would recognize, rather than being someone he expected everyone to recognize. Before Lindsay's rebound had destroyed his summer, he had always conducted himself as the latter. So it was a strange thrill to reconstruct himself as a fictional nobody. He even came up with a new name, compiled from the first and last names of his neighbors. What would Max Malkin wear, and how would he conduct himself online? The possibilities were endless, as the only requirement was to be an ardent fan of his own band. Perhaps he'd also pretend to have played in another forgotten band like Disregard. On the strength of this new identity, he texted Dana for the first time in years. "Going to be in town in a few weeks. U got to see my temporary new look—I've been going undercover! jk :)"

There was indeed a regional transit police training in September that was bringing Eckley to New York, and he elected to bring the tape just in case any NYHC-based buyers materialized during that trip. After moving back to Boston, he had secured a transit police job similar to the one he had held in New York. The conference was taking place at a hotel in Elmsford, and while he hoped to make full use of that hotel room later in the week if Dana was around, on Thursday night he was staying with his dad and stepmom in Yonkers, since he knew they would be pleased to have him visit overnight.

Leading up to the trip, he had made a few cryptic comments about Ministry of Fear and Indignation from a burner Instagram account, but no one seemed to have noticed. The circle of people he had thought to follow was either disinterested or too insular. How could he broaden his audience while continuing to stay anonymous or avoid the trouble of creating a plethora of false Max Malkin profiles online? Message boards used to be the perfect venue for creating fake personas, but they had fallen out of fashion. It was then that he remembered the Controlled board. It was invite-only, and Lindsay had rarely posted, mostly just lurked, but had gotten him invited too. And it was more focused on simplistic '80s NYHC and mid-aughts Boston hardcore than Ministry of Fear's more intricate style, but that might be perfect for Indignation.

The day of the conference, he spotted a thread about zines, which he didn't even know still existed, and when he saw a discussion on riff recycling, the opportunity seemed almost too perfect. He decided to flex some Warzone knowledge he had picked up, in fact, on the Bridge 9 board over a decade ago, and tie in Indignation/Ministry of Fear. Warzone: one of the many bands that David Eckley had never cared for, but seemed to be universally beloved by a variety of age groups. A few hours later, there was a reply from someone who wanted to see the Indignation video. It seemed almost too easy. His plan was already in motion.

After replying to the potential tape customer, Eckley ruminated on another aspect of Ministry of Fear's resurgence that he wished was proceeding more smoothly. He had been talking to Adam Risk about re-releasing the Ministry of Fear LP on his label, Risk Management Records, but was trying to finesse the timing to best suit his own needs, rather than Adam's. In the ideal scenario, the re-release would coincide with renewed interest due to Eckley's clandestine Indignation/Ministry of Fear internet campaign. And then, based on this burgeoning interest, he would try to organize a full lineup to play a reunion show.

Risk had hit some financial difficulties and had somehow gotten the idea that booking a Ministry of Fear reunion would generate some quick cash. Eckley, however, was unsure how they would draw at their first show back, especially if the record wasn't out beforehand and the new kids didn't have access to their material. The guarantee would have to cover Mark flying in from Miami—if Mark and/or Bill were to even be convinced to play—and the general effort and expense of organizing everyone for regular practices. But how to disabuse Adam Risk of the idea that his band was a powerful draw without him losing confidence in the entire project? They had reached a standoff in which Risk didn't want to put out the record unless they had a reunion show booked and Eckley didn't want to go through the trouble of organizing a reunion until there was proof the record was underway.

Lost Indignation

The stalemate continued through the fall, with Eckley losing hope in the idea of a record materializing. Adam was on the verge of being evicted, and on two separate occasions, Eckley saved his ass by lending him money, against his better judgment. Though the infusions of cash hadn't fully resolved Risk Management's issues. Adam had taken preorders for another record that he couldn't hope to put out until more money came in. Eckley half considered investing in the label, though he knew it wouldn't be a lucrative venture. How much clout did running a label get you in 2017? Risk didn't seem to be doing great in the girls department, but then again, Eckley was much better looking. As October turned into November, he managed not to intervene in managing the label, though Adam filled his phone with a steady torrent of texts, along with continually haranguing him in-person about the state of the MOF reunion.

Finally, one night at the bar just before Thanksgiving, Eckley snapped. "I don't fucking know what the deal is with the reunion, OK? If we do it, I want to do it right, and I don't know if some of the guys are going to take it as seriously as I will."

"That and you might still need a few members," Risk added unhelpfully, reading his mind.

"Who knows, maybe I'll find someone when I'm home this weekend?" Eckley mused. It wasn't a terrible idea, though who did he even still know back in Westchester who played guitar and would be willing to commute to Boston for practice? Though he might as well let Adam think he knew more people than he did.

"Same, dude. I'm going home for a few days, too, though I'll be back in town on Saturday if you want to meet up."

"I look forward to it," Eckley responded without an iota of enthusiasm. Fucking Adam Risk! How could he get this guy to leave him the hell alone?

Rather than thinking about Ministry of Fear while he was home, Eckley tried to banish Adam from his mind. He was hoping to encounter Dana, but apparently he had gone way harder than intended on Wednesday night, and was really feeling the consequences on Thursday. He slept for most of the day, and managed to pull himself together at Thanksgiving dinner for the sake of his dad and Jean, but this was the roughest he'd felt in years after a night of drinking. Who the hell had he run into last night? He vaguely remembered seeing Warren Yatrofsky and Paul Pounsenech, an old friend from Crestwood, and then meeting friends of that guy whose wife bought the video ... but then there was also some Scottish actor who drove a cab? He had woken up on Central Avenue, in the backseat of the Scotsman's cab, still drunk, with a devastating headache, and utterly unable to remember the address of his childhood home. The Scottish guy had been kind enough to drop him home, and then bring back his wallet

Becky McAuley

and phone later in the day, after finding it in the car. But the other details of that night would be forever lost to memory.

On Friday night, he briefly considered going to see Outburst and Killing Time in the city. He and Ryan had seen Outburst at CBGB's the day that Indignation broke up, on the show they were supposed to play. David would never admit how badly he had wanted to be a member of Indignation, and that day he practically was, heading down to the city with Ryan to help sell the tapes after the rest of the band and their ride had fallen apart, literally, on the way to the show. But ultimately, he decided against attending this reunion. This was the first time in years that Outburst had played with the original singer, and the show was bound to sell out. And what if that guy and his wife who bought the tape were there again and wanted to drink with him? He was still feeling the effects of Wednesday and couldn't handle another night like that so soon, especially down in Brooklyn. Better to stay local and then head back to Boston on Saturday.

His only regret was not seeing Dana while he was in town. He had been planning to stop by the bar on Wednesday, then meet up with her later, hopefully at her apartment. But even if the evening hadn't ended in a blackout in the early hours of the morning, his phone had died before he could have gotten in touch with her to see if she was still down to hook up. Its loss of battery had doubtlessly been aided by that guy in the trenchcoat who had kept asking him to play Sepultura videos.

That was the last thing he remembered: a wave of anger and sadness, and a wish to get totally annihilated. Could the disheveled Sepultura fan somehow know how he had met Lindsay and be mocking their first interactions at Great Scott when they had kept showing each other the Leeway videos? All he knew was that he didn't want to think about Lindsay anymore, or be in this bar, or even leave to be with Dana. What could he do to turn the night around? Apparently, whatever he'd done to instill a good time hadn't worked, unless waking up in the backseat of a cab was a good time. He supposed it was better than waking up in the back of a police car.

When he got his phone back the next day, he had eleven missed calls and nine voicemails from Dana, all in the early hours of Thanksgiving morning. He had texted her back on Thursday, just before dinner, and followed up with a teasing message on Friday, but she hadn't replied. Whatever—it was her loss. He left for Boston on Saturday, giving up any chance to see her the rest of the weekend. There were also a bunch of texts from Adam asking if he'd made progress on the reunion, which he ignored.

Eckley was back in Boston by late Saturday afternoon, and instead of getting in touch with Adam, he decided to have dinner with his friend Missy—super chic if slightly narcissistic—and her girlfriend Elena, whom Eckley always thought of as her "new" girlfriend, though by now they must

Lost Indignation

have been dating for a year or two. Eckley always felt a little better about himself in Missy's company.

Missy was vain but oddly kind and easy to please but hard to shock. He had once basically confessed to murder in her presence, but she merely responded with, "Oh, Davey! I can never tell if you're serious," and punched his arm (surprisingly hard—she was in excellent shape). Missy worked in investor relations and was a nascent art collector; and, unlike her innate sartorial eye, her taste in art seemed questionable so far. Eckley was waiting for this to pass, along with her other fleeting superficial hobbies, talk of which he good-naturedly indulged until they dissipated. That Saturday, she kept going on about wanting an Alex Preno. "I don't know if you've heard about the artist who's doing those magazine covers? I abso need one."

"I used to paint a little, back in the day," Eckley interjected. He hadn't even planned to say that. And technically Ryan had been the artist, but why not reclaim other pieces of Ryan's legacy as his own?

"Oh really? I'd love to see your work!" Elena tried to avoid rolling her eyes. She'd never warmed up to him like Missy had, and, in fact, Eckley had the distinct idea that she considered him a creative fraud. Elena had some sort of entry level position at the Isabella Stewart Gardner Museum and seemed to regard most of Missy's friends, and perhaps Missy herself, as vapid pretenders.

David tried to remember what he knew about Ryan's artistic output. What had happened to all the art he'd been making in the '90s, and then later when they were roommates? The only time they'd ever had a serious conversation about Ryan's painting was at the Wretched Spaniel the night before Thanksgiving in 2001, when Ryan had given him the extra copy of the Indignation demo. It was the first time in a while that they'd been back in touch and what started his tradition of stopping by the Wretched Spaniel the night before Thanksgiving. In the years before Ryan's death, at those dinners that Eckley always paid for, hadn't Ryan once mentioned something about a storage unit upstate? Eckley made a mental note to investigate if the art was still stored there, even after Ryan's death.

The night with Missy and Elena was exactly what he needed: nothing too extensive, just dinner and a nearby bar, and he was home soon after midnight. He was getting into bed around 1 a.m. when his phone buzzed with an incoming text. It was from Dana and only three words: "I want you."

He sighed. Of course she was resurfacing now that he was back in Boston! He opened the message, then deliberately ignored her as he rolled over and drifted to sleep, waiting until the next morning to reply: "Wish u had told me that when I was still in NY!"

Becky McAuley

At 6 p.m. in Boston in November, it already feels like the middle of the night. Eckley was drinking tea and watching porn (a potentially dangerous combination) when his phone lit up with a text, not from Dana, but from Adam Risk. "Are you back? Want to come by the Half Crown later?"

Eckley did not want to leave his cozy apartment to hang with Adam, who had been increasingly rattled lately. Dude was seriously in debt, and it almost seemed like he expected David Eckley to resolve that situation for him. Even if Eckley had been in the position to reform Ministry of Fear instantaneously, with buy-in from all members, living and dead, he couldn't have guaranteed that the resulting net proceeds from the show would have eased Adam's financial burden, with the way that kids were so fickle these days about shows outside of their narrow niche. MOF was the type of band that transcended genres, but again, a reunion was supposed to be for joy and glory, not to mitigate the financial issues of someone like Adam Risk.

And yet, he consented to meet him at the bar. "I'm down, see you around 8:30?" He wouldn't stay long.

At the Half Crown, Eckley reported that no, he hadn't recruited any band members in New York, though he did pretend that he'd asked Paul to invest in Adam's label, and Paul had graciously declined. While continuing to emphasize these other avenues in which he could offer support to this guy who was not quite his friend, Eckley also tried to be as stern and realistic as possible so that Adam didn't continue to pin all his hopes on Ministry of Fear.

He specifically remembered using the phrase "you need to adjust your expectations" regarding both how hard it would be to get the members together and the result of the reunion. Adam seemed to understand, and despite the disappointing news, they both managed to enjoy their night out. They left the bar together shortly after 11 p.m. and parted ways outside, which meant that David Eckley was the last person to be seen with Adam Risk.

Early Wednesday morning, Eckley was walking into the gym when he saw a familiar face approaching. "'Sup, Dave." It was Bryan Lau, a friend of a friend and a Boston cop whom Eckley saw occasionally at the gym.

"Bryan! What's going on?"

"I need to talk to you about something, but let's take a walk to get away from all these ears." Eckley, uncharacteristically apprehensive, had no choice to retrace his steps and return to the frigid morning outside. They walked around the edge of the building towards the parking lot.

"So this guy Adam Risskov has been missing, and I wanted to give you a heads up that your name has come up in the investigation."

"Fuck, really? When was he last seen?"

"No one has heard from him since Sunday."

"Shit, I know that guy, do you want me to reach out to him?" Eckley considered his face hard to read, and realized that his genuine surprise and concern could be an asset here. Out of all the things he thought might someday result in an inquiry from the police, he wouldn't have suspected Adam Risk to be the source.

"I think people have been trying to reach out to him; that's the issue."

"Well, I hope he's OK." Eckley tried to project concern, as he scanned the mental checklist of defense attorneys he could summon if the cops did in fact want to speak to him. He really did hope Adam was OK, since he did not fucking want to be blamed for a disappearance he had nothing to do with!

"Hey, I'm not here officially, I'm not working the case, so I don't have any reason to make it easier for those prick DT's. I know you well enough to know you weren't involved in whatever's going on with this guy. But I just wanted to let you know in case they try to bring you in to talk to you about him."

"Appreciate it man. And let me know if you hear anything about Adam. I really do hope he's alright. We're not close, but he's a good kid." Fuck, it was 2017. When had Adam Risk stopped being a kid? When had David Eckley?

After imparting this ominous news, Lau continued to his car, and Eckley walked inside, though he wanted to turn around and go back to bed. Fuck! He hadn't done anything to Adam Risk. That little shit wasn't worth harming. Who knew Risk had the presence of mind to disappear and attempt to pin it on David Eckley? Well, it wasn't going to work.

And yet he didn't feel great about continuing to stay at home or frequenting his regular haunts where someone could find him just as easily as Lau had done, but with more nefarious intentions. The fact that he was blameless in Risk's disappearance wouldn't shield him from additional scrutiny for other past actions that needed no revisiting. Should he stay with friends, or get out of Boston entirely? Driving home from the gym, he ran through a short list of buddies he could crash with. From the engineer who lived too far from work, to the fellow transit cop whose wife would likely nix having a visitor, there was no perfect option. And when he had moved back to Boston in 2006, his hardcore friends seemed to have melted away. He could stay with Missy and Elena, but Missy often worked 70 hour weeks, leaving Elena home with the dog, and he wasn't a big animal person. He could stay in a hotel, but was it worth the expense when he would be just as easy to find at work?

By Thursday, Eckley had a plan. He managed to take Friday off of work, and texted Dana after securing his PTO. They'd been texting sporadically all week, Dana all but begging him to come back to New York. If he made it through the rest of his shift, he was free to get the hell out of Boston before the cops made any more inquiries. "So, I'll be back in the 914 sooner than expected," he texted. "How about I come down this wknd after all?"

Chapter 16
2017

By the time a complimentary tiramisu with three forks arrived at their table, Mo was convinced that a murder weapon involved in the demise of Ryan Marnell could be traced back to David Eckley if unearthed. Pat grabbed one more Andes mint for the road before they parted from Anthony in the parking lot, vowing to keep each other updated.

"So that's wild that Anthony might know where to look for a murder weapon!"

"Don't get your hopes up," Pat cautioned as he cradled their box of leftovers. "Who knows if one even exists, if it got buried in that spot, or if it's still there."

"If he saw Ryan and Eckley bury something else, then I agree that's the first place to look." Mo eased the car out of the parking lot. "I also think we should try to get in touch with Ryan's family, if he has any left, to see if they know anything about Eckley and how they feel about all this."

"Well since the trick-or-treating was, ah, unsuccessful—" Mo held up both middle fingers while waiting to turn left onto Main Street "—why don't you try looking some stuff up online or even going to the library? There must have been something in the newspaper when Ryan died."

Mo considered this suggestion. She did love the libraries of lower Westchester, but had never gone there to do research, preferring to wander through the biography areas or pick out her fiction and leave. But Pat was right that there might be more news articles on microfiche, or whatever they used these days, with details about Ryan that she wouldn't find online. Even if just an obituary.

"You know what, I could call that guy who gave Christine his card. Musty the Mustelid or whatever his name was."

Pat found Musty Kherlakian's info in his Google Photos from the night they had met Christine. Mo waited to call him till they had returned to Overlook Street and settled her car into a spot on Westchester Avenue where it wouldn't have to move till Wednesday night. She loved talking on the phone to people she knew, but always balked at cold-calling strangers. But Musty answered affably after two rings and seemed happy to hear his volunteer research services were required. Conveniently, he would be at the Yonkers Historical Society on Tuesday morning, which was located inside the Will Library. A Tuesday morning appointment gave her pause, as she'd have to miss work during the week before fucking Art Basel. But it would be worth it if she could get the information she needed. At work she told them she had a research appointment for school, and while she wouldn't be able to come in on Tuesday, she could stay later on Wednesday, since she had no colloquium. And it was half true, since for her final project for Thursday workshop, she was finishing a story set in Crestwood, loosely based on Ryan and David. Maybe Musty could help her infuse some old-school Crestwood details.

"Mo McRoar!" Musty Kherlakian had an old-school accent and an old-school mustache and was dressed more for a tactical mission or fishing expedition than volunteering at the historical society. As Mo wondered what to expect from their meeting, Musty summarized his history and skills. "I retired from the phone company, and now I do what I like best, which is helping people find what they need. So what are you looking for?"

"I'm looking for information about a person who died in Dobbs Ferry in August 2006. He was hit by a train, so I assume something made it to the newspaper, but I'm not sure which one. And then if there's any information about his family members, I'd like to try to find them too," Mo said carefully. Musty, to his credit, seemed unfazed by the request, suggesting they start with the *Journal News*, and if nothing appeared there, then to move on to the *Crestwood Citizen*, a now obsolete hyperlocal paper. He shepherded her to the reference desk to request use of the microfilm and reader, greeting the librarian by name. Mo handed over her library card and wrote down the time period of the *Journal News* that they were likely to need. She assumed that any sort of news or obituary about Ryan would have appeared by September, or sooner if it included details of an upcoming memorial service. But would there be any mention of him at all, if his family no longer had roots in the area, or if he himself was too isolated from the mainstream world?

Since Musty knew the librarian through volunteering at the Historical Society and was already adept at using a microfilm reader, he and Mo were allowed to proceed unencumbered by further assistance. He loaded the film and described its basic procedure, then let her step up to control the machine. Mo half wondered if there would have been news of the train incident elsewhere in the paper, but it was easiest to start with the obituaries, which were also more likely to note any scant details of his life and survivors. Nothing showed up for the first half of August. But then, on August 17:

Marnell, Ryan D.
Former Crestwood resident Ryan Marnell died in Dobbs Ferry on August 14. He was born in Crestwood in 1971 to Dennis and Eileen Marnell. Ryan was an artist and a musician and is survived by his mother Eileen Marnell. A Mass of Christian Burial will be held at Annunciation Church in Crestwood on Monday, August 21 at 10 a.m. Visiting hours Sunday, August 20, 2006, from 2-4 & 7-9 p.m. Westchester Funeral Home, 190 Main St, Eastchester, NY 10707.

Lost Indignation

Mo paused, hardly believing it was real. OK, so now they had to track down Eileen Marnell, especially if Ryan wasn't survived by any other family members.

"I think I found him!" Mo tried to keep her voice to library levels. "Unless there are any other Ryan Marnells who were artists and musicians and died in Dobbs Ferry that year. It says he was survived by his mom, who is named Eileen Marnell. So now I just need to find her contact info." (And hope she wants to talk to me, Mo silently added.) "Can you show me how to print this?"

"Eileen Marnell!" Musty exclaimed. "I know her! She used to volunteer here. Let me give you her number." Mo sighed, but grinned. Another Petraske's connection that could have allowed her to skip a step all along.

As soon as she had returned the film, left the library, and said goodbye to Musty (who refused any form of payment, but allowed that Mo could buy him a beer at Petraske's sometime, or the Wretched Spaniel), Mo dialed Mrs. Marnell from the car. She hoped this was going to go better than accidentally calling the mother of dead Sean from Power Structure. The number rang through to voicemail, and while younger people never checked their voicemail anymore, old people certainly did. Mo left a vague message, only half-expecting a reply. If Mrs. Marnell did call back, it would hopefully be before school that afternoon. In the meantime she was heading home to finish her penultimate craft class assignment (another perk of not going into the city for work).

But 15 minutes later, just as she was walking into their building on Overlook Street, Mrs. Marnell returned her call. Mo answered immediately. "Mo McGraw? I got your message." Mo crept up the wooden stairs to the third floor. Was she really talking to Ryan's mom?

"Yes, thank you so much for calling me back! I'm a graduate student and I'm writing about your son," Mo said quickly as she unlocked the apartment door, even if this was only sort of true, "so I'd love to speak with you and learn more about his music. I had a research appointment with Mr. Kherlakian, and he gave me your number." Mo had no idea how uniformly Musty was known as Musty, so she went with the safer formal title. She also didn't mention that she thought this woman's son had been murdered rather than committing suicide, but that could come later.

"Musty Kherlakian! I'm glad he was able to help you with your research. I'm at work right now, but if you live in the area, I can show you some of Ryan's music and artwork. Are you in Yonkers?"

"Mount Vernon, so close enough. And I'd love that!" Mo had prepared herself that Ryan's mom could be uninterested in talking about his musical past, but she seemed accommodating so far.

Becky McAuley

"Why don't you come by tonight?"

"Tonight?" Just like the day they had bought the tape, yet this time she was more certain of her conversation partner's identity. "I was going to bring my husband too, if that's OK, and he's working this evening, but I'll see if he can get out early." Pat was working until 8:00, which meant that depending where in Yonkers Mrs. Marnell lived, they wouldn't get there until after 8:30.

Ryan's mom OK'd Pat's attendance, but asked them to come earlier, so Mo texted Pat as soon as she had written down the address of the Marnell apartment on Warburton Avenue. The Musty connection had generated an instant result. Now she just had to hope that meeting Ryan's mom would live up to her outsize expectations, and that Pat could get out early. He always came up with good questions and disarmed people with his local history and dialect.

When Mo got out of craft class at 5:30, she had a new Gchat that Pat could depart at 7:00 since they were fully staffed, if she wanted to pick him up and go straight to their meeting. It had rained on Mo as she was walking home from class, but had tapered off by evening, though the wet pavement shone in the streetlights as she navigated south through Hastings.

"Don't act too surprised," Mo cautioned as they crossed the Yonkers border, "if I mention that I'm writing something about Ryan for school. I might take a non-fiction class next semester, and I'm already using some details for a story. I may have told his mom that's why I'm researching him."

"Already tired of fiction? After one whole semester?"

"Maybe I'm just tired of making up stories when all this real life shit has been so fucking wild."

Mo had thought they might have to park down at the Greystone train station, but she managed to find a space on Warburton, a few buildings south of the address Mrs. Marnell had provided.

"Doesn't Ally live right around here?"

"Yeah, I think her building is one or two up the hill? Though everything in this area looks the same." Pat was correct, that most of the buildings were of a similar style, and were taller and more modern than the six story brick co-ops in Fleetwood.

They managed to find the correct entrance, and Mrs. Marnell buzzed them up. Checking her hair in the mirror in the lobby as they summoned the elevator, Mo was uncharacteristically nervous. In their past meetings, from Zimmer to Christine, or even sending Pat to the bar to ambush Eckley, there had been an element of winging it and using whatever came out of the situation. But with Ryan's mom, it would be difficult to continue the investigation if she was not on board and wanted

Lost Indignation

the past to stay in the past.

When Mrs. Marnell opened the door of Apartment 7B, she looked more or less how Mo had expected: somewhere in her sixties with a medium build and graying hair. She seemed friendly enough while welcoming them, though Mo had the idea that she was keenly observing her guests and hoping to discern more of the purpose behind their visit.

After the initial introductions ("Please call me Eileen," their host instructed), and some small talk about the Aqueduct trail nearby, Mo was itching to ask about anything Indignation-related. Though how much would Mrs. Marnell even know, or remember? If they had been neighbors of the Eckleys, she must have known young David, yet how would they maneuver the conversation towards those topics?

As usual, Mo was glad to have brought Pat. Soon he was talking about growing up in Eastchester and going to some pizza place called Albanese's that Mo had never heard of but the Marnells had also frequented. Though she shouldn't have worried about a segue. Pat next mentioned a record store across the street from Albanese's and asked if Ryan had hung out there.

"I'm not sure if that one was a favorite. Ryan and his friends got around on their skateboards and the train. He was very independent. I do remember they used to go to record stores on Central Avenue and down in the city." Pat nodded, as Mo wondered if "Central Avenue" meant Record Stop or Mad Platters or both—or maybe Rockin' Rex, if it was open yet.

"Speaking of records ... or tapes. I would love to know more about Ryan's band, Indignation! That's how I first heard of Ryan, when I was looking for the Indignation demo tape."

"Well, I couldn't tell you about the music," Eileen smiled, reminiscing. "But I remember driving him to band practice a few times, and how much he loved being in a band.

"I actually have a box of his tapes here somewhere. I'm not sure if there are any last copies of his own demo," she continued, "since Ryan used to sometimes come pick some up to sell them. But I do have one box that he wanted me to keep safe for him. Since I think he knew that he wasn't always in the best position to do that himself."

Mo suddenly felt immense guilt about caring more about the tapes than this person's child. Though once they had started to investigate further, it was hard to separate the two.

"I really wish we'd gotten to know your son," Mo said earnestly. "We've spent so much time learning about his artistic output, but he sounds like such an interesting person too."

Eileen looked wistful. "He really was. Though I'm glad that all these years later, there's a reason people remember him." She paused. "When you say artistic output, have you seen any of his actual art? Not just

Becky McAuley

the band stuff," she clarified. "The paintings."

"No, we haven't, though I did hear that he was a painter."

"Well, let me show you." She started down the hallway, Mo and Pat trading inquisitive looks as they followed.

"This is just some of his work," she continued as she stopped in front of the first door on the right. "There's also a whole storage unit upstate. Ryan always said that if anything ever happened to him," she smiled sadly, "to keep paying for that storage unit no matter what. And it was only ten dollars a month, so I just kept paying. Rather than going up there to see what was inside, for it to be just another reminder that he was gone. And I'm sure it would be more expensive to store it down here."

She switched on the light. The small second bedroom was almost entirely full of paintings, with barely enough room for a twin bed, a bookshelf, and a dresser. There were canvases leaning up against the wall, blocking the dresser, blocking the windows, and others filling a rack on the wall above the bed.

Despite the types of clients represented by CFA, Mo wasn't super knowledgeable about art, and Pat was in fact more interested in outsider art than she was. So while she wasn't an expert, the paintings were undeniably captivating. The canvas nearest to them depicted a record store scene, with a black and white cat lounging in the corner. Another looked unfinished and showed a crowd of people disembarking from a Metro North train. Through their bold colors and hasty brushstrokes, both paintings seemed to embody a sense of movement and excitement, and the one with the cat reminded her of Joseph Bertiers. Mo could see why Pat had spoken of the parallels between hardcore music and outsider art, and it was easy to see how Ryan had been fluent in both forms of expression.

"Whoa. These are amazing!" Mo turned to Pat. "Aren't these really good? I work for a PR company with some art clients, but this guy knows more about art than I do."

Pat stared at the works, transfixed. He had that look where his eyes were so wide that they looked a lighter brown than normal. "I think this is something that a gallerist should look at," he advised. "Someone who's more qualified than us to evaluate it."

"I've always wanted to show it to someone, but I never knew where to start," Eileen lamented. "What if they didn't think it was any good? Plus, I like having everything here with me. It's all here, besides the stuff in storage, and the two that I gave away to his friends." Mo hoped that one of these friends wasn't David Eckley.

"I should put you in touch with my boss, or my coworker Aaron. We represent the Outsider Art Fair and might be able to connect you with a gallery," Mo added. Colette loved outsider art: she always came home from the fair with a substantial haul, and would be captivated by this vast trove created by a possible murder victim.

"I'd love to speak to her," Eileen agreed. Mo assured her that she would approach her boss when she returned from Miami. With the Outsider Art Fair coming up in January, all things outsider art would soon dominate Colette's limited brain space, despite it technically being a small client handled by Aaron.

Eileen sidestepped the paintings and moved towards the closet in the corner. "This was Ryan's room when he stayed here as an adult. Now, it's where I keep his stuff. The tapes should be in here somewhere." She retrieved a shoebox from the top shelf of the closet.

"Here they are." She brought down the box, maneuvered around the paintings to set it on the bed, lifted the lid, and stepped back so Mo and Pat could see.

Mo felt as if an archivist had just brought out a rare treasure for their inspection. The box was full of cassette tapes with handwritten labels, besides a few official demo tapes: she could see a Power Structure tape, a fucking Beyond demo, and—holy shit! Two copies of the Indignation demo!

Mo was stunned. "This is wild. I mean the art is amazing, too, but these tapes ... this is what we've been looking for all along." She bent closer to study the labels. Alongside what looked like some practice tapes and the real demos, there was what might have been the master tapes from the Indignation recording! She was trying to figure out how to ask about buying or borrowing the Indignation stuff when that conundrum was solved for her.

"I want you to have these for your research." Eileen had picked up the box and was holding it out to her. "In the eleven years since he died, you're the only person who's ever asked about his music."

"Are you sure? I mean I would love to have these, and I could always bring them back to you. How about I leave you one copy of the demo?" Mo couldn't believe she was leaving a copy behind, but there was another one in the box, along with the masters and all the practice tapes. Carefully, heart pounding, she slid the tape and insert out of the case.

There was a hand-drawn insert, complete with rudimentary cover art of a guy with his head exploding. Mo wasn't sure if this was a Ryan Marnell original, too, but when she opened it up, it said "art by Eric" right below the track list:

1. Intro/Indignation
2. World v. You
3. Put it Down
4. Now It Can Be Told
5. Religious Instruction

Sure enough, there was someone listed only as "CC - Drums", rather than Matt Zimmer. If an alarmed expression had now replaced Pat's enthusiasm about the art, Mo didn't notice, as enthralled as she was.

"I can't believe I'm holding an Indignation demo!" The only things tempering her excitement were a) trying not to use happy expletives as punctuation in front of Ryan's mom, and b) seeming too obsessed with the tape itself, rather than the legacy of Ryan as a person or the research that she was supposedly conducting.

Mo submerged the rest of her excitement and picked up the box of tapes off the bed. They'd have plenty of time to study these at home, including getting a better look at the Indignation lyrics. In the meantime, they needed to thank Eileen and wrap up the visit so they could get home and have dinner. Could they pick something up at Thai House? Wait, fuck, Thai House was closed on Tuesdays. She took some quick pictures of Ryan's art to gauge the interest of Aaron and Colette. Still chatting about Ryan, Mo and Pat followed their host back down the hall. Mo was zipping herself into her maroon jacket and laughing at Eileen's admonishment of Pat for having no coat (just a hoodie) when she realized there was one more thing she had to ask.

"Thank you again for the tapes and for sharing your time with us tonight. It's been so great to learn more about Ryan. Though there is one more thing I want to ask you while we're here." Mo hesitated. "I don't even know how to say this, but have you ever suspected there was any foul play involved in Ryan's death?"

Eileen gave her a sharp look and suddenly seemed much younger. "You better take your coat off. I've been waiting for eleven years for someone to ask me that, too."

"The first thing you should know," she cautioned as she sat down at the table with her coffee, "is that there have been some mental health issues in my family. So when there was an incident up at school, sophomore year, and Ryan ended up in the hospital, I had a bad feeling. I always knew something might happen to him when he got older, like what happened to my mom. And my fears came true, I did everything I could to try to give him a normal life. I did research, tried to get him to take his medications, but he didn't always want to be here, or for me to interfere. Dennis had died, and I had just sold the house and moved to this apartment. I don't think Ryan liked being shut up in here with me. He lived here on and off, after he dropped out of college, and would store things here, like the tapes. For a few years in the '90s he had a studio over in Irvington, and then he was living upstate before he returned to Westchester for good.

"In his last year with us, it really seemed like Ryan had turned a corner. He was painting a lot and was even going to have a piece in a group show in Hastings. I remember how excited he was. He had just started working on the piece for the show and was walking here to visit me when he said that someone tried to run him over. Showed up here talking about how someone was trying to kill him, how he wasn't safe here." Mo caught her breath, but motioned to her host to continue.

"Now I had heard all kinds of things from Ryan over the years, when he was on his meds or off, but this was different. He seemed much more clear-headed, and I've never seen him so afraid. Like he needed to tell me this in case something happened to him. I tried to calm him down, but he wasn't here that often, said he had found a place where he felt more protected?" She sighed. "That hurt, too—that I could only do so much to protect him. After everything we had been through together. I could have kept a closer eye on him at the end, but was hoping that incident was a one-time thing, that he could stay safe and make it to his show. But that never happened: he died in August, and the show was scheduled for November. He never finished the painting.

"No matter what anyone said, I know there's no way he would have harmed himself before that show. He had never been suicidal at all. But when he died, I think they all just assumed there's this guy with mental health problems, he ends up on railroad tracks, it must have been suicide. How else could he have fallen from the bridge, I'll never know."

Mo was silent for a minute before she spoke. "I heard a recording of someone on a radio show, calling into *Coast to Coast AM*, saying something similar to what you were telling me, that this person thought someone was trying to kill him. He wanted advice from the host, but it almost seemed like ... he was making the call as proof that he was here, that he wanted to tell people what he was going through, in case something happened to him. We weren't sure if it was Ryan, since I've never heard his voice. But he mentioned the protections on this building in Dobbs Ferry. And he called himself ... Arthur Rowe. Like in—"

"*The Ministry of Fear*," they said at the same time. Mo shivered. She hadn't known Eileen was a reader, but it made sense if she had volunteered at the library.

"David Eckley's band," Mo said softly.

"Oh yes, the Eckleys loved Graham Greene," Eileen nodded.

"And Ryan did too?" Mo pressed.

"I know he read some Graham Greene in high school."

"Do you think it's a coincidence that if this was Ryan, he calls into a show using the name of a character in the book that has the same name as David Eckley's band? I don't know if you kept up with David," Mo said quickly, "once he was no longer your neighbor, but he lived in Boston and started a band called Ministry of Fear."

"I knew he was up in Boston, but then he moved back. I think Ryan was actually staying with him at one point? Before he moved upstate. But I haven't heard from him since I saw him at Ryan's funeral."

"Were they ... on good terms at the time of Ryan's death?"

"I don't know. He was acting a bit odd at the funeral, and he never showed up at the wake. But I thought he was just upset. Now with this Arthur Rowe thing ..."

"I'll get you a copy of the recording, if you want to hear his voice, see if it sounds like Ryan," Pat added.

"Yes, I think I should do that."

"There's something else we should show you," Mo continued. "After we heard the person we thought was Ryan on the radio, we went to the building in Dobbs Ferry. And we found this ... it's sort of like a poem, sort of like a painting. Saying that if something happened to the artist, they didn't mean to die. 'I do not wish to die,' I think it was. We took pictures, if you want to see it."

"At the time, it was important to try to make a distinction that it had been an accident, that he wouldn't have taken his own life. But no one wanted to take me seriously. Grieving mother, son passes away, of course no one wants to think their son is capable of suicide, and that their situation is special, you know? It stayed on the death certificate as a suicide, though in my heart, I continued to think it was an accident. At first, I would have never considered a third scenario. But the more I thought about it, I just wanted to know what really happened.

"And then there was his watch, which he wasn't wearing when they found him. I hoped he had taken it off to paint or to keep it safe. But then when I finally got into his car, it wasn't there either. We never found it. And Ryan never took that watch off, once he got out of the hospital the first time. It had been his father's, and his grandfather's before that. I always told him that if he was ever in trouble, he could leave it with me. But he never did. It's just another reason that ..." she trailed off. But Mo had an inkling of the direction of her thoughts. It was one more piece that didn't fit. If Ryan had planned to end his life, what else would he have done differently?

They sat in silence for a moment before Mo and Pat once again attempted to go. They thanked Eileen for dessert and coffee and promised to keep her up to date on any developments involving Ryan.

"We'll get you the radio recording. And that painting-poem-note thing ..."

"I'd like to see that. I mean, maybe I wouldn't. But someone should see it."

"They will," Mo assured her. "We've been talking to a detective in Dobbs Ferry. He's Christine's cousin. Ryan's old girlfriend?"

"I remember Christine! I hope she's well."

"She is," Mo confirmed. "And she mentioned her cousin was a cop in Dobbs Ferry, but we actually met him independently through the music scene. We've been telling him anything odd we've noticed about Ryan's death."

"And he's interested? Those cops back in 2006, no one wanted to hear anything I had to say."

"He is. He wasn't there yet when Ryan died; he was still working down in the city. He's a detective, and he's a little different from what you would expect from someone with the police."

"I hope he knows how important this is," Eileen remarked.

"I think he does."

Mo wondered if for the second time that night, they should offer to make their exit, but Pat tapped her shoulder. "The thing we couldn't read?"

"Oh! I almost forgot. On that painting/poem thing we found in Dobbs, there was something written on the other side that we couldn't figure out. It looked like it said 'say goodbye to Liv.' Would you happen to know who that is?"

"Or it could be 'Viv'?" Pat added helpfully.

"Oh, Viv. She's here with us now ... let me see if I can get her for you." Eileen moved down the hall toward the bedroom, Mo hoping this wasn't what she thought it was ... when their host reappeared, holding what looked like the black and white cat from the record store painting.

"This is Vivian. She was Ryan's, but he ended up leaving her here with me. Sixteen-years-old! I never thought that he would leave us before she did."

Pat clucked at the cat and reached out to pet her. Mo followed his lead, but she was unable to speak. While much of this fall had been consumed by the excitement of unraveling a mystery, seeing Ryan's pet underscored the unspeakable sadness of everything that had transpired. His mom seemed to have come to terms with his death, but who could have imagined that his cat would outlive him by 11 years? It added a whole new dimension.

"Well, I'm so glad she's here with you." Mo fought to keep her voice steady. "And I'm sure he'd appreciate that you're taking such good care of her. And all of this. The tapes, talking to me. That you're keeping his story alive."

"You're the first one who's given me the opportunity to talk about it in a long time. I'm glad you came." That seemed like their cue to leave. Pat gave Vivian a last scratch before she struggled out of Eileen's arms and stalked off. After rezipping herself into her jacket, Mo picked up the box of demos, said their final goodbyes, and stepped into the hallway to wait for the elevator.

Walking to the car, Mo turned from contemplative to animated as she reviewed their successful mission. "Can you believe this? That we got an Indignation tape and got to meet Ryan's cat? His mom is great. I owe Musty a beer or twelve. And Christine." Mo fell silent, realizing how many people and interactions had brought them to this moment. She unearthed the clicker from the depths of her purse to unlock the car. Fortunately, the Camry still had a tape player, as it was 15-years-old and made at the exact time when both tape and CD players were included in some models.

"OK." Pat smiled. "I know there's no way you don't want to listen to an Indignation tape … but which one are we going with first?"

As hard it was not to start with the real demo, Mo wanted to draw out the anticipation a little longer, now that they were finally at the end of the trail.

"Practice tape first," Mo pronounced decisively.

Pat rifled through the box. "9/16/88. That's the most recent one."

Mo stared at the tape. Was it from their last practice as a band? Did they know it was going to be their last practice, any more than the people in Pompeii knew it was going to be their last meal?

Pat ejected Mo's iPod adapter and popped the tape into the deck. The tape wasn't rewound, and it started mid-song, which sounded pretty good, before the chords stopped abruptly, the drums following half a second later, and a bunch of competing voices burst into furious discussion.

"You could slow it down here, then do a spoken word part over it, and then one last even heavier mosh!" Mo froze. That kind of sounded like David Eckley/Max Malkin.

"I don't want to add a whole extra section," someone else replied, sounding annoyed. Could that be Ryan Marnell? It could possibly have been a younger version of the voice on the radio.

"But if you'd just let me make a few suggestions, the songs might come out even better tomorrow," the first speaker continued.

And then another familiar voice entered the conversation, and Mo and Pat started to speak at the same time:

Mo: "Hey, that guy kind of sounds like you!"

Pat: "Oh fuck … that's my dad."

Mo ejected the tape, and for a moment, no one spoke.

"Fuck!" Pat erupted. "Did you ever think that there might be real-life consequences to looking into this shit?"

Mo was, for once, stunned into silence.

"I didn't mean to … all these people were so much older than us …"

"Yeah, apparently one of them was old enough to be my father! But, for the sake of argument, did you think about the fact that these people have families too, and maybe there were things they wouldn't want to revisit?"

"Everyone I talked to so far was so happy to help us!"

"Yeah, because the drummer we met wasn't the one who was my dad, who hasn't wanted to talk to me since 1988! Or uh, hadn't wanted to talk to me." Pat was still not used to referring to his dad in the past tense, as opposed to a vexing mystery who was still walking around out there somewhere upstate.

"All I did was buy a fucking video!" Mo screamed back. "To hear if two bands sounded the same."

"And maybe one of those bands is cursed, just as everyone has been suggesting." Pat slumped in his seat, looking defeated. "I'm sorry." The anger had gone out of his voice. "There's no way you could have known about any of this. It's just a lot to find out that my dad played on that demo by hearing his voice on a practice tape."

And we never got to ask him about it before he died, Mo refrained from saying out loud, since there were a lot of things more significant than the Indignation demo that Pat would have wanted to ask him.

"Fuck," Pat kept shaking his head, but now smiling a little. "I'm part of the reason Indignation didn't play CB's. Or would have been, if my dad wasn't such a piece of shit."

"What are you talking about?"

"My sixth birthday. We were having my party at Sportime and my dad was supposed to be there, but then the day of, he said he had a last minute gig in the city."

"But they didn't play the show," Mo interjected, thoroughly confused until she remembered what Dion had mentioned, that his friend couldn't do the CB's show, as he had "his kid's birthday party or some shit."

Oh, crap.

"So he told Indignation he couldn't play the show, since he had your party, but told your family that he couldn't come to your party, since he was playing a show? Was that really the same weekend?" She tried to remember back to the date on the CB's flyer in the package from Matt.

"We had it a few days early since my uncle was going to be away the next weekend and he was helping us with the party. I specifically remember that."

"Wow. Your dad really was a piece of shit."

"You're telling me?" They sat in silence.

"So CC missed CB's. Hey, did you ever think about the fact that we accidentally named our cat after your dad?"

"I prefer that our cat is named after CC Sabathia. I first had an idea about this when we saw the demo at Eileen's, but I didn't want to say anything while we were there. No one in my family ever called him CC, just some of his friends. But I never made the connection, since drums weren't even his main instrument, and he was more of a rock and metal guy."

"Wait ..." Mo was still caught in the avalanche of revelations due to their discovery. "Does this mean you lived in the same *apartment* as a copy of the Indignation demo?"

Pat laughed ruefully. "Probably not, since this thing was recorded in 1988, right? My parents were already separated. My dad couldn't even bother to show up to my own birthday party. I doubt he gave my mom a copy of the Indignation demo along with her child support check, since he wasn't giving her those either. But if she had one among her David Bowie and Zeppelin tapes, I never saw it. We'll have to ask her."

"How do you think your mom will feel about all this when we tell her?"

"I assume she'll find it fucking hilarious, now that she's gotten over having to wrangle a bunch of six-year-olds at Sportime with one fewer adult than she was expecting at my goddamn party."

A few moments passed. Mo randomly thought about the other Pizza Pizza, the northwest Yonkers one that was not far from here; then again, they could stop at their regular hometown Pizza Pizza as they got off the Cross County Parkway. She was about to ask Pat what he was thinking for dinner when he spoke first.

"There's only one thing left to do now."

"Find proof that David Eckley killed Ryan to give some closure to his mom?"

"No, listen to this Indignation demo!"

"Oh, yeah." Mo couldn't believe it was really sitting there in the car with them while they had been otherwise preoccupied by the recent plot twist. She removed the practice tape, carefully extracted the real Indignation demo from its casing, and guided it into the tape deck. And so, while listening to the tape that they had been looking for all fall, they drove home to Overlook Street, via Locust Street and Pizza Pizza.

The next morning, Mo still couldn't believe that the events of last night had really happened, until she checked for the box of tapes that she had set down on her bookshelf. The Indignation tape existed and was here in their apartment! Once she had galloped through Fleetwood and secured a seat on the 7:46 a.m. train, she started making a Keep note of all the people to tell that she had finally found this tape. And yet the discovery was overshadowed by the even bigger revelations from last night: that her late father-in-law had played on the Indignation demo, that Mrs. Marnell suspected her son had not died accidentally, and was in fact willing to

Lost Indignation

accept that he might have been murdered. Possibly, even, by David Eckley. Maybe Mo should wait on telling anyone about the tape in case some even crazier shit came out in the next week or two.

And a hell of a few weeks it was going to be. Mo couldn't believe she had to focus on the final madness of Art Basel prep with all this other stuff happening, from the hunt for Ryan's truth intensifying to finals and the end of her first semester. Plus the fact that she missed work yesterday and had an avalanche of emails to catch up on. But no matter how hectic today was, they had to get an update to Anthony, to let him know that Mrs. Marnell was committed to finding out what had happened to her son. Mo didn't want to bug him about any follow-up on Sunday's theory, but she couldn't wait for a casual opportunity to ask for updates.

Pat sent an Instagram DM to Dion to confirm the identity of his onetime drummer friend. "Hey, weird question, but was your friend who filled in for Indignation named Chris Catalano? If so, he was my dad"—which elicited the appropriate reply—"oh shit, you're Chris's son!? He was my fuckin' BOY! Was so sorry to hear he had passed, bro."

"That makes one of us," Pat remarked darkly to Mo, but did not extend this cynicism to his exchange with Dion.

The best part was that the Indignation demo tape was just as good as she had imagined. Even if the video hadn't been worth the $20 from the initial park transaction, these five sweet songs on the demo absolutely justified the absurd chase that had transpired over the past few months. After a goofy spoken part that sounded like possibly David Eckley, there was a serviceably moshy intro and song where they rhymed a bunch of stuff with "Indignation." The other four songs varied slightly in style, but all were energetic, original tunes with fun riffs and smart lyrics. If Mo had been a hardcore kid in 1988, she would have loved this shit when it came out, just as she was loving it now.

Mo never enjoyed being separated from a release that had newly hooked her once the songs were stuck in her head, and having this thing on cassette only was not super conducive to listening during the work week. This was 2017, a long time since skaters of the '90s and '00s still used Walkmans instead of Discman CD players so that the music wouldn't skip while skating. Pat's Walkman, acquired for this exact purpose, was long gone. When she mentioned the idea of finding one somewhere after craft class on Tuesday, Pat suggested instead that they should get a device that converted tapes to mp3s. This was a better idea anyway in that Mo wouldn't have to carry a tape and Walkman around all week, plus they could share the mp3s with Anthony, not to mention the members of the band. These converter things were surprisingly less expensive than Mo had presumed, and in stock at B&H, so she could pick one up on the way home on Wednesday. Though if B&H closed at 7:00, the timing was going to be interesting: she was expecting a full and wild day after not being at work since Monday and had promised she could stay late due to no colloquium.

This was the first year without Aby Rosen's annual dinner at the W Hotel, but there was still plenty of Basel-week chaos transpiring, from a last minute Zegna party just before the Young Eef dinner to the Pulse Art Fair after party at the Teixeira Hotel. Plus, on top of everything coming up next week, tonight was also the closing party for Alex Preno's New York show at Fuck Gallery. After a final battle with the yellow cartridge in printer 3, Mo managed to extricate herself just in time to pick up the tape contraption at B&H.

Amidst the Basel backdrop, each day that week brought a new revelation about the Ryan/David situation. Anthony had convinced one of his contacts in Tuckahoe to authorize a dig for a murder weapon in the Abyss. Mo was thankful that Tuckahoe was relatively somnolent and the staff was not backed up working on more dire investigations, since by Thursday afternoon, Anthony had texted Pat that the watch had been found ... with a hammer buried next to it. It was exactly where he had remembered: in the center of a clearing in the Abyss, with a 40 bottle marking the spot. Mo didn't ask if they'd also found the Indignation tape, which might have been requisitioned as evidence. Plus, she now had her own copy that had been sitting in a shoebox for 19 years, rather than out in the woods, not to mention the mp3s they had converted.

And finally, on Friday Mo and Pat had gleaned one more piece of information from Eckley's texts: that he would soon be back in town to see Dana.

When Eckley had texted Dana that he was returning sooner than expected, the original impetus had been to get the fuck out of Boston until some of the Adam Risk heat had subsided. If it earned him another sporadic hookup with Dana, that was a bonus. But as he hurtled down the Merritt, he realized that the visit was imbued with more than mere convenience or the usual benefits of his intermittent partner. What if he somehow got framed for Adam's disappearance, which he'd had nothing to do with, and this was his last weekend as a free man? Or worse, if someone had connected the Risskov thing with Vossen's death—or even Ryan Marnell? Not that anyone had ever been smart enough to connect any dots. Yet on the off chance he wouldn't be in Westchester again for a while, he decided to thoroughly enjoy himself (and Dana) this weekend.

This time, he hadn't even told his family he was coming down, and he wasn't going to waste an evening at the Wretched Spaniel either. And Dana always had creative ways to distract him. As far as he knew, she still had two roommates, but she'd never been shy about fucking in public.

Lost Indignation

Maybe that was exactly what he needed: to revisit various locales where she'd done mind-blowing shit to his dick, or to recast other meaningful Westchester spots into places she would soon be doing mind-blowing shit to his dick.

Jerking off in the Dunkin' Donuts parking lot after getting her number was not the only time he had shot his load in a parking lot in 2005: their first "date" had been at the North White Plains train station, so Dana could shoot him in the tunnel for her photography class. Though before the afternoon was over, other things would be shot besides film. David was getting hard just thinking about it. Yes, coming down here had been a good idea.

Saturday morning, Mo woke up as Pat walked into their bedroom. "Eckley's in New York."

"What? Right now?" It took her a minute to remember what day it was. Sunshine streamed in from the window and she realized it was Saturday.

"Yeah, I saw a text late last night, but I didn't want to wake you."

"Thank you for that," Mo mumbled groggily. She had gotten home from work around 11 p.m. due to the final sprint of Art Basel prep. At least everything seemed reasonably under control this year, and, starting tomorrow, approximately a third of her office would be on their way to Miami. Which, ostensibly, meant one-third less chaos and annoyance, but Mo knew those would be multiplied by the travel aspect and the circus of concurrent events that was Art Basel.

"I already texted Anthony. I'll keep him updated if I hear anything else."

"Already? What time is it?" Mo looked around. She couldn't get used to Pat waking up before her, though 90 percent of the time she loved it. The display on her clock radio showed 8:36 a.m.

"Yeah, I'm riding bikes with him today, remember?"

"Oh, yeah." In any other week, this would have been all she had heard about all week: Pat, Anthony and Sydenstricker were going to ride to the Kensico Dam and back via the Bronx River trail. Mo had received a courtesy invite, but had declined, as she wouldn't be able to keep up with them and didn't want to delay the proceedings.

"Damn right! And we got a good day for it. It's already 40 degrees." Pat dipped across the hall to the kitchen to pour himself more iced coffee and reappeared a moment later with a second cup for Mo. "What are you up to today?"

"Oh, I'll probably write, or pretend to write and actually look at social media."

"Sounds about right. Hey, you should ride over with me for the beginning and then you can split off and do your own ride. We're meeting at Dunkin' Donuts on Bronx River Road."

Mo opted to let Pat head off to the bike adventure and settled herself on the couch with the holy trifecta of a cat, coffee, and magazine. It was amazing not only how many magazines had accumulated on their coffee table, but also that every time she lay down on the couch, she managed to place the coffee just out of reach. With Pat out the door, she let her mind drift to Eckley. What was he doing in Westchester, besides probably meeting up with Dana? Was coming back so soon after Thanksgiving a sign that Eckley thought he had nothing to hide or that there was something he needed to urgently handle? Mo expected that they would find out soon enough, either from his texts or some other disturbance. She managed to be productive during Pat's ride, but all day, in the back of her mind, she was wondering about Eckley.

The night started like one of many between Eckley and Dana: with few specific plans, but the idea that anything could take shape. Dana knew he had always appreciated her spontaneity. But how much was it that he recognized she was chill as fuck, and how much that she knew when to let him take control? Either way she was glad he had capitulated and returned so soon after their missed connection last weekend.

Eckley had seemed distracted ever since he arrived. Today, they had started at some brewery in Elmsford (Dana had wanted to go ice skating nearby, but he had refused), but when they got back in the car, she thought they might be heading to more drinks in downtown White Plains, or maybe dinner, though Eckley had previously mentioned Silvio's in Yonkers. Instead, as soon as they got off the Bronx River Parkway at Fisher Lane, she knew they were headed to the North White Plains train station, the site of their first "date."

When she had first slipped her number to Eckley, Dana had been living in West Harrison and taking a photography class at Westchester Community College. Eckley had mentioned working as a transit cop, so she had asked him to accompany her to the tunnel in North White Plains. It was an assignment on framing, and Eckley was a natural in front of the camera. It was symmetry, she supposed, that she had first sucked his dick in this parking lot, and they were back here today. The night had an air of a valedictory tour, though she couldn't have identified why Eckley was revisiting these places of significance.

Yet tonight's reenactment didn't go as smoothly as their original liaison in 2005: Eckley couldn't seem to get hard. Dana did her best to exhort and encourage him, but soon realized that it wasn't going to happen. After all, he wasn't as young as he had been, though she wasn't going to say that. Dana always had the idea that he'd picked her over her sister not

Lost Indignation

just because of her youth and tits, but because she knew when to shut the fuck up. Eckley seemed annoyed, either with her or with his equipment, but eventually reached the same conclusion.

"Whatever, we can do this later," he snapped as he reassembled his clothing and started the engine. "Why the fuck did you want to come here?" Dana buckled her seatbelt, knowing his frustration might translate into his driving, and didn't mention that it had been his idea to come here, in both senses of the word.

As Eckley drove south on the Bronx River Parkway, Dana was still hoping they were on their way to Silvio's. She was hungry as fuck and could practically taste the chicken parm, so she attempted to hurry things along.

"Are we still going to dinner? I'm getting hungry. Though you could feed me."

"I need to check on something first," he replied peevishly.

"Then Silvio's?"

He didn't answer.

Eckley got off the parkway at the Scarsdale Road exit, turning left towards Tuckahoe rather than right towards his old neighborhood, then parked on a side street. Dana thought this might present another opportunity to resume their activities and put him in a better mood, but he sprang from the car and headed past the Boy Scout cabin towards the bike path as she reluctantly followed. What were they doing here? It was a little cold to enjoy themselves in the woods, not that Eckley looked intent on enjoying anything. Dana caught up to him before they crossed the bridge over the waterfall, but Eckley turned onto a path into the woods. As she activated the flashlight on her phone, Dana vaguely recalled from local lore that teenagers had dubbed this area The Abyss. She was wondering if kids still hung out here when they encountered much more recent evidence of human presence.

"What the hell is this shit?" Eckley had also engaged his flashlight and its erratic beams confronted a profusion of police caution tape, brightly colored flags pinned into the ground, and heaps of recently displaced earth. From his utterly shocked tone to his frantic pacing, Dana surmised that this was something entirely different than he had been hoping to find. She was afraid to ask why he had been sent into such a frenzy by this patch of woods being disturbed, and could only imagine that something significant had once happened here in his personal history.

"This is crazy! Who the fuck told them to look here?" Eckley seemed to answer his own question as he looked over at Dana. "That night on the bridge. You were there." He stared at her, his face a dangerous composition of realization and rage.

"What are you talking about?" Dana was used to Eckley's mercurial moods, but tonight he seemed less in command of himself, and positively deranged.

"The night that Ryan ... And who would believe you weren't? During his wake, you're off fucking his best friend who also happens to be dating your sister? What kind of behavior is that?" David was visibly upset and pacing in front of the entrance to the trail. Dana didn't point out that Eckley skipping the wake and fucking his girlfriend's sister was far more egregious than her own actions at that time, especially because she hardly knew Ryan Marnell, and what the hell did she have to do with any of this, besides the fact that David Eckley had something to hide and seemed intent to drag her down too?

"Obviously, you were worried he had found out about us and was going to tell Christine," David continued as he assembled the narrative. "And everyone thought it was an accident, or a suicide, or whatever."

Dana knew she had to change the subject, though she wanted to ask why exactly David knew so much about that night that Ryan died if he had supposedly just found him on the tracks afterwards.

"I hadn't seen Ryan since 1990, and definitely not the night he died," she said stiffly. "Anyway, what does that have to do with why we're here?"

It was if Eckley hadn't even heard her or didn't realize she was a few steps behind him. "I gave them every clue," he muttered. "These fucking people. And they still went off in the wrong direction. Wait!" he whirled around. "Did you plant that demo on Marnell too? In 2001? So it would come back to Boston and try to discredit me?"

"Again, I have no idea what you're talking about." Dana stood her ground but turned back towards the bike path. Didn't anyone traverse it at this hour?

"The Indignation demo!" David exploded. "That's what this is all about! Thing was cursed from the beginning! I paid for part of it, and later I tried to destroy them all. But they keep coming back to haunt me." He was breathing harder now as his eyes wildly scanned the woods. "So then I tried a different strategy. Tried to release this video that would set the record straight, that I wrote the Indignation songs, which then turned into Ministry of Fear songs. Out into the hardcore ecosystem where hype would do the rest. Someone got the wrong idea and started looking into this Indignation crap. But I am not going to let these people get the upper hand. Believe me, I am still going to destroy every last copy of that fucking demo. But we have bigger things to deal with first!" He whipped around suddenly and grabbed her arm. "Like the fact that you were there the night Ryan died, a fact that has never previously been reported, and I intend to do something about that." When Dana tried to protest, he started to push her towards the car. "Let's go. We have one more stop to make."

Lost Indignation

It was then that Dana really started to worry, since it didn't sound like they were still going to dinner. One more stop before what? She had a feeling they might be heading towards that building on Palisade and the aforementioned bridge. As Eckley merged onto the Bronx River Parkway, she shoved her phone deep into her purse where he couldn't see its light and managed to type "Help! Might be on the way to Palisade?" to Anthony, before turning on location sharing in Google Maps so that he could track their movements. Her cousin had just texted her this afternoon, somehow having known that Eckley was in town, and warned her to be careful. She would have been offended, except that Anthony had managed to remain a neutral party in the family dispute over David Eckley. Now she was glad that he was already apprised of the situation and might be able to intercept them in Dobbs Ferry, either alone or with backup. Part of the allure of sneaking around with Eckley had been his unpredictability, but whatever he was planning tonight had surpassed spontaneity and crossed into danger.

Eckley got off the parkway at the Harney Road exit and raced up the hills towards Ardsley. As they crossed Central Avenue, Dana wondered if her premonition about their destination might be correct, as her sense of alarm increased. They roared across the Sprain Brook Parkway, Dana hanging onto the door handle due to Eckley's rate of speed, then down the hill past the Ardsley village hall and barely made the light before the Ashford Avenue bridge. To the right was Petraske's, which Dana always avoided since her sister worked there. Was it possible she was even working there tonight, and would she even give a shit if Dana was in danger? Dana had always felt a little bad about the Eckley thing, though not bad enough to stop seeing him, and had never tried to apologize. During the few times they'd seen each other at family gatherings since Christine had moved back from California, they had avoided each other as much as possible and exchanged only the minimum conversation.

There was little traffic on Ashford Avenue as they whipped past the park and the hospital toward downtown Dobbs Ferry. Dana was sure they were heading for Palisade Street, unless Eckley was planning a detour to, say, shame her in front of her parents, who still lived nearby. Or would he try to turn her in at the Dobbs Ferry police department for a crime she hadn't committed? Dana had never thought much about how Ryan Marnell had died, or that Eckley could have been involved besides finding his body while he was on duty at work. But now, his insistence on tying her into the story convinced her that he had been there as well.

Eckley zoomed through a yellow light where Ashford met Broadway. Due to the darkness, Dana couldn't see the river as they sped down Cedar Street, but she could sense its presence due to the sheer black space it inhabited. They swung a hard left on Palisade Street. This was her last chance for their destination to change. But as she predicted, Eckley immediately made the right into the familiar driveway and careened down the hill toward the building that awaited them at the bottom.

Dana wasn't sure what was about to happen, but she figured he would drive straight to the railroad bridge—and then what? Try to throw her onto the tracks? Is that what had happened to Ryan? But just as she grasped that idea, they were diverted. There was someone at the bottom of the driveway: was that Anthony's car? It sounded like his sound system, and it was blasting something old and loud and fast, which sounded like a tape that Dana had spirited out of Christine's collection once she left for college—

The music apparently meant something to David too. His eyes widened as he emitted a yowl of rage and jerked the steering wheel, just missing the car in front of them. Suddenly they were speeding toward the pond. Dana reflexively reached to roll down her window, praying this wouldn't be the end, when there was the loudest fucking noise she had ever heard. Merely inches from the water, the engine was stalled, and it sounded like the car was ripping apart. And David was screaming, running, raving, but he didn't get far. For the moment at least, Dana was totally forgotten. And for once, that was OK.

Back on Overlook Street, Mo and Pat were lying in bed, trying to decide if they should order from Pizza Pizza or Jade Garden. Maybe for a real treat, they'd get delivery instead of picking up. Pat was usually the one to walk up the hill to acquire their dinner, but he had just biked 30 miles. Pat, Anthony, and J.P. had had a great ride, though Pat had only been able to pass the barest skeleton of Eckley updates to Anthony without letting in J.P. on the entire thing. At least Anthony knew that Eckley was in town, a situation to monitor for the sake of his cousin if nothing else. Pat had also sent him rudimentary mp3s of the entire Indignation demo from their experiments with the conversion device, as additional context for the investigation.

So it was down to Jade Garden vs. Pizza Pizza when Pat got the first text from Anthony.

"Oh shit, he's at Palisade Street, and Eckley and Dana are supposedly on the way."

"What?" Mo only could only imagine the ominous context behind this. While it had occurred to her that they were putting themselves at risk by getting entangled with Eckley, she hadn't realized that they could have unwittingly flung more people into Eckley's path. They didn't know why Eckley had decided to come back to New York that weekend, but why else would he be heading to 145 Palisade if not in relation to his history with Ryan? Yes, Dana was Pat's manipulative and delusional ex, but she was also a human being, and while it was Anthony's job to investigate people like David Eckley, Mo and Pat were the ones who had corralled him into this chase.

"Damn, as much as I was never a fan of this Dana person based on what I know about her, I hope she's OK."

"She's an adult; she can handle herself," Pat replied. But could she? Eckley had purposely wooed the weaker Eckley sister while Christine had escaped relatively unscathed.

For a few minutes, they sat in silence, wondering what was transpiring across the county. Mo couldn't even think about dinner—even scallion pancakes from Jade Garden. What seemed like eons later, but was closer to 20 minutes, the waiting was punctured by an alert from Pat's phone.

"Holy shit, they got him!" Pat yelled. Mo felt a flood of relief.

"How?!" Mo sat up in bed and looked around, as if expecting to see the crime scene of 145 Palisade on their old TV across the bedroom.

Pat turned to her with a smile. "The Indignation demo. It was the star of the show."

Becky McAuley

Chapter 17
2017

"So once we finally sat down with him and his attorney, he started confessing everything. Including stuff we never would have known." They were at Pizzeria La Rosa again with Anthony, eight days after Eckley had tried to drive himself and Dana into the pond. Parts of the story had made it to the news: first a short item in the police blotter of a local paper that covered the northern Rivertowns describing the incident at the bottom of the hill, and then a more complete account in the *Journal News* that mentioned Ryan's murder, courtesy of an anonymous police source. Eckley hadn't been charged with anything yet besides attempted manslaughter for almost driving Dana into the pond, and Anthony hadn't been the anonymous source, but now that certain details of the Eckley/Marnell situation were public, he had no problem telling them the full story. Mo wondered if it was going to get picked up by the city papers, which might make Ryan and his art even more enticing to Colette. CFA had made it through Art Basel week, and the Young Eef midnight dinner had been surprisingly spectacular after all. Colette was back in the city, having flown home Saturday morning, and Mo had already put a meeting in Google Calendar to tell her about Ryan. Though she knew as well as anyone that Colette was unlikely to stick to her schedule.

"First he starts talking about Ryan, confirming everything you suspected: the murder, the tapes, burying the watch with the hammer. And then he drops the news that he killed some other guy named Tyler while he was living in Boston. So we had to call the Boston PD, and it turns out they were looking into him for potential involvement in a *third* case, for some missing person, in the past week. The third guy turned up though, looks like he tried to fake his own death and pin it on Eckley." Anthony presented all of this so nonchalantly, though Mo looked over at Pat like "what?!" at the mention of the second murder. At least that sort of explained why Tyler Vossen's library card was in his wallet.

Anthony went on that Eckley was being held without bail, due to the severity of the alleged crimes. Mo wondered if she should have been worried if Eckley hadn't been denied bail and had figured out her and Pat's ancillary role in this whole strange tale.

"Why do you think he confessed?"

"Part of it was involuntary. He was already yelling shit when he got out of the car. He couldn't help himself, he was all jacked up from almost driving into the pond until his car got stuck on the sculpture. Dana said he went totally crazy when he saw the Abyss was all dug up. After that, he claimed she had been there the night that Ryan died. Which she has an alibi for, not that I believed for a second she was there."

"Wait, his car got stuck on a sculpture? Maybe it was the same sculpture he tripped over when he was trying to punch this guy." Mo elbowed Pat.

"That sculpture has had a rough few weeks. But he wouldn't have even run into it if my cousin hadn't texted that they might be heading there—and if you two hadn't sent me the mp3s of the demo! As soon as I got that text from Dana, I called for backup and fucking floored it to the bottom of the driveway. And then I thought, 'What can I do to stop this car in its tracks?' The Indignation demo, of course.

"Anyway," Anthony continued, "Eckley must have thought this was finally his chance to be famous, to be the handsome murderer and get a ton of fan mail in jail. Not that the people with the podcasts will care about him if he's only killed two people. Though who knows? He's a good-looking guy. Or at least all my cousins seem to think so." He sighed. Mo almost voiced a third theory: maybe Eckley couldn't resist getting credit for what he'd done and—as he had taunted on Thanksgiving Eve—that everyone had previously been too stupid to figure it out.

She thought back to the line in *The Rebel Angels* about how publishers would fight to print a book by a murderer. Would Eckley try to capitalize on his notoriety? Hopefully, she would get there first. Ever since she had told Mrs. Marnell that she was writing about Ryan for school, Mo couldn't shake the thought this had all been leading to something bigger than hearing Indignation: that the next step was to write about Ryan's life and work. But in what form and context? She was starting small, finding ways to work aspects of his story into her upcoming finals assignment, before planning anything else.

It would have been easy to spend hours ruminating on Eckley's crimes, but the work week was approaching and Mo could only devote so much time to the world of David Eckley and Ryan Marnell. With Art Basel concluded and the CFA team back in New York, focus turned to various neglected clients and the Ethan Mitchell/Winston Alexander lunch that Thursday. Ethan was coming on Tuesday to finalize the seating with Colette. Mo hadn't seen him since the business card incident a few months earlier.

Upon his arrival at the office, Ethan received a boisterous greeting from both Colette and Pierre. Mo half-listened to their seating plan banter in the way she vaguely monitored most client meetings by Carine's desk, like a Google Home listening for the trigger phrase. And then she heard it.

"You need an artist here ... oh you have to come to OAF in January, but you need ... like that guy that Maureen knows, but he was murdered, so we can't seat him ... MAUREEN!?"

Mo scampered towards Colette's office area. She was used to being summoned to recollect the name of a reporter or artist just beyond Colette's grasp, but she hadn't been expecting this. She had briefed her on the Ryan story yesterday morning, while Drew was out with the dog, but Colette had seemed distracted and Mo couldn't tell how much she had absorbed. Now here she was, bringing up the story without Mo's prompting and interjecting it into a meeting with another client.

"Hi, Colette—what's up? And hi, Ethan, how are you?" Mo stood before Colette and Ethan, who were both crouched around the seating plan on the coffee table. She was glad she wasn't wearing anything super embarrassing (maroon sweater, orange skirt, gray tights, gray and red Vandals circa 2007) and looked somewhat put together compared to her recent trash-human ensembles.

"Maureen! Who is your artist, the one who was murdered ..."

"Ryan Marnell," Mo said quickly but clearly. Somehow, she hadn't realized until this moment that she was on stage. "He was an outsider artist and a musician too. That's how I found out about him, through his music, looking for songs from one of his old bands. And then I met his mom and started looking into what happened to him. I'm writing about him too, first something for school, then something more."

Colette nodded over the stickies, Mo having been summoned for this anecdote and then likely to be dismissed, but Ethan looked interested. "Ryan Marnell." He wrote down Ryan's name on a spare sticky and tucked it into his pocket. "What kind of music?"

"Hardcore punk," Mo responded, leaning all the way in to Ethan's history of playing at the Anthrax almost 30 years ago. What kind of band had Future Humans been, at least somewhat hardcore-adjacent, right? It wasn't worth the usual deliberate ambiguity, where hardcore got glossed over as "punk" or something even more innocuous. This was usually around the time that Colette would say something about Mo liking "Grateful Dead music (!?)," with Mo insisting she mostly listened to rap anyway.

"Really. What band was he in?"

"Indignation. They weren't around very long."

"Indignation! I saw them once! At the Anthrax? Late '80s?"

"Yes! Wow. I can't believe you saw them! You were in Future Humans, right?"

"I was." Mo was suddenly aware that everyone in the room was listening to this conversation; that Colette, who was frowning over the stickies, was going to be disgruntled soon (if not already) that Mo had inadvertently hijacked a client meeting. She also needed to leave for class in 13 minutes.

"It sounds like we have a lot to catch up on. I've got your card," Ethan added, not elaborating on the location scouting card in question.

Mo nodded and turned back to her desk. "Yes, you do."

Colette didn't engage her again in the next few minutes as Mo rapidly wrapped up and shut down her computer to leave for class. That interaction had been revelatory, not just because it proved that Colette had been listening as Mo recounted the Ryan/David murder saga, but because Ethan Mitchell seemed interested in Ryan! Of course he could have been feigning polite enthusiasm, but Mo sensed it was genuine and that she was going to get an email from him sooner or later. The hard part would be to put the anticipation out of her mind and focus on way more important shit like all her final papers due that week. And even if Ryan's name couldn't have been added to the seating plan since he was no longer among the living, his name had still been added to a sticky and claimed by Ethan Mitchell.

Mo was imbued with jumpy energy for the rest of the day, including her final craft class of the semester. It was hard to describe why she felt so electrified by today's conversation. It wasn't just the chance to mention hardcore to someone who understood what she was talking about, but also that she had found an opportunity to drop in that she was writing about Ryan. Ethan was in publishing, and the difference between him being curious about Ryan vs. Mo embarking on a long and solitary project without publisher interest would make a difference in, well, everything. For now, she would wait to see if he would reach out, and if he didn't, she could take matters into her own hands.

Now that Colette had acknowledged Ryan's story and in fact mentioned it to another client, Mo was taking this as justification that she could nudge Ryan into the CFA world in other insidious ways, like introducing an invasive species. The first step was to see if there was anything Aaron could do to secure some sort of tangential involvement in the Outsider Art Fair, just over a month away. While finagling Ryan onto a gallery's roster could be seen as a favor for Mo, she was also confident it would increase press coverage for CFA. Per Eileen Marnell, news outlets from outside of Westchester were starting to contact her to learn more about Ryan in the context of Eckley's grisly ministrations. Mo had already advised her to refer to her son as a visionary artist and hint at a large body of work he was creating at the time of his death. And any mention of his involvement in the Outsider Art Fair could benefit all parties.

Colette, Tati, and the events team were scheduled to work the Ethan Mitchell/Win Alexander lunch on Thursday and would be out of the office from late morning through mid-afternoon, so Mo had arranged a coffee with Aaron for noon on Thursday, once the last flurry of RSVP-confirmation or cancellation phone calls should have ceased. It was too cold for the outdoor seating area at the High Line Hotel, but they got a spot on one of the couches in the lobby after grabbing coffee at Intelligentsia. Aaron seemed impressed by Ryan's story and the photos of his work. He suggested some galleries that could fit Ryan's style and made introductions over email that night. And while the Sperling Vieira Gallery emailed back promptly to confirm that they were not taking additional clients at this time, Trisha from Broad Scope Gallery replied that she had seen the Ryan story in the *Journal News* and was interested in his work. It was fortuitous, Mo reflected, that Broad Scope was in Garnerville, NY, which was in Rockland County, and therefore within the reach of a regional article.

It was turning into a snowy Friday, so things were probably quieter at the gallery than at CFA, where the action never abated except when the office was closed during Hurricane Sandy. Before the snow had stopped falling, Trisha had asked to meet with Mo and Eileen that Sunday, to see some of Ryan's output and learn about his history. Mo already liked this woman, who fired off concise emails and seemed to understand the urgency of capitalizing on Ryan's story being in the news. Hopefully the idea of showing him in the Outsider Art Fair would find its way into the conversation. And if it didn't come up organically, Mo had learned from being a hardcore kid that it rarely hurt to ask.

Eileen was available for Sunday, and Westchester only ended up getting a few inches of snow, so their travel would be unimpeded. On Saturday afternoon, Mo was piling on various garments in preparation to check on her car. Hopefully it would be more of a brush-off than a dig-out, but who knew since she was parked on the weird hill on Urban Street. She had finally ensconced herself in hat, hood, coat, scarf and was pulling on her boots when she heard a buzzing from her purse beside the coffee table. Mo dropped her gloves among the riot of magazines and fished out her phone. It was a 212 number.

"Hi, this is Mo?" Pat looked over quizzically, as did Brett and CC from the couch.

"Mo McGraw? This is Ethan Mitchell."

"I answered the phone, and it was this publisher, who I met through work, and he told me he might be interested in publishing a book about Ryan. One that I would be writing," Mo clarified nonchalantly, as she changed lanes for the exit towards the Tappan Zee Bridge. Eileen was in the passenger seat beside her, having been picked up in Yonkers on the way to the Broad Scope Gallery. Pat was in the back, headphones on, but Mo was pretty sure he was listening. His mom lived over in Nyack, so she would be meeting them at the gallery, where they were going to check out the art and walk around the rest of the Garnerville complex and/or hang out in the brewery at its other end while Mo and Eileen talked to Broad Scope about Ryan and showed Trisha more samples of his work.

"And I told him I might be interested, but that I wanted to talk to you first. I'd only do something like this if you were comfortable with it and fully on board. Out of respect for you, but also to get the best story of Ryan."

"I know you're asking me as a formality, and I appreciate it," Eileen replied carefully. "But of course I'd want you to write about Ryan! A few weeks ago, I never would have thought that someone would be interested in his art or his story. And if there's to be a book, it's best if it comes from you."

"But there doesn't have to be a book at all," Mo quickly added, though it crushed her to downplay the possibility. A fucking book! She, who had been selling homemade zines for years— at $2 apiece in person, $3 by mail—had someone interested in publishing her writing, not in just another person's esteemed zine like *Gratitude*, but in an actual book!

"I want people to know his story," his mother stated simply. "And you're the right person to bring it to the world."

"Well in that case," Mo continued, though she was smiling now, "I guess we better get started on some interviews. I wonder if my tape recorder still works?"

Pat was definitely listening. "You should leave that tape recorder in 2004 where you found it. I'll get you set up on an app."

It was a productive Sunday. Mutually energized by the idea that there might be a book about Ryan, Mo and Eileen had a meaningful meeting with Trisha from Broad Scope, who all but told them she was planning to represent Ryan and his estate. They had brought a few more paintings from what Mo was starting to think of as the *Stunt Double* series, where there was always a black and white cat on the edge of the frame, watching the proceedings. Was this merely Ryan's signature or a way to mark that he always felt set apart from everything happening around him?

Since Ryan had no studio, instead of doing a traditional studio visit, Trisha suggested consolidating all his work in one place to evaluate it further. That meant closing the storage unit upstate, which had been untouched for over ten years, and picking up everything from Mrs. Marnell's apartment, all of which Broad Scope was handling. Mo wondered if they needed approval from Colette for any of this Ryan stuff, but Aaron had managed to slip it into an Outsider update just before break that hey, remember that artist that Mo was talking about? The Broad Scope Gallery was probably going to represent his estate, and if that happened, he was likely to have a piece or two in the fair! Mo's heart swelled when she heard Aaron mention that development so casually, but Colette didn't even react: maybe she had already forgotten about the murder element and the adjacent press coverage it could potentially generate.

On a similar note, Mo herself would be helping Aaron with press materials about Broad Scope and Ryan Marnell. Representing an art fair could be both fulfilling and arduous in that there was an exponential web of stories to highlight: 63 galleries were showing at OAF this year, and then multiple artists per gallery, all with compelling narratives and bodies of work. Especially since these were outsider artists with nontraditional backgrounds, who had been institutionalized, ignored, or taught through unusual means. Besides spending a few days with her family over Christmas break, she was going to be home writing about Ryan anyway. Ethan had suggested she start working on a book proposal, news that both elated and scared the shit out of her. The irony of having to create Ryan Marnell press materials was also not lost on her: now she had two different outlets to write about Ryan and Indignation, after having thought about little else that fall.

Mo spent the rest of that very cold week toiling on the book proposal when she wasn't working with Aaron on the Ryan press materials. As a notorious procrastinator, these were the only two things in her life that she wasn't going to procrastinate on, though both were still going when she returned to work in January after the holiday. At least she was still working a part-time schedule, though second semester classes were a few weeks away.

The Outsider Art Fair always took on an outsize importance as it drew closer, overshadowing more remunerative clients, but this year Ryan was officially part of its story, as Trisha from Broad Scope had opted to show two of his paintings. Apparently Colette did remember the significance of Ryan after all, as more than once, Mo heard Colette on the phone exhorting her friends to come to the fair and check out Broad Scope's offerings, including "Ryan Marnell, who was *murdered!*" She felt a little bad that the circumstances of Ryan's death had imprinted him on her boss's brain rather than the power of his art itself.

And finally, it was the day of the fair. Excitement had been building all week: late nights of finalizing RSVPs and then the warm-up events at the Ace Hotel. Thursday was the VIP preview and there were over 2000 people RSVP'd. If Mo did ever leave CFA, she would grudgingly miss the controlled chaos of event day: everyone scurrying around in all black, Big L style, heels clacking and clomping, the color printer whirring, Colette screaming for an Uber or an updated tip sheet. About one-third of the office was working the preview, and ordinarily Mo would have been staying behind with the others and enjoying the quiet in the wake of their departure. But for the first time since CFA had started representing the fair in 2013, Mo was heading over shortly after those working the event. She wasn't on the staffing chart, but she would be attending in a semi-official capacity. She wanted to see the Martín Ramírez that Ricco/Maresca Gallery was showing and the Joseph Bertiers stuff at Ernie Wolfe, but she and Pat were coming back on Saturday, and she realized that if she stuck close to Ryan's pieces, she would be more likely to encounter everyone from his world. Mo had provided a short list of friends of Ryan who might want to attend the opening, or if they couldn't make it today, to come by on another day of the fair. Christine had RSVP'd, as had, surprisingly, Warren Yatrofsky. Eileen Marnell would be in attendance, but a half-dozen art media outlets already wanted to speak to her, as orchestrated by Aaron, so Mo figured she'd be busy. Matt Zimmer was coming down with his whole family over the weekend. Mo had also snuck Shane Perry onto the list. And when the guests arrived, they would find Ryan everywhere: in the Broad Scope booth, in the catalog (he'd made it just in time), and even in the *New York Times* preview.

Mo wound through the throngs in the entryway and was waved through check-in. It was fun to witness the excitement of the VIP preview, though it took a few minutes to find Broad Scope on the map and navigate to its location. She knew she was going the right direction when she saw Trisha from the gallery bustling past in purple tights, her nose ring winking merrily, a pack of collectors in tow. Behind her, Mo heard a heavily accented version of "Marnell" uttered by some dude in outlandish loafers. And though she hadn't yet seen Shane Perry, she swore she heard someone at a neighboring exhibitor introducing themselves as Giuseppe McCleary.

Stepping into the Broad Scope booth, she spotted Christine and Warren standing in front of one of Ryan's *Stunt Double* paintings. She was surprised to see them together, but realized they must have known each other back in the day. And even if they weren't exactly friends, and barely looked dressed for the same event, they were both here because of Ryan. Christine was wearing a long green dress with silver boots and looked fucking spectacular. Warren was in his customary flight jacket and camo pants.

"Look who's here! I'm so glad you both made it."

"The perks of working in the service industry," Christine remarked dryly. "It's not like I have to be at work until 6:00. Though I was working until 3 a.m. last night."

Warren wandered off to look at other Broad Scope offerings. "I didn't know this was a whole series." Christine was gazing at the *Stunt Double* paintings, two of which had made it to the fair: the cat in the record store scene and the cat among the skateboarders in Dobbs Ferry. "Ryan's mom gave me one of these, with the cat in front of my family's house on Chestnut Street. I didn't realize there was one with us skating down at the river too." Mo looked closer at the river scene: in the foreground there were boys skating on the loading dock, and in the background three faceless girls, one of which she had suspected might be Christine. The black-and-white cat looked on from the steps.

Lost Indignation

"I had a feeling that might be you! But I didn't want to put that in the press materials. Should I tell any of the reporters here that you're in one of the paintings?"

Christine grimaced. "No need. It's enough just to see him here, you know?" Looking at the Ryan Marnells hanging in the Outsider Art Fair, Mo knew what she meant.

"When we met his mom, she mentioned giving paintings to two of his friends. I'm glad that one of those friends was you. I was worried one might have been David Eckley."

"No, it was me, and Ryan's friend Leah. She's coming this weekend." Mo recognized the name that Eileen had added to the list. She was about to ask Christine more about Leah, or what else she knew about Ryan's friends, when another familiar figure entered the Broad Scope booth.

"Hi, Ethan! This is Christine, an old friend of Ryan. Christine, this is Ethan, who's interested in Ryan's work." How to even introduce either of them? Should she reveal what she had just discovered, that Christine was depicted in one of the paintings hanging in front of them? Should she have called her Ryan's ex-girlfriend, or was there more power in her only being a friend? And how to describe Ethan: as a client? As her publisher? Or just a Ryan fan?

They chatted for another minute before Ethan stepped back to continue through the fair. "Wonderful to meet you," he directed at Christine, and to Mo: "I'll let you know as soon as I have an update," for she had finally submitted the book proposal. This week had been so busy she hadn't had time to worry about how it would be received. And as much as she liked being in touch with Ethan on a regular basis, she missed when their contact had been sporadic and novel enough for references to "I've got your card."

Mo was going straight home rather than returning to the office once she was done at the fair. What was the easiest way to get to Grand Central from here? It was fucking cold, so she was going to dip into the 1 at 18th rather than trying to walk east to the F or the 6. But as she exited the Metropolitan Pavilion, she had the feeling that she was seeing all of this for the last time. Not the fair itself, as she and Pat would be back here on the weekend, but the process of watching a CFA event take shape. Mo had always been behind the scenes for that process, but how much longer would she be part of the process at all?

Ryan's art was receiving most of the attention, but ever since David Eckley's murders had made the news, there had been a few mentions of Ministry of Fear on the Bridge 9 board and on social media. Things really got out of hand on B9 when someone from Boston posted a news article implicating Eckley in Tyler Vossen's death and made the connection that both had played together in a band. Besides some young guy who was a big Ministry of Fear fan and was devastated that one member had killed another, most posts expressed the sentiment of "I never liked that dude," which was hardly surprising.

Though what *was* surprising was that Eckley's first murder victim had been a member of his former band. Had he been motivated by a similar situation of creative control? (Not that he was even in Indignation in the first place.) Pat wondered aloud if this qualified Eckley as a serial killer, if both murders had occurred in similar contexts, rather than just being crimes of opportunity. Mo was unsure if they would ever find out: if the cases came to trial, the hardcore-related details would remain secondary to the facts of the killing and prior interpersonal relationships.

She also pondered how Eckley would react if her book was someday published, as she was sure he would find a way to procure a copy. It could incite his ire, though maybe he'd enjoy being the center of attention, as Mo grimly expected another wave of renewed interest in Ministry of Fear. Perhaps Eckley would only regret that he couldn't capitalize on it with a reunion, or that he wouldn't be the one telling his story.

Mo was fine with Ryan's notoriety bolstering the interest in his paintings, but was hesitant to exploit the Ministry of Fear/Indignation connection in a musical context. Though there was one forum where she wanted to close the loop for anyone who had been following the original thread. While Eckley had deleted his Controlled Board username, wiping out their chain of PM's along with it, his original post about Warzone, Altercation, Waylon Jennings, Indignation, and Ministry of Fear remained in the thread under "deleted user." Mo quoted his initial post and left an update in the *Gratitude* thread. "Remember this guy? He sold me this messed up videotape that had like 0.5 seconds of an Indignation song ... but it turns out he stole the Indignation songs he's referring to—and then killed the guy who wrote them!" Her fellow posters were suitably excited and alarmed by this development, not least that there had been a murderer among them, even if he had since closed his account. Though only a few people asked the essential question, unrelated to the murder intrigued: were the Indignation songs worth hearing?

They absolutely fucking were, much more so than the Ministry of Fear songs that had been based on them. Mo had given the Ministry of Fear CD a spin or two when it first arrived from Discogs, but without having heard the Indignation songs yet, there wasn't much to compare. MOF was too metal for her, just as she had suspected, though the songs at the end of the CD were better (the ones from the 7"). Once she had the Indignation tracks as well, she wasn't surprised that the 7" featured the most purloined Indignation riffs. Though she still liked the original Indignation versions best of all.

Lost Indignation

Carl Bernstein once remarked that journalism was "the best obtainable version of the truth," and while whatever Mo had been doing that fall wasn't journalism, in the end she had obtained what was as close to the truth as possible. Many of the best mysteries in hardcore remained unsolved, so it was a feat that she had uncovered the unhappy resolution to Ryan and David's friendship and located an Indignation demo only three months after first hearing their name. Just like in the Handsome Boy Modeling School song, Eckley hadn't been able to hide from the truth. And yet there were still so many things Mo didn't know, especially about the last few years of Ryan Marnell's life. While writing about him, she hoped to fill out a better picture of what he had created and endured, bringing closure to his mom while bringing his story to the world.

There was one more story that Mo had to finish, that wasn't for school or press materials or a book: she had to decide what she was going to do about work and school next semester. Mo had signed up for three classes again, though two were in non-fiction, and she was considering switching her program concentration to non-fiction entirely. (Pat had already made a Non-Phixion reference every time she had brought it up, which was one more reason to decide ASAP.) The problem was how the hell she was going to balance it all with CFA. Leaving her day job had never been an option, but between being on Pat's insurance and the potential book contract, it was the first time she could ever consider it. Though did it make sense to leave entirely, or just further decrease her time in the office? Or do project-based hiring and recruiting, rather than a more immersive data role? There were a lot of options among the scale of creativity vs. stability, and she wasn't sure which ones Colette would go for. Though the time had come to stop thinking about what worked for Colette and start thinking about herself.

Like many of the most important decisions in her life, Mo decided to wing it, depending on when she could capture Colette for a meeting and the direction it subsequently took. With one week left between the end of the fair and the start of spring semester, she was running out of time. Mo arrived early on the Wednesday after the fair, a day on which she had confirmed in Gcal that Colette had no morning meetings. The office was quiet: even Pierre was still snoozing, and Colette hadn't come down yet from the third floor. If she was going to do it, the time was now, Side By Side style.

Mo picked up her phone to text Colette, half hoping for an intervention from the world: the front door opening or footsteps on the stairs (canine or human). She had spent so much time over the past seven years in this exact spot. And yet no intervention came. She pressed Send, asking if she could come upstairs to chat. A second later she had a reply:

"Come up."

Heart thudding, Mo stood up from her chair by the door, ascended the treacherous stairs, and greeted Colette and Pierre in the living room. Sitting down on one of the couches (the one least coated in dog hair), she made sure to take note of the room as if seeing it for the last time.

"Listen ..." she began.

THE END

Acknowledgements

First, thanks to all of you for making it this far! "I can hardly believe it" that *Lost Indignation* is real. Thank you John Scharbach and Zack Wuerthner for making this book a reality, taking a chance on another novel, and linking me up with extraordinary cover artist Chris Wilson. I'm so honored to join the elite roster at Shining Life.

Chris Skowronski: I couldn't have asked for a more inspiring, patient and authentic editor. Thank you for winnowing a spring training roster of a draft to a regular season squad of a novel. To intrepid first readers AJ McGuire, Sam Reiss, and Ned Russin, I'm grateful for your invaluable constructive feedback that inspired further edits, like finalizing the roster for the playoffs.

To the people who let me into their worlds and neighborhoods to ensure the details were real: Armando Bordas, Shane Medanich, and AJ McGuire again. Caroline Biggs, Julia Champagne, and Paige Ackerson-Kiely for Sarah Lawrence assists; Anthony Rosini and Mark Yoshitomi on Dobbs Ferry in the '80s; Nina Smith from the Yonkers Riverfront Library; message board mastermind Michael Fairley; and Lars Weiss, Mike Galderisi, Dave Brown, and Gary Agis. And Philadelphians Davin Jael Bernard/Eaten Alive and Marie-Helene Bertino for the epigraphs.

To everyone who intentionally or unintentionally inspired names of bands, characters and bars: Freddy Alva, Edo Zavarella, Henry Apel, Steve Larger, Chris Wynne, Stefan Petraske, and Lisa Miller Steers for the best names of all. To everyone who believed in me, waited for my zine, or was bummed I was trying to finish a novel before IQNM #4.5, #5 or #6. To Charlie Curkin for connecting me to a job and an entire world, and all coworkers in the trenches with me, past and present. (At least two people mentioned in this paragraph own the same Bad Trip shirt.)

The world is such a different place than when I started writing this in 2017, when Philip Roth, Biz Markie and Rich McLoughlin were all still alive, as were both my grandfathers and my cat Goose. Many restaurants mentioned here have closed, though fortuitously, Pizzeria La Rosa opened days before I started the book. A special thank you to Matt DiGesu for being a gracious host and friend.

Thank you to Mike McAuley for the plot walks, '80s video game expertise, Crestwood Halloween 2018, helping shape the psychological profile of David Eckley, location scouting outings, and for the hundreds of ways you supported me during this process, from smoothies to keeping cats out of my desk drawers. To my family: Mom, Dad, Lisa and Brian, my grandparents, aunts, uncles, and cousins and "Thanksgiving Cousins," plus Mike's equally inspiring extended family: I am lucky to be surrounded by fans of books (and baseball.)

And to everyone who loves hardcore, the 914, and hardcore in the 914, I hope this book feels as real to you as it does for me.

At the Outsider Art Fair 2018

Becky McAuley is the creator of *I Question Not Me* and *Double Rabies* fanzines and serveemasentence.com. She has contributed to *In Effect*, *Gratitude Fanzine*, *Lifers*, and *Some Will Never Know*. This is her first novel. She lives in Mount Vernon, New York.